McFARLANE'S PERFECT BRIDE

BY
CHRISTINE RIMMER

AND

TAMING THE MONTANA MILLIONAIRE

BY
TERESA SOUTHWICK

MILLS &
BOON

Dear Reader,

One thing in life is certain: change. Times are a little tougher in Thunder Canyon, Montana lately. The boom created by the gold rush a few years ago is over. And Thunder Canyon Resort, which once gave Vail and Aspen a run for the money, is struggling to stay afloat.

Corporate shark and East Coast power player Connor McFarlane has been going through a few changes himself lately. He's in town for the summer to get to know his estranged fifteen-year-old son and make amends with his sister, Melanie. There's also a rumour he's engineering a takeover of Thunder Canyon Resort.

Connor intends to meet his goals for this Montana summer and go. Until he meets schoolteacher Tori Jones. A recent bitter divorce has left him wanting nothing to do with love. And he never plans to marry again.

But Tori Jones is a very special woman—just possibly the perfect woman for him.

Happy reading, everyone.

Yours,

Christine Rimmer

McFARLANE'S PERFECT BRIDE

BY
CHRISTINE RIMMER

First published in Great Britain 2011
by Mills & Boon, an imprint of Harlequin (UK) Limited,
Eton House, 18-24 Paradise Road, Richmond, Surrey TW9 1SR

© Harlequin Books S.A. 2010

ISBN: 978 0 263 88911 6

23-0911

Special thanks and acknowledgement to Christine Rimmer for her contribution to the MONTANA MAVERICKS: THUNDER CANYON COWBOYS mini-series.

Harlequin (UK) policy is to use papers that are natural, renewable and recyclable products and made from wood grown in sustainable forests. The logging and manufacturing processes conform to the legal environmental regulations of the country of origin.

Printed and bound in Spain
by Blackprint CPI, Barcelona

Christine Rimmer came to her profession the long way around. Before settling down to write about the magic of romance, she'd been everything from an actress to a sales clerk to a waitress. Now that she's finally found work that suits her perfectly, she insists she never had a problem keeping a job—she was merely gaining "life experience" for her future as a novelist. Christine is grateful not only for the joy she finds in writing, but for what waits when the day's work is through: a man she loves, who loves her right back, and the privilege of watching their children grow and change day to day. She lives with her family in Oklahoma. Visit Christine at www.christinerimmer.com.

For all you teachers out there.
The work you do is the most important work there is.

Chapter One

The doorbell rang just as Tori Jones set the snack tray on the breakfast nook table. "Help yourselves." She gave her star student, Jerilyn Doolin, a fond smile and sent a nod in the direction of Jerilyn's new friend, CJ. "There's juice in the fridge."

Jerilyn pushed her chair back. "Thanks, Ms. Jones."

The doorbell chimed again. "I'll just see who that is." Tori hurried to answer.

She'd made it halfway through her great room to the small foyer when the pounding started. Hard. On the door. The bell rang again, twice, fast. Followed by more pounding. Alarm jangled through her at the loud, frantic sounds. Was there a fire?

"All right, all right. I'm coming, I'm coming…"

She yanked the door wide on a tall, hot-looking guy in designer jeans and high-dollar boots.

Before she could get out a yes-may-I-help-you, the guy growled, "That's my son's skateboard." With a stabbing motion of his index finger, he pointed. Tori peered around the door frame at the skateboard that Jerilyn's friend had left propped against the porch wall. "Do you have my son here?" the stranger demanded.

Have him? Like she'd kidnapped the boy or something? Tori felt her temper rise.

She tamped it down by reminding herself that the angry man in front of her was probably scared to death. And then she spotted the gorgeous, gas-guzzling SUV parked at the curb. Had he been driving up one street and down another looking for a sign of his lost child? Thunder Canyon, Montana, wasn't a big city. But the streets would have to seem endless to a man frantically searching for his missing kid.

"I asked you a question." The man raked his fingers back through thick, expertly cut auburn hair.

Tori schooled her voice to a calmness she didn't feel. "Is your son's name CJ?"

"That's right." The man seemed on the verge of grabbing her and shaking her until she produced the boy. "Is he here?"

"Yes, he is. He's—" With a startled cry, she jumped back as the guy barged into her house.

"Where?" He snarled the word at her. "Take me to him. Now."

"Wait a minute. You can't—"

Oh, but he could. He was already past her, striding boldly into her great room, shouting, "CJ, damn it! CJ!"

Jerilyn and CJ appeared from the kitchen, both wide-eyed. But as soon as CJ caught sight of the furious man, he put on a scowl. "Sheesh, Dad. Chill."

"What is the matter with you?" Mr. Hotshot stopped where he was and started lecturing his son. "I had no clue where you had gotten off to. You know you are not to leave the house without telling Gerda where you're going."

CJ's face flamed. He stared down at the hardwood floor, his shaggy hair falling forward to cover his red cheeks. "Come on, Dad," he muttered. "I was only—"

"And what about your phone? You promised me you wouldn't go off without your phone."

"Like it even works in the canyon." The boy was still talking to the floor.

"Speak up," his father demanded. "I can't hear you."

CJ, who had seemed a normal, reasonably friendly teenager before his dad showed up, clamped his mouth shut now. He refused to even look at his father.

Tori realized she'd been standing there speechless for too long. She needed to calm the father down and diffuse the considerable tension. "Listen, why don't we all go into the kitchen and—"

"No, thanks." CJ's dad cut her off with an absent wave of his hand. "We're going. Come on, CJ. Now." He turned for the door. The boy followed him out, head low, feet dragging.

Tori longed to stop them, to get them to speak civilly to each other, at least, before they took off. But she knew that was only her inner schoolteacher talking. In the end, she had no right to interfere. CJ seemed embarrassed by his dad, but not the least afraid of him. And she couldn't see herself getting between father and son unless there was real cause. Overbearing rudeness just wouldn't cut it as a reason to intervene.

Trailing after his dad, the boy went out into the June sunshine, pulling the door shut behind him. Tori and Jerilyn hardly moved until they heard the engine of that pricey SUV start up outside and drive away.

Jerilyn broke the echoing silence first. "CJ hates his dad." She spoke wistfully. "I don't get that. Yeah, his dad was mad. But at least he cares…"

A low sound of sympathy escaped Tori. Jerilyn's mom had died of cancer the year before. Since then, her father walked around in a daze, emotionally paralyzed with grief. Butch Doolin used to dote on his only child. But not since he lost his wife. Jerilyn had confided in Tori that lately she wondered if her dad even knew she existed anymore.

Tori went to her and smoothed her thick black hair. "How 'bout some cheese, whole-wheat crackers and fresh fruit?"

Jerilyn's wistful expression faded. She giggled. "Ms. Jones, did you ever serve a snack that wasn't healthy?"

"Not a chance." She took the girl by the shoulders and turned her toward the kitchen.

As they sipped organic cranberry juice and nibbled on sliced apples and rennet-free white cheddar, Jerilyn talked about CJ. "I've seen him a couple of times before in the past week, riding his skateboard around Heritage Park. I never thought he'd notice me. But today, he stopped and we started talking…" A dreamy look made her dark eyes shine. "It was so strange, the way we connected, you know? It seemed like we could instantly tell each other everything. I felt so…comfortable with him. And, yeah, he dresses like a skater and he wears his hair long and all, but he's very smart. He's fifteen, same as me. He skipped fourth grade, just like I did."

It was good to hear a little about the boy. Tori'd had no time to ask the pertinent questions before the furious father arrived.

She sipped her juice. "You really like him."

Jerilyn smiled shyly. "I hope maybe I'll see him again. He's going to some expensive boarding school back east in the fall. But even if he stayed here in Thunder Canyon for school, he'd probably end up hanging with the rich, popular kids…"

Tori slid her glass across the table and clinked it with Jerilyn's. "Uh-uh. Don't go there. You have no reason to start beating yourself up. You're every bit as good— and twice as pretty—as any girl at Thunder Canyon High."

Jerilyn wrinkled her nose. "You say that 'cause I'm smart and I understand *Moby Dick* better than most college students."

"I say it 'cause it's true. Your being smart is a bonus." She ate a strawberry. "I have to admit, though. I can't help but love a student who stays on top of the reading list and writes a better essay than I can—and though we didn't have much chance to talk, it definitely seemed to me that CJ liked you."

"You're just saying that to make me feel better."

"Jerilyn." Tori spoke sternly.

"Yes, Ms. Jones?"

"If I say it, I mean it."

"Yes, Ms. Jones." Jerilyn sighed. "You *really* think he likes me?"

"I do. I really do. And he seemed like a nice boy."

"I'm so glad you liked him." Jerilyn beamed.

Too bad his dad's such a complete jerk, Tori thought, but didn't say.

"Tall, good-looking, auburn-haired, buttoned-down. Obviously rich. Pushy. And rude?" asked Allaire Traub, who was Tori's dearest friend.

Tori took the fruit and cheese tray from earlier that day out of the fridge and pulled off the plastic wrap. "That's him."

Allaire's two-year-old, Alex, who sat on her lap, started chanting in a singsong. "Rude, rude, rude, rude…"

"Shh," Allaire chided. She kissed his dark brown baby curls. Tori set the tray on the table and Allaire gave Alex a slice of apple.

"Apple. Yum," said the little boy.

Tori slid into the chair opposite her friend. "So…you know him?"

"Well, I know *of* him." Allaire rescued Alex's sippy cup just as he was about to knock it to the floor. She kissed his cheek and commanded adoringly, "Eat your apple and sit still."

"Apple, apple, apple, apple." The little boy giggled. And then he stuck the slice of apple in his mouth. He was quiet. For the moment.

Tori prompted, "And his name is…?"

Allaire frowned. "Who?"

"Mr. Buttoned-down, Pushy and Rude?"

"Oh. Right. He's Connor McFarlane, Melanie Chilton's brother."

Tori put her hands to her cheeks. "Of course. I should

have known." Melanie McFarlane had come to town three years ago determined to prove herself to her rich, snobby family. She'd ended up opening a guest ranch and marrying a local rancher, Russ Chilton. "Connor McFarlane. He runs the family empire, right?"

Allaire nodded. "McFarlane House Hotels." She passed her son an orange wedge. "He's here for the summer, with his son, Connor Jr."

"Aka, CJ."

"That's right." Allaire gave Alex his sippy cup—then took it away when he started to pound it on the edge of the table.

"I thought Melanie and her brother didn't get along."

"Rumor is they're trying, you know? Connor's been taken down a peg since the economy dipped. The way I heard it, McFarlane House had to pull back. A serious retrenchment. They closed a few hotels. The company is holding strong now, but not growing the way it was. And Connor's personal fortune took a serious hit, though I understand he's still a long way from the poorhouse. His wife dumped him. And CJ, formerly the perfect son, has been acting out. Melanie suggested that her brother and CJ come to Montana for the summer. Connor's renting one of those big houses in New Town that all the newcomers built—and then tried to unload when the bottom fell out."

In spite of herself, Tori felt sympathy rising. "His wife divorced him?"

Allaire nodded. "Pretty much out of nowhere, apparently. Story goes that she met someone richer."

Tori shook her head. "How do you *know* all this stuff?"

Allaire lifted a delicate, gold-dusted eyebrow. "To many, I may seem merely a deceptively fragile-looking über-talented art teacher and loving wife and mother. But I also have my finger on the pulse of Thunder Canyon."

"Because you're married to DJ," Tori said with a chuckle.

Allaire shrugged. "You know my husband. He makes it his business to keep an eye on the movers and shakers. Even if they're supposedly only visiting for the summer."

DJ Traub ran a successful chain of mid-priced restaurants with locations all over the western states. When he returned to town to stay a few years ago, he'd opened a DJ's Rib Shack on-site at the sprawling, upscale Thunder Canyon Resort, which covered most of nearby Thunder Mountain. The resort gave Vail and Aspen a run for the money—or it had until the financial downturn. DJ knew everybody *and* what they were up to.

Alex waved his chewed orange rind. "DJ, DJ, that's my daddy!"

"Oh, yes, he is." Allaire hugged him close and said to Tori, "You *are* coming to the barbecue up at the resort Saturday, right?"

"Wouldn't miss it. I thought I'd bring Jerilyn."

"Great. She'll like that. It's really good of you to look out for her."

"It's no hardship. She's a joy to have around."

Allaire gazed at Tori fondly. "She reminds you of yourself."

"A little, maybe." Tori had lost her mom when she was thirteen. Her dad had been really out of it for a while, trying to deal with the loss.

"And *your* dad got better, eventually."

"Yes, he did." Now she had a stepmother she loved and three half brothers ages ten, six and three.

"So there's hope that Butch Doolin will pull it together."

Tori was trying to think of something positive to say about Jerilyn's dad when Alex started pounding his little fist in the table. "More juice," the toddler commanded. Allaire put the cup in his chubby hand. This time, he actually drank from it. "Here, Mommy." He gave the cup back. "I tired." He set his apple core on the table and snuggled back into his mother's arms. In seconds, he was fast asleep.

"Amazing," said Tori with a doting smile.

Allaire made a tender sound of agreement as she smoothed his springy curls. Softly, so as not to wake him, she spoke of the small family reunion she and DJ were hosting out at their ranch that weekend. A couple of Traub cousins, wealthy ones, were coming up from Texas for the event. They would all be at the Rib Shack for the barbecue Saturday.

Tori still had Connor McFarlane on her mind. She asked in a near-whisper, "What do you mean, Connor's 'supposedly' only visiting for the summer?"

Allaire set the sippy cup on the table. "Well, DJ says Connor's been at the resort a lot. Chatting people up, nosing around. And Grant told DJ that Connor's had dinner with Caleb Douglas out at the Douglas Ranch." Caleb Douglas was co-owner of the resort. Grant Clifton managed the place, with help from Riley Douglas, Caleb's son.

Tori frowned. "A takeover? I knew the resort was

struggling lately. But would Caleb do that? The resort is his pride and joy."

"Money's short. Even the Douglases need to tighten their belts."

"But I mean, would Caleb really sell?"

Allaire made a noncommittal noise in her throat. "Can't say for sure. But *something's* going on."

"You're going," Connor said flatly. "And we're late."

CJ didn't spare him so much as a glance. He was busy manipulating the black controller of his Xbox 360 Elite, wearing a headset so he could talk to whomever he was playing with online—and also shut his father out. On the flatscreen that took up half a wall of his bedroom, soldiers in WWII Army gear battled the Germans somewhere in a burned-out city in France. A tank lurched over rubble and belched fire as a building exploded and a couple of hapless Germans went flying in the air, faces contorted with fear.

Connor stood by the bed. His blood pressure had to be spiking. He wanted to shout, *What the hell have you done with my son?* He hardly knew this shaggy-looking, angry, sulky kid. The CJ he knew gazed at him with worshipful eyes and only wanted a chance to spend a little time with his busy, successful dad.

I will not shout. I will not rip those headphones off of his head.

Connor fisted his hands and counted to ten. And then he grabbed the TV remote off the bed and pointed it at the flatscreen.

The screen went black.

CJ slanted him a venomous look. "Turn it back on. Now."

Connor did nothing of the sort. With a calmness he didn't feel, he reached out and gently pulled the headset from CJ's ears. "I told you we were going to the big summer kickoff barbecue." The barbecue, at DJ's Rib Shack up at the resort, presented a useful opportunity to get more face time with people he needed to know better—family and otherwise. "Your Aunt Melanie and Uncle Russ are going. Ryan, too." Ryan Chilton, Russ's son from his first marriage, was thirteen.

CJ groaned and tossed the controller aside. "I'm not babysitting Ryan."

"No one said anything about babysitting. You will, however, behave in a civilized manner and treat your aunt and her family with respect."

"I hate that kind of crap. 'Big summer kickoff barbecue.'" He chanted the words in an angry singsong. "Big whoop."

Again, Connor reminded himself that shouting and threats had so far gotten him nowhere. He spoke with deadly mildness. "Fine. Stay home if you like. Stay home all summer. In this room. With no electronics."

CJ blinked. "You would *ground* me forever for missing some dumb barbecue?"

"Try me."

CJ glared at him. Connor stared steadily back.

And then, at last, CJ put down the remote. "Fine. Let's go." He jumped to his feet and headed for the door in his sloppy skater gear, which included ripped-out, sagging jeans, a wrinkled plaid shirt over a T-shirt that had seen better days. And dirty old-school tennis shoes with the laces undone.

Connor reminded himself that the barbecue was casual and he didn't have time for a wardrobe battle.

CJ stopped in the doorway and turned with a glare. "Well? You coming or not?"

Connor straightened his sport jacket and gave a brisk nod. "Absolutely. I am right behind you."

The resort was packed. People spilled out of the Rib Shack and filled up the huge central lobby of the main clubhouse.

Connor spotted Melanie, Russ and Ryan over by the lobby's natural-stone fireplace, which was on a grand scale, like the rest of the clubhouse. Big enough to roast a couple of steers inside and still have room for an elk or three.

He hooked an arm around CJ's shoulders to keep him from slipping off and worked his way through the crowd, spreading greetings as he went. Melanie saw him just before he reached her. She smiled and waved, her sleek red hair shining in the afternoon sun that beamed down from the skylights three stories overhead and flooded in the soaring wall of windows with its amazing view of the white-capped peak of Thunder Mountain.

She was a fine woman, his sister. And forgiving. All those years he'd looked down on her. And still, she'd welcomed him to her new hometown and seemed to want only to let bygones be bygones. She made him feel humble, an emotion with which he'd had no relationship until recently.

Russ gave him a cool nod. Ryan's face split in a happy grin at the sight of his older cousin.

CJ squirmed a little under Connor's firm grip and said loudly, "Well, we're here. Can we eat?"

Ryan nodded eagerly. "In the Rib Shack. Come on, I'll show you…"

Connor hesitated to let go of his son. "Stay in the building."

"Sheesh, Dad. Awright, awright."

"Stay with Ryan."

"I will, I will."

Melanie caught his eye. "I'm sure they'll be fine."

Russ spoke to Ryan. "Get us a table if you can."

"We will, Dad. Come on, CJ." He bounded off through the crowd, headed for the Rib Shack. CJ followed, kind of shuffling along. Watching them go, Connor actually found himself envying Russ his happy, upbeat son.

Russ was watching the boys, too. "Job's still open," he said in that cryptic way he had.

The job in question was for CJ. Russ and Melanie had offered to hire him part-time for the summer, to work at Melanie's guest ranch, the Hopping H. Russ thought a few hours a day mucking out stables or doing dishes in the ranch house would be good for him.

When Russ had made the initial offer, Connor had turned him down flat. The McFarlane offspring did not do dishes or clean up horse manure. Plus, at that point, Connor had still nurtured the fond hope that CJ might spend his summer catching up on his schoolwork. Just weeks before, the boy had almost been booted out of his expensive New York boarding school due to his suddenly plummeting grades.

However, in the eleven days they'd been in Thunder Canyon, Connor had not seen his son so much as pick up a book. CJ rode his skateboard around town, disappearing for hours at a time, worrying Connor half out of his mind. When he wasn't vanishing into thin air, he sat in his room and played video games.

Connor had started to wonder if he should reconsider Russ's job offer. He asked ruefully, "Mind if I think it over a little?"

Russ and Melanie shared a glance. And Russ answered in a neutral tone. "Take your time. The job will be there if you want him to have it."

A big hand clapped Connor on the back. "Glad you came. Good to see you."

He turned and greeted Caleb Douglas and his wife, Adele. Silver-haired with cool green eyes, Caleb had suffered poor health in recent years. He still had a booming voice and a hearty manner, but Connor could see the weariness in his face, the deep lines around his eyes. He was half owner of the resort, which meant he would feel duty-bound to show up for big events like this one.

But his heart wasn't in it anymore. And times were tougher than they had been. Caleb could be convinced to sell. And Connor's extensive research into the matter had led him to believe that Caleb's silent partner would go along with whatever Caleb decided.

Yeah, Caleb would sell. Hopefully, before the summer was out.

And for a very reasonable price.

Caleb made small talk for a minute or two, then stepped in close to Connor while Adele chatted up Melanie and Russ.

The older man spoke low so only Connor could hear.

"Come on out to the ranch again. We'll…talk some more."

"I'd like that." Connor smiled.

"Excellent—but next week's no good. Adele's dragging me to Hawaii." Caleb grunted. "Lately Adele's got some idea that we should travel more. But how about a week from Monday? Dinner, seven-thirty?"

"I'll be there, thanks."

A minute or two later, Caleb and his wife moved on.

Next, Grant Clifton appeared with his pretty wife, Stephanie, and a Clifton cousin, Beauregard, who was known as Bo.

Bo was good-looking and talkative, a rancher by trade—and a salesman by nature. "I think we need some fresh ideas in this old town. And that's why I'm running for mayor."

Grant laughed. "Come on, Bo. Against Arthur?"

"Arthur Swinton is a staunch conservative," Melanie explained for Connor's benefit.

Russ said, "Been in town politics for years."

Grant added, "Arthur's on the city council and he's running for mayor. It's pretty much a given he's going to win."

Bo laughed. "Nothing's a given, cousin."

Russ suggested dryly, "Don't forget death and taxes."

"You're right," agreed Bo. "And for the sales tax we pay around here, we should get more for our money." Bo went on to explain in detail all the projects he planned to fight for when he won the election.

When Grant and Stephanie finally dragged Bo away, Melanie suggested they start moving in the general direction of the Rib Shack. Connor turned for the wide arch that led through to the restaurant and almost ran into the woman standing behind him.

Slim, with short, wispy, strawberry-blond hair, the woman wore a snug summer dress splashed with vivid pink flowers. He couldn't see her face. She was turned the other way.

"Tori, hey," said Melanie, who apparently knew her.

The woman turned to smile at his sister. But the smile faded when she saw him. She gazed up at him warily, through big, bright hazel eyes.

He stifled a groan of embarrassment as he remembered where he'd seen her before.

Chapter Two

Connor felt like a jerk.

Probably because he'd behaved like one the other day.

"Hello," the woman named Tori said coolly.

Jones, he thought, scouring his brain for the information CJ had reluctantly given up when Connor had grilled him after he got the kid home on Thursday. Her name was Tori Jones and she taught English at the high school. "How are you?" he asked, for lack of anything more original to say.

"Just fine, thank you." And then, finally, she did smile—over his shoulder, at Melanie. "Hey." She even smiled at Russ. And she had that teenage girl with her, the one CJ liked, whose name was Jerilyn.

The girl said, "Hi, Mr. McFarlane."

He cleared his throat. "Uh. Hi, Jerilyn."

"Is, um, CJ here, too?" Her pretty face was open, guileless. And heartbreakingly hopeful.

His sister said, "Ah. So you've met my big brother?"

"Yes, we have," Tori Jones said sweetly. "Just the other day, as a matter of fact."

Connor told the dark-haired girl, "CJ's in the restaurant, with Ryan."

And Melanie said, "Why don't you two join us? We were just going in to eat."

Jerilyn turned her hopeful gaze on the English teacher.

After a moment, Tori nodded. "Sure. Why not?"

So they all went together, easing their way through the crowd toward the packed Rib Shack.

As it turned out, Ryan and CJ had actually managed to save three chairs. CJ jumped up at the sight of Jerilyn. "Jerilyn! Hi." Suddenly he was only too eager to scout out a couple more seats for the dark-haired girl and her teacher.

They went through the serving line and loaded their plates with ribs, barbecued chicken, fat white rolls and coleslaw. Back at the table, CJ worked it so that Jerilyn sat next to him. The girl seemed to glow with pleasure at CJ's attention. And CJ behaved almost like his old self, suddenly—smiling and happy, his face animated as he and the girl whispered together.

Connor ended up with Melanie on one side and Tori Jones on the other. Through the meal, his sister and Tori talked around him—about the barbecue and what a success it was, about the resort and how nice it was to see it packed full of people again.

Since Russ had bought the first beers for the four

adults, Connor did his bit and went over to the bar to get a second round. He eased in next to a blonde woman, sitting alone, nursing a white wine.

She smiled and leaned close to him. "I'm Erin. Erin Castro."

Was she coming on to him?

He decided she wasn't. There was no breathless smile, no fluttering eyelashes. Probably just being friendly. He gave her offered hand a quick shake. "Connor McFarlane."

She seemed to study his face intently. "No relation to the Traubs, the Cliftons or the Cateses?" She had named the town's three major families.

He laughed. "No, but they're thick on the ground around here."

"So I've been told."

He paid the bartender, gathered up the four beers by their necks and headed back to the table, forgetting about the woman named Erin as soon as he turned away from her. Mostly, he was thinking about Tori Jones.

Thinking that he liked the cute spray of freckles across her nose and those big hazel eyes. Thinking that he owed her an apology for his behavior on Thursday. After all, he *was* trying to be a better man. And one of the things a better man did was to say he was sorry when an apology was called for.

Sometimes trying to be a better man could be a real pain in the ass.

At the table, he took the chair next to her again and set one of the beers in front of her. "Here you go."

She met his eyes. "Thanks."

"My pleasure." Holding her gaze, he tried a smile.

She didn't smile back. And yet somehow that look they shared went on far too long.

She glanced away first.

He passed fresh ones down the table to Melanie and Russ and tried to think of how he could smoothly suggest that the schoolteacher give him a moment alone.

Smoothly. That was the key. But for some reason, he didn't feel especially smooth. And that really bugged him. He ran a hotel chain, for pity's sake. It was part of his job to be smooth when a situation required it.

After the meal, which included red velvet cake and coffee for dessert, DJ Traub got up with a microphone and thanked everyone for coming to his annual summer kickoff barbecue. He introduced his visiting Texas cousins, Dillon and Corey, after which he announced there would be dancing out on the patio. Everyone applauded as DJ left the mike.

CJ stood and pulled back Jerilyn's chair for her.

Connor snapped to attention. "What's up?"

His son stiffened. But then Jerilyn gave CJ a gentle look. That was all it took. CJ actually spoke in civil tone. "We were just going to hang around out in the lobby area."

"If that's all right," Jerilyn added, stars in her dark eyes.

"Just the lobby," Connor warned.

CJ nodded.

Jerilyn promised, "Just the lobby, Mr. McFarlane. By the big fireplace."

"All right."

The girl turned her warm smile on Ryan. "Come with us," she offered softly. CJ looked a little sulky about that, but he didn't object.

"Sure." Ryan, his face lit up like a Christmas tree, jumped to his feet and bounced off in the wake of the two older kids.

"She's a lovely girl," said Melanie.

On his other side, Tori made a soft noise of agreement.

Out on the patio, the band DJ had hired struck up a country song. Russ took Melanie's hand and got up. "'Scuse me while I dance with my beautiful wife."

Melanie rose. "We'll be back." Russ put his arm around her.

Connor watched them make their way through the thicket of tables to the open patio doors, leaving him alone with the cute schoolteacher and his chance to make amends.

How to begin?

He had no clue. He felt awkward, tongue-tied as a kid with his first crush. Which was pretty ridiculous, really. He did not have a crush on Tori Jones. He'd just been put through the wringer with the divorce and the last thing he needed was another relationship.

Deeply annoyed with himself for feeling nervous, and for finding the schoolteacher much too attractive, he stared out through the open doors at the patio and the couples dancing there and started thinking about CJ.

And the girl, Jerilyn.

Jerilyn seemed like a kind-hearted person. And she was certainly polite and respectful of adults. But still, he'd better ask around, find out for certain she was really okay.

Being a full-time father was a challenge. You couldn't just tell a kid to get with the program or get out, like you could an employee. The cold fact was that Connor's life had been a damn sight simpler before the divorce, when CJ had been Jennifer's responsibility and Connor was free to wheel and deal around the clock.

It had been Jennifer's idea that he should take the boy to live with him for the summer, leaving her free to float around the Mediterranean on a luxury yacht with her new shipping magnate boyfriend. Connor might have refused. But he had felt obligated to spend some time with his son. Yes, it was probably too little too late. But CJ really needed guidance now and Connor was determined to try to provide it.

Beside him, the schoolteacher shifted in her chair. The movement reminded him that he couldn't avoid facing her forever—and that to keep staring off into space while she was sitting right next to him was borderline rude.

He turned to her.

Those hazel eyes were waiting. A slight, knowing smile tipped the corners of her mouth and he realized she'd been watching him.

"What?" he demanded, knowing he sounded as surly as CJ did most of the time.

She only shrugged, a delicate movement of one slim shoulder.

"All right," he said. "It's like this. I've been trying to figure out how to tell you I'm sorry for my behavior Thursday afternoon. I wanted to be smooth about it, you know?"

Damn. What was the matter with him? Had he actually just said out loud that he wanted to be smooth?

Apparently, he had, because she repeated, "Smooth, huh?"

"You're grinning," he accused.

She tipped her head to the side. "You know, you're kind of cute when you're embarrassed."

He narrowed his eyes at her. "A McFarlane is never cute and very rarely embarrassed."

She laughed then, a full-throated, musical sound.

He heard himself say, "You've got a great laugh."

Her laughter faded as quickly as it had come. She tipped her strawberry-blond head the other way and said softly, "Your apology is accepted. I know you must have been worried sick."

He answered honestly, "Yeah. I was." And then he actually confessed, "Sometimes, lately, I wonder where my son went—and I don't only mean when he disappears on his skateboard and I don't know where to find him."

"Teenagers can be a challenge."

"It's more than that. You should have known him before…" He let the sentence die unfinished. This woman did not need to hear about his broken marriage.

"It will work out," she said. "Just give it time."

He chuckled low. "Is that a promise?"

"Let's call it a professional assessment. I deal with kids his age nine months out of the year and I can spot the ones who are just going through a tough phase. CJ's one of those."

"You think so?"

"I do. And it's good that you're spending time with him."

"I hope you're right. He mostly behaves like he wishes I would get lost and stay that way."

"Don't believe that. He needs you. Maybe he can't— or doesn't know how to—show you. But it matters to him, that you're around and you care."

Another long moment passed. He looked into those big eyes and she gazed back at him. Finally, he said, "Thanks. I appreciate a little reassurance."

"Anytime."

He leaned a little closer to her, got a whiff of her fresh, citrusy perfume. And it suddenly occurred to him that she would be the one to tell him all about Jerilyn. And he did need to know more about the girl, since CJ seemed so gone on her. "I've got a great idea."

The hazel eyes widened. "You do?"

"Yeah. Dinner. You and me. This coming Friday."

She seemed to realize she'd let him get too close and sat back away from him. "Oh. No, really—"

"Yeah. Really. I promise not to yell or say rude things."

"Bad idea. Seriously. Bad."

"What's bad about it?"

She considered for a moment. "Okay, *bad* isn't the right word. I just don't think it's a *good* idea."

"Why not?"

"Call it…instinct."

He laughed. "Your instincts tell you not to go out with me?"

"Yeah. They do."

Should he have been discouraged? He wasn't. He saw the flush of color on her smooth cheeks and knew he could change her mind. "Come on. Take a chance. Friday night, the Gallatin Room right here at the resort. I've heard the food's pretty good."

She laughed again, a softer laugh than the one before, but no less warm, no less musical. "You high-powered types don't take no for an answer."

"So say yes."

Her gaze slid away—and then came back to meet his.

He pressed the advantage. "It's only dinner. What can it hurt?"

Something happened in her eyes. A decision. In his favor. "Good point." She gave him a nod.

"A yes," he said, and felt absurdly triumphant. "You just said yes."

Her gaze dropped to his mouth and then shifted up again, to his eyes. "You remember where I live?"

"I'll never forget."

"Seven-thirty."

"I'll be there."

"You're going out with Connor McFarlane?" Allaire asked in complete disbelief. "Tell me you're joking." She leaned close across the lacy tablecloth. It was Monday at noon. They were having their regular girls-only lunch at the Tottering Teapot on Main Street. DJ was home with Alex so Allaire could have a little time for herself.

The Teapot was famous for really good vegetarian sandwiches and an endless variety of teas, both caffeinated and herbal. All the tables had lace cloths and the food was served on mismatched thrift-store china. Not many men in town ate at the Teapot, but the women loved it.

"Not joking. I'm having dinner with him Friday night." Tori kept her voice low. No reason everyone and their sister needed to hear this conversation.

Allaire demanded, "Why ask for trouble?"

"Because I kind of like him. He can be really charming when he's not terrified something's happened to his son."

"He's a shark. He's trying to take over the resort."

"It's just a rumor. You said so yourself."

"Watch. Wait. You'll see it's more that a rumor."

"Doesn't matter. I like him and I'm going out with him—and will you stop? It's only a date. Not a lifetime commitment."

Allaire pursed her lips in an expression of serious distaste. "You like him a *lot*. I can see it in your eyes."

"In my eyes? Oh, please."

Allaire leaned even closer. "Yep. Right there." She aimed her index and middle fingers directly at Tori and sighted down them. "I can see it. You've got a thing for Mr. Bigshot McFarlane."

Tori waved a hand. "Stop worrying. I'll have a nice dinner and some good conversation. That's all, nothing more."

Allaire made a scoffing sound, but had to quell the rest of the lecture because Haley Anderson came in. In her mid-twenties, Haley went to college part-time and worked at the Hitching Post down the street, a local bar and also a town landmark. She spotted them and Tori waved her over.

"Good news." Haley was beaming. As a rule, she wasn't the beaming type. She'd had a rough time of it, raising her two younger siblings after their parents died. But today, her smile lit up the whole restaurant.

Allaire guessed, "You found a place."

Haley beamed wider. "The price is right and it's just down the street."

Tori thought she knew where. "That vacant storefront down the block from the Hitching Post?"

"That's the one. I met with the property manager, made an offer that's a little lower than what they're asking."

"And?"

"The owner's not in town. The property manager will consult with him and I should get my answer in the next few weeks." Haley hugged herself. "I can just feel it, you know? This is it."

Haley Anderson had a dream. Her dream was called ROOTS. It was to be a sort of Outward Bound/Big Brother organization to help troubled teens. Getting the storefront would mean she had a home base from which to launch the program.

She asked Allaire, "Did you talk with the principal?" She meant at the high school.

Allaire nodded. "He said to bring him a proposal when you're all set up. He really can't do much until then. You should definitely be able to put up flyers around the school, though. I mean, once you're up and running and can show what you're offering."

"Of course. I understand." Haley gave a nervous laugh. "I guess I'm kind of getting ahead of myself."

Tori reached over and squeezed her hand. "It's good to think ahead. And it's a fine project, an important one."

"We'll help all we can," Allaire promised.

Haley went on beaming. "I knew I could count on you two."

The little bell over the door chimed again. It was Melanie Chilton. Ignoring Tori's warning look, Allaire waved her over.

"Join us." Allaire gave Connor's sister a big, sweet smile.

"Only for a minute." Melanie slid in next to Tori. "I've got to get back to the Hopping H." The waitress appeared. They all ordered, with Melanie asking for hers to go. When the waitress left, Melanie asked Allaire, "So how was the weekend reunion?"

"The *mini* reunion," Allaire corrected. "Just the local Traubs and Corey and Dillon. It went great. Both of DJ's cousins say they'll be back in town soon."

"Tell DJ we loved the barbecue. We had a wonderful time."

"So I heard," said Allaire, sending a meaningful look Tori's way.

Melanie glanced at Tori and then back at Allaire. "Okay. What am I not picking up on here?"

Allaire gave an airy wave of her hand. "Oh, nothing."

Tori glared at her, mostly in fun. "You are impossible."

Now Allaire was grinning. "So I've been told."

"What's going on?" Haley demanded.

Tori realized it was kind of silly to try to keep the date with Connor to herself. Everyone in town would know anyway, after she showed up at the resort with him on Friday night. "Connor asked me out to dinner. I said yes. It's not a big deal, but Allaire is trying to make it one."

Melanie blinked. And then she grinned. "I thought there was something going on with you two."

Tori frowned. Everyone seemed to know something she didn't. "You did?"

Haley asked Melanie, "Connor. That's your brother, right?"

Melanie nodded and told Haley what Tori and Allaire

already knew. "He's in town for the summer." And then she lowered her voice so only their table could hear. "He's always been...difficult to get along with, at least, for me. He and my father looked down on me. No matter how hard I worked, I was never good enough, never *man* enough, to be an equal partner in McFarlane House Hotels. But Connor's been surprising me lately. He's different, since his divorce, since he and our father had to sell a couple of failing locations, including the new Atlanta hotel, just to stay afloat."

"You're saying you believe Connor's changed?" asked Allaire, sounding annoyingly doubtful.

"I do," said Melanie. "Or at least, he's not nearly as overbearing as he used to be. Now and then, in the past few days, I even get the feeling he's actually listening to me. And to Russ." And then she chuckled wryly. "My father, though. Donovan McFarlane is a man who'll never change."

"Thunder Canyon, Montana," Donovan McFarlane growled in disgust. "It's a black hole, Connor, and you know it."

Connor reminded himself to breathe slowly and evenly. He ordered his fingers to hold the phone more loosely. "I can get a good deal on the resort. But I need a little time to work on Caleb Douglas, to show him how the best decision for him is to sell."

"McFarlane House does not need a resort in some tiny Montana town. I've seen the numbers on that location. They're not good, trending down."

"Everything's trending down lately." *Even McFarlane House,* Connor thought. "Once we're in charge, we'll start making the necessary changes to get the resort in the black again. We'll cut back, at first, focus on the strongest services, get rid of any staff that isn't ready to—"

"Honestly, I don't know what's gotten into you lately, but I don't like it. First your sister, and now you. Throwing over your life work, your *heritage*."

"Dad. I'm not throwing anything over."

As usual, Donovan wasn't listening "—your sister with her ridiculous dude ranch, you with your sudden burning need to buy that failing resort."

"The Hopping H is doing very well, thanks, Dad. And we agreed that the resort could work for us."

"I agreed to no such thing. I do not care in the least about that resort. I want you back here in Philadelphia right away. I need you here." It was a bald-faced lie. Donovan McFarlane could run the McFarlane House corporate office with one hand tied behind his back and a bag over his head.

"I'll be there next week for the monthly—"

"Not next week. Now. You're welcome to stay with us until you can find another house. Your mother would be only too happy to have you nearby again. Why you had to give Jennifer *your* house is beyond me."

"It was her house, too, Dad."

"What about the prenup? We both know what that prenup said. She had no right to that house. And then she went and sold it, anyway."

"Dad, let's not rehash all this again."

"All right. Come home. You could have at least kept that condo."

"Dad. We discussed this. I sold the condo because when I come back in the fall, I'm going to find another house."

"I've reevaluated and I want—"

"Well, I haven't. Except for the specific meetings and catch-up visits we agreed on two weeks ago, I'm here in Thunder Canyon for the summer with my son."

There was a silence on the other end of the line. A deadly one. Finally, Donovan said, "You could just send Connor Jr. back to school. A summer without distractions, time to focus on his studies. Do the boy a world of good."

"Dad."

"Ahem. What is it?"

"I'm spending the summer here in Thunder Canyon and so is CJ. End of discussion."

"You're very stubborn. You don't get that from me."

Connor almost laughed. It would have been a sound with zero humor in it. "I have to go now, Dad. See you next week." Connor disconnected the call before his father could start issuing more orders.

And then he just stood there, in the study of his rented house, staring blindly out the window at the snowcapped peak of Thunder Mountain in the distance. There had been a time, not that long ago, when he and his dad saw eye to eye on just about every issue.

But now, whenever he talked to Donovan, he hung up wanting to put his fist through a wall. Donovan just didn't get it. Times were changing and a man either swam with the tide or drowned.

Sometimes Connor thought he was a survivor, that he really was changing, working his way toward a better life for himself and the son he'd neglected for too long.

And sometimes he knew he was kidding himself, that

he was actually drowning, going under for the third time and still telling himself he had both feet firmly planted on solid ground.

Chapter Three

"Roses." The schoolteacher looked up at him through those amazing hazel eyes. "You actually brought flowers."

He blinked. "What? That's bad?"

"No, of course not. It's lovely."

He handed them over.

"Thank you." She said it softly. She seemed to mean it. "I should put them in water, huh?"

"Good idea."

She stepped back from the doorway. "Come on in."

So he followed her, admiring the view of her trim backside in a slim-fitting red dress as she led the way through a comfortable-looking great room, back to an open kitchen with turquoise-blue walls and old-fashioned counters of white ceramic tile.

She opened a cupboard by the sink and pointed at

the top shelf. "See that square vase? Could you reach it for me?"

He got it down and she filled it with water and put the roses in it, tugging at them this way and that until she had them arranged to her satisfaction. "So pretty…"

He completely agreed, though it wasn't precisely the flowers he was looking at.

She slanted him a look. "Want a drink? I have a variety of organic juices. And I think I have an old bottle of vodka around here somewhere…a screwdriver. I could make you one of those." She looked so pleased with herself, he almost said yes, just to stand in her turquoise kitchen and watch her bustling around, mixing the drink for him.

Then again… "I'm not really a screwdriver kind of guy."

"Well, okay." She carried the vase over to the breakfast nook and put it in the center of the table. "Ta-da. Looks beautiful."

"Yes, it does."

"You ready?"

"After you."

Tori loved the Gallatin Room. She'd only been there a few times, once before on a date and also for a couple of parties. It was the best restaurant at the resort—really, in all of Thunder Canyon—and had a beautiful view of tall, majestic evergreens and the top of Thunder Mountain. It also had a massive stone fireplace, one that wasn't quite as large as the one in the main lobby. But impressive, nonetheless.

The host led them to a really good table, by the fireplace, with a view of the mountain and the spectacular sky, shot now with orange and gold as the sun set. A waiter came to take their drink orders. Connor ordered Scotch, the really good kind that was older than Tori. She asked for a glass of white wine.

The drinks appeared instantly. They sat and sipped and watched the sunset.

She said what she was thinking. "I love this restaurant."

His dark eyes made a quick scan of the beautiful room. "It's slow for a Friday evening, don't you think?"

She shrugged. "I guess."

"The Scotch is perfect. And the service so far is excellent. It'll be interesting to see how good the food is. As a rule, it's the first thing to slip."

"Uh, slip?"

He sipped his Scotch slowly. "When traffic declines."

She knew what he meant, but still she teased, "Traffic?"

He set down his glass and regarded her lazily. "When business slows down."

She stared at his fingers, which were still wrapped around the crystal glass. They were very nice fingers. Long. Lean. Strong-looking. "Hotelier to the core, huh?"

He didn't deny it. On the contrary, he gave her a rueful smile as he turned his crystal glass and stared down at the amber liquid inside. "I think it's in the blood. My father would certainly say it is."

She suddenly craved total honesty—no matter how unwise. "Your sister says your father's overbearing. And that he'll never change."

"Melanie's become way too frank in the past couple of years."

"I really like frankness in a person. I also heard you're in town to buy out this resort, after which you'll change everything around and fire half the staff."

"Who said that?" His voice was flat.

"It doesn't matter. Is it true?"

"Don't believe every rumor you hear." He studied her—a long, considering look.

"You're not going to answer my question, are you?" She sipped her wine again, set the glass down. "Never mind. I think you *are* in town to buy this resort. Feel free to tell me I'm wrong."

He staunchly refused to confirm or deny her suspicions. "I'm here to spend time getting to know my sister and her family. And above all, for my son. I've neglected CJ for much too long. I'm hoping it's not too late to heal the breach between us."

She believed he was telling the truth about his son. "It's not too late," she said softly. "It's never too late."

Those dark eyes went soft—but only for a split second. And then they were cool and watchful again. "You're an optimist."

"And proud of it." She picked up the leather-bound menu and set it back down without opening it. "It matters, Connor. That you care about your son, that you *show* him you care. And I admire you for figuring out that you need to spend time with him, no matter how long it took you to realize that."

His gaze was locked hard on hers. "I didn't figure it out. Not by myself, anyway. If my ex-wife hadn't demanded that I take him for the summer, I wouldn't have."

"But you did take him. You could have simply refused."

He almost smiled. "You insist on making me seem a better man than I am."

"Hey." She raised her glass to him. "Gives you something to live up to."

He did smile then. And he picked up his menu and opened it to study the offerings within. She opened hers, too.

The waiter appeared when they set their menus down again. They ordered. Connor asked for a bottle of cabernet to go with the meal.

The wine steward hustled over to confer with Connor. Once the choice was made, the wine had to be tasted. Connor nodded his approval. The waiter served them each a glass. He left the bottle, wrapped in a white cloth, within easy reach.

The food came—appetizers, salads and then the main course. Connor had prime rib, she had the trout. Tori found it all delicious, every last bite. If the quality was going downhill, she couldn't tell.

He asked her about her childhood. She told him of her mother's early death and her father's extended depression following the loss.

"Must have been a hard time."

"It was. But we got through it." She spoke of her half brothers and her stepmother. "My dad's happy now. It all worked out."

"What does your dad do?"

"He's a psychiatrist in Denver. Nowadays he does a lot of pro bono work, helping people deal with grief after the loss of a loved one."

"He would be the one to understand what they're going through, huh?"

"Yes. He understands."

"You admire him."

"I do. Very much."

"You were raised in…?"

"Denver, mostly. I moved here about three years ago."

"And you love it."

"Yep. I plan to live in Thunder Canyon till I'm old and gray."

Eventually, the talk got back around to CJ. He said, "My brother-in-law wants CJ to go to work part-time at the Hopping H."

"Doing…?"

"Whatever's needed. Dishes. Clearing tables after meals, feeding livestock."

"You sound reluctant."

"I have been, yeah. But lately I'm thinking maybe a job would be a good thing, a way to make sure CJ has a little structure, you know?"

"I think it's a great idea. Teaches him responsibility, gives him a schedule he has to keep. And a little extra pocket change. What's not to like?"

"Well, when you put it that way…" His eyes were soft again. Was that admiration she saw in them? Maybe so, because then he said, "I like the way you dress. In bright colors. Kind of…fun." The way he said *fun* made her absolutely certain that there hadn't been a lot of that in his life.

"I like things bright," she said. "And cheerful."

"And optimistic."

"Yep. That, too." She wondered about his ex-wife,

about what had happened between them that it didn't work out.

But no way was she asking about the ex on a first date. She'd been out with enough men to know the red flags, and a guy talking too much about his ex when a woman hardly knew him was definitely a bad sign. Usually that meant he wasn't over the other woman yet.

He said, "You're looking much too thoughtful."

"Just considering the various conversational booby traps."

"Such as?"

"If I told you, you'd probably only wish I hadn't— and if you *didn't* wish I hadn't, that would be a total red flag."

"I think I'm confused."

"I think I've been on too many first dates."

He laughed. "What? Things never work out for you romantically? I have a hard time believing that."

"Was that compliment?"

"Only the truth as I see it."

She felt absurdly flattered. And her cheeks were warm. And she could sit there forever, looking across the table into Connor McFarlane's sexy, dark eyes, letting the sound of his deep, warm voice pour over her. She said, "It's not that things don't work out for me. It's just, I rarely say no to a first date. So I go on quite a few."

"And second dates?"

"I look at it this way. A first date is one thing. But why say yes to a second when the spark isn't there?"

His gaze remained locked with hers. "I completely agree."

The waiter came and whisked away their plates. He

offered dessert. They both passed, but he had coffee and she took hot tea.

Connor said, "So tell me about Jerilyn. What's her background?"

Something in the way he said that, *What's her background?* had Tori snapping to wary attention. "Jerilyn's a terrific person. Brilliant. Loving. Thoughtful. A straight-A student."

He sipped his coffee. "You sound defensive."

"And you sound like a snob trying to find out if Jerilyn's *background* measures up."

"Tori." His voice was gentle, understanding, even. "She seems like a fine girl."

"She *is* a fine girl."

"And yes, I was wondering about her background."

She poured Earl Grey from the small china teapot into an eggshell-thin cup. "Similar to mine, actually. Her mom died a year ago and her father's having trouble coping."

"What does her father do?"

She looked into his eyes again. And she did not smile. "Butch Doolin is the maintenance engineer at the high school."

"The janitor, you mean."

"It's honest work, Connor."

"Did I say it wasn't?"

Instead of answering him, she sipped her tea. When she gently set the cup back in the saucer, she said, "CJ likes Jerilyn, a lot."

"I noticed."

"And she likes him."

"He's too young for a girlfriend." His voice was gruff.

She argued, "He's old enough to be interested in a girl—in Jerilyn, specifically—which means he's not too young."

"I just don't want him getting into anything serious. Not at his age."

"And especially not with a janitor's daughter." She didn't even try to keep the sarcasm out of her voice.

He sat very still, watching her face. Finally he said, "You're angry."

"Yes. I just saw a side of you I don't like. The elitist side."

"A person's background does matter." His voice was coaxing and kind. She wished she could agree with him, because she really did like him, was seriously attracted to him.

Talk about sparks…

But she couldn't pretend to agree when she didn't. "Background matters up to a point, yes. I wish it didn't, but I'm at least something of a realist. However, what matters most is who that person is. And Jerilyn Doolin is everything I just said she was and more. She's a special girl. It says a lot about your son that he would show the good taste and judgment to have his first big crush on someone like her."

He sat back in his chair and put up both hands. "Okay. I give up. You've convinced me. Jerilyn Doolin is a wonderful girl. CJ is lucky she's interested in him."

Most of her defensive tension drained away. She hid a triumphant smile. "About time you realized that."

"Maybe so." He still looked doubtful.

"But?"

"I'm just not happy about it. CJ can't afford the distraction."

"Distraction? Boys have been falling for girls since the beginning of time. That's not going to change just because you're not happy about it."

"The last thing CJ needs right now is to get too involved with a girl—any girl."

"Connor, he likes her. She likes him. You can't make that go away. In fact, in my experience, which is reasonably extensive given that I work with teenagers for a living, the more the parents try to come between a young couple, the more the attraction grows." Tori spoke with intensity. With passion, even.

He was staring at her, frowning.

Was she becoming a little too emotional over this? Maybe. But she really believed what she was saying and she wanted to get through to the hardheaded man across from her, to get him to understand. She feared if he didn't, he would only be making things worse for CJ.

"Romeo and Juliet," she declared vehemently. *"Wuthering Heights, Titanic.* Think of all the books and plays and movies about passionate, thwarted young love. It only leads to heartbreak when the grown-ups decide to interfere."

He leaned toward her again. "So, Tori."

"What?" she demanded hotly.

"Tell me what you *really* think."

She blinked. And then she laughed. He laughed, too. "Okay," she admitted. "I try to be open-minded, but when I really believe something, I advocate for it, you know?"

"Nothing wrong with that."

She qualified wryly, "Up to a point, you mean."

"Yeah," he agreed. He was watching her mouth again.

"Up to a point…" The words trailed off. A few seconds of silence elapsed—a silence filled with sparks. Finally, he confessed, "Sometimes I'm at a loss, you know? I have no idea how to get through to my own son."

"Are you asking for my advice?"

"Yeah. I guess I am."

"Okay, then. Here's what I think you should do. Take Russ up on his offer to put CJ to work at the Hopping H. And then tell CJ to invite Jerilyn over to your house."

"Over to the house for what?"

"To visit, to hang out. You know, play video games or watch a movie. Make your son feel that his new friends are welcome at home. Let him know that you're on his side. Start changing the equation from you versus him to you supporting him and really taking into account what he wants and needs."

"Seems to me I already support him."

She let her exasperation show. "You mean by buying him every electronic gadget under the sun and then being frustrated because all he does is play video games?"

"What?" Rueful humor shone in his eyes. "I should take away his Xbox?"

"I can't answer that question. You might just widen the rift at this point by denying him something you gave him in the first place."

"Actually, I think that was Jennifer—my ex-wife— who gave him the Xbox."

"Ah. Blaming the ex, huh?"

He shook his head. "Does nothing get by you?"

"Hey, I teach high-school English. Without a sharply honed sense of what's bull and what's not, I wouldn't make it through the first week of a new semester."

He gave in. "Okay, okay. I'll ask CJ to have Jerilyn

over and I'll take Russ up on his offer, get CJ working at Melanie's guest ranch. Anything else?"

Tori laughed. "I'll be in touch with further suggestions."

Entranced. Captivated. Enchanted.

They were words straight out of some women's novel.

But as Connor sat across that table from Tori Jones, he couldn't help thinking that those words exactly described what the small-town schoolteacher did to him. He might as well stop trying to tell himself he wasn't interested. He was powerfully drawn to her.

Clearly, he should have dated more when he was younger.

He'd married Jennifer while they were both in college. Because she was from the right family and she was gorgeous and ready to get married to the right kind of man. A man with money and good breeding equal to her own. It had seemed a very suitable match. The perfect match.

Plus, with the marrying and the settling down out of the way early, he'd been free to concentrate on his career in the family company. He'd never looked at another woman during his marriage. He had a wife and a son, a beautiful home—and his ambitions for McFarlane House, which were considerable. What else was there?

Just possibly, a whole lot more, he was discovering.

There had been a couple of other women, since Jennifer walked out on him. The sex had been good with them, which it never really had been with Jennifer.

But he had never been entranced. Or captivated. Or enchanted.

Until now.

He wanted her—*her,* Tori Jones, in particular. Not just someone suitably attractive and well-bred, as Jennifer had been. Not just someone sophisticated, sexually exciting and discreet, which pretty much described the two women he'd dated after his marriage had crashed and burned.

It came to him that he...he *liked* this woman. And that feeling was new to him. He liked her quick wit, her wisdom and her big heart. He liked the passion in her voice when she talked about things she believed in.

He liked *her.* And suddenly it mattered all out of proportion that she might like him, too.

Was he losing it? He couldn't help but wonder. Was he cracking under the strain—of the soured economy, the McFarlane House setbacks, his divorce, the scary changes in his son? Of the changes he'd decided he needed to make in his life and himself?

Strangely, right then, on his first date with Tori Jones, he didn't care if he just might be going over the edge. He was having a great time—having *fun,* of all things—and he didn't want it to end.

They lingered at the table for over an hour after the meal was finished, talking and laughing, sharing glances that said a lot more than their words did. Finally, reluctantly, he took her home.

At her house, hating to let her go, he walked her up to the door.

She turned to him and said what he'd been praying she might. "Want to come in for a minute?"

He held her gaze, nodded. They shared a warm smile.

Inside, she offered coffee. He accepted, more as a matter of form than because he needed any extra caffeine.

She made more tea for herself and they went out to her comfortable great room and sat on the sofa. He drank the coffee he didn't really want and thought about kissing her, about holding her in his arms.

About how, once he did that, he would have a hard time letting go.

"I should say goodbye," he finally admitted aloud. "It's almost midnight."

"You sure you don't want another cup of coffee?" Those hazel eyes teased him.

"I'm sure." He rose and held down his hand to her. "And it wasn't the coffee I came in for, anyway."

She put her fingers in his. The contact was electric. He had to remind himself forcefully that he was not going to grab her against him and crush her mouth with his. "I'm glad," she said softly as she stood.

He couldn't resist. He lowered his head. She tilted her mouth upward, the sweetest kind of offering.

And, at last, he brushed her lips with his own. Her fresh scent surrounded him and her mouth was soft as rose petals.

She was the one who kept him from deepening that first, too-short kiss. She did that by lowering her head slightly, and taking a step back.

He didn't know whether to applaud her good sense— or reach out and haul her near again. And then she was turning, leading him to the door. He followed.

Out on her front porch, the night was dark velvet.

She touched his arm. The light caress seemed to burn all the way to his soul. "Thank you," she said. "I had a really good time tonight."

"Sunday," he said, his voice lower, rougher than he should have allowed it to be.

"What about it?" She gazed up at him. In her eyes, he saw that if he tried to kiss her again, she would let him.

He didn't try. A little restraint never hurt—or so he told himself. "Melanie's having us out to the Hopping H for a picnic Sunday. CJ and me."

"Great," she said approvingly. "That's what I'm talking about. Make opportunities to spend quality time with him."

"Come with us."

A slight frown tightened her brow and she tipped her head to the side, studying him. "Are you sure? It sounds more like a family thing."

"I'm sure. Come with us. You can keep an eye on me, see how I'm doing, interacting with CJ. Then later, you can give me more advice."

She laughed, the sound like a song in the night. "Oh, so that's it. You want me around to help you improve your relationship with to CJ."

"That's my story and I'm sticking to it. Come with us."

"Why do I get the feeling you're after more than parenting advice from me?"

"Wait."

"For what?"

"For this." He dared to take her gently by the arms and pull her against him. And then he kissed her a second time. A longer kiss. Deeper, too. He wanted to go on like that, kissing her forever in the cool almost-summer darkness. But then he remembered that he was exercising restraint and carefully put her away from him. "I would call that a spark. A definite spark."

"Yeah," she answered breathlessly, her eyes bright as stars. "Guess so."

"So, then. I get a second date, right?"

Her expression turned a little bit sad. "Connor. It's problematic. You know it is."

He told her the straight-ahead truth. "I want to see you again—and not so you can help me out with CJ."

Her eyes widened. But then her soft mouth twisted. "It's only—"

"Say it. Tell me. I can't overcome your objections if you don't tell me what they are."

"Oh, Connor. You're here for the summer and then you'll be gone."

"Just like CJ, with Jerilyn. Why is that okay for them, but not for us?"

"Well, because they're kids and we're not."

"And because we're not kids, we have to live for the future. Is that what you're telling me?"

"No, not exactly. I'm just saying that a summer romance is one thing for two fifteen-year-olds. For adults, it's—"

"What? You won't let yourself live in the moment just because you're all grown up?"

She laughed. "You know, Connor. You can be incredibly persuasive when you put your mind to it."

Triumph flared within him, a sudden bright heat. He was sure he had her. "So that means you'll come with us?"

She glanced out toward the velvety night beyond the

porch, and then met his eyes again. "There's something else."

The flare of triumph died. But he refused to give up. "Tell me."

"I…get a sense that you're a good man deep down. But, well, you're still one of those guys who think they own the world, someone who doesn't care who gets hurt as long as he gets what he wants."

Apparently one of her friends had been saying harsh things about him. Probably whichever friend had told her he was trying to buy out the resort. He wasn't particularly surprised. "Ouch," he said lightly. "Don't feel you have to pull any punches."

"I don't. I won't."

"I noticed." He still wasn't giving up. "You do believe I'm an okay guy—at least, essentially, right?"

"Yes, but—"

"Forget the buts. Just go with that. After all, it's only a second date. Being essentially a good guy should be enough to get me a second date with you—I mean, given the all-important presence of the spark."

"You are incredibly persistent, you know that?"

"I can be, when I want something bad enough."

She moistened her lips. "Um, how bad is bad enough?"

He thought again about another kiss. But he didn't try for one. He only gazed down at her, steadily, trying his best to look both determined and hopeful.

She sighed. "You're right, I suppose."

"Of course I am," he declared with firmness. And then he arched a brow at her. "Er, right about what?"

That soft mouth was trying really hard not to smile.

"Well, that it's only a second date. And there *is* the spark—"

"Exactly. Come with us on Sunday."

She did smile then. For Connor, that smile was like the sun coming out on a rainy day. "Yes," she said. "All right."

Now he had what he wanted, he almost couldn't believe it. He stared down at her, speechless.

"What *are* you thinking?" she demanded, when several seconds had passed without a single word from him.

"You said yes."

"You're surprised?" Her eyes sparkled.

"I guess I am."

"Well, Connor, you were very convincing—but there is a condition."

"Name it."

"I'm inviting Jerilyn, too."

Chapter Four

Connor drove home in a pleasant haze of satisfaction. In spite of her objections, Tori had agreed to a second date. He felt pleased all out of proportion.

And Sunday wouldn't be the end of it. There would be a third date. And a fourth. And more after that. He was certain of it. The summer ahead was looking potentially brighter and more enjoyable than he ever would have imagined.

Until tonight, he'd seen this summer as a series of unpleasant but necessary steps, of things that he needed to do to get his life back on track: to try to get to know his son, to be a better brother to his sister. And to acquire a new property in tough times and make that property profitable in spite of everything.

Now, there was pleasure involved, too. Because of

a certain strawberry-blonde schoolteacher with a cute smattering of freckles across her nose.

At home, Gerda, his live-in housekeeper, was already in bed. Light bled out from under the door of CJ's room. Connor listened for the sounds of weapons firing and objects exploding.

Nothing. Just silence. CJ probably had his headphones on.

He looked at his watch. Almost one.

With a weary sigh, he tapped on the door. No answer. He tapped again, louder.

"What?" Muffled, annoyed, from inside.

Connor pushed the door open and went in.

As expected, CJ sat on the end of the bed, fully dressed, wearing headphones and working a controller. "What?" Eyes on the screen, thumbs flying.

Connor said nothing. He went over and sat next to his son on the bed. He watched the violence on the silent screen while CJ continued to play his game.

Several minutes passed. Connor felt his own impatience rise. He ignored it. He breathed slowly and evenly and he stared at the screen, sitting absolutely still.

Finally, CJ paused the game, took off his headphones, and glared at him. "I asked you, what?"

Connor spoke in a friendly tone. "I had a date with Tori Jones tonight. Had a really good time, too."

CJ gaped. For some reason, Connor found his son's surprise inordinately satisfying. "Ms. Jones? She went out with *you?*"

Connor played it cool. "That's right. And she's coming with us to the picnic Sunday."

"What picnic?" CJ pretended not to remember,

though Connor had told him more than once that they were going.

"Out at the Hopping H."

"Oh, great." Meaning it wasn't. "Forget it, okay? I'm not going to any picnic out at Aunt Melanie's ranch."

"Suit yourself."

CJ slanted him a suspicious look; Connor usually didn't give in that easily.

Connor got up and crossed to the door, turning back to deliver the zinger. "I'm sure Jerilyn will be sorry you couldn't make it." He stepped over the threshold.

CJ stopped him before he shut the door behind him. "Okay, wait."

Connor faced the room again. "It's late. Turn off the game and go to sleep."

"You're serious." CJ squinted at him, as though trying to see inside his head. "Jerilyn will be there."

If she accepts Tori's invitation. "I'm serious."

"Okay, fine. I guess I don't mind going."

Connor remembered Tori's advice. "Another thing."

"What?" CJ asked in a guarded mumble.

"You should ask Jerilyn to come over to the house. And any other new friends you've made in town."

"What for?"

"I don't know, just to…hang out. Plus, I'd like to get to know your friends a little."

CJ frowned as he turned Connor's suggestion over in his mind, no doubt looking for the catch. He found it. "Get to know them? Why? So you can ask them all kinds of questions?"

Connor suppressed a sigh. "No. Because they're your friends, that's all. I would like to meet your friends."

CJ thought about that for a minute. Apparently, he found Connor's reasoning acceptable. He gave out a grudging, "I'll think about it."

"Good. And go to bed."

"Oh, all right." CJ grabbed the remote and turned off the flatscreen.

"Good night," said Connor, as he pulled the door shut after him.

Faintly, he heard his son mutter, "Night."

In the morning, after breakfast, Connor shut the door to his study and called his sister. One of the college girls she had helping out at the ranch for the summer answered the phone.

"Hi, Mr. McFarlane. She's in the dining room, visiting with the guests."

"Have her call me when she gets a moment."

"Hold on. She just came into the kitchen…"

Then Melanie was on the line. "Connor. Hi."

"You sound breathless."

"We've got a full house." Even in the lagging economy, she was making the Hopping H pay. "And it's Saturday breakfast, which is always hectic."

"Just called to give you a heads-up. About tomorrow? I invited two more people. I hope that's okay."

"No problem. The more the merrier. Who? Do I know them?"

"Tori Jones and Jerilyn Doolin."

"Ah," Melanie said. It was a very knowing kind of sound.

"What does *ah* mean?"

"Not a thing."

"Liar."

"Well, if you must know, I ran into Tori at the Tottering Teapot last Monday."

"The Tottering Teapot. Is that a restaurant?"

"That's right. On Main. We all love it."

"We?"

"It's more of a woman's kind of place, actually," she explained. That news didn't surprise him in the least. "Lots of fresh salads. About a thousand different varieties of tea."

"I get the picture," he said without a lot of enthusiasm. "So you talked with Tori…"

"I did. She mentioned she was going out with you. And Grant dropped by early this morning. You two were spotted in the Gallatin Room last night."

He shook his head, though his sister couldn't see. "News travels at the speed of light around this town."

"It does, absolutely." Melanie lowered her voice. "Did you enjoy the evening? Isn't Tori great? I'm glad to see you dating again. It's about time."

"I did. She is. And come on. It's only been a year since the divorce. For your information, I *have* dated before last night, though the two other women I spent time with were nothing like Tori Jones."

"You never told me." She faked a hurt tone.

And suddenly, he could see her as she was at seven or eight years old. A skinny little red-headed thing, wanting attention from her big brother. And never getting it.

He swallowed down the sudden lump of guilt in his throat and kidded her, "Melanie, no matter how well we get along now, I'm not telling you everything."

"And just when I thought I knew all your secrets." Her joking tone turned distracted. "Hold on a minute…"

He heard her giving instructions to someone. Then she came back on the line. "Where were we?"

"I'm not going to keep you. But I did want to ask…"

"What? Name it."

"About that job offer Russ made, for CJ?"

"Still open. Just say the word."

"Great. But I'm thinking CJ's more likely to agree to the idea if it comes straight from you—or from anyone but me. Somehow, whatever I say to him nowadays, he thinks it's an order. An order he's honor-bound to reject out of hand."

"All right, then. Sunday, when the time is right, I'll offer him a job."

Tori called Jerilyn at nine Saturday morning to invite her to the Sunday picnic at Melanie's guest ranch.

The teenager answered the phone in tears. "Oh, Ms. Jones, I don't know what to do…"

"What? What's the matter?"

"Can I…would it be all right if I came over?"

"Yes. Right now. Do you want me to come and get you?"

"Oh, no. It's okay." The girl paused to stifle a sob. "I can ride my bike. I'll be there in ten minutes."

"You're sure?"

"I'll be right over."

When Jerilyn appeared, pedaling fast down the street, Tori was waiting for her, out on the porch.

"Oh, Ms. Jones…" Jerilyn dropped her bike on the front walk. Fresh tears welled. She ran up the steps and into Tori's waiting arms.

Tori pulled the girl inside and shut the door. "Shh... shh. There now. Okay..."

When the sobbing settled down a little, Tori led her to the sofa, passed the tissues, and got the story out of her.

"My dad got a warning Thursday. From his supervisor. My dad hasn't been getting the summer maintenance done. And if his work doesn't improve in the next two weeks, he's going to get fired."

"Oh, Jerilyn." Tori hugged her again. "Did your dad tell you this?"

Jerilyn blew her nose. "No way. He doesn't tell me anything. I found the warning notice on the kitchen table, wadded up in a ball. And he started drinking Thursday night. He called in sick yesterday. He drank all day, late into last night. He was still at it when I finally went to bed. This morning, he won't get up. I made breakfast. Just what he likes, scrambled eggs and home fries, sausage and English muffins. I tried to get him up to eat. He just growled at me to leave him alone."

"Has he...hit you?" Tori hated to ask, but she knew that she had to. "Or hurt you in any way?"

Jerilyn sobbed and shook her head. "Oh, no. He just sits at the kitchen table and drinks and doesn't say anything. Sometimes...he cries."

Tori grabbed her close again. "Aw, honey. It's okay. It's okay." As she gave out the familiar litany of reassurances, she knew that in reality, it wasn't okay. Not okay in the least.

"He would never hurt me." Jerilyn swallowed more sobs. "Except that when he loses his job and we can't pay the bills and...well, that will hurt me. That will hurt me really bad."

"That's not going to happen."

Jerilyn sagged against Tori with a long, sad sigh. "Yeah. It is. It is going to happen."

Tori took her by the shoulders. "Look at me. Do you trust me?"

"You know I do. Totally."

"I'm going to call someone who can help, okay? I'm going to do everything I can to bring your dad back to you, to make sure he doesn't lose his job."

Jerilyn blinked away the tears. "Who are you going to call?"

"Someone who's been through exactly what your dad's going through. Someone who managed to survive. Someone who will know what to do."

Tori's father, Dr. Sherwood Jones, caught a one-o'clock flight to Bozeman and rented a car. By four that afternoon, he was sitting in Tori's living room.

"I can't promise anything," he warned a pale-faced Jerilyn, who looked at him through red, puffy eyes. "And I can't even talk to him unless he's sober."

"He should be, by now. Unless he's started in drinking again."

"You say he's never hit you or been in any way violent with you?"

"No. He wouldn't. He...hasn't. Not ever. He's just so sad and lonely for my mom. They were always so close. She was his very best friend in the world. Without her... it's killing him, Dr. Jones. It's hurting him so deep."

"I understand." He glanced over at Tori, who sat across the coffee table from him and Jerilyn. Tori gulped down the sudden lump in her throat. Her dad did understand. They both did. He told Jerilyn. "Tori and I lost her mother when Tori was a couple of years younger than you are."

Jerilyn's eyes filled with tears again. She turned her gaze to Tori and tried a wobbly smile. "I know. Ms. Jones told me that, right after my mom died."

Sherwood clasped Jerilyn's shoulder. "I think we should go to your house now, see if maybe your dad is sober, and willing to talk with me. Are you okay with doing that?"

Jerilyn's dark eyes were wide—and determined. "Yes. I think we should. We should go now."

"Well, all right then," Sherwood said, with that gentle smile that always warmed Tori's heart.

They were at the front door when the phone rang. Tori told them, "I'll just get that and be out in a sec."

Her dad and Jerilyn headed for the car as Tori answered the phone on the side table in the great room.

It was Connor. "I just called to tell you I really hope Jerilyn said yes about tomorrow. I told CJ she would be there and suddenly he can't wait to go to a picnic at the Hopping H."

His voice, so warm, threaded with wry humor, made her wish he was there, right then, at her side. She would lean into him and he would put his strong arms around her and she would feel she could handle anything, even the rough family problems of her star student—and what was she thinking?

He was never going to be the kind of man she could lean on. She really had to remember that. He was leaving when summer was over—and in the meantime, he was going to cause trouble in the town that she loved.

"Tori? You there?"

"Right here. I…haven't invited her yet."

"What is it? What's happened?"

"It's a long story, one I just don't have time to go into right now."

"What can I do? Anything."

She almost smiled. When he talked like that, so ready to rush to her side if she needed him, she could almost forget that in his real life, he was a ruthless corporate shark determined to buy out the Thunder Canyon Resort and throw a bunch of people out of work. "No, really. Thank you."

"Are you in trouble?"

"No. Don't worry, please. It's not about me. I'm perfectly okay. And I'll explain it all later. Right now, I have to go."

"Call me. As soon as you can. I mean it."

"Yes. All right. I'll call this evening. I promise." She said a hurried goodbye and then rushed out to join and Jerilyn and Sherwood in his rental car.

Jerilyn lived in a small, run-down house in a South New Town neighborhood that had seen better days. The siding needed fresh paint and the porch boards creaked.

Inside, they found Butch Doolin sitting at the cluttered kitchen table in a T-shirt and a ragged pair of sweatpants. His bloodshot eyes were puffy from too much alcohol the day before and he sported a couple of days' worth of dark beard.

But he had a cup of coffee in front of him—no liquor in sight. He looked hungover, but sober.

And more than a little surprised to see Jerilyn, her teacher and some man he'd never met before standing in the doorway to his living room. "Jerilyn? What's going on?"

Tori's dad stepped right up. "I'm Sherwood Jones, Mr. Doolin. We're here to see if we can help."

Butch frowned. "Help?" And then he slowly shook his head. He turned to Jerilyn and spoke with weary resignation. "Sweet girl, what have you been up to?"

Jerilyn put her hand over her mouth, swallowed hard, and then let her hand drop. "Daddy. I saw that warning letter. You're going to lose your job. I had to do something. You can't keep on like this."

Tori had never seen a man so shamed as Butch Doolin was right then. He hung his head. "Sweet girl, I'm so sorry. So damn sorry. I don't know what to do, how to keep going. Without your mother, it all seems so pointless…" His big shoulders shook.

Jerilyn would have gone to him. But Tori's dad stopped her. He tipped his head back the way they had come. "You two go ahead," he said low. "Let me talk to him for a while." He tossed Tori the keys to the rental car. "I'll call you…"

Tori took Jerilyn's hand and led her back out through the small, dim living room. They returned to Tori's house to wait. Time crawled by. Tori offered dinner, but Jerilyn only shook her head.

Finally, at a little after seven, Tori's dad called for them to come and get him. Sherwood Jones was waiting for them out in front when they got to Jerilyn's again.

Jerilyn jumped out. "My dad? Is he…?"

Tori got out, too, and came around to join them on the cracked sidewalk.

"Your dad is okay. And I think he's going to be a lot better, Jerilyn," Tori's dad said. "I think he's ready to get help. We talked for a long time. He poured out all the booze in the house and he'll be going to regular AA meetings. Plus I've given him the names of a few good counselors he can choose from, as well as a local grief recovery group. And he has my number. I'm always available to him if he needs me." He gave Jerilyn a card. "And I'm available for you, as well. You can call me here, directly, if there's anything you want to ask me. And especially if you find yourself worried about him again."

"You really think he's going to get better?"

"I do. Sincerely. It's not going to be easy, but I think you'll see a definite improvement now."

Jerilyn let out a low cry and grabbed Tori's father in a hug. "Thank you, oh, thank you."

He hugged her back. "Call me if you need help. I mean that."

Then Tori offered Jerilyn that dinner she hadn't accepted before, but she was eager to go in, to talk to her dad. She grabbed Tori close, quickly let her go and turned for the house.

Tori remembered the picnic tomorrow. "Wait. I almost forgot. You're invited to a picnic at the Hopping H tomorrow."

"Will CJ be there?" The sad dark eyes were suddenly brighter.

"Yeah. But I'm sure he'll understand, if you'd rather—"

Jerilyn put up a hand. "Please. I want to go. My bike's at your house. Can you pick me up?"

Tori named a time and Jerilyn said she would be ready.

As Tori and her dad got back in the rental, she offered, "Hungry?"

Her dad shook his head. "Butch gave me a sandwich. And I need to get to Bozeman. There's a flight to Denver at ten to nine."

They drove back to Tori's house.

"That's one shiny SUV," her dad said when he pulled to a stop behind the expensive vehicle. "And there's a man on your porch."

Tori glanced over and saw Connor sitting on her top step, wearing pricey jeans, expensive boots and a dark-colored knit shirt. The sight of him caused her heart to do a happy somersault inside her chest. Which was ridiculous. *And* physically impossible. "It's Connor. He's…a friend," she said, sounding absurdly breathless. Connor rose and came down the steps. She added, "I'll introduce you to him, Dad."

Connor was already at her side door. She rolled her window down. He was smiling. But his eyes were cool. Maybe he wasn't all that happy about watching her drive up with a strange man.

"Hey," he said. "I got worried about you."

"Connor, this is my father, Dr. Sherwood Jones."

Suddenly, his dark eyes had warmth in them again. "Dr. Jones. Hello."

Her dad stuck his arm across the seat. "Good to meet you, Connor." Connor put out his hand, too. Tori leaned out of the way so they could shake.

Then Sherwood gunned the engine. "I hate to run off. But I have to get a move on or I'll miss that last flight. And while your stepmother is a very understanding woman, she insists I save Sundays for her and the boys."

Tori leaned across the console and kissed his cheek. "Thanks, Dad."

"Anytime."

"Kiss Lucille and hug my brothers for me."

"Will do."

Connor opened her door for her and she got out. With a final wave, Tori's dad drove off.

She felt Connor's hand settle at her waist. A little thrill went through her at the contact. She chided him, "I said I would call."

"I should be more patient, I know."

"Yes, you should. Especially considering that we've only had one date."

"Two, if you count tomorrow."

She laughed. "It's not tomorrow yet." And then she confessed, "I'm glad you're here."

"Me, too." He pulled her closer to his side. "What was that all about?"

She looked up into those beautiful eyes of his and wanted to trust him—even if he *was* a shark. "I'm starving."

"Are you going to tell me what happened today?"

"Probably. But right now, I want to eat."

"You want to go out?"

"You know, you're sneaking in a third date on me and we haven't even gotten through the second one yet."

"It's true. That's exactly what I'm doing. We could go to—"

She didn't let him finish. "No. I've got some stuffed shells in the fridge. And I'll make a salad. You want pasta?"

"I ate with CJ. But if you twisted my arm, I'd have a little something."

"Jerilyn will be coming with us tomorrow."

"Terrific. I wasn't looking forward to telling CJ otherwise."

They went up the walk together, circling Jerilyn's bike when they got to it. Tori made a mental note to take it up to the porch before she went to bed.

Inside, Connor pushed the front door shut behind them and caught her hand when she would have headed straight for the kitchen.

"Wait a minute…" His warm, strong arms came around her.

"Oh, Connor…"

"Shh." He lowered his mouth to hers.

It was a beautiful kiss. Slow, lazy, gradually deepening. His arms felt so good around her and her body seemed to hum in response to him, as if she were somehow tuned to him—to his touch, to his strong body pressed so close to hers, to his lips that were doing magical things to hers. Even to the scent of him, which was clean and so manly. He tasted of mint. And of heat. She never wanted to pull away.

But she did. "Dinner. I mean it."

In the kitchen, she warmed up the giant herb-and-cheese stuffed pasta shells and put a salad together. He ate two shells and two pieces of garlic bread. She sat across from him at her breakfast nook table and couldn't believe how comfortable it felt having him there.

Comfortable. And kind of thrilling. Both at the same time.

Was that good?

Or just plain dangerous? The last thing she needed was to fall for Connor McFarlane, who would wreak havoc up at the resort, cause people to lose their livelihoods—and then go back east before the first snow.

"Does Melanie know you're planning to take over the resort?"

He set down his fork. "The shells were really good. And who says I'm planning to take over the resort?"

"Well, if you were—and she didn't know—that might not be such a great thing for your relationship with her, that you might be doing something that affects her community and you haven't even bothered to tell her. I mean, if you're not going tell me, you at least should tell *her* what you're up to, don't you think?"

He had picked up his water glass. But he set it down without taking a drink. "Yes," he said blandly. "I suppose, if I were planning a buyout of the resort, that maybe I ought to tell my sister what I have in mind."

"Will you, then? Will you tell her?"

He only gazed at her, his face a mask, unreadable.

Suddenly, she was furious with him. But why?

Self-preservation, maybe. She could still feel the warm, exciting pressure of his lips on hers, still remember the thrill of his arms wrapped tightly around her.

Really, she was much too attracted for her own peace of mind.

She said, too softly, "You want me to tell you what happened this afternoon, to trust you with something that's private to someone I care about, but you won't even tell me honestly whether you're thinking of buying out the resort or not."

He took his napkin from his lap, wiped his mouth, and slid it in beside his plate. "All right, Tori."

"All right, what?"

"I can see this is an ultimatum."

"I didn't say that."

"You didn't have to. It's all over your face, clear in your voice."

"Look. The word is out that you're sniffing around the resort. People aren't blind around here. And if I'm going to be spending more time with you, I want to know the truth. I can live with this thing between us ending when the fall comes. But I can't live with you lying to me."

"I haven't lied to you."

"By omission, yes. You have. I want to know for certain. I *need* to know—at least, I do if we're going to keep dating."

"Why do you need to know? What possible good will the information do?"

She considered his question. And she answered truthfully. "It's about honesty, Connor. It's about basic trust. Are you hoping to buy out the resort, yes or no?"

A silence. A long one. And then, finally, "I would need to know ahead of time that you would keep what I tell you to yourself."

"Uh-uh. No way. Is there some reason it has to be a secret—especially considering that everybody already knows anyway? I mean, come on. You talk about how you want to change things in your life, with your son. With your sister. Maybe being straight in your business dealings wouldn't be such a bad idea, either. I'm not saying you have to tell me all the diabolical details of your takeover plan. I'm just saying why deny what you're after when everyone knows your denial is a big, fat lie anyway?"

He arched a brow. "Diabolical?"

She waved a hand. "Sorry. That was a little over the top. But still, you know what I mean."

He refused to give in. "As a rule, it's not a good idea to show your hand, even if the player across from you already knows you have aces."

"We're talking about people's lives, Connor, not a card game."

He pushed back his chair and stood. "This conversation is going nowhere."

She knew he was right. They were arguing in circles. She said gently, "Yeah. I guess so."

"Good night." His voice was soft, his eyes troubled.

"Good night, Connor."

He went out through the great room. She heard the front door open and close. And a minute or two after that, she heard the SUV start up and drive away.

She sat there at the table for a long time after he left her, feeling sad and weepy—but refusing to cry. Connor McFarlane was not the man for her. She had to accept that. It was better that he had left, that his thing between them went no further. Getting into it with him would only lead to hurt and heartbreak.

Alone at the table, she nodded to herself and swallowed down the lump of tears that clogged her throat. Yes. Really. It was better that he was gone.

Chapter Five

Connor was halfway back to his rented house, feeling like crap, trying to come to grips with the fact that his enjoyable summer with Tori Jones was over before it had even begun, when he realized that he'd left her without canceling their plans for tomorrow.

At the house, after spending a few minutes in CJ's room, watching him play his endless video game, he went to his own room. He took a shower and sat in front of the television, channel-surfing with the sound down, paying very little attention to the images that flashed in front of his eyes.

He kept reliving what it felt like to hold her in his arms. He'd been really looking forward to doing that again, and frequently. And he'd done some serious fantasizing over what it was going to be like the first time they made love. It would probably be really good, if the chemistry between them was any indication.

Maybe she would call and tell him formally that she wouldn't be coming to the picnic tomorrow. Maybe he ought to call her.

But the phone didn't ring. And he decided it would be easier just to go ahead and proceed as planned tomorrow. At worst, she would call it off when he and CJ came to pick her and Jerilyn up. He could live with that.

And if she decided to go through with it, well, he could stand that, too. It would be awkward, yes, but at least CJ would be happy to have some time with the girl he liked.

In the morning, Connor had breakfast with CJ and then went to his study to look over some paperwork from the main office. The phone rang at eleven. He jumped at the sound.

But it was only his father, making the usual demands, that he come back to Philly immediately, to stay. That, if he insisted on doing the resort deal, he get on it and get it over with.

Connor made noncommittal noises and told his dad to give his mother his love.

An hour later, he and CJ left the house.

"You okay, Dad?" CJ asked him as they drove the quiet Sunday streets on the way to Tori's house.

Connor almost ran a red light. It was the first time in the past year or so that his son had expressed the slightest interest in him or anything he might be doing or thinking.

It was a clear sign that he was actually making progress with the boy. He should have been ecstatic.

And he was. But the thrill was muted by the

knowledge that whatever progress he was making with CJ was mostly due to the excellent advice of a certain strawberry-blonde schoolteacher. And then there was also the possibility that whatever gains he'd made would be lost if Jerilyn was not at Tori's house when they got there, if Tori had decided to call the afternoon off.

Really, he should have discussed the picnic with her before he walked out on her last night. Or called her later.

But he hadn't. And now he was stuck with having no clue what would happen when they got to her house.

Bright move, McFarlane.

He pushed his dark thoughts away and sent his son a warm glance. "Thanks, I'm okay."

"You're really quiet."

"Just…thoughtful, I guess."

At Tori's house, the bicycle that had been on the front walk the evening before was propped up on the porch. But other than that, everything looked just as it had last night. He still had no clue whether Tori and Jerilyn were coming with them, or not.

CJ jumped out of the car and was halfway up the walk before Connor got out and followed him. It was CJ who rang the doorbell. Connor was just climbing the steps when the door opened.

Tori, in jeans, boots and a cute, snug Western shirt, grinned at CJ. "Right on time."

Relief, sweet as cool water on a hot day, poured through Connor. They were going. He'd never been so pleased about anything in his life.

Jerilyn, also in jeans, peered over Tori's shoulder. "Hey."

"Hey," CJ replied, his voice cracking on the

single syllable. He cleared his throat and said it again. "Hey."

Tori's gaze shifted to meet Connor's. She gave him a careful smile and a nod. He did the same.

"I packed a basket," she said. "Some cheese and fruit, some whole-wheat crackers. Some juice…"

Jerilyn pulled a face. "All totally healthy," she added. And she and CJ groaned in unison.

"Ready to go?" Connor asked.

"Yes, we are," Tori replied, her gaze sliding away from his. "I'll get the basket and we can be on our way."

His relief that she wasn't backing out on him faded. He could see the day stretching endlessly out ahead of them. A day of careful smiles and sliding glances, of unacknowledged tension.

But there was nothing else to do but gut it up and get through it. The muscles in his shoulders knotting, he turned and went back down the steps toward the waiting SUV.

It was a good day, the sky clear and blue, with only a few fluffy white clouds gliding slowly toward the west.

Russ had horses picked out and tacked up for each of them. Connor, who had learned to ride six years before when he opened McFarlane House Louisville at a former horse ranch, got a big palomino mare. Tori got a handsome bay gelding. CJ's gray seemed calm and steady-natured, as did Jerilyn's blue roan. Russ, Melanie and Ryan all rode the horses they favored for everyday riding at the Hopping H and at Russ's original ranch, the Flying J, which abutted the H.

Melanie had pack saddles full of food and drinks. She tucked the stuff Tori had brought in with the rest, and they rode out.

In a wide, rolling pasture dotted with wildflowers, they spread a couple of blankets. Melanie and Tori put out the food. They ate as the hobbled horses cropped the grass nearby.

The kids were finished with lunch in no time. They wandered off to explore, CJ and Jerilyn side by side, Ryan happily trailing along behind.

The grown-ups chatted about casual stuff. Melanie said she and Russ were turning a nice profit with the guest ranch. Russ talked about buying more land. Connor dared to kid him that if he didn't watch out, he'd become a land baron. Russ laughed and said maybe he would. His easy response pleased Connor. He was making progress healing the early breach with his cowboy brother-in-law.

Tori mentioned some Outward Bound–type program, ROOTS, that a local woman, Haley Anderson, was trying to start up in a storefront in town. Melanie said she was so happy for Haley, to have found the right place for ROOTS at last.

And then Melanie wanted to know if Tori had met Erin Castro, who was new in town and apparently going around asking questions about the Cateses, the Cliftons and the Traubs.

Tori frowned. "No. I haven't met her."

Russ said, "Grant told me that woman started in on him at the Hitching Post. She had a thousand and one questions."

Connor remembered the blonde woman he'd spoken to at the bar at DJ's. "I met her at the summer kickoff barbecue. She introduced herself." He described their brief conversation.

Russ grunted. "She's up to something…"

"But what?" Melanie wondered aloud.

Russ added, "Grant said she has this tattered yellowed newspaper clipping, a picture of some old-time gathering of—"

"Let me guess." Connor predicted, "The Cateses, the Cliftons and the Traubs."

"You got it."

"Maybe she's writing a tell-all," Tori suggested lightly. "The secrets of Thunder Canyon, Montana, revealed."

"She better watch herself," Russ muttered darkly. "Folks around here don't like strangers poking in their private business."

And the conversation moved on.

Connor didn't say much to Tori. She returned the favor. He didn't think his sister or her husband even noticed that they kept their distance from each other and avoided eye contact.

He couldn't help glancing Tori's way, though, when he thought no one was looking. She was so pretty, strawberry-blond hair shining in the sun, her skin like cream. There was something about her, even beyond her fresh good looks, something that drew him. He couldn't explain it, and he certainly didn't understand it. It just *was*, like the blue sky above, the wide, rolling pasture below.

And it's going nowhere, so get over it, the voice of wisdom within advised.

The kids wandered in and out of their view, sometimes disappearing into a small stand of pines on a ridge to the northeast, sometimes coming near, but then turning to head off in a different direction before they got too close to the adults. Their laughter and chatter rang out across the rolling field.

Once, when they were all three in sight, near a weathered fence that separated the pasture from the next one over, Melanie got up. "Time to talk a little business." She set off toward the three by the fence.

"Business?" Tori glanced at Connor—and then apparently caught herself actually looking at him. Her gaze slid away.

Russ, stretched out on his back, with his hat over his eyes, said lazily, "Connor's decided it's not a bad idea if CJ does a little honest work this summer."

Tori sent Connor another swift glance. What? She was surprised that he'd taken her advice.

He gave a curt nod and looked away.

Russ, still with his hat over his eyes, continued, "He and Red agreed that she should make the offer." According to Melanie, Russ had always called her Red. Even back when she didn't like it in the least. Now, though, it was his pet name for her.

Melanie had reached the three teenagers. Connor—and Tori, too, he noticed out of the corner of his eye—watched as the scene played out. Melanie spoke.

CJ instantly started shaking his head, backing away. It looked like a no-go.

But then Jerilyn said something. Melanie nodded and offered her hand. The girl took it.

And then CJ spoke up again. Melanie turned to him and said something. He nodded. And Melanie shook *his* hand.

Ryan shot a fist in the air and they heard him exclaim, "Yes!"

Russ lifted his hat enough to glance toward the scene by the old fence. "Mission accomplished, if you ask me."

"Looks that way," Connor agreed. "Your wife is amazing."

"She certainly is." Russ spoke with deep satisfaction. Then he put his hat back over his eyes and let his head drop to the blanket again.

Melanie returned to them. Connor thought she looked sort of bemused. "CJ starts tomorrow," she told him. "Nine to one, Monday through Thursday. I guess we'll have to take turns driving him out here—Jerilyn, too."

"Either Gerda or I will do it, no problem." Connor would slip his housekeeper a little extra for the inconvenience. "So you've got two new employees, then?"

"Oh, yes, I do. CJ turned me down flat. But then Jerilyn spoke up and said how she'd love to work at the Hopping H. So I offered her the job."

Connor could guess the rest. "And then CJ suddenly changed his mind."

"And it's great. I can put them both to work, and Ryan will love having them around." She added, sounding bemused again, "I really do like that girl."

Connor almost turned to share a glance with Tori, to give her a nod of acknowledgment, since what had just happened was all at her urging. But then he remembered that he and Tori were finished sharing glances.

They were finished, period.

As the day went by, Tori became only more certain that there really was no hope for her and Connor. The picnic at the ranch was just one of those final obligations they both felt duty-bound to fulfill.

By Sunday evening, when Connor pulled the SUV to a stop in front of her house, she was beyond positive. It was done between them, finished. All without ever really getting started.

She tried to remind herself yet again that it was for the best. But somehow it didn't feel that way in the least.

CJ and Jerilyn jumped out first, but only to load Jerilyn's bike in the back. They would take it to her house when they dropped her off.

That left Tori and Connor momentarily alone.

She said, each word falsely bright, "Well, thank you. It was a beautiful day."

"Yeah," he replied without looking at her. "Great weather."

"I'll be seeing you, then." She leaned on the door.

He turned as the door swung wide and he looked at her. A look that burned her right down to the core. She had the impossible, overwhelming urge to leap across the console and kiss him so hard...

Uh-uh. No way. Not going to happen.

She tore her gaze free of his and got the heck out of there, somehow managing to wave goodbye to Jerilyn and CJ as they put the bike in the back of the SUV.

In the house, feeling totally bereft and hating that she felt that way, she called Allaire. But no one was home. They were probably off at some Traub family Sunday dinner. Tori hung up without leaving a message.

About then, she realized that she'd left her picnic basket in the back of Connor's SUV. It wasn't a big deal. She could get it later. Much, much later.

Or maybe he would have CJ drop it by.

It was all just too sad and depressing. She'd finally found a guy who made her heart turn somersaults, and he was a ruthless corporate shark unwilling to be straight with her.

She took a long bath and turned in early.

And at midnight she was still lying there, wide awake, telling herself that she hardly knew Connor. They'd only spent a total of maybe fifteen hours together—if you counted the picnic just that day, when they'd each been doing their level best to pretend the other didn't exist.

Really, she needed to get over this and move on. She needed to shut her eyes and get some sleep.

But sleep was not in the offing. She kept seeing his face at that last moment before she got out of the SUV, seeing the hunger there, the stark longing for what was never going to happen between them. She kept thinking that maybe she had been too uncompromising.

After all, she knew darn well he was trying to buy out the resort. His confessing the fact in so many words wouldn't make much difference in the end.

Except that, well, what kind of relationship would they have, if he couldn't even be honest with her about his real intentions? It all had to start with honesty, and with trust, too. If they didn't have honesty and trust, they had nothing.

Time crawled by. She tried not to look at her bedside clock. It only reminded her how miserable she was—and how little sleep she was getting.

And then, out of nowhere, at ten after one, the doorbell rang.

At the unexpected sound, her pulse started booming in her ears. And her chest felt so tight, it hurt to breathe.

Either it was Connor, unable to wait to tell her he wanted to work it out with her. Or it was some awful disaster that couldn't be put off till daylight: a fire; Jerilyn with bad news about her dad…

Terrible dread and impossible hope warring for prominence in her heart, Tori yanked on her robe and ran to answer. Breathless, frantic, she pulled the door wide—and when she saw who was on the other side, her pulse thudded all the louder.

Connor.

He stood there on her doorstep in the same jeans and fancy boots he'd worn that afternoon, her picnic basket in his hand, looking exhausted—but determined, too. She realized as she gaped at him that he was the handsomest man she'd ever known.

"You left this in my SUV." He held out the basket. "And yes, I'm planning to buy the resort."

Connor waited, his stomach in a knot and his throat locked up tight. He had no idea what would happen next. She just might grab the basket and shut the door in his face.

But no. Those amazing hazel eyes had gone misty. That had to be a good sign, right?

And then she stepped back and tipped her head toward the great room, inviting him in.

He cleared his throat. He felt he owed her…something. A more thorough confession.

What the hell was happening to him? He wished he knew.

He found his voice. "I've been walking the floor half the night, thinking about you—" And then it was like a damn bursting. The words came tumbling out of him.

"Thinking about how I've never met anyone like you and I can't stand to think it's over with us when it never even got started. I decided at least fifty times that I would come over here—after which I decided not to, that in the end, I would be leaving when the summer is over, so what was the point, since I know you want more than a summer romance?"

She gazed up at him, her eyes so soft. "Connor."

"Yeah?"

"Will you please come in so that I can shut the door?"

He frowned, wanting—*needing*—her to be certain about letting him into her house. It was insane. Where had these silly scruples come from? He'd never been troubled by them before. "You're, uh, sure?"

She only looked at him, still misty-eyed, and slowly nodded her red-gold head.

So he stepped over the threshold. She shut the door behind him and turned the lock. And then she took the picnic basket from him and set it on the narrow entry-area table.

"Come on." She turned. He followed her through the great room to her cozy kitchen at the back of the house. "Sit down." She gestured at the table.

He sat, hardly daring to believe he was actually here in her kitchen again, that not only had he come here in the middle of the night, she had answered the door. She had let him in.

Maybe it wasn't over, after all.

He watched, dumbfounded, as she put water on for the tea she liked and loaded up the coffeemaker for him. She looked more beautiful than ever, he thought, with her hair a little wild, her face scrubbed clean of makeup, wearing a lightweight yellow robe that revealed a lot of sleek bare leg and adorable bare feet with toenails painted the color of a ripe plum.

She pushed the brew button on the coffeemaker and took the chair across from him. "What else?"

"Uh. Excuse me?"

"It seemed as though you had more to say."

"I did. I do."

She folded her hands on the tabletop. "I'm listening."

He raked his fingers back through his hair. "It's only…I'm sorry, but I can't give you more than this summer. This, right now, that's all I'm ready for. I'm not…cut out for anything more."

Her red-kissed brows drew together and he knew he wasn't making much sense.

He confessed, "I, well, I was a lousy husband, you know?"

"No. I didn't know."

"I was. Just lousy. All that really mattered to me was my work. I wanted to take what my father and grandfather had started and make it *more*. New, exciting locations, each one-of-a-kind, each a luxury boutique hotel with stylish rooms, signature restaurants, bars and destination spas. I considered marriage and children as no more than something that was expected of me, something I needed to get out of the way so I could focus on my work, on growing the McFarlane House brand. So I fulfilled what I saw as my obligation to acquire a spouse, to procreate. I found a beautiful woman with the right pedigree and I married her."

"You…you didn't care for her at all?"

He shrugged. "Looking back, I think I told myself I

cared. But really, being brutally honest now, I didn't care enough. Yes, I told my ex-wife I loved her, but it was just because I knew it was something I was supposed to say. And it's only by necessity that I'm trying to figure out how to be a halfway decent dad for CJ."

"But, Connor, you *are* trying. That's what matters."

"No. I'm doing what I have to do, fulfilling my responsibility to my son. Period. I live for my work, and I'm not husband material. I can't see that changing. I'm just not a family man."

She caught her lower lip between her even white teeth—and then let it go. "Clearly, it's not going to do any good to tell you that you're a better man than you think you are."

He stuck with the truth, painful as it was to reveal. "I think you *want* me to be a better man."

She gazed at him for a long time. And then, finally, she conceded, "Yes. That may be true, to an extent. I would like you to be the best you can be. Tonight, though, I see that you already are a good man. A man capable of honesty. Of trust. And I understand what you're telling me. I already knew—or at least, I knew the part about how you're not up for anything long-lasting. We talked about it before, remember?"

"Of course I remember. I remember everything. Every look. Every smile. Every word we said." He swore low. "I sound like an idiot, some hopeless fool..."

"No. You don't." She reached out her hand to him. He met her halfway, in the middle of the table. Palm to palm, they wove their fingers together. "You don't sound like a fool, not in the least." Her soft mouth trembled on a smile. "I'm so glad that you're here. That it's not over, after all."

He shoved back his chair and stood. She stood with him. And then, hands still joined, in unison they stepped toward each other around the table. Once she was close enough, he reeled her in. She felt like heaven in his arms.

"No, it's not over," he said, staring down into those beautiful misty eyes. "Not yet…"

"Not yet…" she echoed, lifting her mouth to him. He took it. Wrapping her tighter, closer, he kissed her deeply, learning all the sweet, wet surfaces behind her parted lips.

When he lifted his head, it was only to slant it the other way and claim her lips again. He could have stood there in her kitchen, holding her, kissing her, until the sun came up.

But then the kettle whistled and the coffeemaker beeped. He let her go so she could brew her tea and pour his coffee.

They sat across from each other again.

He stared at his untouched mug, at the fragrant curl of steam rising from it. "Jerilyn told CJ what happened Saturday, the crisis with Jerilyn's father. He said your dad flew in from Denver to help. Jerilyn says she has hope now, that things will be all right."

"CJ told you what Jerilyn told him?"

"He did."

"I think I would call that actual communication—and the beginnings of trust, as well."

"So would I. Due in large part to you, Tori. I'm trying, I really am, to take your advice, to let him know I'm on his side, that he can count on me. I think it just may be working—at least a little."

"I'm so glad."

"You haven't touched your tea."

She tipped her head to the side the way she always did when she was studying him. "And you aren't drinking your coffee."

He confessed, "I'm thinking about holding you in my arms again. And I'm also thinking that if I start kissing you, I won't want to stop."

"Would that be...so bad?" Her voice was shy, hesitant. Her eyes were anything but.

"Uh-uh. Not bad at all. It would be really, really good. But I don't want to rush you into anything you might regret."

Her smile was full of feminine intent. "How long do you plan to stay here in town?"

"I have to leave Wednesday, for meetings in Philadelphia. But I'll be back by Friday afternoon."

Steadily, she held his gaze. "I meant, how long are you planning to be living in town? When will you be leaving for good?"

"If the resort deal works out, I'll be here into the winter, at least. But after CJ returns to school, I'll make my home base back east, and only be in Thunder Canyon on and off."

"And CJ starts school...?"

"At the end of August."

"A little over two months from now."

"That's right. Is that somehow significant?"

"Yes. Very."

"Because?"

She pushed her chair back again, leaving her tea still untouched. "Because two months will go by too fast. And it seems to me that we shouldn't waste a day, an hour, another *minute* of the time we have together."

He stared at her. And then, slowly, he rose to his feet. They faced each other, with only the round kitchen table between them. He asked, rough and low, "What are telling me, Tori?"

She approached him slowly, untying the sash of her robe as she came. When she reached him, she dropped the sash to the floor and eased the robe from her shoulders. It fell away without a sound. Underneath she wore a short summer nightgown with tiny satin straps that tied in charming little bows at her shoulders. That nightgown revealed a lot more than it covered.

His desire, carefully banked until then, flared high. "You are so beautiful."

"Take me in your arms, Connor," she whispered, lifting on tiptoe, her breasts brushing his chest, making the flare of desire burn all the hotter. "Take me in your arms and hold me all night long."

Chapter Six

Connor's newfound conscience urged him to argue with her, to tell her she ought to think twice about this, to grab her by the shoulders and put her firmly away from him, to speak reasonably about taking their time, to remind her again about not rushing into anything she might regret later.

But she had it right, after all. They didn't have a lot of time. Just one short summer.

And wasting a minute of it, now they were both on the same page about where they were going?

Uh-uh. No way.

He wrapped his arms around her, good and tight. And he kissed her, deeply. Endlessly. His mouth locked to hers, drinking her in, he bent to scoop her up high in his arms.

She pulled her soft lips from his just long enough

to fling out a hand in the general direction of the great room and to whisper, "That way…"

He claimed her mouth again and started walking, carrying her out of the kitchen, across the great room, to her bedroom not far from the entryway. The door was wide open. He went in.

At the side of the bed, he lowered her feet to the rug. Dizzy with the scent of her, with the taste of her, and the soft, arousing feel of her body so close to him, somehow he still managed to break the incredible kiss.

He knew that they had to be at least a little bit responsible. "I should have thought of this."

"Of what?"

"I don't have condoms…"

She surged up, caught his mouth in a swift, hot kiss, and then sank back to her heels again. "It's okay." She rested her small hands, palms flat, against his chest. "I have them." Her dreamy gaze turned rueful. "I always wanted to be ready, in case it ever felt right with someone. It never did—not in the whole time I've lived in Thunder Canyon. Not until tonight…"

"Well." He ran his palms down the silky skin of her arms. So smooth. And she smelled so good. Like fresh, ripe strawberries and sugared lemons, both at the same time. "Okay, then."

"Just okay?" she teased him.

He chuckled. "Better than okay. Way, way better."

"Then kiss me, Connor." Her eyes were mossy green at that moment, and shining so bright. "Kiss me again…"

He didn't have to be told a third time. He caught her sweet lips and she opened for him, letting his tongue in to play with hers. And as he kissed her, she turned slightly, moving them both around, until the backs of his legs touched the side of the bed.

She guided him, gently pushing him back, until he lay across the tangled white sheets. And she came down with him, soft and sighing, her mouth so wet and sweet. He couldn't get enough of her kisses, couldn't get enough of *her*.

But then she pulled away and rose up on an elbow. She gazed down at him, her lips soft and swollen, her eyes making tempting erotic promises as she tugged on his shirttail, sliding her fingers beneath the knit fabric to caress him.

He groaned at her touch, at the way her soft fingers glided over his flesh, tenderly, teasingly. And he wanted to feel her, all of her, skin to skin. So he sat up, kissed her once, hard and fast, and ripped his shirt up and over his head. Swiftly, he yanked off his boots and got rid of his socks. He undid the button at the top of his fly, and tugged the zipper down. Lifting his hips, he shoved the jeans and his boxer briefs halfway down his thighs.

She helped him, getting hold of the jeans and the briefs, sliding them off the rest of the way, tossing them over the edge of the bed.

At last, he was naked. He felt her gaze on him, sweeping upward over his body to meet his waiting eyes.

She breathed his name on a long sigh. "Connor..." And she swayed against him.

Magic, the feel of her smooth skin pressed to his. He caught her, pulling her close, tucking her tightly to his bare chest, reveling in the silky feel of her hair against his flesh, in the delicacy of her body, the way it curved into his, in the scent of her, so fresh and clean and sweet.

"Tori." Her name sounded so good on his tongue.

She tipped her head back to him with a questioning sound.

"Tori..." He kissed her. And that time, while he kissed her, he touched her, clasping her slim upper arm, palming the firm curve of her shoulder.

Such soft, tempting skin, and all of it his to caress. He traced a finger inward, skimming the bows that held her nightgown in place. And then up, along the velvety skin of her neck, until he reached the heated flutter of her pulse, waiting there for him, in the vulnerable cove at the side of her throat.

He laid his whole hand, flat, against the satiny warmth of her upper chest. Lower still, he curved his fingers around a high, firm breast. She moaned when he did that, and moaned again as he found her nipple through the thin cloth of her nightgown and teased it, rolling it tenderly between his thumb and forefinger.

Those sweet little bows at her shoulders? By then he couldn't resist them. He made short work of them, pulling the end of one and then the other. They fell apart, taking the top of her flimsy little gown down with them.

Her breasts were revealed to him, round and firm, compact, the skin so fine, the delicate blue veins showing faintly beneath. He eased her to her back, bent his head and took her pretty pink nipple into his mouth. She groaned deep in her chest when he did that, and pulled him close to her. He drew on her breast, strongly, and she bowed her slim torso toward him, lifting her breasts, offering him more of her.

The hem of her short gown rode high on her smooth thighs. He reached down, guided it higher.

She wore nothing beneath. He touched her belly, stroking, loving the feel of her, enjoying the eager way she gave herself, so openly, without holding anything of herself away from him. She groaned and clutched his head even tighter to her breast.

And he let his hand wander lower, over the warm silk of her lower belly, to the place where the soft curls were waiting. She lifted toward him, urging him on.

He touched her, dipping a finger into the feminine heart of her. She was wet. Hot. He explored the silky folds and she encouraged him with tender little moans and sighs, as she lifted her hips, opening her thighs to him, so eager. Hungry for more.

So he gave her more. He kissed his way down her body, sliding her gown even higher, until it was no more than a tangled, satin band around her waist. He kissed her belly, dipped his tongue into her navel, and breathed in the musky, sweet scent of her excitement.

He had to taste her. Now. Immediately. He kissed the silky red-gold curls and lower, putting his mouth where his wet fingers had been.

She was writhing by then, her hands clutching his head, fingers speared in his hair, urging him onward. He ran his tongue along the slick wetness, drinking in the taste of her, driving her higher, finding that it aroused him beyond all reason to be giving her pleasure, to know that she liked it, that she wanted him to kiss her in this most intimate way.

And then, all at once, she was crying out his name. She broke, shuddering. He tasted her completion, felt it pulse against his tongue.

Her satisfaction drove him higher, gave him something so good, so right. Something he had never known he craved, something hot and bright and beautiful. Something good and true.

Who knew it could be like this?

Not Connor.

He had never been what anyone would call an attentive lover. With his wife, the sex didn't matter anyway, except for the necessity of producing his son. And with the women he'd dated in the past year, he'd been utterly selfish. He saw that now. They gave him pleasure in the form of sexual release. And he took them out to the best restaurants, showered then with pricey gifts.

But with Tori…

Everything was different.

He got pleasure from *her* pleasure, took satisfaction from knowing she was satisfied.

She sighed, and a little laugh escaped her. "Oh, Connor." Her fingers, now, were gentle in his hair. "Who knew?" Good question. He certainly hadn't. She whispered, "Come up here, up here to me…"

One last press of his lips against those wet red-gold curls and he obeyed her, kissing his way up the middle of her body, over her soft, tempting belly, between her small, perfect breasts. He paused to dip his tongue into the groove at the base of her throat. Never would he get enough of the taste of her, sweet and slightly salty now, with the sweat of their lovemaking.

He kissed her throat, her chin, and finally, with a sigh, he settled his mouth over hers and tasted her more deeply. He was aching, aching in a good way, hard and ready, needing her so bad.

She caught his face in her two soft hands. "The drawer, in the nightstand…"

He reached for it, his mouth still locked with hers.

Finding the knob, he pulled it open, felt around inside, his fingers closing over a pen, a notepad, a small flashlight. But nothing that felt like the condom he was groping for.

She pushed gently at his shoulders. "Let me," she suggested.

Reluctantly, he let her up, and sank back against the pillows. He admired the gorgeous curve of her slim back as she got up on her folded knees and slid the drawer all the way open.

"Got it." She pulled out a box from way in back and swiftly peeled the lid wide, taking out a single sealed pouch. She held it up.

He reached for it.

But she only laughed and snatched it away and looked at him from under her thick lashes. "Let me. Please."

He settled back against the pillow again and folded his hands behind his head. "Absolutely. Be my guest." He spoke teasingly, though he wanted only to grab her, roll her under him and bury himself deep in her waiting softness.

She was kind. She didn't fool around. She had the pouch open and the condom sliding down over him within seconds. The touch of her hand as she guided it into place, snugging it neatly, evenly, at the base, almost undid him.

But not quite. She bent over him, so her lips were no more than a breath away from his. "Good?"

He refused to move. If she wanted to take control, so be it. "Excellent."

She slid a leg over him and went up on her knees astride him, but away from him. Her eyes weren't so teasing anymore. They were hungry. Ready.

He resisted the powerful urge to grab her hips and surge up into her.

She bent close, though she didn't lower herself down onto his waiting hardness. She whispered, "You're gritting your teeth."

"And you're driving me wild."

"I'm so glad to hear that." She kissed him, slowly, a brushing kiss that turned deeper—and then deeper still.

"Come down to me, Tori. Now..."

Impossibly, miraculously, she actually obeyed him. He felt her against him—there, where he needed her—and then he slipped inside.

She was wet and hot and, oh, so welcoming. He couldn't stop himself from reaching for her then. He took her hips and pulled her down onto him.

She moaned then. So did he.

And she rode him, kissing him, her hips working in a rhythm that shattered him, that broke him into a thousand tiny pieces—and then somehow put him back together again.

At the last minute, as he knew he was losing it, he grabbed her more firmly by the round curves of her bottom and he rolled her, so he was on top. She lifted her legs and wrapped them around him, holding him, rocking him, murmuring his name.

He muttered, "Tori," and then again, "Tori," as the world spun away. He saw utter darkness behind his eyes. And then, at the last possible moment, as she turned him inside out, the darkness turned to shimmering light.

They must have slept.

When he woke, the bedside clock said it was almost

five. Tori lay beside him, her face so innocent and sweet in the light of the lamp they'd left on, her strawberry hair bright as sunshine spilled across the pillow.

He tried to slide his arm out from under her head without waking her. But her eyes drifted open.

"Connor..."

"Um?"

"What time...?"

"Five to five."

"You have to go?"

"Unfortunately." He bent close, brushed a kiss on her forehead. "Tonight I'm going out to the Douglas Ranch. Caleb invited me to dinner."

She made a low, knowing sound. "More hush-hush negotiating, huh?"

"We aren't quite at that point yet. Want to come with me?"

She shook her head. "I think I'll just stay out of that, if you don't mind."

He kissed the tip of her nose. "Tuesday, then? I'll take you to dinner."

"I have a better idea."

"What could be better than you, me and dinner?"

"You, me, CJ, Ryan, Jerilyn...and dinner."

He groaned. "Dinner with the kids. Not exactly the romantic evening I had in mind."

She chided him, "You know it's a good idea."

"Yeah, I suppose it is." He planted a kiss on her sweet mouth and slid his arm out from under her. "Okay. Tuesday. Dinner with the kids—and I have to go." He jumped from the bed and grabbed his briefs and his jeans. When he was fully dressed, he bent close to her for a final kiss. "Every summer should start this way."

She twined her arms around his neck and lifted her mouth to his. "I couldn't agree with you more."

"You *didn't*." Allaire wore an expression of total disbelief. She sent a quick glance around the Tottering Teapot, clearly worried that someone might have heard what Tori had just said.

"Yeah," Tori answered, after savoring a slow bite of her avocado and swiss sandwich with sprouts. "I did. *We* did. And it was wonderful."

Allaire leaned closer across the lace tablecloth and pitched her voice barely above a whisper. "But you said yourself he admitted he's buying out the resort—and then leaving town."

"I like him. I like him a lot. I want to be with him, for as long as it lasts."

A look of concern crossed Allaire's face. "I just don't want to see you hurt, Tori."

"I know you don't. And I realize that I might be hurt."

"Might?" Allaire demanded.

Tori busted to the truth. "Okay. I guess it's likely, in the end. But I want to be with him more than I want to protect myself against heartbreak. Sometimes you just have to go for it, you know? Go for it and not count the cost."

Connor couldn't stay away from Tori.

She drew him like a bee to a flower, a kid to a cookie jar. He stopped by her house that afternoon and confessed that he couldn't bear to keep away. Tori said she understood completely, that she felt the same.

That night, he went out to the Douglas Ranch, as

planned. Riley Douglas, who was Caleb and Adele's son and Grant Clifton's partner in running the resort, showed up, too. Riley was silent through most of the meal—silent and watchful. When Caleb and Connor discussed the resort, Riley said that he was sure he and Grant could turn things around, given time.

Caleb looked at his son and said in a weary tone, "Money's tight. You know that. And time is the one thing I don't have a lot of."

"Just don't rush into anything," Riley warned.

"I'm not rushing," Caleb replied, sending Connor a telling glance. "I'm considering the options, son. Considering them fully."

When he left the Douglas Ranch, Connor went straight to Tori's. She didn't ask if Caleb had offered to sell him the resort—or anything about what had happened during his visit with the Douglases. He knew she didn't want to know.

And he was more than content to say nothing of his meeting with Caleb. He only wanted to take her in his arms, to feel her soft body pressed close to his.

Tuesday morning after he took CJ and Jerilyn out to Melanie's, he got a call from Grant Clifton. Grant wanted to speak with him alone.

Connor drove up toward the resort, stopping off at the office complex down the mountain from the main lodge. Grant led him to his private office and shut the door.

Grant was furious, Connor could see that in the tightness of his square jaw. He said he'd talked to Riley Douglas that morning.

"Riley clued me in. I get the picture now, and I don't much like what I see. You want the resort and when you get it, people who matter to me, people who have worked hard here, are going to be without their jobs."

"Grant, come on. Let's not get ahead of ourselves."

"I *liked* you," Grant said with deadly softness. "I heard you were here to be with your son, to smooth over past differences with your sister. I admired that. Yeah, I also heard the rumors that you were interested in the resort. I didn't listen to what they said."

"Grant, there's no reason for—"

"You're right." Clifton cut him off. "Getting you here in my office and reaming you a new one isn't a very smart thing for me to do. But I'm just pissed off enough that I don't give a damn what's smart. I just want you to know that *I* know now you're not who I thought you were. You're no better than a vulture, McFarlane. And I wanted to say that to your face."

Connor said nothing. With a curt nod, he turned for the door. Grant made no move to stop him.

As he drove down the mountain, Connor tried to remind himself that he'd been called worse things than a vulture. In the past, he'd never cared. He went after what he wanted and he got it and what people said didn't mean a thing.

Now, strangely, Grant Clifton's harsh words rankled. And he found himself worrying about Melanie and Russ, about their reaction when they learned he had plans for the resort. Tori had warned him he'd better tell Melanie what he was up to.

So he detoured to the Hopping H. He found Melanie in the kitchen, baking cookies. The kids, she said, were out in the barn with Russ.

She took a sheet of great-smelling snickerdoodles from the oven and set them on top of the stove. And she turned to him. She frowned when she saw his face. "What? You look like somebody stole your dog."

"I never had a dog."

She chuckled. "Mother never would have allowed that. 'They are so filthy, darlings.'" She imitated their mother's cool, aristocratic tones. "'And the shedding.'" She faked a delicate shudder. "'No. Impossible.'"

He laughed—and then instantly grew serious. "There's something I need to tell you."

Now she looked worried. Really worried. "What? Is it about CJ? I think he's doing much better."

"He is. It's not about him."

"Well?"

He laid it on her. "I came here this summer for him. And to spend some time with you."

"I know that, Connor. And I'm pleased that you're here."

"And also to buy the Thunder Canyon Resort."

"Yes," she replied. "What else?"

"What do you mean, what else?" he demanded grimly. "That's it."

"That you want to buy the resort?"

"Yes. I want to buy the resort and I thought you should know."

She took off the fat oven mitt and waved her hand airily. "Oh, that. I knew that."

He groped for a chair and lowered himself into it. "You did?"

"You're my brother, Connor. I know you. I know how your mind works. The resort is a different type of property than McFarlane House usually takes on. That makes it a challenge and you love a challenge. Plus, you can probably get it for an excellent price. Of course, you'll go after it."

His mouth was hanging open. He snapped it shut. "You knew all along."

"I did. And I knew that you'd tell me about it eventually, when you were ready to discuss it."

He confessed bleakly, "Grant Clifton just called me a vulture."

Her eyes grew sad. "Yes, well. Grant found his calling, managing the resort. It's killing him to watch it fail. I'm sorry to hear he lashed out at you. Please don't take his cruel words to heart. He'll settle down in time. And my guess is that when he does, you'll get an apology."

"But…he and Russ are best friends, aren't they?"

Now her expression was tender. "You're worried about Russ being angry with you?"

"Think about it. Russ and I didn't exactly get off to a great start. I've felt like we're slowly getting on a better footing. But I'm afraid if he gets an earful from Grant, I'll lose all the progress I've made with him."

She sat down at the table with him and put her hand over his. "A girl could do a lot worse than to have a brother like you."

Her words pleased him. Very much. "Thanks. That means a lot."

"It's only the truth."

"Well, lately, at least."

"At least." She chuckled. "And don't worry about Russ. He never liked the resort, thought it brought a lot more growth and questionable 'progress' than Thunder Canyon ever needed. And he always believed that Grant was meant to be a rancher like his father and his father before him. Russ is not going to resent you because Grant might have to consider a career change."

That night, as planned, Tori had Connor and the kids over to her house for dinner. She thought it went well. And she couldn't help but notice that CJ actually looked at his father when he spoke to him.

Plus, there was a new contentment about Jerilyn. She said she liked the job at the Hopping H. And her dad seemed better. The day before, Butch had found a therapist from the list Tori's dad had provided. Insurance would pay the therapist's bill.

"It's a start, I think," Jerilyn told them.

At a little after nine, Connor left with the kids. He would take Jerilyn home. Ryan would come with him and CJ to their house to spend the night. Gerda would take the boys out to the ranch in the morning, stopping to pick up Jerilyn along the way.

Tori stood out on the porch and waved as they drove away, and wished that he would be coming back later to see her alone. But Connor would be leaving first thing in the morning for Philadelphia, gone until Friday evening. She missed him already and wished they'd had a little privacy to enjoy a more intimate farewell.

But then she chuckled to herself. If she'd wanted to be alone with him tonight, she shouldn't have engineered dinner with the kids. She went inside, took a long, hot bath, watched some TV—and wasn't all that surprised when her doorbell rang at ten past twelve.

She didn't say a word. Just held out her eager arms to him.

Connor headed for Bozeman at five the next morning to catch his flight. The trip took longer than it would have in the past. In an effort to cut costs, he flew commercial rather than enjoy the pricey comfort and privacy of a McFarlane House jet.

In Philadelphia, the meetings were endless and both his father and his mother were on his case every chance they got. They wanted him back home. Now. His father argued that the Thunder Canyon Resort was too big for their purposes, too much to take on. McFarlane House had always been a boutique brand. Sprawling resorts—especially failing ones—just weren't a good fit.

Connor listened and nodded. And then reminded them that there was a plan and he was sticking with it, that times were changing and McFarlane House had to change with them.

The flight back was a nightmare. Every plane he boarded had some mechanical issue or other. By late afternoon, he ended up calling everyone—Gerda, CJ and Tori. He told them he would be stuck in an airport hotel in Kansas City for the night. Tori said she missed him. He missed her, too, all out of proportion to the short time he'd been away. CJ asked permission to spend the night at Russ's ranch, the Flying J. One of Russ's mares had just foaled and another was about to. CJ hoped to be there to see the new foal born.

More calls ensued, to Melanie and Russ, who said CJ was welcome to bunk at the Flying J for the night. And that Russ would be glad to drive into town and pick CJ up.

So it was settled. Connor hung up the phone feeling really good. CJ had sounded so excited about the whole thing. More and more, he dared to hope that he was getting his son back, that CJ would move beyond the trauma and pain of his parents' divorce, that he would be okay, after all.

The early flights the next morning, through Denver to Bozeman, went off without a hitch. By a little after ten, he was in his own SUV and on his way back to Thunder Canyon.

At the house, he was alone. Gerda had left a note saying she'd gone for groceries and his lunch was in the fridge. CJ was still out at the Flying J. He hauled his suitcase into his bedroom suite and grabbed the phone to call Tori.

The doorbell rang as he was dialing. He put the phone down and went to answer.

The last person he'd ever expected to see in Thunder Canyon was waiting on the other side. "Jennifer."

She was looking gorgeous, as always, all in white. Her gold hair was streaked with platinum and her skin was a golden brown—no doubt from long, lazy days lounging in the sun on Constantin Kronidis's yacht. At the curb behind her, a gleaming black limo waited.

"Hello, Connor." She pushed her giant, diamond-accented Versace sunglasses up over her forehead and anchored them in her hair. "I need to speak with you."

This was not sounding especially good. But then again, what could she do to him now? The divorce was final, the property divided, custody of CJ settled.

He ushered her inside, into the living room, and gestured for her to sit. She took the sofa. He offered, to be civil, "Can I get you anything?"

She looked up at him, her beautiful face a cold mask. "My son, please."

Last time I checked, he was my son, too, Connor thought. But he kept his mouth shut. The words would only come across as a jab. And at least until he knew what she was up to, he would refrain from antagonizing her.

He sat in the club chair across the coffee table from her. "CJ's out." Instinct had him holding back on telling her where.

Of course, that was her next question. "Out where?"

He cut to the chase. "What do you want, Jennifer?"

She cast a dismissive glance around the room, which was attractive, high-ceilinged and expensively furnished, but certainly not up to her standards of luxury. "Constantin has asked me to marry him."

"Congratulations," he said with reasonable sincerity. "I hope you'll be very happy."

"I'm sure we will. As for CJ, I've changed my mind."

He didn't ask her what she'd changed her mind about. He knew she was going to tell him anyway. He braced himself for the bad news.

And she hit him with it. "On deeper reflection, I don't want my son spending the summer here. It's a waste of his precious time. He's behind in his studies and he needs desperately to catch up. So I've found a fine school in Switzerland, MonteVera, and enrolled him for the summer."

Chapter Seven

Connor sat very still as he resisted the powerful urge to leap across the coffee table, grab his ex-wife by her slim shoulders and shake her until a little warmth and good sense spilled out.

He reminded himself that she *was* the mother of his child. And he hadn't been a good husband to her—in fact, he hadn't been much of a husband at all. She *had* taken good care of CJ in the past. Yes, she'd always been a distant and distracted mother. But she'd been there for CJ when Connor hadn't.

He thought of his own parents, for some reason. His mother had always been a lot like Jennifer. Present, but emotionally unavailable.

His father's voice crept into his mind. *You could just send Connor Jr. back to school. A summer without dis-*

tractions, time to focus on his studies. Do the boy a world of good.

For a moment, he wondered if somehow Donovan McFarlane and Jennifer were in on this thing together.

But then again, no. Jennifer and his parents had never really hit it off. And his father might think he owned the world, but he did have certain principles. Donovan would have considered it unconscionable to scheme against his only son with the woman who had disgraced the McFarlane name by divorcing said son.

"What's the matter, Connor?" Jennifer cooed. "I seem to have struck you speechless."

In a carefully modulated tone, he reminded her, "In case you've forgotten, it was your idea that he spend the summer with me."

She adjusted her sunglasses on top of her head, smoothed a hand down her hair. "Of course I haven't forgotten. But as I said a moment ago, I've rethought the situation. He needs to be closely supervised and this way, he'll have the summer to get on top of his studies and make up for his failure last year. Also, I know he's a burden to you, Connor. And I'm willing to take him off your hands."

"No, thanks."

She blinked her delft-blue eyes. "Excuse me?"

"I think you were right to send him to me. And it's working out well. It's good for him to get to know me, to spend time with his father. And I'm perfectly happy with having him here. He will stay with me. And I'll be more than happy to pay whatever penalties the school in Switzerland demands when you tell them that CJ won't be going there after all."

"This is not about fees, Connor. This is about the welfare of our son."

Our son. Well. Progress. Of a sort. "Yes, it is about CJ's welfare. He and I are getting to know each other this summer. I think you'll agree that it's about time. He seems…happier every day. As to his schoolwork, he's catching up." Okay. Total lie. But Connor would see to it that CJ hit the books, starting immediately.

Jennifer looked pained. "How is he catching up, here, in some nowhere town at the end of the earth?"

The lie reached his lips—and he let it out. "He has a tutor. A very qualified one, as a matter of fact. She teaches at the high school, on the advanced track." Hey, that was partly true, at least. Tori did teach advanced placement English; he knew that for a fact.

"Some country schoolteacher is not good enough. He deserves the best. And MonteVera is world-class." A slight frown creased her satin-smooth brow. "And I don't understand this. I thought you would be pleased to have him taken off your hands."

Two weeks ago, she would have been right. If she'd shown up then to take CJ away, he'd have been only too happy to see his son go. But now…

Uh-uh. Maybe if he was honest with her, straightforward. Okay, it was a novel idea, but it might work.

He leaned toward her, willing her to understand. "Jennifer. The answer is no, he's not going away. The end of August is soon enough for him to go back to school. Try to see his side. He needs this time, here, with me. He's enjoying himself. And he and I…well, when we got here, he would hardly speak to me. That's changing. Slowly. If I send him away now, he won't ever forgive me."

She flipped a thick swatch of that pale hair back over her shoulder, impatient. Thoroughly annoyed. "Connor. Will you listen to yourself? It's always about you, isn't it?"

So much for hoping she might understand. He sat back in his chair, putting as much distance as he could between them while still remaining seated. "I don't think *you* were listening. No, it's not about me. It's about CJ. The divorce has been hard on him."

She huffed, turned her head away, wrapped her arms tightly around herself. "Now you're blaming me."

"No, I'm not. I'm saying he's been hurt enough and he deserves a break. He likes it here in Thunder Canyon and I'm not taking this summer away from him because you've suddenly decided to go back on your own agreements and ship him off to Switzerland."

"I am hardly *shipping* him off. I only want what's best for him."

"Then let him have his summer here."

She shot to her feet. "I want to see him. Now."

"Not until you agree that you won't take him away with you."

"I'll agree to no such thing. What I will do is call my lawyer."

He gazed at her steadily. "Now, you're threatening me?"

She threw up a hand. "You have been a terrible, neglectful father, Connor."

"I could have been better, true. I'm working hard at doing better now."

"You're not hearing me. I'm about to remarry. Constantin can buy and sell you ten times over. I can trample you in court. Do you understand?"

"So, it's all about the money, as always, isn't it, Jennifer?" He said the words wearily. He really didn't want to fight with her. He thought they had both moved on.

Apparently he'd thought wrong.

She drew herself up. "I am telling you to think about it. Take a day or two. And if by Monday morning, you aren't ready to agree to send CJ to Switzerland, I'll be suing you for full custody. And I will win, too."

The last thing he needed right now was another court battle with her, especially considering that she was absolutely right about her fiancé. Kronidis had very deep pockets.

But Connor wasn't going to back down on this. CJ's welfare was at stake. And in the past couple of weeks he'd learned at last that his son—and his son's high regard—meant a lot to him.

"I'll sue you right back," he said icily. "And *I'll* win. Because I'm getting married, as well—to a wonderful, warmhearted woman. A woman who'll be there for CJ, a hands-on kind of mom. A teacher, as a matter of fact— CJ's tutor, whom I mentioned before."

Dear God in heaven, what had he just said?

But the whopping lie was almost worth it—just for the look of stunned shock on his ex's face. Spots of flaming color rode high on those amazing cheekbones of hers. And the blue eyes shot sparks.

He added triumphantly, "Her name is Tori Jones. CJ is crazy about her. Almost as crazy as I am."

Jennifer's sculpted nostrils were flaring. "Oh, you're crazy, all right. You are out of your mind."

"No," he answered with a slow smile. "In fact, I'm saner than I've ever been."

"I seriously doubt that."

He rose. "I think we've said about all we have to say to each other."

If a look could kill, she'd have him dead where he stood. "I'll be back Monday," she said. "Have CJ ready to go. I can find my own way out, thank you."

"CJ is going nowhere." He dropped back to the club chair as she turned for the door.

Once Jennifer was gone, Connor paced the floor, considering his options. They didn't change. It seemed very clear to him what he needed to do next. Too bad it was wrong. And a really big lie.

Not to mention totally unfair to Tori, whom he honestly cared about and had hoped never to hurt.

Still, at this point, he saw no other way out than to call his lawyers and let it go, count on them to fight Jennifer off. Her lawyers were at least as good as his.

And she had Kronidis's billions at her disposal.

No. He was going to fight this every way he could—if it turned out that Tori was willing to help him.

Willing to help him.

Strange. He'd been pacing back and forth for a half an hour, going over the various possibilities, and it had never occurred to him until that moment that he might try lying to Tori, too. That he could propose to her, tell her he'd changed his mind about everything, that he loved her and wanted to marry her and make a home with her, right there in Thunder Canyon. And then when the summer was over, he could plead cold feet and break it off with her.

He almost smiled. First off, she was smarter than that. She would know something wasn't right, for him to flip-flop like that, out of nowhere. Also, she was way too likely to find out about Jennifer and her threats. She'd figure out what he was up to then, for certain.

But even beyond the low probability he could pull it off, he just wasn't willing to lie to her. If she went into this with him, it should be with her eyes wide open.

He called the Flying J. Russ answered and went and got CJ from the barn.

"Dad, hey. You're home."

Home. The way his son said that word...it was everything. The last of Connor's doubts about asking Tori to help him with this fell away. He would do anything to keep CJ where he wanted to be for the whole damn summer.

"I'm here," he said, and meant it in more ways than one. "What's up with the baby horses?"

CJ chuckled. "Foals, dad."

"Right. Foals. Well?"

"Ryan and I are trying to decide on a name for the one born Friday. And the other hasn't come yet. So I was wondering..."

"You want to stay over another night, is that it?"

"Yeah. I was hoping it might be okay."

"What does Russ say?"

"He says it's okay."

In the background, he heard Russ's voice. "Fine with me."

"All right. Until tomorrow morning." They had a few big things to talk about. And they needed to do that before Jennifer came back Monday.

"Okay, Dad. I really gotta go. That foal is coming any minute now, I can just feel it."

Connor murmured a goodbye and heard the click as CJ hung up. He called Tori.

She answered on the first ring. "You're back."

The sound of her voice made his arms ache to hold her. "I want to see you." The words came out low. Rough. Hungry. Not all that surprising, since he *was* hungry. For her.

A low laugh escaped her, a laugh that teased him. "I'm home. Come over right now."

Tori was at the door, waiting for him, when he rang the bell.

She yanked it wide and sighed at the sight of him, so tall, so handsome. Her own personal corporate shark, who had somehow turned out to be the man she longed for. The kind of man she could believe in. She beamed up at him. "I thought you'd never get here."

His dark gaze ran over her, head to toe and back up again. "I know exactly how you feel." And then he reached for her.

She swayed toward him, lifting her mouth for that first, delicious kiss. He covered her lips with his, wrapping his arms good and tight around her, lifting her feet right off the floor, so he could carry her back across her threshold and shove the door shut behind them with his foot.

He kept walking, to the open door just beyond the foyer and right through it. The second he lowered her feet to the rug by the bed, she started tugging on his shirt, unzipping his trousers.

As she undressed him, he did the same for her. He took her camisole top by the hem and pulled it up and off. He undid her shorts and pushed them down. She was naked in no time.

And so was he. They fell across the bed together

rolling, kissing as they caressed each other, each so eager, starving for the simple thrill of the other's hungry touch.

She needed no slow seduction. Not today. Her body was ready for him just from his kiss, from his long, knowing fingers parting her, stroking her. She stuck out a hand and fumbled for the small drawer by the side of the bed.

Since their first time, she'd moved the condoms front and center, with some loose and waiting, outside the box. She grabbed one, broke their endless kiss long enough to rip the top off the pouch with her teeth.

"Now," she whispered to him.

"Oh, yeah…" He rolled them again, so they were on their sides, facing each other.

She reached down between them, loving the hard, hot length of him, as well as the way he moaned when she positioned the condom and rolled it down over him, fitting it smooth and tight.

"Now," he groaned again, and rolled her under him. She opened for him, so ready.

And then he was in her. She wrapped her legs around him. There was only pure sensation, of his body pressed to hers, his hardness filling her, his hips rocking into hers in a rhythm she knew by heart.

She grabbed him closer. She held on so tight. The pleasure bloomed wide, and then contracted in a shimmer of sparks and light.

Her bathtub wasn't that large, but it was big enough for two.

They went in there and filled it and sank into the welcoming heat together. He made his body a cradle for hers and she leaned back against his strong chest and shut her eyes.

"Heaven," she whispered on a sigh. "This, and the rest of it. I love it when you're touching me." His arm, dusted with silky dark hair, rested on the rim of the tub. She ran a wet finger along the strong length of it. "And I love touching you…"

He nuzzled her neck. "It's mutual. Take my word for it." And then he pulled away enough to rest his dark head back on the towel she'd given him to use as a pillow. He was still.

Too still?

Some sharp instinct had her turning to glance over her damp shoulder at him. "Connor?"

"Umm?" He had his eyes closed, his head back, cradled by the towel.

"Is everything…okay?" She wondered why she'd asked that as soon as the words escaped her lips.

But then he sat up straight again and met her gaze levelly.

And she knew that her weird instinct was true. "What is it?"

Suddenly, his eyes were bleak. "I need to ask you something. A…favor. And I'm afraid that when I do, you'll not only say no, you'll ask me to leave. And not to come back."

She moved, then, gripping the tub sides, sloshing water as she turned around to face him. "I think you'd better just ask, then."

"All right. Here it is. I want us to pretend, for the summer, that we are engaged."

She sputtered, "B-but whatever for?"

"Hear me out, okay, before you give me an answer?"

She raked her damp hair back off her forehead. "Okay, then. Explain. And this had better be good."

Chapter Eight

Tori listened, not sure what to think, as Connor told her all of it: the visit from his ex-wife, her demand that he let her send CJ away. Connor's refusal. His ex's threats. His lies—that Tori was tutoring CJ, and that she was his fiancée.

When he was finished, she got out of the bathtub, grabbed a towel and wrapped it around herself. She handed him one, too, and waited as he rose, the cooling bathwater slicking off his fine, hard body.

He dried himself and entered the bedroom, where he pulled on his trousers. She traded her towel for the terry cloth robe that hung on the back of the bathroom door.

They went into the kitchen. Neither of them said a word as she made coffee for him, prepared tea for herself. They both sat at the table.

She sipped her tea. "As to the tutoring. Yes, of course."

"Thank you." He lifted his coffee cup, drank. Set it down.

"But as far as the other…" She felt uncomfortable saying it right out: *pretending to be engaged to him, playing at being his fiancée.* No matter how she chose to put it, it sounded like a foolish thing for two grown people to be doing.

A foolish thing—and a lie.

"As far as the other…" She started again, let the words fade off a second time. She rested her elbows on the table and leaned toward him. "Do you think it's really necessary? I mean, won't the summer be over before she can get any kind of judgment taking him away from you?"

He sipped more coffee. "Legally, she might be able to get some judge to order me to turn CJ over to her within a week or two."

"But don't you share custody? Don't you have as much right to be with your son as she does?"

He looked away—and then faced her again. "It's like this. We share legal custody, but she has physical custody and I have open visitation rights—meaning when I want a weekend with him, I call at least two weeks in advance and she, within reason, has to let me have him, up to a possible total of thirty weekends a year." He set his cup down and turned to gaze blindly out the window again. "That seemed fine with me, at the time of the settlement. I never dreamed I'd want to spend that much time with him, anyway. Frankly, at that point, I wasn't looking forward to the occasional weekend I'd feel duty-bound to take him." Connor continued to stare out the window. Even in profile, she could see how disgusted he was with himself.

She had to actively resist the need to reach across, to cover his hand with hers. "But then Jennifer guilted you into taking him for the summer…"

He looked at her again. "And I've slowly discovered I want to be a real dad, after all."

She reminded him, "CJ's fifteen. Isn't that old enough to have a say in this? You *are* going to tell him what's going on, won't you?"

He nodded. "He's at the Flying J overnight. Tomorrow, when I pick him up, I'll talk to him about it. Find out for sure what *he* wants."

"If he wants to stay—which I'm guessing he will—that should be enough, shouldn't it, to sway any judge? That a fifteen-year-old boy should get the summer with his father, the summer that his mother set up in the first place?"

"I'm hoping it won't come to CJ having to face a judge over something that was supposed to have been settled already."

"To…choose sides between you and his mother in court, you mean?"

"That is exactly what I mean. I just want to give him—give both of us—this summer we didn't even know that we needed. I don't want to lose the ground I've gained with him. And if she gets a judge to order me to let her take him away…well, he's been making real progress. His attitude about me, about life…about himself, really—it's all so much better. He even seems *happy* at times lately, you know? I don't think I can bear to let Jennifer snatch that away from him."

Tori looked down into her teacup, but found no

answers there. "I'm still not sure that pretending I'm your fiancée is going to help you with this."

"You're a respected schoolteacher. You're likable. A good person. The kind of woman who would be the perfect stepmother for him, an ideal choice for my wife. If I can tell my lawyers that you're going to marry me, going to help me provide the kind of home CJ will thrive in when he's with us, and that's why I've decided to sue for joint custody, they should be able to hold the line on Jennifer until at least the end of August."

Hold the line, she thought. *He wants to hold the line.* He thought that she, Tori, would make the perfect wife and mother. But he still wasn't offering to make it real between them. He wanted to play at being married, just long enough to keep his ex at bay.

Oh, it would be so easy to get angry with him now.

But no. She had known who he was, what he was and wasn't capable of, when she decided to snatch this one beautiful summer with him. She refused to suddenly start expecting more of him than he was willing to give.

"Connor. Has it occurred to you that maybe your lawyers can hold the line anyway, without me having to pose as your fiancée?"

"Yeah. It's occurred to me. But I'm willing to play every angle I've got to keep my son where he wants to be, to make sure he gets his summer in Thunder Canyon. If I let Jennifer send him away now, I'll lose what progress I've made trying to show him that I want to be a real father to him. I can't afford that. *He* can't afford that."

When he said it that way, she wanted to say yes, to

promise she would be his pretend fiancée if he needed her to, to do *anything* to help him and CJ.

And yet...

"What about when the summer's over?"

He sighed. "Frankly, Tori, I'm not looking that far ahead."

"Don't you think maybe you should?"

After a moment, he nodded. "Yeah. All right. When the summer's over, we would...break up. It does happen, you know."

"And *then* what about your custody arrangement?"

"I'm hoping I'll have joint physical custody by then. And I *am* CJ's father. Once I have joint custody, it's going to be very hard for Jennifer to convince a judge to take it away."

"You think you can settle a custody battle in two months?"

"I don't know. Maybe not. But I can keep Jennifer from sending CJ away for that long. With your help, I know I can keep CJ here, where he wants to be, until school starts. With your help, I'll have two months to prove to my son that I really do intend to be a father to him."

Tori got up, went to the counter, got a fresh tea bag and poured more hot water over it. She purposely kept her back to him the whole time.

Finally, she turned to him. "I can't make this decision today. I need a little time to think about it. And I think you need to talk with CJ, make absolutely certain that he actually wants what we're both so sure he does."

"I understand." He pushed his coffee cup away and rose. "I have to know your answer by tomorrow, so I can call my lawyers first thing Monday morning."

She picked a random deadline out of the air, because he needed one—and because she did, too. "Tomorrow afternoon."

"Two o'clock?"

"I'll be here."

After Connor left, the house seemed emptier than usual. Tori ran a load of laundry, dusted the living room, changed the sheets on the bed. The simple, everyday actions brought her no closer to having a decision to offer Connor.

She hoped that by the morning, she'd have made up her mind.

Allaire called at a little after three and invited her over for dinner that night. "I mean, if you haven't got a hot date with you-know-who..." Allaire's voice was teasing, free of any hint of judgment. Whatever her private opinion of Connor, she wasn't going to put him down while Tori was going out with him.

Tori wondered wryly what her friend would say if she announced tomorrow that she and Connor were engaged.

"I would love to come. What time should I be there and what can I bring?"

"That yummy salad you make with the mandarin oranges and roasted pecans. Six?"

"I'm there, on time, with the salad."

The evening was a good one. Dinner was delicious and Tori got to help tuck Alex into bed. Later, she considered confiding in her best friend.

But she dismissed that idea about a minute after she thought of it. Allaire would tell her she was crazy to even consider such a thing, that perpetrating a big, fat lie would do no good for anyone—and likely cause everyone involved a world of hurt.

Plus, well, whatever Allaire's reaction might be to the news that Connor had asked Tori to pose as his bride-to-be, it just wasn't right to tell her. It wasn't right to tell *anyone*. Connor had confided in her, put his trust in her. She would not betray that trust, whatever decision she made come tomorrow afternoon.

Before Tori left for the twenty-mile drive home from the small ranch Allaire and DJ owned, Allaire asked her if she had something on her mind. Tori put on a bright smile and lied through her teeth.

"Nope. Not a thing. Thanks. It was a good evening." She hugged her friend, said good-night to DJ, grabbed her empty salad bowl and took her leave.

At home, she turned on all the lights in spite of the waste of electricity. But pushing back the shadows did little to banish her apprehensions. So she turned most of them back off again and she stayed up until after two watching movies she'd already seen before.

There was something so comforting about knowing how it would all come out in the end.

At ten the next morning, Connor collected CJ at the Flying J. CJ talked steadily through the whole drive back to the house in New Town. The second foal had been born, though they'd had to call the vet since the foal was breech and Russ couldn't get it to turn.

"Dad. It's gross. But kind of amazing, you know? Uncle Russ just stuck his arms inside that mare, past his elbows, and tried to turn that foal around. And the vet did the same thing—and it worked that time. The foals are so cute, little spindly legs, and those great big eyes."

Connor glanced over at his son. "So you had a good time, huh?"

CJ grunted. "Dad, I had a *great* time."

Connor decided to wait till they were at the house to discuss Jennifer's demand.

But as soon as they got there and got CJ's duffel and pack inside, CJ announced, "I have to call Jerilyn," and disappeared into his room.

Connor waited. A half an hour later, CJ was still in his room with the door shut. He waited another fifteen minutes before he tapped on the door.

"Yeah?"

Connor turned the doorknob and stuck his head in. His son was sprawled on the bed, the phone to his ear.

"Hold on," CJ said, and took the phone away from his ear. "Dad, can I go over to Jerilyn's?"

Why not? "Sure, but I need a minute or two first. There's something we should discuss." He tried to sound easy and casual, not to get CJ upset before they'd even started talking.

But the kid must have picked up something. "What's wrong?"

Connor put on a smile. "Tell Jerilyn hi for me and say you'll be over soon. Then we'll talk."

Not sixty seconds later, CJ joined him in the living room. He dropped to the sofa. "So...what's up?"

Connor, in the club chair across the coffee table—the same chair he'd sat in when Jennifer laid down her ultimatum—had no idea how to begin this conversation, though he'd been rehearsing it in his head since he left Tori's house the day before.

"Dad?"

Connor sucked in a breath—and laid it right out there. "Your mother came here yesterday. She came to pick you up. She's arranged for you to spend the summer at the MonteVera School in Switzerland. She wants you to get a chance to focus on your schoolwork, to get caught up for next term."

CJ said a very bad word, followed by a single syllable in the negative. "No."

"I'm going to ignore the swearing in this situation."

"Gee, Dad. Thanks." CJ ladled on the sarcasm. And then he asked, with more hope than anger, "What did you tell her?"

"I told her absolutely not. That we had an arrangement already in place for the summer and I intended to stick with it, that you were enjoying your stay here in Thunder Canyon and I saw no reason to send you to Switzerland."

CJ's face lit up. The sight not only tugged at Connor's heartstrings, it also made him all the more certain he'd called it right in this case. "You did? You said that?"

Connor nodded. "And I put her off, refused to tell her where to find you. I wanted to get this chance to speak with you first."

CJ spread his knees, braced his elbows on them and linked his hands between them. "Good. That's good."

"I wanted to be certain that you really want to stay here for the summer."

"Are you kidding me?" CJ bounced on the couch cushions, unable to contain himself. "Of course I do."

"You should be sure. If you do stay, your mother has threatened to take legal action."

CJ made a scoffing sound. "Oh, right. Suddenly she gives a crap."

"CJ, I'm sure she's doing what she thinks is best." Actually, he wasn't sure. But she *was* CJ's mother and as such he refused to let CJ disparage her.

"She doesn't care what's best for me, Dad. She cares about her new boyfriend and his big boat and all his money."

Connor just looked at him, levelly. "CJ. Stop."

CJ's red-brown hair, still badly in need of the services of a good barber, fell over his eyes as he stared at the floor between his knees. "You mean it? You'll tell her you want me with you, that I'm here for the summer the way that we said from the first?"

"Yes. I mean it. I will tell her—I've already told her—that you're staying, that we're sticking with the original plan."·

"Well, okay." CJ glanced up, shoved the hair out of his eyes. "Thanks."

"Don't thank me yet. She said she'll be back Monday to get you."

"But she's *not* getting me, right, she's not sending me away?" He looked so worried that Connor would let him down. And why wouldn't he be worried? Connor had been letting him down almost since the day he was born.

"No." Connor spoke slowly. Clearly. "You're staying here, as we agreed. And when she comes tomorrow, you'll have to be here, you'll have to speak with her."

"Why?"

"CJ, she can't only hear this secondhand, from me. She needs to hear it from you. You have to tell her what *you* want."

CJ stared. And then he shook his head. His hair fell over his eyes again. But then, at last, he shoved it back and nodded. "All right. I will. Whatever."

"When you tell her, you'll do it respectfully, please."

"Yeah. Okay. Respectfully."

"And there's another thing…"

"What else?"

"Since your mother was concerned about your wasting the summer without making any effort to catch up on your studies, I told her that Tori was tutoring you."

CJ's eyes grew wide. "You lied."

If his son only knew. "I did. Since then, I've discussed the problem with Tori. She's agreed to help. If you stay, you'll have to be willing to turn my lie into the truth. You'll have to work with Tori, every day, five days a week, starting Monday. And you'll have to do the assignments she gives you. With your job at the Hopping H and the time you'll need to put in on your studies, the summer will be a busy one."

"Ms. Jones will tutor me…" He seemed to consider the idea.

"Yes, she will. And you will have to work hard on the school stuff, no slacking. I need that agreement from you."

CJ looked down between his spread knees again. And when he glanced up, it was to give a firm nod. "You got it, Dad. I'll study with Ms. Jones."

"This will be your opportunity to prove to your mother, and to me—and most of all, to yourself—that you don't need to go to Switzerland to get your studies back on track."

"And I will prove it, Dad."

Connor made a low, approving sound. "I believe that you will."

"Thanks, Dad. I really mean that." The look in CJ's eyes said it all.

They had come a long way, the two of them. Connor was more determined than ever to make this the summer when he healed the past wounds he'd inflicted on his innocent son.

Ten minutes later, CJ was out the door, on his way to see Jerilyn. He'd been invited to her house for lunch, but he promised he'd be back home for dinner.

After he left, Connor called Melanie to explain that CJ's mother was coming by sometime Monday morning, so CJ would be late for work in order to have a little time with her. Melanie said it was no problem. And Russ or Butch Doolin would see that Jerilyn got a ride out to the ranch.

Then she said, in a tone that managed to be simultaneously cautious and offhand, "I thought Jennifer was in Europe for the summer."

"Yeah," Connor answered bleakly. "So did I."

Melanie was quiet for a moment, before asking gently, "Something going on?"

"It's a long story."

"I'd like to hear about it if you feel like telling me."

He surprised himself by doing exactly that. He told her all about Jennifer's visit. And about the conversation he'd just had with CJ. He told her that Tori would be tutoring CJ for the summer.

Yes, he left a gap. A big one. He failed to mention the part about how he'd told Jennifer that Tori was his fiancée. And since he didn't mention that particular whopper of a lie, there was no need to explain how Tori was still deciding whether to pretend to be engaged to him or not.

When he was finished, Melanie said she was proud of him. "I know it means the world to CJ, that you're sticking by him, that now he's found out he likes it here, you're keeping your word about this summer."

"Yeah. It's kind of funny. If you'd told me three weeks ago that CJ would be working at the Hopping H and was willing to study hard with a tutor in order to be allowed to stay in Thunder Canyon with me for the summer, I would have said you were out of your mind."

"He was angry at you, acting out. But deep down, what he really wanted, even then, was to be here, with you— and to know that you wanted him with you."

"Maybe. But now I do know, for certain, that he wants to be here. He's said so himself."

"And you're going to fight for him."

"Yes. I am."

Tori's doorbell rang at two on the dot.

Her pulse suddenly on hyperdrive, she went to answer. "Hello, Connor." He looked so serious, and handsome enough to break a thousand hearts. She wanted to fling herself into his strong arms, to swear she would do anything he wanted, anything to help.

Somehow, she managed *not* to throw herself at him. He didn't reach for her, either. She ushered him in.

She still had no idea what to say to him. Should she go with the passionate urging of her foolish heart and tell him that, yes, she'd be only too happy to be his fake fiancée for the summer? Or did she refuse to help him in this lie—and in the process, end up helping his ex to hurt him *and* CJ?

They ended up sitting at either end of her couch. Once they were both settled, there was a silence. An excruciating one.

Finally, he spoke in low, restrained tone. "I talked with CJ this morning."

"And?"

"He said he wants to stay here for the summer. He wants it very much. He's agreed to study with you, to be guided by you and to do his homework faithfully."

"Great."

"I was thinking, Monday through Friday, in the afternoon—say, two to four? And then homework for him, to amount to a couple of hours five nights a week."

"That sounds fine with me," she said. "I'd be happy to do it."

He named an hourly rate that was higher than she would have asked and added, "Starting Monday?"

"Yes. The rate will be fine and I can start Monday."

"Whatever you think, Tori. You know what you're doing."

As a teacher? Yes, she did.

As a woman and potential phony fiancée?

Not so much.

More silence. She had no idea where to begin. Apparently, neither did he.

Finally, she ventured, staring straight ahead and not at him. "People could be hurt if we did it."

He didn't ask what *it* was. He knew as well as she did. She glanced his way and saw him looking at the far wall. She watched as he shrugged. "That's how life is. Sometimes you get hurt."

"I don't mean just you and me. CJ, too. He could get hurt. He could get his hopes up."

He turned to her, then. A frown creased his brow. "About?"

"You and me, making a permanent home, here. In Thunder Canyon. Since he likes it here so much, he could decide he wants to live with us."

Connor was still frowning. "So we'll just tell him we haven't decided how we're going to work out the details of where to live, of where our home base will be. That we're playing it all by ear and the only thing we do know is that he will go back to his boarding school in the fall."

She chided, "He could still be hurt when it doesn't work out."

"Not as much as he'll be hurt if I let Jennifer send him to Switzerland."

She happened to agree with him on that. "If we did it, we would have to agree to tell no one else. No one. Not Melanie."

He was on the same page with that. "And not your friend Allaire."

"That's right. No one."

"No one," he echoed, in the tone of a man swearing a solemn oath.

Her pulse had started knocking again, her heart beating so hard against the wall of her rib cage. It was time to decide. She needed to tell him—yes or no. They were both facing front again.

She slid him another glance. "It would have to look

real. Which means you would have to propose, so I would have a proposal story to tell."

"A proposal story?"

"Yes." *Men,* she thought. "A woman will always tell her proposal story—where they were when he proposed, what he said, if he went down on his knees. If we want to be believed, I've got to have my proposal story."

He cleared his throat. "Fair enough. I'll make sure you have one."

"And a ring. There would have to be a ring. I would help you pick it out. And, of course, I would return it when things…don't work out."

"A ring," he repeated. "Absolutely." They were looking at each other again. In a voice barely above a whisper, he asked, "Well, then?"

She swallowed, hard. And nodded. "Then yes, all right. I will be your fake fiancée for the summer."

He blinked. "You just said yes. Tell me you just said yes."

"Yes."

He stared, unmoving, for several heartbeats.

And then, without further prompting, he got up, picked up the coffee table and moved it out of the way— and he got down on his knees.

She giggled, a silly, girlish sound. At the same time, tears blurred her vision. "Oh, Connor."

He took her hand, kissed the back of it, gazed up at her through dark eyes suddenly filled with light. It could have been real. And she couldn't help herself. She wished that it was.

"Tori, you are the most amazing woman I have ever met. I love everything about you—the sound of your laughter, the beauty of your smile. Your strawberry hair and the cute freckles on your nose."

She groaned. "You just *had* to mention the freckles."

He put a hand to his heart. "Yes. I love those freckles. Because they're yours. I love all of you, every inch. I love the way your lips feel when they're pressed to mine. I love the way you sigh when I touch you, the way you moan when I—"

She put up a hand.

"What?" He pretended to scowl.

She gazed down at him adoringly. "You can be so romantic."

"Thanks. I'm trying."

And then she shook a finger at him. "But don't get overly graphic, okay? A proposal story should be G-rated, PG if you must, but that is really pushing it."

"Yes. All right. G-rated. I understand." And then he kissed her hand again and pressed it to his heart. "Marry me, Tori. Please. I love you. Say you'll be mine."

She beamed. "Excellent."

He prompted, "Well?"

And she gave him her answer. "Oh, Connor. I love you so much. With all my heart. Yes, of course, I'll marry you."

He swept to his feet, dragging her up with him and he wrapped her tightly in his arms. "Right answer," he whispered against her lips.

"So glad you liked it. As far as the lead-in—"

"The lead-in?" He lifted his head and scowled at her.

"Yeah. We need a lead-in. Meaning, what made you decide to propose today?"

"Ah. Well, I…was away for three days. I missed you unbearably. I knew the minute I saw you again, I'd be on my knees. And I was."

"Wow. That's good."

He was the soul of modesty. "I kind of thought so."

"Except that it doesn't add up. I mean, you saw me yesterday, after your trip."

"Okay, then. How's this? I waited a day, though it was hell for me, just to make certain I couldn't live without you."

She laughed. "Connor. Get outta here. You're *really* good at this."

"I do my best." He brought his lips down so close to hers again.

She could drown in those dark eyes of his. She whispered, prayerfully, "You should kiss me now."

"My thoughts, exactly." He claimed her lips in a kiss that stole the breath from her body and made stars dance behind her eyes.

And then, their mouths still fused, he scooped her high against his chest and turned for her bedroom.

That was when the doorbell rang.

They groaned in mutual disappointment and he whispered, "Get rid of whoever it is. Do it fast."

She chuckled. "You're so eager. I like that in a fiancé, even a fake one."

"Just answer the door," he growled as he let her slide to the floor. She straightened her shirt, smoothed her hair and went to see who it was.

"Hey, Ms. Jones," Jerilyn and CJ chimed in unison when she opened the door. Both were grinning, windblown and pink-cheeked.

CJ added, "We were just riding by…" He tipped his

head toward the front walk, where his skateboard and Jerilyn's bike lay as they'd dropped them. "We saw my dad's SUV..."

"Come on in." She stepped back and called to Connor. "It's the kids." They trooped in. "Thirsty?"

Jerilyn laughed. "We were hoping you would ask."

"There's juice in the fridge."

"Thanks, Ms. Jones."

"Hey, Dad," CJ greeted his father as he went by.

Tori went to stand beside Connor as the kids disappeared into the kitchen. They heard cupboards opening, the clunk of the icemaker, followed by cheerful clattering sounds as ice cubes dropped into glasses.

Connor wrapped an arm around her, nuzzled her hair. "I guess it wouldn't be nice to tell them to get lost."

She laughed. "They won't stay long."

CJ appeared carrying a glass of juice. "You guys look...happy."

Connor squeezed her shoulder and captured her gaze. "Good a time as any, don't you think?"

She felt like a diver, poised, suspended in that last split second before she sailed off a cliff into dangerous deep waters far below. But the decision was made. She took the plunge. "Yes. I think so."

By that time, Jerilyn, with her own full glass, had come to stand with CJ. "A good time for what?"

Connor squeezed her shoulder again. "We want you two to be the first to know."

The teenagers shared a bewildered glance. And CJ asked, "Know what?"

Connor announced with pride, "That Tori has just agreed to be my wife."

Chapter Nine

For a moment, Connor worried that CJ was angry, that he hated the idea of his dad planning to marry again. The two kids just stood there, gaping.

And then Jerilyn gave a gleeful laugh. "How great."

And CJ let out a whoop. "Score!"

Connor blinked, unsure. "Uh. That's good, right?"

"Totally, Dad. Sweet," CJ confirmed.

Jerilyn came rushing over. She set her drink on the coffee table and grabbed Tori. "Oh, I'm so happy." She pulled her favorite teacher close, hugging hard. "You're perfect for him, Ms. Jones. I knew it right from the first."

Tori hugged her back. "Um, you did?"

Jerilyn took her by the shoulders and held her away, beaming at Tori with complete satisfaction. You would have thought CJ's girlfriend had engineered the engagement herself. "Well, maybe not that *first* day." She sent a glance at Connor. "That first day, you were kind of scary, Mr. McFarlane."

Connor felt a little abashed. "Yeah. I suppose I was. Sorry."

"But up at the summer kickoff barbecue. That was when I got the feeling you guys might get together."

Now Tori laughed. "No."

"Oh, yeah." She grabbed Tori's left hand. What was it about women? Even the really young ones went right for the ring finger. "Wait. Where's the ring?"

Tori blinked. "Well, um, we…"

On the fly, Connor came up with an answer. "I couldn't wait to ask her. And we've just agreed to drive over to Bozeman today and choose one."

"Wow, Dad," said CJ. He actually looked a little misty-eyed. "This is pretty cool."

Looking at him, Connor could almost feel guilty for deceiving him like this—but not that guilty. After all, he was doing what he had to do, to keep CJ with him.

"So when's the wedding?" Jerilyn demanded.

Tori shook her head. "Slow down, we just got engaged. Let us enjoy the glow for a while before we start in about the wedding."

CJ said, "Hey. So are we moving here, for good, then, Dad? That would be so sweet. If we lived here, I could go to Thunder Canyon High."

Connor felt a shiver down his backbone. Already his son was dreaming of a future in Thunder Canyon—a future that was never going to happen. "We've made no plans yet. None. Enjoy the summer, CJ. Leave it at that."

"I will, Dad. But if you're—"

Connor didn't let him finish. "CJ."

CJ hesitated. But he didn't exactly give up. "Well, we can talk about it later, huh?"

Connor knew he had to draw the line on this or he'd never hear the end of it. "You will go back to boarding school, as always." He spoke flatly. "I can get you your summer, CJ, even though your mother wants it otherwise. But you can't push me beyond that."

CJ stared at the floor. Finally, he sighed. "Okay, Dad."

Connor nodded. "Good, then." Tori and Jerilyn were looking uncomfortable. In Tori's hazel eyes, he saw again all the ways their fake engagement could cause more problems than it would solve. He put on a cheerful tone. "So. You two want to come with us, to pick out the ring? We can all go out to dinner afterward."

Jerilyn was already shaking her head. "Oh, no. You guys have to do that alone."

Connor laughed. "What? That's some kind of requirement?"

"Well, yeah. It's a totally romantic moment, choosing a ring. You don't need us there for that."

Connor happened to glance at CJ, who made a big show of shrugging and shaking his head. "Don't ask me. I know nothing about that stuff."

Jerilyn held firm. "*I* do. You two should choose the ring together, just the two of you." And she added with a glowing smile, "Plus, well, my dad and I are having dinner together tonight. Sunday dinner, as a family, we both agreed."

So it was decided that the teenagers would continue with their afternoon, as planned. And Tori and Connor would make a quick trip to Bozeman.

Ten minutes later, the kids were on their way to Main Street and the park nearby and Tori and Connor were in the SUV, headed out of town.

She sent him a glance across the console. "Just think. If we weren't pretending to be engaged, we could be having wild sex right now. Instead, we're off to buy a ring that will probably cost you a whole lot more than you want to spend."

He held her gaze for an extra second before turning his eyes back to the road. "This won't take long at all. I think we can fit in the wild sex when we get back to your house."

She tried to stifle a laugh. "Oh. Well. I'm so relieved to hear that."

"I knew you would be. And as to the ring, whatever it costs, you're worth it."

She chuckled, and then grew serious. "You realize, don't you, that already CJ's imagining his new life here in Montana—year-round?"

"I made it clear to him that he's going back to school."

She spoke softly. "I know you did. But that doesn't mean you've heard the last of it from him. Now he's got it in his head that you might make a permanent home here in town, he's going to keep trying to get you to agree that he should live here with you."

He captured her hand, brought it to his lips. "It's going to work out fine. You'll see."

"I sincerely hope so."

They found a jewelry store that was not only open on Sunday, it also had a really nice selection of engagement diamonds.

As Connor expected she might, Tori tried to choose something inexpensive and plain.

He wouldn't let her. "Don't forget my rep as a rich corporate shark—I say that one." The ring he indicated had a giant princess-cut stone surrounded by lots of tiny pavé diamonds. More pavé diamonds, channel-cut, glittered in the platinum band.

Tori's eyes lit up. "Oh, that's much too extravagant."

Connor sent the jeweler a wry smile. "She wants to try it on."

"Yes, of course." The jeweler beamed back at him, dollar signs shining in his eyes.

"Connor. No. Really."

"Now, now." The jeweler clucked his tongue. "You must at least try it on." He winked at Connor as he took her hand and slid the gorgeous rock onto her finger. "Ah. Yes. It's beautiful on you. Just exquisite."

"She loves it," Connor said. "We'll take it."

"Oh, Connor—"

He didn't even let her get started. "No more discussion. It's settled." He passed the jeweler his credit card.

Tori looked down at the ring—and then up at him again. "I knew you would do this. You are much too extravagant. You realize that, don't you?"

He framed her face. "Not extravagant in the least. My perfect bride deserves the perfect ring."

And then he kissed her. She smiled against his lips and for a moment or two, he almost found himself believing that they really were a couple in love, that the ring on her finger meant the start of a lifetime—*their* lifetime, together.

But it didn't, of course. And he needed to remember that.

Tori tried not to spend the whole drive home admiring the ring.

She tried to remember that the ring might be real, but the engagement wasn't. That the gorgeous diamond he'd just put on her finger was only for show and she would be returning it at the end of August. That she must keep her head, above all. Not get too attached. To the ring.

Or to him.

At her house, he shut and locked the front door behind them. And then he took her in his strong arms, claiming her mouth in a kiss that lasted forever and made her doubts fly away. He peeled off her clothes and his own, leaving a trail of shirts and shoes and jeans and underwear as he waltzed her backward to her bedroom door.

By the side of bed, he clasped her bare shoulders and guided her down so she sat on the edge. Holding her gaze, he sank to his knees.

With tender hands, so gentle and slow, he eased her thighs apart. And he kissed her, deeply, there at the heart of her womanhood, a long, wet, lovely kiss, a kiss that was so intimate, it was almost beyond bearing.

But, oh, she did bear it. She reveled in it. She clutched his dark head, her fingers buried in the silky strands of his hair. And she offered herself, shamelessly, completely, without holding back.

When her climax rushed over her, he went on kissing

her, drawing the last drop of pleasure from the sweet, endless pulsing, making the fulfillment go on and on.

And then, after that, when he rose up above her and came down across the white sheets with her, she lay dazed and limp beneath his expert caresses, only wanting more of him. Wanting everything.

All he would give her.

All the pleasure, all the excitement, all the pure joy they would share in this too-brief summer allotted to them.

He kissed her breasts, her belly. And then slowly, his soft lips trailed back up again, along the center of her body. He kissed her throat, scraped his teeth along the curve of her chin. And then, at last, he claimed her mouth. She tasted her own desire on his lips, musky and hot.

Consumed by his burning kiss, she was vaguely aware that he reached out and pulled open the drawer in the nightstand. He lifted his mouth from hers.

She groaned and tried to pull him back.

He whispered, "Wait…"

Wait?

She did not want to wait.

With another groan—one of protest, this time, she opened her eyes. And understood.

With amazing, swift dexterity, he had a condom out and ready. He rolled it down over himself.

"Now?" she whispered on a pleading note.

He granted her a slow smile. "Now."

"Come here, then. Hurry." She moaned again, reaching for him, tugging at his hard shoulders, urging him to come to her.

And he did, he covered her, all corded muscle and

burning heat. She reached down between them, encircling him, loving the way he groaned against her lips when she touched him, when she guided him into her, lifting her body up, offering him everything.

He took what she gave, took *her*. And she was ready, so wet and eager. Primed to accept him. He slid in as though he were made for her, made to be with her.

When he moved, she went with him, taking the cues his body gave her, answering back in kind. Wrapping her legs around his lean hips, holding on so tight, she felt for a moment that they were one body, so fully joined there was no separating them.

She cried out when she reached the finish, her body pulsing around him. And he joined her. They rode the wave of completion together. The whole world narrowed down to a hot pinpoint of soaring light and pleasure. She rode the light, up and over, to the edge of fulfillment, and then finally over, with a long sigh, into limp satisfaction.

Connor relaxed, too, on top of her. They were both sweating, breathing hard. She kept her arms and legs wrapped around him for the longest time, wishing she would never have to let him go.

He didn't want to leave her. But it was almost five.

Reluctantly, he eased his body to the side. He kissed her sweat-damp shoulder. "I have to go…"

She touched his hair, brushed a finger over his cheek. "I know."

"Want to have dinner at my house with me and CJ?"

She lifted up on an elbow and braced her head on her hand. Her face was sweetly flushed. Even the freckles on her nose were slightly pink. And her strawberry hair was wild, tangled.

He thought he'd never seen anyone so sexy in his life.

"It's tempting," she said. "But you two need a little guy time now and then. You've been gone most of the week."

He leaned close, stole one last quick kiss. "I guess you're right."

She frowned. "But I was thinking…"

"About?"

"Tomorrow. You said your ex-wife was coming, supposedly to pick up CJ, in the morning."

"Yeah."

"Do you want me to be there?"

He chuckled. And not really with humor. "You think you're up for that? Jennifer can be a complete bitch when she's not happy about a situation."

"It's okay. I can take it. I'm a teacher, remember? I'm used to smiling sincerely no matter what, staying diplomatic and upbeat in the most uncomfortable situations. And, well, if I met her, she and I might just hit it off. Maybe she would rethink her unreasonable demands."

"Seriously, Tori. You don't know Jennifer."

"In any case, it wouldn't hurt for her to see that I really exist and I'm relatively harmless, would it?"

Actually, he thought it was a great idea. At least in theory. "If you're volunteering, I'm more than happy to accept the support. But I warn you, it could get ugly."

"I can take it."

He kissed her again. "And you have to promise that no matter what she says to you, no matter how rude she is, you won't let her change your mind about you and me."

She put on a very solemn expression. "I promise, Connor. I will be your bogus fiancée until the end of August, no matter what your ex-wife does tomorrow morning."

"Excellent." He kissed her again and wished he could linger.

But she pulled away. "Go on, now. Have your evening with CJ."

He dragged himself up and out of her bed. Then he followed the trail of clothing that led out toward the entry area, separating his from hers and getting dressed as he went.

She pulled on a robe and joined him at the door. "What time tomorrow?"

"Jennifer didn't give an exact time. Just another of her techniques to keep everyone off-balance. Be there at nine?" He waited for her nod. "I'll call you if she shows up earlier than that."

CJ was already at the house when Connor arrived. They had dinner together. CJ talked about Jerilyn, about his job at the Hopping H.

"I got paid Friday," he announced with pride.

Connor gazed across the table at him and felt real satisfaction at their progress in the past few weeks. His son *was* doing better. And he was also growing up.

It wouldn't be too many more years before CJ was old enough to make his own decisions, about his future. About the kind of life he wanted to lead.

And it was Connor's job to make sure CJ had the tools and abilities he needed to enjoy a successful, productive, reasonably happy adult life.

"When will you and Ms. Jones get married?" CJ wanted to know.

"We haven't decided yet."

"Did you get her a ring?"

"Yes, I did."

"Is it a nice one?"

"I think so. And she seems pleased with it."

"Well, Dad. Cool."

"After dinner, I was thinking we would look through the books you brought with you, kind of get you focused on your studies again, review what you see as your strengths, where you're caught up. And where you need work."

CJ groaned. But it was a good-natured sound. "Do we have to?"

"It'll give Tori a starting point for your first tutoring session tomorrow."

CJ ate a big bite of the meat loaf Gerda had prepared for them. He chewed and swallowed, took a gulp of his milk and set the glass down firmly. "Yeah. I think you're right, Dad. Something to start with. That would be a good thing."

They worked for three hours that night, going through the schoolbooks from the year before, marking the points where CJ needed more work. They went online and got copies of his grades, so that Tori could see which classes he was weak in.

At ten, they knocked off. CJ put the books away and then came to sit next to Connor on the end of the bed.

"Dad? Do I *have* to be here when Mom comes tomorrow?"

Connor completely understood his son's apprehension.

But there was no getting out of dealing with Jennifer—for either of them. "Yeah. You need to talk to her. You need to tell her how you feel, what you want."

CJ made a low sound. "Like she'll listen."

"Respectfully," Connor reminded him.

"I know, Dad. I remember."

Connor wanted to hug him. But he'd never been physically demonstrative with CJ. Would it freak the kid out if suddenly Connor started with the hugs?

It kind of freaked Connor out, to think about it.

He settled for firmly clasping his son's shoulder. "It'll be fine."

CJ snorted. "Come on, Dad. You know Mom. She wants things her way, always has. It's not exactly gonna be fine."

"She does love you," Connor said, and wished the words didn't sound so weak. CJ only grunted. Connor added, "You'll get through it."

"Yeah." CJ spoke in the affirmative—but he was shaking his head. "I guess I will."

"Tori will be here when your mother comes."

"Why?"

Connor had no idea what his son was thinking. He asked cautiously, "Does that bother you, if Tori's here?"

"No, Dad. It's only…that could be weird."

"Maybe. But Tori says she can handle it. And I think it's a good thing. For your mother to meet my fiancée, to see that we're, all of us, moving on with our lives." His fiancée. So quickly, the lie was getting to be second nature. He kept having to remind himself that it *was* a lie, to draw the line in his mind, between the roles he and Tori played and their real relationship, which was amazing.

But not destined to last.

"Dad?"

"Yeah?"

"You kind of spaced out there for a minute. You okay?"

Connor shook himself. "I'm fine." He got up from the edge of the bed and went to the open door. "Good night."

"Night, Dad."

Tori was up and dressed and ready to go by seven the next morning. She wanted to be able to head for Connor's instantly if his ex should show up before nine.

But the phone didn't ring.

At nine on the dot, she stood at Connor's door. He opened it and pulled her inside before she even had a chance to ring the bell.

He kissed her. One of *those* kisses. The kind that stole her breath and curled her toes and reminded her of all the lovely things he did to her when they were alone in bed.

Eventually, with great reluctance, she pulled away. "Where's CJ?"

"In his room."

"Your ex-wife…?"

"Not here yet. Tea? I think Gerda has some around here somewhere."

"Yes. All right. Tea." Tea would be good. Something to do with her hands—to keep them from reaching for him.

She followed him into the kitchen, which had

everything a gourmet cook might desire: gleaming granite counters, custom cabinets, name-brand stainless-steel appliances. He heated a mug of water in the microwave and stuck a tea bag in it.

"Thank you." She put her hands around the cup, taking comfort from the warmth of it.

There was coffee already made. He was pouring a cup for himself when the doorbell rang.

Connor set the half-filled mug on the counter and put the pot back on the heating pad. "Well. I guess this is it."

Her stomach lurched. But she answered with a smile. "Yes. I think so."

They went back down the central hallway together. She detoured to the living room as they passed it. "I'll wait here. Don't want to overwhelm her at the door." He gave her a nod and continued on to the entry.

Tori perched on a chair in his big, well-furnished living room. She heard the door open, and then a woman's voice—tight, controlled. Connor said something.

And then two sets of footsteps approached.

Connor and a beautiful, very angry-looking blonde appeared in the doorway to the hall. "Jennifer, my fiancée, Tori Jones."

The blonde dismissed her with a look and said to Connor, "Is CJ ready? I want to get going right away."

Tori kept her smile in place as she rose. "It's so great to finally meet you."

Jennifer granted her an icy glance. "Yes, well." And instantly turned back to Connor. "CJ. Where is he?"

Connor shrugged. "In his room."

"Take me to him. Now."

"Sure. This way." Connor sent her a rueful look over his shoulder as he and Jennifer left the doorway.

Tori waited, too nervous to sit back down, until he returned a couple of minutes later.

"Gee," she said when he entered the living room. "That went well."

He let out a heavy sigh. "Sorry. Really."

"Don't be sorry. I volunteered to come, remember? And I still think it's good, that she's met me, that I'm... real to her, you know?"

"Yeah. I guess so."

She frowned. "So...what now?"

"I don't know. We wait, for a few minutes anyway. Give CJ his chance to say what he needs to say."

"What if she tries to drag him out of here?"

Connor actually chuckled. "She's no bigger than he is anymore. And he can be seriously un-draggable when he's made up his mind about something." He took her hand. "Come on. Let's sit down." He led her to the sofa and they sat together.

A tense couple of minutes passed. They held hands; they were quiet, waiting.

And then Tori heard the sound of high heels swiftly, furiously tap-tapping the hardwood floor in the central hallway. The blonde appeared in the doorway again.

"Connor. I told you to have him ready to go. He's not packed. He says he's not going."

"Jennifer, I don't know what more to say to you than I already have. We all agreed he's staying here for the summer and we are keeping that agreement."

Jennifer fumed. Tori could almost see smoke coming out of her delicate, diamond-bedecked ears. "Get him ready. Get him ready now."

Connor let go of Tori's hand and stood. "No, Jennifer. I will do no such thing." Tori rose to stand beside him. A show of solidarity couldn't hurt.

Jennifer looked ready to take Connor's head off with her perfectly manicured hands. "You know what you're asking for, don't you? I will call my lawyers. I'll get a court order. He's going, one way or another."

"I've already called *my* lawyers," Connor said calmly.

"You're bluffing."

"Jennifer. Why would I bluff about such a thing? I called them two hours ago, at nine sharp Eastern time. I told them I'm getting married again and I'll be able to make a fine, supportive family environment for my son. So I'm suing for joint physical custody."

Jennifer's plump red mouth dropped open. "You're not serious."

"Yes, I am. I've also told them about our agreement for this summer and your decision to go back on it. I've explained that CJ wants to stay with me."

"How dare you?"

"I am his father, Jennifer. He's fifteen and his say in this does matter."

"I will have him physically removed from this house."

"No, you won't. My lawyers are aware of your threats and taking steps to block your efforts as we speak."

Jennifer pressed her fingers to her temples, as if suddenly stricken by a really bad headache. "I cannot believe that you're doing this to me."

Tori started to speak, to try to ease the tension a little—though she had the sinking feeling she was completely out of her depth here. That it had been unwise of her to come.

Connor spoke before she did. "I'm not doing this to you, Jennifer. You are not the issue here. CJ is. And I'm doing this for him."

"You are a selfish, selfish man."

"I'm sorry you feel that way." He grabbed for Tori's hand again. Aching for him, she gave it, twining her fingers with his. He said to the blonde in the doorway, "You are more than welcome to see CJ anytime this summer, if you'll simply do us the courtesy of calling in advance. But for now, I think it's best that you go. Please."

"What do you care, you bastard?" she demanded. "You never cared."

Connor didn't defend himself. Which was probably the best choice at that point. "You should go," he said again. "Now."

For maybe thirty seconds, Jennifer stood frozen in place. And then, with a small, enraged sound, she announced, "You will hear from my lawyers."

"Got that. Loud and clear."

Jennifer still refused to go. She hovered there, for an endless moment longer. Tori feared she was going to say something really terrible, something that would finally do it, would serve to break Connor's iron control.

But in the end, she simply whirled on her designer heel and headed for the door. Tori counted it a small blessing that at least she didn't slam it on her way out.

Chapter Ten

Connor sank to the sofa again. Tori sat, too.

He said, his voice stark, barely more than a whisper, "God. She hates me. She's the mother of my son and she hates my guts."

"Connor, don't."

"I thought for a while that she was over all that, that we'd each moved on with our lives. But no. She still hates me."

Tori had kind of figured that out already, but with Jennifer's angry words echoing in her head, the truth became all the more agonizingly clear. She wished she hadn't come—at the same time as she remembered the way he'd grabbed for her hand. As if he needed her, took strength from her presence there.

He seemed to sense the direction of her thoughts.

"I was glad you were here. Just more proof of what a selfish bastard I am."

"You're not, Connor. You're not."

"But I really hate that you had to witness that."

"Not your fault," she reminded him. "It was my idea." She felt she just had to say something in his defense, since he seemed unwilling to do that for himself. "It takes two to make a bad marriage, or at least, that's what I've always believed."

He gave her a rueful glance. "Don't defend me. Please."

"Well, okay. What do I know, anyway? I'm just the fake fiancée."

"You know a lot." His voice was tender. "And as bad as that was, I still think I'm doing the right thing, for CJ."

"Me, too."

There were footsteps in the hallway. CJ appeared and stood in the open doorway where his mother had been. "She's gone?"

Connor replied, "Yeah."

"She was so mad, Dad."

"Yeah. She was."

CJ raked his shaggy hair back off his forehead. He looked very young right then. And there was way too much hurt in the eyes that were so much like his father's. Hurt and determination, too. He stood up straighter. "I think I need to get to work, you know?"

"Good idea," said Connor. "I'll take you now."

CJ gave Tori a shy glance. "See you at two, Ms. Jones."

She sent him a bright smile. "Yes. I'm looking forward to working with you, CJ."

"You could ride along with us," Connor suggested.

Nervously, Tori twisted her engagement ring, caught herself doing it, and made herself stop. "I have lunch at noon with Allaire. And you two might have a few things to talk about. I'll just go back to my place, thanks."

CJ was silent on the drive to the Hopping H. And Connor couldn't think of anything constructive to say then, anyway. Plus, he was worried about Tori.

He never should have allowed her to be there when Jennifer showed up. Tori shouldn't have to deal with crap like that. It wasn't her problem and he feared that the unpleasant encounter had only made her have second thoughts about their temporary engagement.

Halfway to the guest ranch, he knew he was going to race back to Tori's place as soon as CJ got where he needed to go. But then, as he pulled the SUV to a stop in front of the ranch house, he decided that he would leave her alone for the rest of the day.

The woman deserved a little time to herself now and then.

If she changed her mind about everything, so be it. He would certainly understand why.

"Thanks, Dad." CJ got out of the vehicle and ran up the steps to the front door. He went in.

And Melanie came out. She waved at him to wait and then ran to his side window.

He rolled it down.

She made a funny, disbelieving face at him and then accused, "Jerilyn says you and Tori are getting married. Is it true?"

Great. More lies to tell. "Yeah."

"Connor. Since when?"

"Yesterday afternoon. I got down on my knees and begged her. She said yes. We went to Bozeman and bought the ring."

Melanie let out laugh. "Seriously? Really?"

He felt like a jerk for deceiving her. But he continued to do so anyway. "Yeah. Seriously."

She was shaking her head. "You're a fast worker, big brother."

"I see what I want, I go after it."

She reached in the window and patted his shoulder, a fond sort of gesture that made him feel even more like a lying creep. "You certainly do. And I'm happy for you. She's a wonderful person."

"Yes. She is."

"When's the wedding?"

He groaned. "Hold on, will you? We just got engaged."

"All right, I won't push for the details. Yet—and I have an idea."

"Uh-oh."

"Don't be so negative. You haven't even heard what it is."

"No, but I have a feeling you're going to tell me."

"We need a party." She gave a firm nod. "An engagement party. I'll call Allaire. We'll get right on it."

This was getting out of hand. "Hold on. Don't make a big deal. Please."

"Oh, come on. It will be fun. And you and Tori together, engaged to be married, that calls for a celebration. "

"Would you mind if I checked with Tori first? I don't even know if she's told Allaire."

"Of course, she's told Allaire. They're best friends."

"Melanie. I mean it. Wait."

She folded her arms across her middle. "Fine. Talk to Tori. And get back to me. Soon."

"All right. I promise. I'll talk to her."

"How did it go with Jennifer?"

"About as expected. She was furious. She's calling her lawyers. I already called mine."

"It will work out."

"I hope so."

"You did the right thing—and I mean it about the party. Talk to Tori. Get back to me. I'm giving you twenty-four hours on it and then I'm calling Tori myself."

"I can hardly believe it," Allaire said with a combination of wonder and disbelief. "He asked you to marry him and you said yes?"

"That's right. I love him," Tori said simply. She neither choked nor stumbled over the words. And when they came out, they sounded true. Real.

Yes, she'd spent the two and a half hours since leaving Connor's house wondering if she ought to call a halt to this dangerous charade before they got in any deeper.

But then she'd come to the Tottering Teapot for the weekly girls-only lunch and she'd sat across from Allaire at their usual lace-covered table. And she'd made the announcement, simply and directly. With no fanfare.

And no hesitation.

Allaire sat back in her chair. She studied Tori's face for several seconds that seemed like a lifetime and a half. And then, finally, she nodded. And she smiled. "I'm happy for you. And he's a lucky, lucky man."

Tori couldn't help nodding back. "Yes, he is. And I'm a happy woman."

Allaire looked at her sideways. "Ahem. Your left hand."

"Yes?"

"It's under the table."

Tori giggled like a high-school girl. "Yes."

"Come on. Let me see it."

Tori lifted her hand and held it out across table.

"Wow," said Allaire. "Just…wow." She grinned at Tori. "I take back every small-minded thing I ever said about him. That is one gorgeous ring."

"I know. I love it."

Allaire raised her teacup. "To you, my dear friend. And to Connor. And to all the happiness that love can bring."

Tori clinked her cup with her best friend's. They sipped in unison.

Strangely, at that moment, beaming across the table at Allaire, Tori didn't feel like a liar or a cheat.

She felt happy. And hopeful. Like a woman in love.

Connor dropped CJ off at two, as planned. He didn't come in, just waved from the SUV when Tori opened the door.

CJ and Tori worked for the agreed-on two hours. He'd brought his grade reports and several books he and Connor had bookmarked the night before, so he could show her where he was in the classes he'd taken the previous semester.

By the end of the session, Tori felt the tutoring was

going to work out well. CJ seemed seriously committed to getting caught up. And he was a very smart boy. Now he was willing to apply himself, she had little doubt that he would be ready for his junior year when he went back to school in the fall.

At four, as they were finishing up, Jerilyn appeared.

CJ confessed he'd invited her. "I hope that's okay, Ms. Jones…"

She told him it was great and ushered them into the kitchen for snacks and juice. The doorbell rang again.

"That's Dad. He said he'd come get me this time in case I had too many books to carry on my skateboard."

Tori left the kids in the kitchen and went to let him in.

"All finished?" he asked when she pulled open the door.

"We are." Strange how her heart felt lighter, just at the sight of him. "And Jerilyn got here a minute ago, too. Want some juice and crackers?"

He glanced past her shoulder. "Where are they?"

She almost laughed. "In the kitchen—and you're whispering."

"Yeah, well. After this morning, I've been a nervous wreck, waiting to ask you…"

"What?"

"Are we…still on with this?"

"I have to tell you, I did have second thoughts."

He looked stricken. "I knew it."

"But then I went to lunch with Allaire…and told her we're getting married."

Those dark eyes of his were velvet-soft. He

stepped over the threshold and took her by the arms. "Seriously?"

"Seriously." She moved back a step. He came right with her and nudged the door shut behind him.

For a moment, they simply regarded each other. Looking up at him, so close she could feel the heat of his body, seemed to steal all the air from her lungs. And strangely, a thousand butterflies had somehow gotten loose in her stomach.

He lowered his dark head. She raised hers. They shared a kiss as sweet and tender as any kiss could be.

When he lifted his head, he said, "Melanie insists that she's calling Allaire and setting up an engagement party."

She chided, "Don't look so grim. Tell your sister thank you. When people get engaged, the ones they love want to celebrate."

He grumbled. "That's pretty much what Melanie said."

"Shakespeare has a quote for this."

"I know, I know. The one about tangled webs, right?"

"That's it. So I think we should just go for it, you know? We're in this and, unless you want to back out now, Connor, we're staying in it for the next eight weeks or so."

"I don't want to back out—I just keep thinking that *you'll* want to." His voice was gruff.

"Well, stop. I'm not getting cold feet, okay? I agreed to do this and I'm sticking by my agreement. Stop second-guessing me."

He pretended to look chastised. "Yes, Ms. Jones."

"That's better—now come on in the kitchen before the kids come looking for us."

CJ and Jerilyn were at the kitchen table, each with a large glass of orange juice and a plate of organic potato chips.

"Dad, I had a good lesson," CJ announced proudly. "Didn't I, Ms. Jones?"

"We made great progress, yes."

"Dad, can Jerilyn come over for dinner? Afterward, she says she'll help me with my homework—if *her* dad says it's okay, I mean."

"Of course," Connor said. He arched a brow at Tori. "Join us?"

"I'd love to. Yes."

In the sunny summer days that followed, Tori and Connor were together every chance they got. They shared dinners with CJ—at Connor's and at Tori's. Connor would come over to her place in the mornings when CJ was at the Hopping H. And sometimes he also showed up late at night, after his son was in bed. They went out to romantic dinners, once to the resort again, and once into Bozeman to Tori's favorite restaurant there.

Word of their engagement spread fast in Thunder Canyon. There were congratulations on everyone's lips. And each one seemed sincere.

They told his parents and hers. It seemed the wisest course. They didn't want them to hear it from someone else. Her dad and stepmom gave their blessing. His parents didn't sound too thrilled. But at least they were polite in their chilly, distant way.

After they talked to the McFarlanes, Tori teased him

that she now knew of at least two people who wouldn't be the least bit sad to see their engagement come to an end.

Connor grabbed her close and kissed her until her head was spinning. "Don't talk about it ending," he growled. "We've barely begun."

She almost said, *It doesn't* have *to end, you know.*

But shouldn't he know that? Of course, he did. He cared for her a lot. But he'd made it painfully clear that he didn't intend to marry again. She had to remember that it wasn't forever, that the fantasy they were living was just that. And it was destined to end before the leaves started to fall.

On Thursday, the first of July, a week and three days after Jennifer declared she would sue for full custody, Connor was served with papers from her lawyers. He shrugged and told Tori that Jennifer would be getting his countersuit that same day. She thought he seemed pretty confident.

But then, he always did. He had another meeting with Caleb Douglas that Thursday evening. Caleb's mostly silent partner, Justin Caldwell, showed up that time, too, with his wife, Katie. Justin was Caleb's illegitimate son. And Katie was a close friend of the Douglas family, who had spent several years living in Thunder Canyon as something of an honorary daughter to the Douglases.

Later that night, in her bed, Connor told her that Justin seemed fond of his father and of his half brother, Riley, as well. Connor said Justin wasn't a factor in the sale. Justin was willing to do whatever Caleb decided.

"I got the feeling that he *wasn't* willing to invest any more money, though. And that he'd be happier if Caleb either decided to sell—or found a way to get more investors to put in some green until the economy picks up enough steam that they start seeing real profits again."

She scolded, "Why are you telling me this? Didn't I say I wanted nothing to do with your takeover plans?"

He kissed the tip of her nose. "You *have* nothing to do with them. This is just pillow talk."

"You'd better watch yourself, Mr. Corporate Shark. I'll sell all your secrets to the highest bidder."

He chuckled. "Oh, come on. Corporate spying is not your style."

She pointed at her nose. "These freckles? This school-teacher act? All designed to lull you into trusting me so I can ferret out all of it, learn every trick you have up your sleeve—and pass it on to people who will pay well to know what you're up to."

He bent close, blew in her ear. And then he caught her earlobe between his teeth and bit it just hard enough to make her moan. "I'm in control here."

"Ha. So you think."

He kissed her. Long and deeply.

"Okay," she said when they came up for air. "I see your point."

He kissed her again.

"I forgot." She put on a dazed expression. "What were we talking about?"

And he kissed her a third time.

After that, Tori forgot everything—except the feel of his hands on her body and the touch of his lips to hers.

The next night was Friday, the second of July—and the date of their engagement party.

Melanie and Allaire had managed somehow, on extremely short notice, to get the upstairs ballroom in the town hall on Main Street for the party. This was quite a feat, as it was the weekend of the Fourth with all kinds of community events in the works.

From what Tori heard, practically everybody in town pitched in on the party. They wouldn't let her help. But all day Friday, the ballroom was full of Tori's friends and students—including Jerilyn and CJ, who had gotten a day off from his lessons with Tori so he could help with the party.

Jerilyn came by Tori's house in the late afternoon and reported that they'd spent the day setting up tables and chairs. And decorating. Jerilyn was really proud of the way the decorations had turned out. But she refused to tell Tori anything specific about them.

"Because you should be surprised, Ms. Jones. That's part of the fun."

Tori did know that they were having potluck, with everyone bringing something, to be served buffet-style. And DJ was not only providing condiments and a few side dishes from the Rib Shack, he'd also hired the same six-piece band that would be playing at the Independence Day dance Saturday night. The band didn't mind picking up an extra gig, as long they were in town.

Tori and Connor were given instructions to be there at eight. Not before, not after. Melanie and Russ picked up CJ at six and Jerilyn was getting there with her dad.

Connor, dressed for the occasion in jeans, tooled boots and a gorgeous Western shirt, showed up at Tori's door at seven forty-five. "My sister ordered me to cowboy up for this thing." He didn't look happy. But he sure did look good. Not like a real cowboy—more like a movie star *playing* a cowboy.

She said, "Hey. Works for me."

He came inside and shut the door. "I like that dress. What color is that?"

"Teal blue."

"It matches your eyes."

"My eyes are hazel."

"And right now they look blue-green." The dress was sleeveless, perfect for a summer evening. With a lazy finger, he traced the low, square neckline. "Beautiful."

"Thank you—and why do I get the feeling it's not my dress that interests you?"

Dark eyes gleamed. "Maybe because I'm thinking about what's underneath."

"Don't get ideas. We have to be there at eight sharp."

"I can be quick when I have to."

She gently slapped his hand away. "Uh-uh. I just got ready. You are not messing up my hair—or my makeup."

"I can be careful."

"You are incorrigible."

"So I've been told."

"It's going to be great," she told him. "You'll see." She turned to grab her purse from the entry table. "Now, let's get going."

He scowled. "I think there's some kind of surprise brewing. I don't like surprises."

"Relax. Let all your control issues go, just for one evening. It's going to be fun."

"Control issues?" He arched a dark brow. "I have no control issues."

She wisely refrained from arguing the point.

CJ was waiting on the front steps of the town hall. "I'm supposed to take you up," he said.

Clearly there *was* some kind of surprise brewing.

Connor narrowed his eyes. "What are they plotting?"

CJ wasn't telling. He was trying not to grin. "Come on, Dad. You'll see."

Inside, with CJ in the lead, they mounted the wide, slightly creaky wooden steps that led to a large landing. Wide-open double doors gave way into the hall itself. The lights were off in there—and it seemed much too quiet.

"Come on, you guys." CJ, several steps ahead of them, turned back to signal them onward as he made the landing. But he didn't wait for them. He went on through the doors, vanishing into the large shadowed room beyond.

"I don't like this," Connor muttered out of the corner of his mouth.

She took his hand. "Be brave," she teased.

He grunted but said no more. They reached the landing. Beyond was darkness, punctuated only by the random sparkle of what looked like Mylar streamers hanging from the ceiling. Connor held back.

Tori couldn't suppress a giggle. "This is so exciting."

"Yeah, right."

"Coward," she teased.

"Fine," he grumbled. "Let's get it over with."

Side by side, they stepped into the shadows beyond the doorway.

The lights popped on, blindingly bright, as shouts, applause and catcalls erupted. Simultaneously, the band started playing "Here Comes the Bride," only flat, with a horrible-sounding horn.

And suddenly, an enormous clump of glittery confetti fell from above. For a moment, as the horn played on, they were engulfed in a snowfall of shiny foil and bits of bright paper.

Then everyone came rushing forward to shout congratulations and grab them in bear hugs. That went on for at least five minutes. Tori lost sight of her confetti-covered fake fiancé as each of them was hugged, passed down the line, and hugged again.

Finally, they all seemed to settle down. The band stopped mid-note.

Tori glanced toward the stage at the far end of the hall. Allaire was up there, at the mike, wearing a pretty pink dress, her hair shining like spun gold under the lights, looking like a fairy princess.

"Connor McFarlane," she said. "Congratulations. You are a very fortunate man."

Tori blushed. And everyone started clapping and whistling again.

Allaire raised her hand. "And, Tori, we love you. May you find all the happiness you so richly deserve."

The guests clapped even louder.

Tori shouted, "Thank you. What a great party. Thank you, everyone!"

Tears filled her eyes and guilt tried to creep up on her. All these people, people she cared about, wishing her and Connor well, not knowing it was a lie.

The band struck up a lively tune. The guests dispersed from clogging the doorway, pausing only to clasp Tori's shoulder again, to offer more good wishes. Some coupled up and danced. Others grabbed plates and got in line at the buffet tables.

Connor appeared. "There you are. Lost you there for a minute or two."

She swallowed her tears of guilt and whispered in his ear, "That wasn't so bad, was it?"

He grunted. "Okay, I admit it. It could have been worse."

Laughing, they brushed at each other's shoulders and hair, thinning out the confetti snowfall a little.

CJ and Jerilyn came toward them. Both were grinning wide. CJ called, "Sweet, huh, Dad?"

"Yeah," said Connor dryly. "Sweet."

It seemed to Tori that the whole town was there. The kids from her classes, everyone from school, every Traub and Clifton, every Cates and every Douglas, too.

She and Connor found a table with a couple of free seats. She admired the decorations, which involved flags and Uncle Sam hats and patriotic bunting, everything doused with glitter, in red, white and blue. And the ceiling? A sea of shining Mylar streamers.

Connor went and got them soft drinks—no liquor allowed in the hall. Later, they went through the buffet line, loading up their plates with more than they would ever be able to eat.

They danced. He was an excellent dancer. She filed that information away in her growing store of knowledge about him. Funny, how she felt she could never know enough about him. She could spend the rest of her life learning his ways. His likes. His dislikes. His numerous and considerable abilities. His failings, of which there were more than a few.

There would never be enough time, not even in a whole lifetime, to know everything about him, every secret dream, every favorite thing. And they didn't have a lifetime.

They had only right now.

He brushed his lips to her temple, then tipped up her chin with a finger so that she met his eyes as they swayed through a slow song. "You look...almost sad." His voice was low, for her ears alone.

She made her lips tip up in a smile. "I'm not, really. Not sad—or if I am, it's only a little. Mostly, I'm happy. Happier than I've ever been."

He held her gaze, searched her face. But only for a moment. And then he pulled her close again and they danced on through the rest of that song and the next one, too.

Later, when the band took a break, they returned to their table. Russ and Melanie joined them and a few minutes later, Grant Clifton and his wife, Stephanie, came by. Steph said how happy she was for Connor and Tori. And Grant, looking very proud, announced that they were having their first baby in February.

Russ got up and clapped his lifelong friend on the back. "Now that's good news. Boy or girl?"

"Not a clue," said Grant.

Russ raised his Pepsi. "Here's to baby Clifton."

"To baby Clifton," everyone at the table echoed in unison.

Stephanie laughed and patted her still-flat tummy. "Grant's already trying to get me to take it easy. I tell him to back off. I've got a ranch to run."

Grant wrapped an arm around his wife and pulled her close for a quick kiss. And then Melanie was up and reaching for a hug from Steph. Tori got up, too, to congratulate Steph with a hug of her own.

When Tori took her chair again, Grant was leaning close to Connor, saying something in his ear that the rest of the table couldn't hear.

"Sure," said Connor. "Monday at ten."

Grant nodded. Tori thought he looked way too serious. And worried, as well. "Thanks."

The band started up again. Grant took Steph's hand and led her out onto the floor.

Tori leaned closer to Connor. "What was that about?"

He put his lips to her ear. "Long story. Later."

Tori shrugged and let it go. She sat back and enjoyed the rest of the evening, which went by in a warm blur of good company, music and laughter.

At the end, CJ went back to the ranch with the Chiltons. He seemed happy to go and looking forward to visiting the foals at the Flying J. That left Tori and Connor with a whole night to themselves.

At her house, they agreed that the party had been terrific. And they also agreed that they refused to feel guilty that the whole town had just celebrated an engagement that would never get all the way to the altar. It had been a town event at minimal cost to all involved and everyone had seemed to have a good time.

They made unhurried love.

Later, as they lay side by side in her darkened room, slowly drifting toward sleep, she remembered that strange moment at the table, with Grant. "So..."

"Um?"

"What was that about with Grant tonight?"

He touched her, smoothing a hand down the curve of her thigh. "Do we really need to talk about Grant?"

"Come on." She caught that wandering hand of his, brought it to her lips and then twined her fingers with his. "I do want to know."

He pulled his hand away. "Tori…"

"Come on." She nudged him in the arm with her elbow.

And finally, he gave in and told her. "Grant wants to meet with me. At his office, one-to-one, up at the resort. Monday morning. I'm not looking forward to it."

"Why not?"

"Last time I met with him, he called me a vulture."

"Not Grant."

"Yeah. Grant."

"When was that?"

"Before I left for the trip to Philadelphia."

"You never mentioned that."

"You didn't want to hear about it then, remember?" Tenderly, he guided a strand of hair off her cheek. "That was before you decided to seduce me and steal all my corporate secrets."

"But what happened? Fill me in."

"Not much. He'd been in denial, I guess. And he finally had to admit to himself that I really was likely to end up buying the resort. He didn't like it. And let me know that in no uncertain terms."

"Poor Grant. He loves that resort so much." She canted up on an elbow and peered down at Connor's face through the dimness. "I'm sure he wants to meet with you in order to work things out with you."

"There's nothing to work out."

"Of course there is, if he was out of line."

Connor was silent.

She asked softly, "You'll keep him on, won't you, when you take over?"

His shadowed eyes gave nothing away. "It's still if, not when."

"Oh, please. You can't fool me. And you didn't answer my question. Will you keep Grant on?"

Again, he didn't reply for the longest time. Then, finally, "It's doubtful. For a number of reasons."

"What reasons?" She asked the question a little too heatedly.

"Tori. Look." Suddenly his voice was weary. "Can we not get into a fight over this?"

"I'm not getting in a fight. I just want to know why you can't keep Grant on."

"Because I have to have someone I can work with, not someone who resents me for taking over 'his' baby. Because he's the one who's been in charge while things went from bad to worse."

"It's not his fault that the recession hit. His ideas *and* his follow-through were stellar. And the resort is everything to him. And for crying out loud, his wife's having a baby—"

He hooked a hand around her neck and brought her face down close to his. "Stop." And he kissed her, hard.

She refused to return the kiss. And when he let her go, she flopped over onto her back again.

He lay beside her, unmoving. They were both silent for a long time.

Finally, she spoke again. "I'm sorry. I just hate it, that's all, when things don't work out for good people."

He shifted beside her and pushed back the covers. "I understand." He was on his feet, reaching for his clothes. Leaving, apparently.

She sat up. "Connor, wait."

He had his boxer briefs on, his jeans in his hands. "It's okay. Seriously. I know exactly what you're telling me. I get it. And I'm not angry at you."

"Then why are you going?"

He didn't answer, only shoved his feet into the jeans.

"Stay," she whispered softly.

"No. Not tonight." He sat in the chair in the corner and put on his socks and his boots. Then he grabbed that fancy Western shirt off the back of the chair and stuck his arms in the sleeves.

She still didn't get this. "But I don't—"

"Just let it go." He rose again and buttoned his shirt. "Please."

She realized that he really was leaving and there was nothing she could do or say to make him change his mind.

"Good night," he said softly.

She only nodded. And she closed her eyes as he turned from her so she wouldn't have to watch him go.

He called her when he got back to his house. "I'm sorry I walked out like that. Honestly. And I meant what I said. It's not about you."

"So then why did you go?"

"You think I like firing people? I don't. But it's business and I have to do what's necessary."

She felt absurdly hopeful. "It does bother you, then,

to fire a man even though the only thing he did wrong was to be in charge when the economy went down the tubes?"

"Fine," he confessed low. "Yes, it does bother me. It bothers me more than it used to."

"That's *so* good to hear."

"For you, maybe. From where I'm standing, it's pretty damn scary. In the past, I was tougher. And a man needs to be tough, especially in times like these."

"You're still plenty tough, believe me. Maybe too tough."

"A man can't be too tough."

"Yes, he can. I'm glad it bothers you," she said, with conviction. "It *should* bother you."

"Tori. Look. Can we just leave it at I'm sorry? And I don't think we should talk about the resort anymore."

She reminded herself that he wasn't really her fiancé, that she didn't need to get to the rock-bottom of this issue—or any issue—with him. She didn't need to know all his secrets.

Too bad something in her hungry heart kept driving her to learn them.

But he was right. She could let it go. Just like she would be letting *him* go in August.

"Tori. You still with me?"

She took a long, slow breath. "Right here."

"Good. First thing in the morning, then? Come to my place. I'll cook breakfast."

She thought of the engagement party, how much fun it had been—how somewhere deep in her heart, she wished that celebration could have been real. She wished that her beautiful engagement ring actually meant forever. She wished that *they* were forever, bonded for a lifetime, she and Connor.

But they weren't. And that hurt. It hurt way too much.

Oh, she should have known it would be like this, shouldn't she? Who had she been kidding? The attraction had been much too strong, right from that first night when he took her to dinner at the Gallatin Room. She should have seen this coming, should have know that this would happen.

She swallowed a groan as the revelation came at her.

She was in love with him. In love with Connor.

How could that be? It was impossible. Falling in love with Connor was never the plan.

But somehow, it had happened anyway.

Chapter Eleven

"Tori?" Connor's voice broke through her thoughts.

"Yes. What?"

"Are you all right?"

No. I'm not. Not all right in the least. And what were they talking about?

She remembered. Breakfast. "Yes," she said tightly into the phone. "I'll be there."

"Terrific."

She had to get off the phone, to be alone with her misery. *In love with Connor.* It was impossible. And also true. She schooled her voice to a bland tone. "Eight o'clock?"

"See you then."

And he was gone, just like that. Dead air on the other end of the line. Smart man, not to give her even a second to reconsider.

She should be that smart. Or at least, smart enough not to fall for the local corporate shark. Smart enough not to pretend to be engaged to a man she could never have in any lasting way.

She hung up the phone and pulled the covers close around her. Which was pointless, really. She loved Connor McFarlane. It was a disaster. No way was she going to be able to sleep.

But she did sleep. And soundly, too. The next thing she knew, it was after seven and sunlight streamed in between a space in the curtains.

At eight on the dot, Connor saw her coming up the walk and breathed a sigh of pure relief. He answered the door as she mounted the steps. "You're here."

"I said I would be."

His damn heart felt constricted in his chest. "God. You're so beautiful."

She looked angry, almost. Probably still ticked at him over last night. She said, "If you know what's good for you, you won't say a word about my freckles."

He didn't care if she was angry. She would get over it. He was just so damn glad to see her. He didn't even try to hide his slow grin. "You stopped me just in time." He grabbed her hand and pulled her inside and into his arms where she fit perfectly.

"I don't know if I want to kiss you." She scowled up at him as he lowered his head.

"Kiss me anyway."

She didn't argue further, so he claimed her sweet mouth. It was one of those kisses that made steam come out his ears and had him wanting only to take her straight to bed.

But he'd promised her breakfast. He took her hand and led her to the kitchen. They had omelets and fresh fruit. Coffee for him, tea for her.

And *then* he took her to bed.

Later, they met Russ, Melanie and the boys in town, for the third of July street fair the merchants put together. They all had lunch at the Hitching Post, which had once been the town's most notorious house of ill repute. Now it was a tavern, the neighborhood kind, where the kids could be included.

Connor saw the blonde woman, Erin, the one he'd met at the summer kickoff barbecue. She was sitting with Haley Anderson, who wore the Hitching Post uniform, but appeared to be on a break.

He also spotted Grant Clifton, with his pretty pregnant wife, at a table across the room. Their eyes met. Grant waved, but didn't smile. Connor waved back and thought about the argument with Tori the night before.

He shouldn't have walked out on her, shouldn't have let the things she said get to him so completely. But he really hated the situation, hated that he agreed with her. It sucked to know that he would be a fool to keep Grant on the payroll when the deal was done.

Which was ridiculous. In business, a man did what he had to do. He tried to play fair, but he couldn't afford to let sentimentality take over. He had to be practical, to make the necessary decisions, no matter how ruthless such decisions might seem to others.

Sometimes, lately, Connor wondered what the hell kind of sap he was turning into. Yes, he'd set out to make a few changes in himself, to heal the rift he'd created with his sister, to have a real relationship with his son. To be a better man.

But not too damn much better. It was getting so he hardly knew the man he saw when he looked in the mirror. It was not a comfortable feeling, to be a stranger inside his own skin.

That evening, Tori made dinner at her house for him and for CJ. He took CJ home at a little after eight and he was back at Tori's door at midnight.

"I missed you," he said when she opened the door.

"You've only been gone a few hours," she chided.

"I know," he whispered. "I missed you anyway."

She didn't say anything more, only searched his face with shadowed eyes. Which was probably just as well. He came inside. She shut the door.

And then she took his hand and led him to her bedroom.

Sunday was the Fourth of July. There was an annual parade along Main Street and a rodeo afterward at the fairgrounds. Melanie had them all out to the Hopping H for dinner. Jerilyn and her dad came, too. They got a large table in the dining room. Since every room was booked, all the other tables were full, too.

Connor went to Tori again that night. They made love for hours. And then they must have dropped off to sleep. He woke in the deepest part of the night, alone in the bed.

Groggily, he dragged himself up against the pillow. "Tori?"

"Right here." She materialized out of the shadows as she rose from the corner chair.

"Everything okay?"

She didn't answer right away. Instead, she came to the bed and dropped her lightweight robe from her shoulders. "Everything is fine." Her pretty body tempted him, smooth and curvy. Her skin had an otherworldly glow in the darkness.

He reached for her. She came down to him and kissed him. They made love again.

Afterward, before he left, he held her. She felt perfect in his arms. He never wanted to let her go.

But somehow, he felt that he was losing her. It was, just barely, the fifth of July. They were supposed to have weeks yet.

But he couldn't shake the feeling that it would all be over much sooner than that.

The first thing Grant did Monday morning was to apologize.

"I was wrong to blame you, Connor. It's not your fault that we're in trouble here, not your fault that we can't go on as we have been." He gave a rueful smile. "And, no, I didn't get you up here to try to convince you that I should stay on when you take over. I can see how that would be a bad idea."

Connor offered his hand. "No hard feelings."

Grant took it. "None."

Connor studied the other man's face. "What else?"

"An hour of your time."

"For...?"

"Let me take you around, introduce you to some of the staff."

"I've met a lot of the staff."

"Humor me. Hear my take on things. Can't hurt."

"That's true."

"And you never know. You might see the resort in a whole new light."

Connor almost smiled. "Now you're scaring me."

"Yeah, well. These are scary times. What do you say?"

"Lead the way."

The tour took longer than an hour. It started at the front desk, where Connor met Erika Rodriguez, who was young and pretty, polite and very professional.

"She's a great worker, smart. Efficient. And dependable," Grant said after they moved on. "And she has a toddler she's raising on her own."

"I get it," said Connor. "You want me to keep *her* on, at least."

"Hell. I want you to keep *everyone* on. It's no secret."

"That won't be possible."

Grant's lopsided smile was way too charming. "I know that. But you can't blame a man for trying."

The rest of the tour was more of the same. Connor met housekeepers and bartenders, spa workers and grounds people. Grant made sure he understood why each and every one of them not only needed the job, but deserved to stay on.

After the tour, Grant convinced him to have lunch with him in the Gallatin Room. Nothing had changed there. Both the food and the service were top-notch. By the time Connor left the resort, he and Grant were on good terms.

And he was even more ambivalent. About everything.

The more time he spent at the resort, the more he second-guessed his decision to take it over. Maybe his father, in trying to manipulate Connor into returning early to Philadelphia, had made a valid point, after all: the resort didn't fit the McFarlane House brand.

Until lately, Connor had been going on the theory that this was a good thing, that McFarlane House needed to try something new, to expand on its own template, to re-create itself during the recession. But now he couldn't help thinking that there were more ways than one to effect the change that was needed.

That afternoon, when he went to Tori's, she didn't ask him how the meeting with Grant had gone. He kind of wished she had. He really wanted to talk with her about it.

But he had suggested they not discuss the resort and she was only doing what he had asked of her. He should be happy with that. He *would* be happy with that.

The summer days sped by. He cherished every moment with Tori. Sometimes he noticed a certain reserve in her manner—a certain watchful distance. But when he asked her if anything was wrong, she would smile and tell him there was nothing.

CJ was doing really well with his studies, and he loved his job at the Hopping H. Twice in the week and a half following the engagement party, CJ broached the subject of staying in Thunder Canyon for the school year.

Both times, Connor insisted that was never going to happen—while, at the same time, he was beginning to wonder why CJ *shouldn't* go to school here. CJ loved his life here. He had his aunt and uncle, his cousin. He had *family* here. Going to the best prep school in the country wasn't everything, after all. For a kid to feel part of a community, to feel loved and supported…that mattered, too.

Connor dropped by the Hopping H often to see his sister and share a cup of coffee when she had a spare moment, or to have a beer with Russ. Once, when it was the three of them alone in the Hopping H kitchen, he even brought up the possibility of CJ staying in town for the school term.

Both Melanie and Russ said CJ would be more than welcome to stay with them. That they loved him, and Ryan idolized him. It would be good for Ryan, to have his cousin around.

"It's not going to happen, of course," Connor ended up insisting. "I was just talking hypothetically."

"Well, if it did," his sister said, "we would be absolutely thrilled to have CJ with us whenever he needed a place to stay."

He got a report from his lawyers concerning the custody suit. His countersuit was officially filed, the legal battle set in motion. The process server had found Jennifer in Greece and laid the papers in her hand.

Connor met with Caleb and Riley and Justin Caldwell again. Nothing was decided. But he knew it was time to call in the McFarlane House legal team, time to put the offer together and lay it on the table. His monthly trip to headquarters was coming up the nineteenth. He would set everything in motion then.

And he kept thinking how quickly the end of the summer would be upon him. That CJ would go back to school. That he and Tori would break up, according to the plan. That he would go home to Philadelphia, buy another house…

About there, he would finally stop himself. He would

remind himself for the umpteenth time that it was only mid-July. He had more than a month left—with Tori, and with his son, in Thunder Canyon. He really needed to stop thinking it was over when so much time still remained.

Then, on the fourteenth of July, he got a call from Jennifer.

"I'd like to…meet you with tomorrow," she said in a tone that was troubling in its hesitancy. "Is that possible? Could I come to your house at ten? And could you have CJ there when I arrive?"

All those questions. The strange lack of hostility. What she was up to now?

"Connor," she said when he didn't answer immediately. "Will that work for you?"

It was very short notice. He could have refused.

But why? He didn't want to deny her contact with CJ. Not really. He just wanted the joint physical custody he should have demanded in the first place. He wanted to make certain CJ got the summer he was enjoying so much. Not to mention a father. For too many years, Connor had denied his son a dad. Not anymore. Never again.

"Of course," he said. "Ten a.m. CJ will be here."

As soon as he hung up, he went straight to Tori's house and explained what was happening. He really wasn't going to ask her to be there. It just wasn't right to put that on her, to keep dragging her into it when he had to deal with his ex.

But she said, "I'd be happy to be there—I mean, if that would be helpful to you."

He should have told her it wasn't necessary. That in the end, he would have to deal with Jennifer on his own anyway. But he didn't. "That would be terrific, if you could. Solidarity is a good thing, I think."

She agreed she would be there.

So the next morning, CJ, looking a little grim, stayed home from work to see his mother. And Tori was there with Connor when the doorbell rang.

Connor opened the door to discover Jennifer, dressed to the nines as always, and clutching the arm of her fiancé, Constantin Kronidis. Up until that moment, Connor had never met the man. But he'd seen pictures. Short, powerfully built and in his early fifties, Kronidis had curly black hair streaked with gray and piercing black eyes. He also possessed the considerable magnetism of a man who had made billions and loved living large.

Kronidis stuck out his hand right there at the door. "Connor, hello. I am so pleased to make your acquaintance at last."

Connor managed to hide his surprise at the unexpected appearance of the other man. "Constantin. Good to meet you." He nodded at Jennifer. "Jennifer."

She actually forced a smile. "Connor."

"Come on in…"

CJ and Tori were waiting in the living room. Connor made the introductions. There were handshakes and greetings. Kronidis was courtly to Tori and warm toward CJ. Connor found himself thinking his ex-wife could have done a whole lot worse in her second husband.

"How about some coffee?" Connor offered.

Kronidis turned to Jennifer and she met his dark eyes. Connor, stunned, saw real affection in that shared glance. Kronidis said, "Yes. Coffee. Thank you."

So Connor went to the kitchen and gave Gerda the go-ahead. She had it all ready to serve.

There was polite conversation while the coffee was poured and sweet rolls and muffins offered around. Kronidis had a sip or two, and then he rose.

"Well. I know important issues are to be discussed here. I only wanted to meet you. I felt it was about time." Jennifer stood and they shared a quick kiss. "I shall wait in the car." Connor started to rise. "No. Please. I am perfectly capable of seeing myself out."

Kronidis took his leave.

When the front door shut behind him, Jennifer spoke. "CJ, I wonder if we could have a few minutes alone."

Without a word, CJ rose and followed Jennifer down the hall.

"Well," said Tori softly as soon as they were out of sight, "this isn't what I'd expected."

"I have to agree with you there."

"I wonder…should I stay?"

He looked in those amazing hazel eyes. And knew he should let her go. But when he spoke, it was only to tell her, "I hope you will."

She said no more. He drank his coffee and she nibbled a muffin and they waited for whatever was happening in CJ's room to end.

The next ten minutes or so seemed like forever. But finally, CJ and his mother reentered the room. There was no mistaking the wide smile on CJ's face. Something good had happened.

The only question was what?

They learned soon enough. CJ bounced over and sat in the far chair.

Jennifer sat next to him, across the coffee table from Connor and Tori. "I hope it's all right that I brought Constantin in with me. He really did want to meet you."

"Of course," said Connor, wishing she would hurry up and tell him what the hell was going on here.

"He's…a family man at heart, Constantin. And he has not been pleased with me lately." She had her hands folded neatly in her lap. She glanced down at them, and then, with a slow breath, raised her head and straightened her shoulders. "He said I had to choose, between a life with him and a life battling my ex-husband. He said it wasn't right, for me to try to—"

She paused to swallow. And then continued. "To take CJ away from his father. That we should all be working together, so that everyone can have a better life. He said—" She looked directly at Connor then. And waved a hand. "Well. It doesn't matter what he said, exactly. What matters is that I did listen. I did see that perhaps I've been…bitter. Angry. Thinking of getting back at you rather than doing the right thing."

Connor could hardly believe what he was hearing. Somehow, he managed to keep his expression composed, though he kept wanting to pinch himself. Could vindictive, cold-hearted Jennifer really be saying these reasonable things?

And then Jennifer said, "So I'm going to drop the custody suit. If you will drop your countersuit, I think we can agree to share both legal and physical custody."

It was true. This was really happening. Jennifer, of all people, was changing—and in a good way. "I would be only too happy to do that," he said with a slow nod. "I'll get with my lawyers and tell them that we've come to an agreement on our own."

"That will be fine," she said, sounding relieved. "Have them contact my lawyers. We'll still need to settle it all legally."

"Yes, I know. I'll do that."

Beside her, CJ was beaming.

Jennifer rose. "Well, that's all then." She aimed a careful smile at Tori. "I'm sorry about last time."

"No problem," Tori answered, rising. "Honestly."

"It's lovely to meet you." If she didn't sound exactly sincere, well, at least she was making a good-faith effort. "I hope you and Connor will be…very happy."

"And you and Constantin, too." Tori bestowed one of her most gracious smiles.

Jennifer glanced at CJ. He bounced to his feet and hugged her. Then she turned to Connor. "Walk me out?"

"Of course." Connor got up and followed his ex-wife to the door.

Once it was just the two of them, on the porch, she said quietly, "I wanted to discuss this last issue where CJ couldn't hear."

"All right." *This last issue.* It sounded ominous.

"CJ wants to stay here for the school year."

"Yes." He hurried to reassure her. "I've made it clear that it isn't going to happen."

"He told me he's doing well, studying with Tori?"

"Yes. He's doing very well."

"Then I wouldn't be averse to his staying here to go to school."

If what went before had seemed improbable, what Jennifer had just said was downright incredible. Connor had to consciously stop himself from gaping like a dumbstruck fool. "You're serious?"

"Yes, I am. I would want him with Constantin and me on a regular basis, for at least a few months total in the year. But he's growing up now."

"Uh. Yes, he is."

"He has a right to make a few decisions for himself."

"He, uh, he certainly does."

"Discuss it with him. Call me."

"I will."

Inside, CJ was not only beaming at the way things had turned out, he was also ready to go to work. Tori wanted to go on home. Connor told her he'd be over to see her, as soon as he took CJ to the Hopping H.

On the ride out to Melanie's ranch, Connor told his son what Jennifer had said out on the porch.

CJ knew what he wanted. "Well, Dad, I do want to go to school here." His brown eyes were shining.

So it was settled, except for the thousand and one details. Connor would have to speak with Melanie and Russ again about this, ask them if they'd meant it when they said CJ could stay with them. And CJ's visits with his mother and Constantin would have to be scheduled.

"All right, then," Connor said, as he pulled into the yard at the Hopping H ranch house. "We can work everything else out as we go along."

"You bet we can, Dad. It's all going to turn out fine." CJ sent him a big, warm smile before shoving open his door. "See you at one?"

"I'll be here."

"Dad?"

"Yeah."

"Now and then, even men need a hug."

"Yes, they do." And he leaned awkwardly across the console and hugged his son.

"I love you, Dad," CJ said in a whisper.

"And I love you, son."

Connor drove back to town thinking about miracles. Because somehow, in the past month, the sulky, troubled CJ had disappeared. His son was back on track, and more. He was a happy kid now, working hard at his studies, comfortable in his new hometown. The change was all that Connor might have hoped for—and more.

He thought about Tori. And he wished…

What? That he could ask her to marry him and really mean it this time? That they could have forever, together, after all? Live happily every after in Thunder Canyon, Montana?

That was not going to happen. He lived in Philadelphia. He traveled a lot. His work was his whole life. Tori deserved so much more than he could ever offer her.

Plus, she belonged here. She loved it here. She'd told him once that she planned to live in Thunder Canyon until she was old and gray. He believed that.

And even though he seemed to have made a kind of peace with his ex-wife, he was far from ready to try marriage again. Not even to someone as terrific as Tori.

He made the turn to her house, and felt the eagerness rise in him. To see her. To be with her. To take her in his arms.

No, it wasn't going to last forever. But while it did, he intended to make the most of every moment.

Chapter Twelve

Tori was waiting for Connor to arrive.

She had a few things to say to him. Important things. Difficult things. And her intentions must have been there, written clearly on her face. Because he knew it instantly when she opened the door to him. She watched his expression change from glad—to apprehensive.

"What?" he said. "What's happened?"

She led him into the kitchen, poured him some coffee and slid into the chair across from him. "The custody battle is over. And everybody won."

He looked at the cup in front of him, but didn't touch it. "Yeah. Good news, huh?"

"Good news." She forced a smile.

He added, "And it also looks like CJ will be staying here for the school year."

That surprised her. It was, apparently, a day for surprises. "Wow. When did that happen?"

"When I walked Jennifer outside. She told me it was time that CJ got to make a few decisions for himself."

"You talked to CJ about it?"

He nodded. "On the way to the Hopping H. He's excited."

"I'll bet he's floating on air." Did that mean Connor would be living full-time in Thunder Canyon? Hope rose within her, but she tamped it down.

He said, "I think Melanie and Russ will take him, when I'm not around."

"Ah." She should have guessed. She asked carefully, "Do you…trust that Jennifer will keep her word about all of this?"

"I do." His answer was firm. "Mostly because of Constantin. After seeing them together today, I think he really loves her."

"And she loves him."

"Yes. I think he'll keep her honest."

Her chest felt tight. She drew in a slow breath. "Yeah. I see that."

"Tori. What's going on?"

She folded her hands on the tabletop. The showy engagement diamond he'd bought for her caught the light and glittered brightly. "We started down this road so CJ could have his summer here. Now we know he will have the summer—and the school year, too."

His eyes were dark as the middle of the night. "What are you telling me?"

"That I think it's time we…talked."

"We *are* talking."

"I mean, about us."

"What about us?"

"About how we're going to end this fake engagement of ours."

There was a silence. A bleak one. Tori tried to gauge his response. She couldn't read him.

He took his coffee cup by the handle, but only to move it a few inches to the right. He didn't raise it to his lips. "We already talked about it. In August, we'll tell everyone we broke up."

She looked at him patiently. "Connor. Please. There's no reason to wait for August now."

He did drink then. He lifted the cup, knocked back a gulp, set it down again. "Right now? Is that what you're saying? You want to end it now?"

"No."

"Then what are you getting at?"

"I don't… I think it's time we started stepping back."

"Stepping back." He echoed her words with hollow precision. "And just how do you want to do that?"

"We need to begin to…drift apart. I'll still wear your ring." She twisted the gorgeous thing on her finger, caught herself. Let it go. "But I think we should stop spending so much time together. I think we should stop…sleeping together."

Again, he echoed her. "Stop sleeping together…"

"Yes. I, well, I'd like a little time, you know? I need to separate what's real from the story we made up. And the best way for me to do that is not to, um, make love with you anymore."

"When did you decide this?"

"I've been thinking about it for a while now."

"And yet you kept telling me that everything was fine." It was an accusation.

"Oh, Connor. It was bound to end. We both knew that. I'm only saying I want to get real about this. Now that Jennifer has come around, we don't have to pretend anymore. And I want that, I want to stop pretending, at least when it comes to the two of us, one on one."

"Let me get this straight. You want to break up—to end it now, as far as what we *really* have together." His voice was hard. Flat. "But until the end of August, we'll go on pretending that we're still engaged."

"Or not. That's okay, too. We can end it right now, if that's better for you. I just thought, since you'll be here full-time at least until then, it would be better for you if you didn't have to deal with all the questions, with everyone in town wondering went wrong."

"I don't give a damn what everyone thinks. Now the custody issue is resolved, it's fine, okay? Whatever you want."

She longed for him to understand. But she could see that he didn't. Softly, she chided, "You don't *act* like it's fine."

His face was a cold mask, showing her nothing of the man within. "Well, it is. It's fine."

"I don't want to hurt you. I really don't."

"Did I say I was hurt?"

"No. No, of course, you didn't. I just need…some time, that's all. Time to get over you." Her throat was so dry. She swallowed convulsively. She felt like such a coward, to be dancing around the real issue like this. To be going on about getting over him, about needing time, without once having said the main truth, without putting the scariest words right out there. She babbled on. "I need to be reminded that this engagement is just an act. And I can't do that this way, with us being lovers. I keep…losing track, forgetting where the line is, between what's real and what's not."

His cold expression didn't change. "You've been building up to this for a couple of weeks now, haven't you?"

She couldn't deny it. "Yes. That's true. I have."

"Since that night I woke up and you were sitting in the corner…"

"Oh, Connor." And she edged a little closer to the emotional precipice. "It was a day or two before that, if you want to know the exact date."

"What day?" It was a demand.

"It was the night of the engagement party, the night we argued over your plans to fire Grant."

"Why that night?" He sounded like a lawyer. A lawyer cross-examining her, determined to force her to reveal her deepest secret.

She stared at his beloved face across the table. And she knew she was going to do it, was going to lay her heart wide-open, to tell him the hardest truth.

"Why that night?" he commanded a second time.

She trembled. It was so silly, to be this upset. If he loved her, if he'd changed his mind about the future, if he wanted it to end differently than they'd always planned, he would have said so by now.

At least, if she didn't tell him, she could salvage some pride. "You don't want to know, Connor."

"Yes," he said coldly. "I do." He was so very angry.

But she saw right then that his anger was no more the issue than her pride was. There was so much more going on here than hurt feelings, than mere pride. She saw that she needed to tell him. She needed to say the all-important words.

Tori told the truth. "Because the night we argued about Grant was the night I realized I'm in love with you."

Connor's world seemed to tip on its axis.

Should he have known? Why hadn't he known, why hadn't he realized?

And why the hell did he feel so damn happy, all of a sudden?

There was nothing to be happy about. Love wasn't in the deal. He wasn't…ready for that. He didn't think he would ever be.

The sudden joy vanished as quickly as it had risen, leaving him empty. Drained. And disgusted with himself—for the interrogation he'd just put her through, for being such a complete ass about this.

He had nothing to offer her, no right to make demands of her, to badger her into this corner, to force her to reveal to him what would have been better left alone.

All she'd wanted was what she had every right to ask for. To be free. To be done with this beautiful, impossible lie they were living.

He stood up then, the movement so swift that she gasped in surprise. "Tori, I'm sorry. So damn sorry."

She let out a slow breath. And a sad little laugh escaped her. "Well. Not really the response I was hoping for."

"I don't know what's the matter with me, to treat you so badly, to put you through this…inquisition.

After all you've done for me and for my son. That was unforgivable of me."

"Connor. It's all right. Don't—"

He chopped the air with an impatient hand. "No. It's not all right. You're an amazing woman and I've been the luckiest man alive, to have had these few incredible weeks with you. I...didn't want it to end, that's all. Even though it has to end, even though, after what happened today with Jennifer, it's *time* for it to end."

She sat there, gazing up at him. Her hazel eyes were blue-green again, and deep as oceans. "Connor, if you think you need forgiveness from me, you've got it. But as far as I'm concerned, there's nothing to forgive. It's okay that this was difficult for you, okay if you had to be a little hard on me to get through it. I'm not angry at you. I don't *blame* you. I went into this with my eyes wide-open."

"Well, you should be angry at me. You should hate me."

"No. I shouldn't. And I don't hate you. And, Connor, the only reason this has to be over now is because you aren't willing, you know? You don't want this to go anywhere. And I do. And that's why it's time we parted ways."

What could he say to that? She was a million miles ahead of him. "I know. You're right."

She took off the ring, held it out to him.

No way. "Keep it. Sell it. Whatever. I...I can't take it back, Tori. I couldn't bear that."

Her smile was so soft, so full of womanly understanding. She set the ring on the table. "All right, then."

"About CJ..."

"You'll tell him it didn't work out with us—but of

course, I'll still tutor him, at least until school starts when we will evaluate his progress. Unless you've changed your mind about that?"

"No. It would be great if you would. He'll be here at two, as usual?"

"Yes, that's fine."

There was nothing more to say. "Goodbye, Tori." He turned to go.

"Connor." She spoke to his retreating back.

He halted in midstride, but he didn't turn.

"Thank you," she said.

He whirled on her, furious all over again. What was the matter with her, to speak so gently, to gaze at him through tender eyes, to be so…kind? He didn't deserve her kindness. She should be angry with him. Yet she only stood there watching him, the saddest, sweetest smile on her beautiful face.

"Thank you?" he demanded, his voice low and rough. "How can you say that? What are you talking about?"

A tear slid down her cheek, gleaming bright. "All my first dates," she whispered. "It seemed like a thousand of them. And no man was ever right. The timing was always wrong—oh, once or twice in college, I told myself I was in love. I even *made* love. But it was never right. It was never real. I…I couldn't admit to myself, until now. Until *you,* Connor, that it was me."

He still didn't understand. "Tori, I don't—"

She put up a hand. "I've been so afraid, deep in my heart, you know? Afraid of loving. Of losing it all. The way my dad and I lost everything that mattered when my mom died." Another tear fell. She didn't even try to brush it away. "Somehow, I missed the main lesson. That a person has to take a chance, to accept the risk of losing, of having to live through the pain and loneliness. Because of you, Connor, *for* you, I took the risk." A small, trembling laugh escaped her. She shook her head. "I took the risk. And it looks like it's turning out just as I always feared, that I have loved and now I'm losing."

He couldn't bear this. "Tori…"

"Uh-uh. Let me say the rest. Let me tell you that I feel…braver, now, because of loving you. Stronger. I know that I can bear the pain and the loneliness when you're gone. I won't like it. Sometimes I'll cry, missing you. But still, I find, deep in my heart, that I'm glad. So glad to have known you. To have called you my love. You *are* a good man," she said, her words soft and gentle as a benediction. "You can stop punishing yourself, stop blaming yourself for everything that hasn't worked out as you intended it to."

He had no answer for her, nothing more to say. He turned and started walking again.

And that time she made no attempt to stop him. She let him go.

Chapter Thirteen

"Ms. Jones, my dad told me. That you're not engaged to him anymore."

"Yes. It…didn't work out for us."

"I wish it had."

"So do I, CJ."

"But you'll still…be my friend?"

"Yes, I will."

"Still let me stop by for juice, with Jerilyn?"

"Definitely. Anytime. With Jerilyn or even if you're by yourself."

"And my dad said we could keep on with the tutoring, even after today. At least until school starts. That it was okay with you."

"That's right. I think it's important."

"Me, too."

"So we'll keep on."

"That's good."

"I agree. Shall we get to work?"

"Yes, Ms. Jones. Let's get to work."

Somehow, Tori got through the rest of the day. And the long night that followed. Her bed seemed huge and empty without Connor in it, holding her close.

Without the possibility that Connor would ever be in it again.

Friday morning, Allaire called. "How about lunch? DJ took Alex up to the resort with him. I'm a free woman until two. The Teapot?"

Tori almost said no. She felt so sad and lost and weepy. The last thing she needed was to break down in tears in the middle of their favorite restaurant.

Then again, if she had Allaire over to her house, she *knew* she would end up in tears. Maybe telling her friend about the breakup in a public place would provide at least some insurance against an emotional scene.

"Tori? You still there?"

"I'm here. And lunch would be perfect. At the Teapot. Noon?"

"I'll be there. Haley's coming, too. She's jazzed. It's a done deal. She got the storefront for ROOTS."

"Great. I want to hear all about it." More insurance against losing it, if Haley was there.

Allaire was waiting for her, alone, at their favorite table. One look at Tori's face, and her best friend knew something was very wrong.

Tori slid into the chair she always sat in.

Allaire said, "My God. What?"

"Where's Haley?"

"She called and said she would be late. Now what's

the matter with you? Something's happened and I want to know what."

Tori put her left hand on the table.

"What?" Allaire demanded again. Then she looked down at Tori's ringless finger. "Oh, no."

Tori nodded. "Yeah."

Allaire leaned closer. "When? What happened?"

"Yesterday. It…didn't work out, that's all."

The waitress appeared. They ordered their usual.

The minute she left them alone, Allaire put her hand over Tori's. "Oh, I can't believe this. You two are so in love."

Tori almost laughed. But she was afraid, if she did, it would only bring on a river of tears. "Well, I love *him,* at least."

"And he loves you. It's so obvious, Tori. I saw it in his eyes every time he looked at you. And I know that you two will work it out. I feel it. I'm sure of it."

Tori did laugh then. "But…you can't stand him."

"Hey. I have a right to be wrong now and then. I know now I judged him too harshly. I mean, if you're in love with him, how bad can he be?"

"Oh, Allaire…"

"It's going to work out."

"I don't think so." She stared across the table at Allaire. And it came to her. She couldn't go on lying to such a dear friend. "Allaire, I…"

"Tell me. Please. I want to hear."

"Yes. All right. And I want you to know." And then, in a whisper, leaning across the table toward her friend, swiftly and without fanfare, Tori told all.

She had just finished when the waitress approached.

They said nothing as she set their tea and sandwiches before them.

When she finally left again, Allaire said, "You should have told me. I can't believe you didn't tell me."

"Well. Now you know."

"I'm glad, at least, that CJ will get to stay here in town."

"Me, too."

"And I think Connor's a fool to let you go."

"He's... I don't know..." The insistent tears threatened to fall again. She swallowed them back. "I think he has trouble letting himself be happy."

Allaire raised her teacup. "Here's to him coming to his senses. And soon."

"I don't think that's going to happen." Tori raised her own cup and touched it to Allaire's. "But I'll certainly drink to the possibility."

A few minutes later, Haley showed up. She was beaming from ear to ear. ROOTS was going to become a reality at last. They congratulated her on her success and discussed how they would all pitch in to fix up the new ROOTS headquarters in the storefront down the street.

Allaire had Tori over for dinner that night. And Saturday, Melanie called. Connor had told his sister that the engagement was over.

"Are you okay?" Melanie wanted to know.

"I'm getting by," Tori replied.

"Want some company? I'm coming into town in an hour."

Tori started to say no, that it wouldn't be a good idea.

But she liked Melanie. And she wouldn't mind a little company—in fact, she'd appreciate some.

Melanie came over. She confessed that Connor had told her everything. "I love my brother," she said with a rueful sigh. "But I told him he's messing up royally, to even consider letting you go."

"Melanie, the engagement was never real. You know that. You said he explained it to you."

Melanie made a low sound in her throat. "Of course it was real. Everyone saw it. You two were meant to be together."

"But we're not together. And we're not going to be."

"That's what I thought about Russ and me. And look at us now."

"I don't see the parallel. You and Russ are nothing like Connor and me."

"Yes, we are. Russ and I married for all kinds of convenient reasons, not one of them love. Or so we thought."

That was hard to believe. "You're not serious. Not you and Russ—"

"Yes, I am. He wanted the Hopping H and I needed help making the guest ranch work. It was a strictly business arrangement. Or so we told ourselves at the time."

Tori couldn't afford to get her hopes up. "It's not the same."

Melanie only smiled at her and said gently, "Love matters. When there's love, all kinds of impossible dreams end up coming true."

Tori nodded. She agreed with Connor's sister. At least, she did in theory. As she had told Connor the day it ended, she believed that love—that having loved *him*—was worth the pain.

But right now, well, she was suffering through the worst of it. It wasn't easy. It hurt a lot. Sometimes, she forgot that love was worth it. Sometimes, she thought that impossible dreams were simply that—impossible.

Sometimes she almost wished she'd never loved him at all.

Connor had the monthly meetings in Philadelphia starting Monday.

He gave Gerda four days off, since CJ wanted to stay with the Chiltons, and he flew out early Sunday. He had dinner with his parents that evening.

They asked after Tori. He said she was fine.

Yes, he should have gone ahead and told them that the engagement was off. But he couldn't bear to do it, couldn't stand to see that cool flare of satisfaction in his mother's eyes. Couldn't sit there and listen to his father tell him how it was all for the best. That the schoolteacher from Montana was not the right woman for him and they were glad he had realized it before he got in too deep.

In too deep.

He was already there. Deep and going deeper. He missed her. He missed her really bad.

And his own sister had told him he was an idiot. Melanie had said she didn't care if he thought he'd gotten engaged to Tori just to improve his chances of getting custody of his son. "Wake up, Connor. You're in love with Tori Jones. If you know what's good for you, you'll go and tell her so, right now."

Of course, he hadn't. He wasn't going back to Tori. He wasn't ready for any of that. Not ready for love.

Or so he kept telling himself. Constantly. Over and over.

As if maybe, when he'd said it enough times, he would actually believe it. He would be able to forget her, to get on with his life.

Monday was one meeting after another.

Tuesday, he gave his presentation on the Thunder Canyon Resort buyout. He shocked the hell out of all them at that meeting.

His father looked like he might have a coronary when Connor said, "I want to invest in the resort instead of buying them out. My prospectus is in front of you. When you've had time to study my new plan, I think you'll see that the numbers are solid. We'll leave the current management team in place, and I project we can see a profit from our investment within the next two years. They need capital. We can give it to them. And then share in the returns."

His father sputtered. "But it won't be a McFarlane House project."

"No. It will be a McFarlane House *investment*. I'll look elsewhere for our next project. As you've mentioned more than once, Donovan, the resort doesn't really fit our brand. But the Thunder Canyon Resort can be profitable again. And that means we will profit, too."

There were hours of arguments, of objections and retrenchments.

But Connor refused to back down. In the end, he convinced them all. Even his father couldn't argue with the numbers Connor had provided. And besides, Donovan had never liked the idea of a sprawling ski resort bearing the McFarlane House name.

Connor stayed over that night. He had dinner with his parents again. Donovan was anxious for him to move back home, to get to work on the next acquisition. They did need to start growing the business again, though more cautiously than before.

His mother said, "And of course, we are looking forward to meeting this fiancée of yours."

He put them off. On all fronts.

And he flew back to Montana first thing Wednesday morning.

Thursday, he called Caleb and set up a meeting for that night, at the Douglas Ranch. He asked that Grant and Riley both be there. And Justin Caldwell, too, if possible.

Caleb said they would all be there. And he was as good as his word.

After dessert was served, Connor told them of the offer he was planning to make, that he would invest McFarlane House capital and work with them to get the resort in the black again and to build the Thunder Canyon brand. That the management team would stay the same. "If that's acceptable," he said, "we can go ahead and call the lawyers, put a formal contract together."

When he finished speaking, Caleb rose from his place at the head of the table. "Adele, let's break out the bubbly. It looks to me like we've got ourselves a deal here."

There was agreement all around. Champagne flowed and toasts were offered.

Later, Grant took Connor aside and shook his hand. "It's a fine thing you did, Connor."

"It's a good investment. We're all going to benefit."

"You're a good man."

"Well. Not everybody thinks so."

"Whoever 'not everybody' is, they're full of crap. I liked you from the first. Yeah, I had my doubts there for a while. I made no secret of them. But my first impression was the right one. I'm looking forward to working with you. And to calling you a friend."

The next morning, Connor got in touch with Frank Cates, who with his son Matt owned Cates Construction. He told Frank he was going to need a new house. Yes, the house would be vacant several months out of the year. But when he could be there, he wanted CJ to have a place to call home.

Frank said to come on down to the office. "And bring that pretty schoolteacher of yours with you. You know she's gonna want her say. A woman always does."

Connor opened his mouth to tell Frank that Tori wouldn't be with him, that she was no longer his fiancée. But the words refused to take form. He thanked Frank, set an appointment for Monday and hung up the phone.

"You okay, Mr. M?" Gerda stopped rolling out pie dough long enough to send him a worried look.

He realized he'd been sitting there at the kitchen counter, staring blindly into space for a minute or two, at least. "Uh. Yes, Gerda. Fine. Just fine."

"I have to tell you, you've looked better." She went back to rolling her pie dough. "Men," she muttered under her breath. "Some of 'em got no idea what's best for 'em."

Connor pretended not to hear her as he watched her

expertly lift the flattened crust and lay it into a pie pan. Swiftly and cleanly, she pinched the edges so they were attractively fluted.

She glanced up again. "Get on with you, now. Go see that sweet Ms. J and tell her you can't live without her."

If he'd been his father, he would have fired her on the spot. Or at the very least informed her that his activities were none of her affair and she would be wise to remember that.

But he wasn't his father.

He wasn't even really himself anymore—or not the hard-charging corporate shark he had once been, anyway. Somehow, he'd become someone altogether different.

Someone who actually spent time with his son. Someone who had healed the lifelong breach with his sister. Someone Gerda felt she could lecture. Someone Grant Clifton called a friend.

He jumped up from the counter stool. "I have to go out."

"About time," Gerda grumbled.

He hardly heard her. He was already halfway down the hall.

When Tori opened the door, the sight of her stole the breath from his body. In bare feet, old jeans and a Thunder Canyon High T-shirt, she was the most beautiful woman he had ever beheld.

"Connor?" She said his name disbelievingly. Her hazel eyes were blue-green as oceans again. And suddenly, he wasn't sure what to say.

"I'm not buying out the resort. I'm investing in it. And Grant Clifton says he's proud to be my friend."

"Oh, Connor…" She swiped at those gorgeous wet eyes. And her sweet mouth was trembling.

"I called Frank Cates. He's going to build me a house."

"A house. Of course. How wonderful."

"Frank said to come down to the office. And to bring you. That you would want to have input, that women always do. I didn't tell him that we weren't together anymore. I couldn't bear to say it. And I didn't tell my parents it was over, either. I couldn't bring myself to do that, to tell them we had ended it."

She searched his face. "Connor. Come in. Please. Come in."

He stumbled forward.

She shut the door, then turned and leaned against it, as if her legs were too shaky to hold her up. She whispered, "What are telling me?"

"I…" There was so much to say. Where in hell should he start? "I…know you love this town, that you want to live the rest of your life here."

She put her hand to her throat. "But, Connor, wh-what are you *telling* me?"

"Oh, Tori. I'm, uh, I…" Words had completely deserted him.

But she knew. She understood. "It's happening, isn't it? You and me, it's going to happen. It's going to be okay."

Wordlessly, he nodded.

She whispered, "I have to tell you, I did doubt you. I doubted all of it, all I thought I had learned, doubted you would ever come back, wondered if love was worth it, after all."

He cleared his throat and somehow found his voice.

"And why wouldn't you doubt? Why wouldn't you wonder? I've been such a fool."

She laughed then, a joyous sound. "Oh, yes, you have." And then a small sob escaped her. She drew in a ragged breath. "As to the question you were trying to ask me, I do love it here in Thunder Canyon. But I can be…flexible. When I said I'd never leave, well, that was before I fell in love with you. Love changes people. Love…opens us up to new possibilities."

"New possibilities."

"Oh, Connor. Yes."

"We could…play it by ear then, as far as where we live?"

"We could. Absolutely. I'd be open to that."

He took her hand. "Tori."

"Yes, Connor. Yes."

And he went down on one knee. She made a soft, surprised sound when he did that.

He said, "You have to have your story."

"Yes," she said wonderingly.

"Your proposal story."

"I do. Oh, yes, I do."

"Tori, you've been telling me for weeks that a man *can* change. That I'm a *good* man. Well, I *have* changed. And the man I am now is more than ready. For love. For marriage. For *you*, Tori. Because I love you. And I'm so sorry I didn't admit it to myself and to you earlier, that I caused you pain."

She looked down at him reproachfully. "It's true. You did hurt me. You hurt me terribly."

"I hope you can find it in your heart to forgive me."

And she sighed. "Oh, Connor. Yes. Always. Yes."

"I don't have a ring yet."

She laughed again. "I still have my ring. Did you imagine I wouldn't? I was keeping it. I would have always kept it. Whether you ever came to your senses or not."

"Well, okay. Now would be the time to go and get it."

"I will. In a minute."

"Marry me, Tori."

"Yes, Connor. I will."

He stared up at her, hardly daring to believe that she would really be his. His wife. His lover. His best friend for life.

"Connor."

"Yes?"

She tugged on his hand. "Come up here. Take me in your arms."

He didn't have to be told twice. He swept to his feet and pulled her close. "I love you. Did I say that?"

"You did. But that's okay. You can say it again. You can say it over and over. 'I love you' never gets old."

"I love you, Tori Jones."

"I love *you*, Connor McFarlane."

He kissed her then. A long, deep, thorough kiss. A kiss that promised her everything. His love, his devotion, his absolute commitment to her and the future that would be theirs, together.

"We're getting married," he said in a voice full of wonder. "We're *really* getting married."

She nodded. And then she kissed him again. And then she led him to her bedroom, where she took the ring from a secret compartment of her jewelry box. She gave it to him. And he slid it onto her ring finger where it belonged.

And then he took her in his arms again. He kissed her some more. With love.

And with wonder, too.

A month ago, if someone had dared to tell him this would happen, he would have called that person deluded, misinformed, a silly, romantic fool.

But it *had* happened. Connor had found true love. Their sham engagement had turned real. He would have the life he had finally learned he truly wanted: a life with Tori at his side.

Did it get any better than this? He didn't see how.

But then he gazed down into Tori's shining eyes. And he realized it just might.

Because they had each other. They had love. And with love, anything was possible.

* * * * *

TAMING THE MONTANA MILLIONAIRE

BY
TERESA SOUTHWICK

First published in Great Britain 2011
by Mills & Boon, an imprint of Harlequin (UK) Limited,
Eton House, 18-24 Paradise Road, Richmond, Surrey TW9 1SR

© Harlequin Books S.A. 2010

ISBN: 978 0 263 88911 6

23-0911

Special thanks and acknowledgement to Teresa Southwick for her contribution to the MONTANA MAVERICKS: THUNDER CANYON COWBOYS mini-series.

Harlequin (UK) policy is to use papers that are natural, renewable and recyclable products and made from wood grown in sustainable forests. The logging and manufacturing processes conform to the legal environmental regulations of the country of origin.

Printed and bound in Spain
by Blackprint CPI, Barcelona

Dear Reader,

Have you ever wondered what might have been—romantically—with a guy from your past? I definitely have and the writer in me can't resist playing "what if."

That's why this particular story in the MONTANA MAVERICKS continuity appealed to me so much. From a chance kiss in the past until she tames her Montana millionaire, Haley Anderson's Cinderella tale was so much fun to write. She's strong, vulnerable, and sassy, a combination bad boy Marlon Cates finds irresistible. Especially since he's done his share of wondering about the shy girl who showed such grace and courage in the wake of tragedy and crushing responsibility.

The "opposites attract" scenario is always a favorite of mine and I hope you enjoy reading *Taming the Montana Millionaire* as much as I enjoyed writing it.

All the best,

Teresa Southwick

To Christine Rimmer who gave us a fantastic start to this series. Thanks for the plotting, fun and friendship.

Teresa Southwick lives with her husband in Las Vegas, the city that reinvents itself every day. An avid fan of romance novels, she is delighted to be living out her dream of writing for Mills & Boon.

Chapter One

She needed another challenge like she needed a sharp stick in the eye.

Haley Anderson was trying to get this small, dingy store-front space whipped into shape to house the teen mentoring program she called ROOTS. It had to be a place where kids would actually want to hang out. She'd hoped it would be ready to open up when the school year ended, but it was already the first of August and she hadn't secured the lease until the end of July. Now the real work started.

The empty area needed furniture, games, a TV, DVD player and probably a computer. But she didn't think bring-ing in any of that while the walls needed a makeover was prudent.

She'd only had time to paint the one that faced Thunder Canyon's Main Street, a background for the mural she was in the process of doing. It was the first thing teenagers would see when they peeked in the window. She wanted warm, empathetic, inviting images. Since she was taking a chance with community donations to open ROOTS, why not amp up the pressure factor with her first, very public art project?

As if all of that wasn't challenge enough, she was a full-time waitress at The Hitching Post, the bar and grill just down the street. Although her brother and sister had part-time summer jobs at Thunder Canyon Resort, she was the main breadwinner of the family. It was the kind of thing that built character, or so she'd been told. From her perspective, she had enough character for a small but determined army.

And now she was staring at yet another challenge. He was still outside. The guy who'd walked all over her tender heart that summer after high school graduation, just before her life really fell apart—correction, before she really started building character.

Marlon Cates. MC. Major Crush. But that was so yesterday. Now the MC stood for major caution.

There was nothing wrong with him standing outside—except it was looking like he planned to come inside. But maybe she was borrowing trouble. Maybe he'd walk on by.

That hope disappeared in a poof when he noticed her watching, lifted his hand and smiled. The grin got to her like nothing else, probably because it was fueled by that wicked twinkle in his eyes. It was the down payment on flirtation and fun and made her heart beat faster even though she knew he was a player. He didn't live in Thunder Canyon now, but he still had family here. Every couple of months he showed up at The Hitching Post and women flocked to him like compulsive gamblers to a deck of cards.

He never left with the same woman twice. Her heart

knew better and shouldn't have beaten faster as he opened the door and walked inside, but it did. Apparently her heart had a mind of its own. When he pushed the door open, the bell above dinged. She hoped it covered the sound of her groan.

"Hi, Haley."

"Marlon."

He was six feet of long legs, lean muscle and broad shoulders. In worn jeans and a black, chest-hugging T-shirt, he looked every inch the bad boy of his high school and college days. His brown eyes glittered with reckless promises and the short dark hair was meticulously mussed. His jaw was shadowed with sexy scruff. She told herself it would rub her face raw if they kissed, but her one personal experience with him hadn't been long enough to rub anything raw except stirred-up yearnings.

Still, a part of her was willing to risk a close encounter with scruff and she planned to choke that part of her into submission. Along with the part of her that desperately wished she wasn't in old, torn, paint-splattered jeans and her brother's too large T-shirt. She also wished her straight brown hair wasn't twisted up off her neck and held with a clip that made it stand out like feathers from a freaked out turkey.

Marlon moved closer and glanced at the mural she'd sketched of kids, computers, books and sports. She was in the process of painting in the lines, but put her brush down on the small rusty metal table she'd brought from home for her art supplies.

"That's impressive," he said, nodding his chin at the wall. "Did you draw this?"

"Yeah." She couldn't remember a time when she didn't have crayon, paint or charcoal pencil in hand. Some art classes in high school and junior college had improved her technique and she soaked up his praise like rain on tinder-dry brush. "Thanks."

He looked down at her, his gaze assessing. "How've you been?"

"Good. You?" It hadn't been that long since she'd seen him. "Weren't you back last month right around the Fourth of July?"

"Yeah." He glanced down and shifted his feet. "Now I'm taking a working vacation."

"Oh."

In college he'd created a line of silk-screened T-shirts, jackets and hats with a Montana theme. A venture capitalist staying at the Thunder Canyon Resort had seen the items displayed in a restaurant on the premises and approached him about backing a bigger business enterprise. Marlon then expanded into MC/TC, primarily a jeans label. When the Hollywood "it" girl he was dating was photographed wearing the brand and turned up in multiple national magazines, the company took off and became phenomenally successful. And still was. But Haley didn't know anyone who wasn't feeling the effects of the recession, and wondered about the state of his company.

This teen program, ROOTS, was dependent on donations and people were struggling, just one of the reasons the opening was later than she'd hoped. But there was still about a month until school started and she wanted the kids to be able to take advantage while they could.

"How's business?" she asked.

"So-so."

She waited for more information, but he was looking around. The room was small and square. And obviously empty.

"I know it doesn't look like much now," she defended, "but I have plans. With used furniture from the Second

Chances thrift store the interior will really pop." She pointed to a doorway. "There's a bathroom and tiny storage area through there, with a door leading to the parking lot. It's big enough to put in a refrigerator, microwave and cabinet for snacks and paper goods. If my brother is anything to go by, teenage boys have bottomless appetites."

"How's Angie?"

"Good," she said. "Trying to figure out what she wants to be when she grows up. She's taking classes at the junior college and changes her major every other month."

"And Austin?"

"He just graduated from college. Engineering major," she said, her voice full of the pride she couldn't hide. "There was a time when I didn't think he would graduate from high school, let alone go to college and get a degree."

"Why is that?"

"He never had a father figure and was only sixteen when mom died. That's a tough age under the best of circumstances, but the two of them were especially close. It hit him really hard."

Her brother wasn't the only one. It had been the worst time of her life and she suspected her sister Angie felt the same way.

"Yeah. I can see where that would happen."

"I'm convinced it's our roots here in Thunder Canyon that tipped the scales in his favor."

"How's that?" he asked.

"The people in this community took us under their wing. Neighbors helped out, especially Ben Walters."

"Isn't he the rancher who lives near your place?"

"Yeah. He's a widower." She sighed. "That's probably why he spent a lot of time with Austin, called him on his crap when necessary because Austin refused to pay attention to me. I'm only his big sister. Sometimes Ben just listened when the kid needed a man to talk to."

"Ben always was a saint."

The critical tone made her feel defensive for some reason. "He was a father to my brother and I'll never forget it. In fact, that's really how ROOTS started in the first place."

"Oh?"

She nodded. "They hired me at The Hitching Post when I needed a job to support the family. Folks stepped in to watch Angie while I was working. And Ben kept Austin out of trouble. We were teens without a mom and Thunder Canyon put their arms around us. I wanted to open a community clubhouse where teenagers can come. Hang out. Talk if they want. Or not. It's just a place where you don't have to feel alone. Like the way people here in town made me feel."

"ROOTS?"

"The name is from an embroidered sampler of my mother's that we keep on the wall at home. It says 'There are but two lasting things we give our children—Roots and Wings.' I intend to pay that message forward."

"Good for you."

Her eyes narrowed on him. Was he laughing at her? "I wouldn't expect a big shot entrepreneur like yourself to understand something that isn't about making money. Especially when it fell into your lap—"

He reached out and put his index finger to her lips, to silence her. "Success didn't just happen. I worked damn hard for it and still do. That wasn't a criticism. Obviously you've got one nerve left and apparently I stepped on it."

"Sorry." That happened when your buttons got pushed, and not any of the good buttons. "It's been sort of an uphill battle—finding the money, convincing the mayor and town council of the need... Thunder Canyon High's principal and faculty have been incredibly helpful. And my special adviser is Carleigh Benedict, from county social services." She took a deep breath. "There will be strict curfews enforced. And adult supervision when the doors are open. I want to make sure I get everything right."

He looked down for a moment, then met her gaze. "Sounds like an ambitious undertaking. Could you use an extra pair of hands?"

Surely he wasn't talking about himself. "I'm definitely going to need volunteers. When it becomes the coolest hangout in town, which is what I'm hoping for. But right now it's just me."

"That wasn't me gathering information. It was a sincere offer to be of assistance," he explained, his expression wry.

"You want to help out?" she asked skeptically.

"Don't sound so surprised." His eyes turned a darker shade of brown, but hurting Marlon's feelings seemed like a long shot since there'd never been an abundance of evidence that he had any. "Like I said, my schedule is loose and not being busy makes me nuts. It seems like a win-win."

"You could give your dad a hand," she suggested helpfully. His father, Frank, owned Cates Construction where Marlon's identical twin, Matt, worked, the twin expected to take over the business some day. She marveled at how different the two men with the same face were. Matt was serious and a stay-put kind of guy. Marlon was a charmer who never stood still.

"I plan to help out my dad if he needs it," he said. "But you know as well as I do that things have slowed down in construction and he's doing his best not to lay off workers. Especially the ones with families."

"Times are tough. That's going to affect a lot of kids," she agreed.

"So let me help you out."

On top of more surprise that he wouldn't drop the idea, Haley's suspicions kicked in. His reputation had bad boy written all over it. Whoever supervised at ROOTS would have to be someone the kids looked up to. Not that she thought Marlon was a threat, but he wasn't positive role model material either.

"I don't think there's much to do right now," she lied.

"Could have fooled me." One of his dark eyebrows rose as he looked around at the empty space and three remaining dingy green walls. "Look, Haley, you'd be doing me a favor and I could return it."

She bit her lip as she looked up at him, trying to figure out how to say this in the nicest possible way. "The thing is, Marlon, what I'm trying to do here is important. These are kids who have been let down in one way or another. Like you said, people are losing their jobs and the bad stuff filters down to the kids. In a world where nothing is in their control they need someone they can count on."

"And you don't think I'm reliable?"

From personal experience she knew he wasn't. A long time ago he'd kissed her and promised to call. He never did. She'd waited by the phone, slept with it next to the bed, constantly checked for messages. There was no way she would have missed his call, if there'd been one. On top of that, he breezed in and out of town whenever he felt like it. He couldn't be counted on.

When she didn't answer immediately, he said, "What's your point?" His facial expression didn't change, but there was an edge to his voice.

Darn it, she thought. He was going to make her say it straight out. She looked up at him, way up, and took a deep breath. "I just don't think commitment is one of your strengths, Marlon. But I really appreciate the offer. Thanks anyway."

He nodded once, then left without another word, which made her one part sad and two parts grateful. Her crush was part of her past, but it didn't seem wise to test that theory by having him underfoot. Although when she looked around and thought about her to-do list, she had a sinking feeling she'd just cut off her nose to spite her face.

"Just once," she whispered to the grungy walls, "I'd like to get what I wish for."

She wished Marlon hadn't walked in. And that he wasn't still the handsome scoundrel she remembered. Most of all she wished to be someone he might be interested in. But she knew better than most that life was filled with challenges you had no control over and some you did. And Marlon Cates was one she just wasn't willing to take on.

Commitment wasn't his strength?

After several hours of stewing over those words, Marlon Cates pushed aside the see-through lace curtain as he stared down on Main Street from the window of his apartment over The Hitching Post. He'd rented the western-themed place, with brass bed, antique chifforobe and its own bath, for a month. It was within walking distance of ROOTS where he'd intended to do his court-mandated time to get back his driving privileges. His parents and three brothers knew what had happened and his mother didn't sugarcoat anything when she said it served him right. Three speeding tickets in less than a year landed him in front of a judge who yanked his license and gave him thirty days of community service.

From this vantage point he could see the storefront where he planned to do his time. When the court clerk gave him a list of places, he'd spotted Haley Anderson's name and decided it might not be so bad after all.

But she'd told him very politely, thank you, no. She was definitely not like the girl he'd kissed all those years ago. He remembered the sweet little sound she'd made when their lips touched, but not how pretty she was. He also didn't remember this confidence, with just enough contrariness to make her interesting. And really artistic judging by the mural she was creating.

He could have told her why he'd offered to help. He'd actually planned to because she would have to know eventually. There would be legal paperwork from the court that she had to sign off on. The thing was she'd gone on about why she was starting the program. Raising her younger siblings after her mom's death. Being part of the community. Bending over backward to get the teen meeting spot right.

Her earnestness was daunting. It seemed pure, but he'd had a costly lesson in misjudging women. A mistake he wouldn't repeat. Still, he just couldn't bring himself to tell her the whole truth of his offer to help. Since he wasn't getting out of Thunder Canyon without a driver's license, he had to persuade Haley to give him a chance. He'd prove himself trustworthy and indispensable, then break the news about community service. It was a good plan and there was no reason to doubt that he'd achieve his objective.

Sales were his business and women found him charming. Mostly. Because there were so few exceptions, they were memorable. There was the girl in college who could give lessons in sales. She'd made him fall for her and even propose. She'd insisted wedding should come before bedding but she wouldn't feel right about marrying him until she paid off a large debt—medical bills from her father's open heart surgery.

Marlon knew now he hadn't been thinking with his head when he wrote her name on a check with a lot of zeroes and handed it over. It was the last time he saw her.

His most recent charm-resistant woman was the judge who'd revoked his license for thirty days. Her Honor just didn't understand the need for speed on the empty, open highway and how it cleared a guy's head. And he was a guy with a lot on his mind.

He'd found his community service. Unfortunately it was for another woman who didn't seem to get his charm. He could go to the next organization on the court's list, but Haley Anderson's turndown had tapped into his mother lode of stubborn. He was going to change her mind. And the prospect was more entertaining than he would have expected.

Marlon saw Haley's old, beat-up blue Ford truck go slowly by The Hitching Post, pull around the corner and into the parking lot behind ROOTS. There was a refrigerator in the truck bed and he got an idea that might solve his problem.

He grinned. It was time to amp up the charm.

He left his apartment and walked down the wooden stairs, leaving by the back entrance to avoid going through the bar and grill. The breakfast and lunch rushes were over and the place sounded pretty empty, but it was too easy to get pulled into a conversation. He was a man on a mission.

He rounded the building, then walked down Main Street, turned right on Nugget Way and into the parking lot behind ROOTS. Haley was standing in front of the half-glass, half-wood door, unlocking it.

"Hi," he said.

She whirled around at the sound of his voice and pressed a hand to her chest. "You scared me."

"Sorry." The sound of his boots on the paved parking lot was loud enough to wake the dead. She must have a lot on her mind, too. "I thought you heard me."

She shook her head, then tucked a strand of hair that escaped her ponytail behind her ear. Earlier when she was painting, her hair had been twisted up and held with a comb thing. An image of that shiny brown silk loose around her shoulders flashed through his mind as the need to run his fingers through it banged around in his gut. He folded his arms over his chest to rein himself in. Distractions were not permitted to men on missions.

She'd changed out of the earlier ratty jeans and oversize T-shirt into a red tab-front, collared shirt with a yellow horse and bridle above the words The Hitching Post on the breast. The shirt was tucked into the waistband of a pair of denims that hugged her curvy hips and thighs. Her big brown eyes assessed him warily. The expression reminded him of a potential client at a sales meeting, wondering what he wanted them to buy and how much it was going to cost.

From experience he knew it was best not to lead with his bottom line. Get your target's guard down.

"Nice day," he said, glancing up at a blue sky with wispy white clouds floating lazily by.

Haley looked up, then back at him. "Yes, it is. A little warm, though," she added.

"Really? You think so?" Maybe *he* was making her warm, which wouldn't be a bad thing. Unless it increased her caution quotient. One look at her lips pressed tightly together told him that was the case. He let his gaze wander to the towering peaks in the distance. "The mountains here are different from the ones in L.A."

He had a condo near the beach in Marina del Rey, a short drive from where his company MC/TC was headquartered.

The high energy of the bustling business center couldn't be more different from Thunder Canyon, Montana.

"How are they different?" Haley asked. "Other than the fact that here you can actually see them."

"Ah, a subtle Los Angeles smog dig?"

"Was that subtle? I didn't mean to be."

"For your information, the California emission standards are actually making a difference in air quality."

"Good to know. But I prefer not to see the air I'm sucking in. I hope Thunder Canyon never has to clean up what we breathe because of too many cars on the road."

Now he was feeling the heat. Cars were not a subject he wanted highlighted in this conversation, since for the next month it would be illegal for him to drive one. Not only that, her eyes were still wondering what he was after.

He glanced at her truck, standing beside them. "I couldn't help noticing you have a refrigerator in your vehicle."

Her full lips curved up for a moment, chasing the guarded look from her eyes. "Nothing gets by you, does it?"

He laughed. "Just a little something you picked up?"

"It's a donation to the teen center," she explained.

"How are you going to get it inside?"

"That's a very good question." She looked from the big white appliance to the back door of the center. "I figured I'd grab some burly men at The Hitching Post and impose on their good nature."

"I'm burly and here now. And my good nature is legendary. Impose away."

She folded her arms over her chest. "You're going to move that heavy white albatross and put it where I say?"

"That's the plan."

"Don't tell me," she said. "There's a big letter S on your chest. The superhero swoops in to save the day."

He eyed the appliance critically and shook his head. "I was thinking more of two planks, a dolly and some strategically placed straps, then rolling it inside all by my lonesome."

"And just where would you get all that paraphernalia?" she asked suspiciously. "Wait, in your back pocket."

He shook his finger at her, a teasing reprimand. "You're going to be sorry for mocking me."

"It's worth the risk." The distrustful look slid back into her eyes.

The expression on her face spoke volumes about the fact that she didn't expect him to follow through. Based on their brief contact six years ago, he supposed it was understandable. But this was now, they were adults, and he had something to prove.

"Just remember," he said. "An apology is always good form when one is confirmed to be in the wrong."

Marlon reached for his cell phone and made a quick call to the Cates Construction office. "Give me thirty minutes and I'll have that big boy inside ROOTS for you."

"Right," she said skeptically.

While he waited for his twin brother to bring what he needed, he helped Haley unload the paper goods from the cab of her truck. There were bags of plates, napkins, cups. They carried them into the small storage area off the main room.

When they came out again, there was a truck parked behind hers with the words Cates Construction painted on the side. His twin brother, Matt, hopped out.

"Hi, Haley," he said.

"Matt. I guess you're here to bail out your brother and make good on his promise?"

"Nope. I just brought the stuff he asked for. He's on his own. I've got work to do."

Marlon helped Matt unload everything, thanked him, and watched him drive back to the construction site for Connor McFarlane's new house.

Haley was staring after the truck, then met his gaze. "When you look at your brother is it like staring into a mirror?"

He laughed and shook his head. "We're pretty different. My mother doesn't have any trouble telling us apart. Although she did admit to being challenged when one of us calls her on the phone."

"Double trouble," Haley murmured. "Okay, hotshot, let's see if your burly body can cash the check your big mouth wrote."

"Oh, ye of little faith."

He let down her truck's tailgate and settled the two sturdy planks side by side about the width of the dolly's wheels. Then he put it in the bed, hauled himself up and muscled the refrigerator onto it. He strapped it on, tilted it back, and wheeled it easily down before rolling it toward the open door.

"Where did you want this?" he asked.

"In the storage room. There's an outlet in there to plug it in," she explained.

He moved it inside and followed her instructions. The sound of the fridge humming made him grin when he met her gaze. "Anything else?"

Her sheepish expression was satisfying. "Thank you very much."

"You're welcome." He arched one eyebrow. "Is there anything more you'd like to say?"

"It's not very gentlemanly to make a woman grovel."

"Hmm." He leaned an arm on the dolly's curved handle. "I believe I warned you about mocking me."

She rubbed a finger across the side of her nose. "Okay. I'll say it. I was wrong, Marlon. I appreciate your help."

"What would you do without me?"

"Same as I do when you're not here," she answered. "Wing it."

"The thing is, Haley, I'm here now. Let me help you out."

"That's okay. I'm used to handling things on my own."

Marlon wasn't used to women turning him down and that was twice she'd told him no. It was really starting to tick him off. The next time he asked she *would* say yes.

She just didn't know it yet.

Chapter Two

Haley waited for Marlon to take the hint and leave, despite feeling kind of bad about it. He really had saved her a whole lot of time and a great deal of trouble.

"Look, Haley—" His easygoing manner didn't change, but something slid into his dark eyes that looked a lot like determination. "With my help, you can accomplish twice as much in half the time."

There was no way to refute that. She was racing against the clock, even if it was her own self-imposed deadline. But the Marlon she remembered wasn't all that enthusiastic about helping others. And the Marlon standing in this tiny storage room seemed to fill up the small space.

She could smell the pleasantly masculine fragrance of his skin and feel the heat from his body. Either was enough to short-circuit rational thought, but the combination made her lightheaded and jumpy. She walked out into the big, empty room with its half-finished mural.

"Two heads are better than one," he continued, following her.

"And that would be helpful—how?"

He rested his hands on lean hips and looked around. "I assume you're going to put something in here."

"Furniture," she confirmed.

"I could help."

"Uh-huh." *If* he was around—and that was a very big if.

"And I can provide a guy's point of view."

"For?" she asked.

"When the kids come around. If they're having a problem, I can give you the male slant on it." There was a serious expression on his face, but the twinkle in his eyes gave him away. "This might come as a big surprise to you, but men and women don't think the same way."

She found herself fighting a smile. "Actually, I think I knew that."

At least she'd probably read something about it in a magazine or seen evidence in a movie. Real life, not so much. She hadn't dated in high school, and the short time she'd spent in college didn't give her the chance to really know the guy she'd been seeing. Then her mom died and she'd come home. A personal life was so far down her priority list it never happened.

"Okay, so you can see the benefit I could provide."

"It's the content of that benefit that concerns me," she said.

"How so?"

"The kids need a role model." She stopped there and hoped he would fill in the blanks.

He stared at her for several moments. "From that I take it you don't think I would be a positive influence?"

Bingo. "Word on the street is that you're a rule-breaker and envelope-pusher."

"Some would say I think outside the box. That's not necessarily a bad quality."

"The thing about breaking rules," she said, "is that you have to know what they are before pushing them. The kids are in that vulnerable limbo where they're figuring things out."

"I can help with that."

Like he'd helped her six years ago? That's not the kind of lesson she wanted the teens to get from ROOTS.

"How?" she asked skeptically.

"You always did the right thing and can't understand the thought process of walking on the wild side. I can give you a different slant."

"Is that an admission of guilt?" she asked, surprised.

"It's a confession insofar as I admit to getting away with 'stuff'. My point being that not much gets by me. But you don't have the same experiences that give one a certain skill set. We would come at any problem of the kids' from two different viewpoints."

"I appreciate the offer, Marlon—"

"Don't say it," he warned.

"What?"

"You were going to say you appreciate the offer, *but* I shouldn't hold my breath."

"I guess you're a mind reader." Not.

If so he'd know how real rejection felt. For days after he'd promised to call it felt as if she'd held her breath. When she finally realized he didn't plan to contact her, it had hurt a lot. But she figured a man like Marlon didn't know what it was like to be let down.

His eyes narrowed. "You know, Haley, this is beginning to feel personal."

"Excuse me?" Her heart started to beat a little faster and the question might buy her some time to slow it down. "I think of it as practical, actually."

"And I disagree." He ran his fingers through his hair. "Practical would be taking what's offered because you need the help. Since you're turning me down, it's got to be personal."

"How do you know I don't have a long waiting list of offers?" she bluffed.

"For starters, you'd have lined someone up to help you get that refrigerator inside. But you planned to wing it."

So she wasn't a very good bluffer. He was way too close to the truth with that personal remark. Who'd have guessed that Marlon Cates was so perceptive? There was no way she would give him the satisfaction of knowing that his rejection still tweaked her on any level, no matter how small.

"It's not personal," she assured him. "I just have to do what's best for the center."

"So we're back to me being unreliable."

"Everyone knows you have a multi-million-dollar company to run," she hedged. "It's just common sense that you can't be counted on when you have to focus on your business."

"Shouldn't I be the one who gets to decide how much time I have to spare for a worthy cause?" He stared at her intently. "And aren't you, as the driving force behind this venture, the one who takes whatever anyone is willing to donate?"

He had a point, darn it. If he hadn't started his multi-million-dollar company, he could easily have gone into the practice of law. He'd certainly backed her into a corner that was going to take some slick maneuvering to get out of gracefully. What she wanted to say was, *what happens when you leave again?* Because he was leaving. His life wasn't in Thunder Canyon anymore.

"Look," he said when she was quiet. "How about this. I'll commit to a certain number of hours per week for the next four weeks. If I prove to be unreliable, I'll do the right thing and admit I was wrong."

She sighed. "Okay."

He opened his mouth, then shut it again and stared for several moments. "What?"

"I agree to your proposal." She met his gaze. "But it's only fair to warn you that you're on probation. *My* probation. If you mess up even once, you're gone. I can't take the chance with the kids."

He held out his hand. "Done."

She stared for several moments and her gaze slid up his strong arm. Finally she settled her fingers into his palm and shook on the deal.

"You won't be sorry."

When the words were followed by a signature Marlon Cates grin, Haley was already sorry. The fluttering in her stomach and the tightness in her chest made her sorry. He still affected her. His presence made her feel things it wasn't safe to feel.

But really, it was one month. Thirty days. Not enough time to do any damage because she was wise to him. She knew to not expect anything.

Only a fool with stars in her eyes would let her guard down and Haley Anderson hadn't had stars in her eyes for a very long time.

Several hours later Haley was willing to admit, if only to herself, that Marlon's help had come in handy. And his timing for offering it couldn't have been better. Second Chances had agreed to donate furniture to her cause.

With Marlon's help, she'd moved over an eight-foot sofa with worn seat cushions and a threadbare loveseat that didn't match. There was a faux leather recliner that didn't recline, coffee and end tables with cigarette burns and scratches. Carved into the top of one were the initials CS+WR, with a heart surrounding the whole thing. Very romantic. The big, ugly donated lamps covered some of the dings, but she arranged it so the heart still showed.

They also got a TV. Since broadcast television had switched from analog to digital, quite a few sets had been discarded. Haley was more than happy to let the thrift store donate one to ROOTS because she had a converter box. Now it was all set up on a stand in the corner.

She brushed her forearm across her forehead and grinned. "Awesome."

"You think?"

Haley heard the doubt in his voice. "Beauty is in the eye of the beholder."

Marlon stood beside her and folded his arms over his chest as he surveyed the room, his gaze settling on the place where stuffing was coming out of the gold-and-brown striped sofa cushion. Then he looked at the green-and-pink loveseat sitting at a right angle to it. "You call this beautiful and can actually say that with a straight face?"

"I still have a little money left from donations to buy some ready-made slipcovers that will just make this room pop." She looked up at him and could almost hear her heart making a popping sound.

It was best to ignore that and concentrate on the good stuff—like being way ahead of where she'd expected to be right now. The only plan she'd had was for her brother and sister to get off work at Thunder Canyon Resort and stop by to help. But there was a flaw in Plan A, which Angie and Austin had pointed out in tones that bordered on whiney.

After work they'd be hungry and tired and not in favor of moving furniture. They'd reluctantly agreed to help, but now it wasn't necessary.

Because she'd had Marlon.

No, he wasn't hers. She didn't *have* him. She had the time he'd donated. No more, no less. And she still couldn't figure out why he'd insisted on helping. One of these days she'd stop looking a gift horse in the mouth while waiting for the other shoe to fall.

"I say it looks good," she said, nodding firmly.

His expression said he disagreed. "That depends on your definition of good and your standards."

"That's the beauty. It's not my standards that matter. This is for the kids. It's going to get trashed, anyway. They don't need to worry about ruining something that's brand-new. This room says come on in. Be comfortable."

"And you couldn't have done it without me," he teased.

"I could have," she said, then reluctantly added, "but not this fast. Seriously, Marlon, thank you."

"You're welcome."

The deep, slightly husky quality in his voice scraped over her skin and seeped inside, tying her in knots. On top of that she was tongue-tied, too. He was a glib, quick-witted, millionaire man of the world and she was a nobody from a small town in Montana. It shouldn't matter, but it did. And as silence stretched between them, she felt more and more awkward and unsophisticated.

Just before she wished the earth would open and swallow her whole, the door opened and her brother and sister walked in. Relief flooded through her. "Austin. Angie."

Her brother was as tall as Marlon and at twenty-two he wasn't that much younger. His brown hair was cut short and with a lot of time and product, he got it to stick out in the trendiest possible way. His navy blue T-shirt set off the dark brown eyes that were studying the man beside her.

"Hey, Marlon." He stuck out his hand.

For some reason the gesture seemed especially manly of her brother and made Haley proud.

"Austin." He shook her brother's hand. "How are you?"

"Good. You?"

"Can't complain." He nodded to Angie. "You look more like your big sister every time I see you."

The slender, twenty-year-old's cheeks turned as pink as her T-shirt. She tucked a strand of straight, shiny, shoulder-length brown hair behind her ear. "Is that a compliment?"

He glanced down at Haley and winked. "Of course."

Like she believed that. What was he going to say? The Anderson sisters shouldn't go down Main Street Thunder Canyon without bags over their heads? Charm and blarney were his specialties.

Austin's gaze drifted past them to the furniture in the center of the room, arranged in a cozy square to cultivate conversation. "So, we're too late to help?" he asked, grinning.

"Try not to look so disappointed," Haley said, wryly.

"Darn, I was really looking forward to lugging stuff around." If anything, his smile grew wider.

"Marlon was kind enough to help me."

Austin nodded. "I owe you one, man."

"No one's counting. I'm happy to be of service." The man looked down at her. "And believe me, it wasn't easy."

That goes double for me, Haley thought, meeting his gaze. "The point is that the basics are in place and I'll get the word out that the kids can come on in."

Angie nodded at the half-finished mural. "It looks good,

Haley. I like what you did with the cell phones, computers and books. The sports stuff is cool, too. Very yin and yang."

"Balance. It's a subtle message up there, but it's the goal." Haley glanced over her shoulder and smiled at her work in progress.

"And a good one," her brother said. "But I really am glad Marlon gave you a hand. It's been a long day."

"Austin works in engineering at the resort," Haley explained.

"Maintenance actually," he clarified. "Angie's in housekeeping."

Her sister shrugged. "It's a job."

"You should be grateful to have it," Haley pointed out.

"So you keep telling me." Her sister's lips pulled tight.

"Hey, sis," Austin said, nudging his younger sister's arm with his elbow and effectively filling the tense silence. "Now that we don't have to help, we can eat sooner. Remember we're starving."

"Yeah."

Haley nodded. "Okay. I've done all I can here for tonight. You guys head on home and I'll be along to get dinner started."

"I can make dinner," Angie offered.

"That's okay." Austin's expression kaleidoscoped from horror to sympathetic understanding. "The last time you got near the stove and tried anything but a sandwich or cold cereal, the scream of the smoke detector took out my hearing for hours."

"It was a blessing in disguise," Haley said. "Always good to know they work."

But when Angie's brown eyes darkened with temper, it was clear she didn't appreciate the good-natured joking.

"And you've never let me try again. How am I going to learn?"

"Have you ever heard the expression where there's smoke, there's fire?" Austin's mouth curved up in a teasing smile. "I kind of like having a roof over my head. Especially with winter coming."

"You're a jerk." Angie punched him in the arm.

"Ow." He rubbed the spot and said to Haley, "She hit me. Are you going to let her get away with not using her words?"

"When are you going to stop treating me like a kid? I'm older than you were when mom died." Angie glared at her, then turned on her heel and walked out, slamming the door behind her.

"She's a little touchy." Austin shrugged. "I better go after her. I'm her ride."

"See you at home," Haley said.

When they were alone again, she and Marlon both spoke at once.

"I'm sorry—"

"They grew up—"

Haley shrugged. "You go first."

"I was just going to say that your siblings grew up well, thanks to you."

She stared out the window where dusk was just settling over Main Street. "I was just going to say that I'm sorry you had to see that."

"What?" he asked innocently.

"Angie's meltdown. She gets snippy when she thinks I'm babying her."

"Looks to me like you were just taking care of your own." He shrugged.

"She doesn't see it that way. She thinks twenty years old is all grown up."

His brown eyes turned the color of rich chocolate when sympathy slid into them. "She's right, though. She is older than you were when—" he shifted his feet then looked at her "—when you took over as head of the family."

"I did what I had to. What anyone would have."

"I'm not so sure that's true. A lot of people would have just walked away from all that responsibility. Not you."

"I couldn't. They're my family." She shrugged as if that explained everything.

"And family is there for each other. But that's not how it looked to me. From what I saw, you take care of everyone else. I can't help wondering who takes care of you."

"Like I said, I don't need anyone. I'm just fine on my own."

He shook his head as he stared down at her. "I'm two parts awed and one part bothered by that."

"Why?"

"As the song says, everybody needs somebody sometime. Like you needed me today."

"That's the thing, Marlon. If you hadn't been here, I'd have rounded up some guys. Austin would have helped. He has friends. I'd have gotten it done somehow."

She remembered back to those first weeks and months after her mother died. They'd gone through the motions of living, but it was like being among the walking dead. They were in shock. In spite of that, she'd had to make sure her siblings went to school, ate, did their homework. That evolved into supervising who their friends were, where they went and with whom. All the things a parent would do. What her mom had done for her.

"You're pretty amazing, Haley Anderson."

"Thanks."

His praise warmed her clear through, in a place that she hadn't realized was frozen over and numb. But it was dangerous to allow it to thaw. If that happened, feeling would return and with it the pins and needles of nerve endings awakening and the pain that went along with it. She'd gotten through her mom's death, but never ever wanted to lose someone again. She just didn't think she had it in her to go on without someone she loved.

And Marlon Cates, happy wanderer and world traveler, was not the person she wanted to talk to about this. It was like exposing her soft underbelly and left her feeling too vulnerable, too raw.

She angled her head toward the door. "I have to go. The hungry hordes are waiting at home."

"Right," he said. "Me, too."

"Okay." She grabbed her purse from the floor and slid the strap over her shoulder. "Good night."

"Wait." He put his hand on her arm to stop her. The feel of his fingers rolled heat all the way to her heart, which started popping like a bag of microwave popcorn. Just barely, she stopped the quiver that his touch generated.

"What?" she asked, a little too breathlessly. With luck he didn't notice.

"What time do you want me here tomorrow?"

Putting a finer point on the question, she didn't really want him there at all. Because she would look forward to seeing him. And she didn't want to.

But apparently whatever selfless kick he was on hadn't let up because he was waiting for an answer. "I'm working the breakfast and dinner shifts at The Hitching Post, but this mural needs work so I plan to do that for a couple of hours in between. You could scrub the walls." His narrowed gaze made her add, "I can't afford more paint, but it needs to be cleaned up. Just a little elbow grease." A task that just might flip the off switch on this altruistic streak of his.

"Okay. See you then."

When he took his hand off her arm and walked out the door, Haley released the breath she'd been holding. Anticipation stretched inside her, a sensation she hadn't experienced for a long time. If she could have stopped it she would have because it *so* wasn't a good idea. But the fact was, she found herself looking forward to tomorrow—and dreading it.

What else would he talk her into doing against her better judgment?

Chapter Three

When Haley arrived at ROOTS the next day Marlon was there waiting. She pulled up at the curb, then grabbed the bags of stuff sitting on the seat beside her and hopped down.

"Hi."

Just like that, his voice and smile kick-started that popping inside her, even though she'd had a whole lot of hours to brace for another face-to-face. "Hi."

Clever comeback, she told herself.

"Let me take those," he said, reaching for the bags.

Their hands brushed and her chest felt tight. "Thanks."

He hefted one. "Do you have rocks in here?"

"You caught me." Slightly more clever on the comeback scale.

He peeked inside and saw the bottles of cleaning supplies along with a bag of candy. There was a wry expression in his eyes. "Nutritious."

"Special treats," she defended. "There's a couple cases of soda in the truck. I'll get them."

He set the bags down by the door and said, "Allow me. You be the brains. I'll be the brawn."

Don't have to ask me twice, she thought, letting herself look at his back as he walked to her truck. She was twenty-four-years old and had never had sex, but inexperience didn't stop her from admiring his broad shoulders and excellent butt. She didn't even know the criteria upon which veteran, male-watching women relied to determine whether or not a man had a bonafide excellent backside, but to her way of thinking, Marlon definitely did.

The muscles in his arms and back rippled and bunched as he stacked the cases of soda one on top of the other then lifted. A flutter moved from her belly to her throat and all of a sudden she couldn't draw a deep breath.

As he turned, she quickly stuck her key in the door and hoped he hadn't caught her staring. That was all she needed. Having him around was a challenge, but she wouldn't know how to handle his teasing about man/woman stuff, highlighting her lack of sophistication. She just wouldn't be able to stand it if he pitied her.

He stopped beside her and frowned. "Is there a problem with the door?"

"Lock's a little stiff," she mumbled, turning the key and twisting the knob to open the door for him.

He walked in ahead of her and she picked up one of the bags outside before following him. Inside, she saw that he'd stopped dead-still and everything about his body language screamed tension.

"Haley?"

"What?" She moved around him and glanced at the room.

It wasn't the way she'd left it. The back cushions on the

sofa had been moved. There were junk food wrappers and beer cans on the coffee table.

"Did you have chips and beer for dinner here last night?"

"No." The one word came out on a whisper as apprehension ballooned inside her.

"Did you let some kids in?" he asked.

"I left right after you. ROOTS isn't officially opened yet. And if it were, I wouldn't be serving beer."

Marlon set the cases of soda down on the scarred coffee table. "Stay here."

"Why? Where are you going?" She automatically started toward the back and he put out his arm to stop her.

"What part of 'stay here' did you not understand?"

"The part where you're going all special agent, covert op. This is my project."

"And there could be someone back there who knows it and is waiting for you." He glared down and there was no trace of humor in his eyes, which was more alarming than the tension in his voice. "Stand by the open door. I'm going to check the place out. If necessary, you go for help."

"But, Marlon, you might need me—"

"No," he said firmly. "Stay here."

"Okay."

It took less than a minute for him to look around the storeroom and bathroom, but it felt like days. Bad stuff always seemed to last longer than the good.

"It's all clear." He appeared in the doorway, his face grim. "But you've got a broken window in here."

She hurried back and saw that the glass in the top half of the door had been shattered. Shards were on the floor. "That's how they got in."

"Yeah."

"Why can't I catch a break?"

The words popped out before she could stop them. She'd been so excited when she left last night. The kids would have a place to sit and TV to watch. Now someone who only wanted a place to party had violated her sense of trust.

"Sometimes life is just not fair—" Emotion flooded her and she caught the corner of her top lip between her teeth to keep from giving in to it.

Marlon pulled her into his arms. "Don't go to the bad place."

"I don't have to go. It broke in and made itself at home."

His big palm rubbed up and down her back and the heat of his body warmed hers. She hadn't even realized how cold she was.

"Don't let it get to you. We'll talk to the cops and see if there's anything they can do. Look on the bright side."

"Is there one?" She forced herself to step away from him. "No, wait, this is where you say things could have been worse."

"It's true."

"Yeah? How?"

"There wasn't anything here to take. And they brought their own beer and snacks," he added.

She fought a smile and felt better for it. God help her, she was glad he'd been here. She wasn't used to anyone looking out for her. Leaning on him was different. And not totally bad. This was a side to Marlon that she'd never seen before. Kind of heroic, which was out of character. She remembered him being a scoundrel and everything she'd seen and heard had supported that impression.

"Let's not wallow," he suggested.

"Not even for a couple minutes?"

He shook his head. "Action is what you need. I'll sweep

up the glass. Do you have a measuring tape?" When she nodded, he said, "You measure for a new window. Then we'll go to the hardware store. It'll be good as new."

It was impossible not to perk up the way he was snapping out orders. She wondered what he was like to work for.

Haley handed him the broom. "So, do your employees cower in fear when they see you coming?"

"No. I'm the world's best boss."

"How do you figure?"

"I'm not in the office all that much."

"Where do you go?" she asked.

"The better question is where don't I go." He pulled the trash can over, then squatted down and picked up the biggest pieces of glass.

"Okay. I'll bite. Where don't you go?" she asked.

"Fiji. Polynesia. Tahiti." He looked up and grinned.

"Seriously."

"I've been all over the U.S. San Francisco. Seattle. New York. Washington, D.C."

"Why?"

"I'm a salesman. It's my job to meet with business people and convince them that the MC/TC brand will fly out of their stores."

"I bet you could probably sell beachfront property in Las Vegas," she said.

"It wouldn't be easy." He looked up and grinned. "But challenge is my middle name."

"Have you been to Las Vegas?"

"Quite a few times. They say New York is the city that never sleeps, but Vegas is the real deal. Very exciting. A buffet for the senses."

"How so?"

He stood and leaned on the broom. "The first thing you notice are the lights. The Strip is all neon and turns night into day. Then you go inside and there are more lights, this time with the sound. Dings, bells, sirens. Any kind of food you can imagine is there. In fact, any decadence you're looking for you can find."

"Wow." She couldn't help wondering how many decadences he'd had. "Where else have you been?"

"The beach. Caribbean beaches are spectacular, but Malibu, Santa Barbara, Santa Monica—there's an excitement to the California coast."

"I've never seen the ocean," she admitted.

He met her gaze and his expression was perilously close to pity. "No?"

She shook her head, then busied herself pulling out the jagged glass remaining in the top of the door. "I've never been out of Montana."

"Be careful. Don't cut yourself," he warned.

"Don't worry about me."

"Easier said than done," he muttered, then asked, "Wouldn't you like to travel?"

"I don't think I'd find anything as beautiful as I've got here."

"I'm not saying Thunder Canyon isn't spectacular. But it's exciting to see other places."

"I guess I'll have to take your word on that," she said measuring the empty space where the window used to be.

She didn't cut herself on the glass, but that didn't mean she wasn't dinged. For those few moments when he'd held her in his arms she'd been able to forget that he didn't hang his hat in Thunder Canyon. But now his words brought her down to earth. It was a reminder that he might have family in town, but this wasn't where he made his home.

However generous he might be with his time right now,

he'd be leaving and she shouldn't get used to having him around permanently.

But those few moments in his arms had been nicer than she would ever have imagined, much sweeter than she wanted them to be.

"Look, you don't have to stay here with me, Marlon, It's nearly midnight."

And Marlon had been alone with Haley since it got dark. He knew he was going to have to tell her pretty soon why he was volunteering at ROOTS, but now wasn't the time. Another night had passed, another break-in had occurred and she was determined to get to the bottom of it. She had a lot on her mind and he was more than happy to use the excuse that it was wrong to add to her burdens. Mostly he was dreading the look of betrayal in her eyes when she found out. Call him a coward, but it could be put off just a little longer.

"No way I'm leaving," he said.

"Seriously, go home and get some sleep."

"Right," he said wryly. "Like I could sleep while you wait here alone for a serial killer."

"He hasn't killed anyone yet," she pointed out.

"That we know of," he reminded her.

Marlon was having serious doubts about his decision to stay and it had nothing to do with danger and everything to do with the scent of Haley's skin. They were sitting on the floor at ROOTS, resting against the back of the ratty old sofa, out of sight from the front window and facing the doorway to the rear entrance.

It was dark, not pitch black, but enough that he couldn't see her features clearly. But he could smell the sweet, floral fragrance of her and there was a knot of need twisting in his gut. He was having a hell of a time *not* kissing her. And since all his senses besides sight were heightened, he could practically hear the soft, moany, girlish noise she'd made the first, last and only time he'd kissed her.

That was six years ago and the memory picked *now* to torture him.

"Did you hear me, Marlon?"

It was like she could read his mind. "What?"

"I said, you really should go. If the guy comes back I'll just call 9-1-1. I've got my phone."

If only he could. Life would be less complicated. But his mother would give him hell and his father would have his hide. He might bend the speed limit rules, but he wasn't a slug who would leave a defenseless woman to face an intruder.

"I'm not going to argue with you, Haley. Two nights in a row someone got in—"

"That's because the hardware store didn't have the size glass I need. We knew the patch was iffy." She shifted on the hard floor and bumped him. "And the someone is a he."

"How can you be so sure?"

"The toilet seat was left up," she said confidently.

"So speaks the crime scene investigator. All the more reason I should stay and back you up."

Against the wall with his mouth against hers, kissing the living daylights out of her. And he told himself he wasn't completely selfish. If she had as much pent-up passion inside her as he thought, an explosion of it would chase the sadness from her eyes.

It was always there, hovering, unless she was excited about something, like this project to pay it forward. Or when she was ticked off at him. Wouldn't it be interesting to see if she was as responsive as he suspected in other ways? If kissing her wouldn't complicate the hell out of everything, he'd do it and move on because concentrating on life after community service was hard when she looked so sad.

"Okay," she said, yawning. "You can stay. But I hope he comes soon."

That went double for him. When her shoulder brushed his arm, his skin caught fire and the blood drained from his head and pumped to points south of his belt.

Haley squirmed around, trying to get comfortable. "If he doesn't want to get caught, you'd think he'd pick somewhere else to break in."

"You wanted this place to be somewhere the kids would feel welcome," he reminded her. "Obviously this guy got the vibe."

And speaking of vibes, he needed to take his mind off the ones that urged him to pull her into his arms. "So what do you think about Bo Clifton running for mayor?"

"I'm all for it. He's my best friend's cousin."

"I didn't know you and Elise Clifton were friends," he said and felt her shrug.

"She was a year older than me, but somehow we bonded. I think it had something to do with the fact that neither of us had a father."

Elise Clifton's father had been murdered when she was twelve years old. Marlon didn't know Haley's story, but he heard the sadness in her voice. Though he couldn't see her expression, he knew there would be sadness there, too. "What happened to your dad?"

"Beats me. He just left. I don't really remember him."

Marlon waited for her to say more, but she didn't. "Do you want to talk about it?"

"No."

"Okay, then." He moved off of the sensitive subject.

"What chance do you think Bo has in the election, now that he's thrown his hat in the ring?"

"It's hard to say. Arthur Swinton has been around for years. He's experienced and everyone knows him. It's hard to argue against a family values platform."

It would be especially important to someone like Haley who had stepped into a difficult situation to take care of family, he thought. "What do you think of Bo?"

There was silence for a few moments before she said, "He's young and has fresh ideas that could shake things up. That's not a bad thing. Especially with the economy in such big trouble."

"You got that right."

"Has your company been affected by the downturn?" she asked.

"Oh, yeah." It was one of the things on his mind when he'd been pulled over for speeding. He'd been wondering whether to tough it out or sell out. The latter option would mean putting a lot of people out of work. That was something he didn't take lightly.

"What's wrong, Marlon?"

"Why?"

"I could hear it in your voice. Something's bothering you."

Apparently he wasn't the only one whose other senses were heightened in the dark. "I just have some business things to work through."

"Anything I can—" A noise at the back door stopped her. "Did you hear that?" she whispered.

"Yeah. Stay here." He put his hand on her arm and actually felt it when she was about to argue. "I mean it, Haley."

"Be careful, Marlon."

He nodded, then rolled to a standing position and

soundlessly moved to the doorway and peeked into the storeroom. A shape was backlit by outside lights in the open door. Marlon ducked back and waited in the main room for the guy to move past him. When he did, Marlon grabbed him from behind.

"Hey, man—"

One of the lamps switched on and Marlon blinked against the brightness, but didn't loosen his hold. "Haley, call the cops."

"He's just a kid, Marlon."

"I didn't know anyone was here." The young voice cracked with the pleading tone. "Let me go. I won't bother you again."

"Don't hurt him," Haley said.

"Hurt him?" This jerk had spoiled a day that should have been happy for her. And all she could think about was not hurting this kid who had no respect for locks and rules? "Are you serious?"

"Look at him. He's more scared than we are." She moved closer. "What's your name?"

There was no sound except heavy breathing from the exertion of their recent scuffle. Marlon tightened his arms, just a little pressure to give the aspiring delinquent something to think about.

"The lady asked you a question."

"Roy. Robbins," he added.

Marlon eased his grip and dropped his hands, then moved to the side to get a good look. Haley was right. He was just a kid, about sixteen or seventeen. Looked like a young Brad Pitt, but skinny and not much taller than Haley.

"What's your deal, kid?"

"None of your business."

"That's where you're wrong. When you broke in here

and scared Haley it became my business." He glanced at the woman in question, who was looking back at him like an alien had popped out of his chest. "Do you know him?"

She shook her head. "You need help, don't you, Roy?" There was no answer, which spoke volumes. "The thing is, kiddo, you didn't need to break in. But you picked the right place. ROOTS is all about helping kids in trouble."

"I'm not in trouble—"

"Wrong again, kid." Marlon watched him closely, waiting for any movement that would indicate he was planning to run for it. "Breaking and entering is a crime. Call the cops, Haley," he said again.

"It's not necessary."

"How can you say that?" Marlon demanded.

"He's just a kid. Probably a runaway. Not dangerous. The authorities have enough to do. This isn't something we need to generate a lot of paperwork for. When my brother was about the same age, he ran away and I was frantic." She looked at the kid. "Let me call your parents to come get you."

"No way." Testosterone-fueled anger wrapped around the words.

"Your mom and dad are probably worried sick about you, Roy."

"They could give a crap," he said bitterly.

Haley frowned. "Did they hurt you?"

"It's not like that," he said quickly.

"Tell me what it's like," she urged.

The kid ran his fingers through his short, spiky, dirty-blond hair. "I just had to get out of there."

"To clear your head?" Haley asked.

"I guess." He lifted a thin shoulder.

Marlon was impressed that she seemed to get him, to understand a guy's need to be alone. Maybe she would comprehend his own need for speed and the resulting community service.

"Go ahead. Call the cops," Roy challenged, his voice sullen and resigned.

It grated on Marlon, but Haley just smiled.

"I don't think that's necessary," she said again. "I'm glad you weren't out on the street. You just needed a place to spend the night."

"And that justifies breaking and entering?" Marlon demanded.

"He didn't take anything."

"That's because you didn't have beer in the fridge," Marlon said wryly.

"That wasn't the best choice you could have made," Haley gently chided the teen.

Roy just shrugged. "Can I go now?"

"Do you have a place to sleep?" she asked, knowing full well he didn't or he wouldn't be here.

"What do you care?" the teen asked.

"That's not an answer." Haley folded her arms over her chest. "I'd give you permission to sleep here except my permit doesn't allow anyone under age to be here without adult supervision."

"Then I'll split and find somewhere else to crash."

Haley sighed. "Look, it's late. I'm tired. And I won't sleep if I'm worried about you."

Hey, Marlon thought, that was his line. He didn't like where this was heading.

"You don't have to," the kid told her.

"Doesn't mean I won't. You can come home with me."

"What?" Marlon stared at her and wondered if her bleeding heart was starving her brain of oxygen. "That's crazy. What do you know about him?"

"He's in trouble. That's all I need to know." She held

up her hand to stop him when Roy started to deny it. "He reminds me of Austin when he was that age. It's why I started this program. How can I turn away the first kid who needs help? Where would my brother be if he'd been turned away when he needed it?"

"But, Haley—" Marlon met her stubborn gaze and slid the kid a wary look while trying to think of something to change her mind. "He's a total stranger. Bad things happen, even in Thunder Canyon."

"No one knows that better than me."

"Look, I didn't mean to—"

"Don't worry about it. The thing is, I'm a pretty good judge of character," she insisted. "And, if you're worried, you can follow me home."

No, he really couldn't. Not legally. "I don't have a car," he hedged.

"No wheels?" the kid said. "That's harsh."

"I didn't think I'd need any," he defended. "And if I did, I could borrow a truck from my dad's construction company."

"Well, I don't want to drive you back to town just because you have big-city induced trust issues," she said.

"I'll sleep on your couch."

She glared at him for several moments, then nodded, apparently getting the message that he wasn't backing down. "Roy can sleep on an air mattress in Austin's room."

"Okay."

That was a lie, Marlon thought, because nothing was okay. A night on her couch was the last thing he wanted but he couldn't let her drive out to her place all alone with a kid she didn't know anything about, and a runaway to boot. Damn this protective feeling. It was darned inconvenient.

It wasn't bad enough that he'd sat in the dark with her

for hours, wanting to kiss her. Now he'd be spending the night under her roof.

On the other hand, it was the least he could do. She didn't just talk the talk. She walked the walk and was willing to put herself out there to help a kid in need. She was a really good person in addition to that sweet, sexy thing she had going on. She wasn't a taker, but a giver and for reasons he couldn't put his finger on, he found that incredibly appealing.

Marlon had a feeling he wouldn't actually get any sleep on her couch—and it had nothing to do with whether or not it was comfortable. Spending the night under the fascinating do-gooder's roof would give him ideas that would test a saint's will power.

And he was no saint.

Chapter Four

The next morning, Haley sat in a booth at The Hitching Post next to Marlon, with Roy across from them. This place, with its cowboy ambience and distressed hardwood floors, was home away from home to her. Manager Linda Powell had given her a job when she badly needed one and that bought a lot of loyalty.

Since no wall separated the restaurant side from the bar side, she was glad that Roy's back was to it. Over the original bar from the 1880s saloon was a picture of owner Lily Divine wearing nothing but gauzy fabric strategically placed to keep her from being completely indecent. There was a better than even chance the teen had seen nude female pictures before, but it wasn't happening on Haley's watch.

She would have fed these two at her house, but cold cereal and toast were not the sort of comfort foods to inspire a troubled teen to loosen his tongue. Breakfast here where she worked was the plan because she'd heard that the way to a man's heart was through his stomach.

Marlon chose that moment to shift and brush his shoulder against hers and the resulting heat shooting through her made her wonder if the saying was true. Not that she wanted his heart—she didn't. She wasn't even sure she liked him, let alone trusted him. Besides, something bothered her about his explanation for not having a car. And why was he really helping at ROOTS?

But none of those questions stopped the heat from pooling in her belly when he brushed against her again. He smelled good, clean and manly. After they'd arrived this morning he'd gone upstairs to his apartment to clean up. She hadn't expected him to come back, but he'd surprised her. The two guys had eaten a full breakfast—eggs, bacon, hash browns and pancakes—but she'd lost her appetite the moment Marlon slid into the booth beside her.

The waitress on duty stopped by the booth with a pot of coffee in her hand. "I hope you enjoyed your breakfast?"

"Best pancakes I've ever had," Marlon said.

"Everything was really good, Shirley," Haley added, glancing at the teen who didn't look up. When he ordered coffee, she'd started to overrule him as being too young. Marlon touched her thigh, just a warning gesture that trapped her protest in her throat. She would never be sure whether she let it slide because being a guy Marlon knew more about guys, or simply that the sizzle generated by his touch zapped it from her mind.

Shirley Echols was a green-eyed redhead who'd grown up in Thunder Canyon. She went away to college, but came back every summer to work. Holding up the coffee pot she said, "Warm up?"

Haley shook her head as her two companions slid their mugs closer for refills, then remembered that this was the other girl's last day. "It's been great working with you this summer."

"Yeah. Me, too. I'll miss you."

"Where are you going?" Marlon asked.

"Back to college. UCLA. Senior year, finally."

"It's a great school," he said approvingly. "And West-wood is a nice area. Close to L.A., Hollywood, Santa Monica. The ocean. Some happening places."

"I know." Shirley slid him a flirty little smile.

Haley was suddenly less concerned about losing a co-worker and covering those shifts than the fact that she didn't like the way Marlon was returning the smile. It could be that a sense of nagging envy was responsible. The two of them shared knowledge of a place Haley had never been and had no expectation of ever going. She was a hick who'd never been out of Montana and had no business wondering if the way to Marlon's heart was through his stomach. Or anything else about him, for that matter.

But darn it, what she was feeling seemed a lot like jealousy. Not that she'd had much experience with the emotion what with her lack of any dating history, but she couldn't deny that resentful pretty well described the knot in her stomach. She wasn't proud of it, but wouldn't deny it, either.

She might be a hick, but she was a polite hick. "Good luck with your last year of school."

"Thanks." Shirley started to walk away then said over her shoulder, "If you need anything else, let me know."

"Count on it," Marlon said with a wink.

Haley bit back a retort because it wasn't any of her business. But the boy across from her was. If she was going to help him, she had to get him to talk.

"Okay, Roy, so tell me again where you're from."

"I never said." He slouched lower in the seat, his empty plate in front of him.

"It was worth a shot." She tried to think of something to draw him out. "What brought you to Thunder Canyon?"

"The trucker I hitched a ride with."

The whole scenario sent a chill through her. "Taking rides from total strangers isn't very safe."

"Really?" Marlon's tone oozed sarcasm. "Carting around complete strangers isn't what smart, savvy people do?"

"I wouldn't hurt her," Roy said.

"I'd like to believe that." Marlon leaned back in the booth. "But you won't tell us more than your name. We don't have any way to check out that you're telling us the truth. Smart money is on keeping you under surveillance."

"He's just a kid," Haley protested. "Cut him some slack."

"Yeah," Roy chimed in. "You don't understand anything."

"So tell us about yourself." Haley wrapped her hands around her mug. "What grade are you in?"

He thought for a moment and apparently decided sharing that couldn't give too much away. "Twelfth."

"So you'll be a senior," she confirmed. "Last year of high school. Graduation. Prom."

"No way." He looked more sullen if possible.

"Do you play sports?" she asked.

"Some."

"I was on the football team in high school," Marlon shared.

Roy folded his arms over his chest. "Big deal."

It was to Haley. She remembered watching him play. If there was a girl at Thunder Canyon High who didn't have a crush on him, she didn't know her. She'd quietly observed him on the field and in the halls, wishing he'd notice her, but half afraid that if he did, she'd make a fool of herself. And then he'd kissed her, just a freak encounter at a football fundraiser the summer after she graduated and he was home from college.

He'd kissed her and she was foolish enough to believe that the earth actually tilted for both of them when he promised to call her. When he never did, she realized that the earth only moved for her and felt like the worst kind of fool—the lovesick kind.

Fool me once, shame on you. Fool me twice, shame on me, she thought.

"Are you on a team?" she asked Roy.

"Football," he confirmed. "And basketball."

"Does your high school play Thunder Canyon during the season?" That information might narrow down where he lived.

"Maybe. Maybe not."

"Nice try, Haley," Marlon said.

"You can't trick me into telling you anything," the kid said. "Everything sucks and I'm not going back."

"What about your family?" she asked. "Your parents?"

When he didn't answer, Marlon said, "You do have parents?"

A sullen look slid over the teen's painfully young face. "Maybe. Maybe not."

Marlon rested his forearms on the table and studied the boy.

"Your parents probably care about you."

"Didn't say I had any."

"Assuming you do, they're probably worried. Although if it were up to me I'd be pretty ticked off at ungrateful offspring like you."

"Whatever. I can take care of myself."

"I'm sure you can," Haley agreed. "But when you care about someone, you worry."

"Who says I care about anyone but myself?" the teen argued.

"It's pretty clear you don't," Marlon snapped. "The least you can do is call them."

"Why should I? They don't care."

"So that would be a confirmation on having parents." Marlon nodded with satisfaction.

"I didn't say that," Roy said quickly.

"No one here is buying it. You need to let them know you're okay."

"Not gonna happen."

"Roy, they must be so worried. If I didn't know where my brother or sister was, I would be frantic."

"It's not like that where I come from."

"Someone cares enough to pay big bucks for the jeans and T-shirt you're wearing," Marlon pointed out. "Isn't that the MC/TC brand?"

"So?"

"It's expensive."

He should know, Haley thought. It was his. "I agree with Marlon."

"You do?" Marlon sounded shocked.

She glanced at his half-amused, half-surprised expression. "Yes, I do. Roy, you have to call your folks and let them know you're not dumped by the side of the road. Or starving. Or sick."

"You can't make me."

True. Now what was she going to do? Try to reason with him. But so far that hadn't worked. She could threaten, refuse to help unless he cooperated. But it wasn't a good idea to make threats you weren't prepared to follow through on. She couldn't turn him out in the cold. And she wasn't quite ready to go to the cops and see if anyone reported him missing. He might just run away again and not be lucky enough to find help.

Marlon blew out a breath. "Okay, tough guy. How about a shoot-out?"

Haley nearly got whiplash when she turned to look at him. "What? You think pistols at ten paces will get the truth out of him?"

"Not guns. Basketball," he explained. "One on one."

"I'd kick your ass," Roy scoffed.

"Really?" Marlon nodded. "Okay, how about this. If you beat me I get Haley to back off."

What? She didn't like where this was going. "Wait a minute—"

He held up a hand to stop her. "If I win, you call the folks and let them know you're alive and well."

Doubt flickered around the edges of his bravado. "I don't know—"

"Just what I thought. No guts."

"Says who?"

Haley could almost see the testosterone arcing back and forth but wasn't so sure this was the way to get information.

"Look, kid," Marlon said, "You've got a big mouth, but so far I haven't seen anything to back it up. What have you got to lose?"

"Nothing." Blue eyes flashed with anger. "You're on. It should be easy to beat an old guy like you."

"Old?"

Haley felt him tense and saw his outraged expression, which was hilarious. She couldn't stop the laughter that bubbled up. "Who knew that at twenty-five you were over the hill?"

"You're only a year behind me," he grumbled. "It won't be so funny three-hundred-and sixty-five days from now."

Probably not, she thought. But it wasn't often the legendary Marlon Cates looked like he did now, and she planned to enjoy the experience while it lasted.

Marlon couldn't wait to tell Haley that the "old guy" was victorious. He and Roy were at ROOTS, hanging out inside after unlocking the door with the key she'd given him. He grabbed two cold sodas from the refrigerator and handed one to the kid who was sitting on the old sofa, humbled and quiet.

"Gotta work on your jump shot, kid," he said.

"Whatever." The tone attempted defiance and failed miserably. He took the soda, popped the top, and downed at least half in one long drink.

Marlon did the same, then looked around. This place was taking shape. The mural was nearly finished—Haley had outdone herself. The wall depicted teens listening to music, playing video games, typing on the computer, reading books. She'd drawn a boy with braces on his teeth, a girl with a zit on her cheek, groups of kids talking.

In every scene, Haley had captured a reality and warmth that were emotionally true. They said writers had a "voice," and looking at her talented depiction of the teen world, it occurred to him that artists did too. He could see her sweetness, caring and sense of humor in every brush stroke on the wall.

The front door opened and in walked the artist herself, looking young enough to pass for one of the teenagers she was so passionate about helping. If she had makeup on, he couldn't tell. But that didn't make her any less beautiful. In fact, she was more lovely, more appealing than high-profile models and actresses all over L.A. and Hollywood because of her naturalness.

Her shiny brown hair was pulled into a ponytail and wisps of bangs teased her forehead. Her Hitching Post knit shirt, green this time, was tucked into a pair of jeans without any label, but the inexpensive denim hugged her hips and legs and made his fingers itch to cup her curves.

"Hey," she said, looking from him to the teen on the couch. The basketball was at his feet. "Well?"

Marlon grinned. "Old guys rule."

"You won?" She moved farther into the room, a shocked expression on her face.

"Don't sound so surprised."

"I'm surprised," Roy mumbled.

"I can't believe it," she said.

Roy leaned his elbows on skinny knees. "He got lucky."

Marlon happened to be looking into Haley's shining brown eyes and couldn't help thinking about a different kind of lucky. Then he pushed the thought away. She wasn't the type of girl a guy casually played around with, which made him a jerk for even thinking it. But he was also a guy and couldn't help wondering what it would be like to touch her....

"I'm very impressed," she said, then looked intently at Roy. "And have you held up your end of the bargain?"

"I was sort of hoping you'd let me scrub floors and toilets instead." There was a pleading expression in his eyes.

She shook her head. "Not a chance. Phone home."

"I'm not telling them where I am," he said stubbornly.

"No one says you have to. The deal was you let them know you're okay. Do you want to use my cell?"

"No. I don't want them tracking me."

Marlon leaned his forearms on the back of the recliner. "Unless they work for an elite law enforcement agency and are expecting your call, I don't think they can triangulate your position."

"Very funny," Roy said, but he was fighting a smile.

"I thought so."

"I'm waiting." Haley crossed her arms over her chest.

The teen huffed out a breath, then pulled out his phone and thumbed through his address book and hit dial. He waited and they could all hear when a woman answered.

"Ma? It's me. I'm fine. That's all I wanted to say." He rolled his eyes, then interrupted, "No. All you need to know is that I'm okay. Tell Dad whatever you want." Without another word he hung up. He finished his Coke, set the can on the coffee table, then grabbed the basketball and stood. "I'm going to shoot some hoops."

"You forgot something." Haley nodded at the empty can.

"There's a recycle container in the back room. Rule number one is pick up after yourself."

He rolled his eyes, huffed out another breath then grudgingly did as instructed. Then he walked to the front door and said, "Now can I go?"

"You need the practice," Marlon commented.

"Yes, you can go," Haley said.

Without another word, shrug, eye-rolling or huffing breath, Roy was gone.

Haley set her purse on the coffee table. "You didn't have to rub it in."

"Yeah, I really did."

"Because of the 'old guy' crack?" Her full lips curved up at the corners.

"Pretty much. Although, just between you and me, he

almost beat me. In the end, it was experience that gave me the edge. That, and a killer jump shot."

"So you won because you're old?" she asked.

"No. I'm experienced."

"And vain."

He thought about that. "Maybe. But did he have it coming? Oh, yeah. The kid needed to be taken down a peg or two. Humility is a building block of respect."

"What about his self-esteem?"

"What about mine?" he countered.

"You're an adult. You should be above that sort of thing."

"Call me shallow, but I felt the need to teach him a lesson. And, contrary to what most do-gooders—excluding yourself, of course—would have you believe, self-esteem isn't shaped by everyone telling you how wonderful you are. It's formed by putting in the work. You carn it by putting one foot in front of the other, day after day. Running away from your problems doesn't solve them. They just trot right along after you."

She tilted her head to the side as she studied him. The ends of her ponytail teased her shoulder and gave him more ideas a guy shouldn't have about a girl like her.

"What?" he asked warily.

"Is it possible I was wrong about you?"

That was unexpected. He shook his head. "I think there's a problem with my hearing."

"Why?"

"I could have sworn you said you were wrong about me."

"No." She fought a smile. "I said it was possible."

"Same thing." When she opened her mouth to protest, he held up a hand to stop her. "What is it you were wrong about?"

One of her eyebrows rose questioningly. "I never would have guessed that self-esteem was one of your issues."

"Humor me."

"Okay." She sighed. "Maybe I was wrong about a bad boy like you being able to relate to kids."

"Wow. And?"

"And what?"

"You questioned my role model qualifications," he reminded her.

"I was wrong. Seriously, Marlon, I understand now what you meant when you were talking about thinking outside the box. Roy never would have called his mom because I asked him to. You were right about understanding a guy's point of view. It never would have occurred to me to challenge him to one-on-one basketball, let alone be able to beat him. I'm sorry for misjudging you."

"Apology accepted."

"I'll go even further. Maybe—" she held up a finger in mock warning "—just maybe, you're a good man and actually as sincere as you seem."

When she smiled at him with genuine warmth and admiration, Marlon felt something shift and tighten in his chest. He'd vowed to get her respect. Mission accomplished. Having it felt even better and more satisfying than he'd expected. It was way past time to confess the real reason he was volunteering and assure her that he would do every last hour of his community service.

He straightened away from the chair and moved in front of her. "There's something I need to tell you—"

Music coming from her purse interrupted him. "My cell."

It took her a few seconds to rummage through her pocketbook before finding the phone. She flipped it open. "Hello. Hi, Linda. Sure, I can come in and help train the new girl. No problem. See you later." She hung up and looked at him. "Sorry. You were saying?"

"About why I wanted to give you a hand with this program—"

Just then the front door opened and a guy in postal service light blue shirt and gray-blue shorts walked in. "Hi, Haley."

"Hey, Bob. What's up?"

"I have something for you. Addressed to ROOTS."

She smiled. "My first mail here."

He handed her a packet. "It's from the Thunder Canyon Justice Center. The county clerk requires a signature."

"This makes me feel official," she said.

It made Marlon feel like crap. He had a pretty good idea what was inside. He watched her sign and hated that her first official mail for her pet project was about him and not in a good way.

When they were alone again, she ripped open the envelope before he could stop her.

"Haley, there's something I need to say—" But the words stuck in his throat when she looked up from the letter and the joy drained from her face, followed closely by the respect and admiration that had been there just moments ago.

"You had your license revoked for reckless driving," she accused.

"It wasn't exactly reckless. I was in complete control of my vehicle."

"And driving way over the speed limit."

"That's what I was trying to tell you," he said.

"So wanting to help the kids was a lie."

"Not exactly. I really do want to help them."

"Only so you can get your license reinstated. Not because you care." The warmth in her eyes was replaced by anger and disappointment.

He missed the warmth. "Yes, but—"

"But nothing. It's just like you said. You know all about trying to get away with stuff. Maybe you should try the truth for a change."

"Haley, you have to listen to me."

"No, I really don't." She shook her head and for a split second the sheen of tears glistened in her eyes. "My responsibility is to the teenagers who come here. I won't tolerate lies from them or anyone who's around them. You're fired, Marlon. Please leave."

He was a salesman and knew when to push and when to exit quietly. He chose the latter and walked out, closing the door behind him.

Losing an account had never felt as bad as this. He'd gone from hero to zero in a heartbeat. For one shining moment she'd admired how he handled the kid. He liked having her good opinion.

And he wanted it back.

He hadn't achieved success in the retail market by going quietly and he wouldn't do it now. Not because it was about community service.

Now it was personal.

Chapter Five

She'd fired Marlon, but Haley was the one who was hot. Even several hours later during her lunch shift at The Hitching Post, she was mad. He'd had her snowed for about thirty seconds before she found out he couldn't be trusted. That must be a world record and a definite warning not to buy into his charm. Clearly she'd been wrong—he hadn't changed at all.

"I'm so stupid," she mumbled, distractedly setting a hamburger and fries down in front of Ben Walters.

"Hey. Whoa."

She stopped. "Did you need something else?"

"Yeah." He pointed to the seat on the other side of the table across from him. "Sit."

She sat. She never said no to Ben Walters, and not just because there weren't any thanks big enough for his support after her mom died. He was a big bear of a man with a thick barrel chest, pale blue eyes that saw too much, and gray hair. A widower in his mid-fifties, he had a deep voice and no tolerance for attitude. He was also her friend and she loved him very much.

He came to The Hitching Post nearly every day for breakfast, lunch or dinner. Sometimes all three. And always sat in the same place. In fact, they called it "Ben's booth", the one with an unobstructed view of Lily Divine over the bar.

Was it only a couple hours ago that she'd sat close by with Marlon and Roy, fretting about the teen seeing the nearly naked picture?

Ben unscrewed the top from the ketchup bottle, turned it upside down and hit the side with his huge palm until his fries were barely visible through the mound of red. "Tell me what's bothering you."

"Nothing."

His gaze jumped to hers. "So you look mad enough to spit and call yourself names over nothing? I never knew you to tell fibs."

That stung. It put her in the same column as that fibbing Marlon Cates. "Okay, you're right. I'm ticked off at someone."

"Who?"

"Marlon Cates."

"Heard he was in town." Ben took a bite of his burger and held her gaze.

Haley hadn't planned to bore him with details, but they just came pouring out. "He claimed he wanted to help me with ROOTS."

"That's disturbing."

"I know. The thing is, I couldn't figure out why he would volunteer."

"Doesn't sound like him," Ben agreed.

"Turns out he got his third speeding ticket in a year and

his license was revoked. The judge gave him community service and he's doing it at ROOTS. But he neglected to tell me that so I fired him."

Ben's ruddy face grew redder. "That kid was always wild. I knew way back when that he was trouble."

"No kidding."

"Nothing he's done since high school has changed my mind." He picked up the napkin and wiped his mouth. "Although he seems to have a head for business. That company of his turned out pretty well. They say he's worth millions."

"That's what they say," she agreed.

"Who knew jeans and western type stuff were worth so much?" He shook his head. "Always said Marlon Cates had a sales personality and it wasn't necessarily a compliment."

"It's a good thing he's successful," she said. "He can afford to pay his speeding tickets."

Ben nodded and finished chewing. "Did you hear about the time a few years back that he and his twin, Matt, got engaged to twin girls?"

"Yeah." As much as Haley wanted to ignore Marlon Cates talk, in a small town stories spread like the flu. "I heard his parents put a stop to it in a nanosecond."

Ben grinned. "Scandal sticks to that boy like white on rice. Since Thunder Canyon resort opened, if he was around some Hollywood 'it' girl was always hot on his heels."

The reminder pricked a part of Haley that she thought was buried much deeper. "For sure his scandalous escapades border on urban legend here in Thunder Canyon."

"True enough," Ben said. "Good for you, booting his butt out of your place."

"In all fairness, he did help me with the heavy work.

I'm not sure how I'd have moved the fridge and furniture without him."

"He's got an angle—"

Linda Powell, the Hitching Post manager, stopped by the table. "Who are you bad-mouthing now, Ben Walters?"

"No one who doesn't deserve it," Ben said. His blue eyes twinkled at the dark-haired woman and she smiled back, a decidedly flirtatious expression in her green eyes.

Haley noticed the attractive, dark blond-haired young woman beside her boss. She'd seen her in here before, but they hadn't met yet. Clearly that was about to change.

"Haley," Linda said, "I'd like to introduce Erin Castro."

"Nice to meet you, Erin." Haley held out her hand and the other woman shook it.

There was something about her that Haley couldn't really define. It had nothing to do with looks, because Erin was really pretty. Her worn jeans and white T-shirt, if anything, were simple and did not draw attention to how beautiful she was, even with her long hair pulled back into a simple ponytail. But there was a needy expression in her blue eyes.

It was just a feeling but if anyone knew what needy felt like it was Haley. Kind-hearted people in this community had pulled her family through the worst time that anyone could imagine. She knew from experience that compassion was always appreciated.

Linda tucked a strand of shoulder-length hair behind her ear. "I just hired Erin to replace Shirley."

"Welcome to The Hitching Post family," Haley said. So this was the new girl she was going to help train. "Meet Ben Walters, my friend and one of our best customers."

"I like my burger medium well." His voice was friendly-gruff.

"Just write 'hockey puck' on the ticket and the cook will know who it's for," Linda teased.

"Thanks for the tip," Erin said.

"I haven't given you one yet." Ben studied her intently. "Gotta see how the service is first."

"Don't be mean, Ben," Linda said.

"Not mean. It's the God's honest truth."

"That's good," Erin said. "I'd rather have the truth than live with a lie."

Haley noticed a spark of intensity in the words, but chalked it up to nerves starting a new job. "Have you ever waitressed before, Erin?"

"I'm so grateful for this opportunity. Linda is taking a chance on me and I'll work hard not to let her down," she said, not really answering. "How long have you lived in Thunder Canyon, Haley?"

Haley noticed the one-hundred-eighty-degree turn away from herself, but didn't point it out. Instead she responded truthfully. "All my life. I grew up here."

"Wow, you must know everyone in town." Erin toyed with the end of her ponytail.

"I know a lot of people," Haley said.

"We were just talking about one of them when you walked up," Ben said. "That Marlon Cates is a piece of work."

"I haven't met him. Do you know him well?" Erin asked her, that edge of intensity slipping into her tone again.

If kissing him meant she knew him well, Haley did. But that wasn't something she was willing to share with her friends, let alone a stranger. "He was a year ahead of me in high school."

"Stay away from that one," Ben warned.

"Why?" Erin asked.

"He's not so bad," Linda chimed in. "Just a high-energy person."

"You call it high energy," Ben said frowning. "I call it bad news."

"Why?" Erin asked.

Haley didn't miss the girl's acute interest in Marlon and wondered about it, trying to ignore the sting of unwanted jealousy.

Another good reason for firing Marlon. He brought out the worst in her.

"It doesn't matter," Haley said. "He lives in Los Angeles and isn't staying in town long."

"I didn't mean to interrupt your lunch, Ben." Linda smiled. "Just wanted you both to meet the new girl."

"I look forward to working with you," Haley said honestly.

"Same here. Nice to meet you both."

As they walked away, Haley studied the newcomer's trim back and slender figure. She sure asked a lot of questions, but maybe it was an attempt at female bonding. Finding common ground for friendship.

The suspicious thoughts made her feel just the slightest bit hypocritical. After all, talk was the foundation of friendship. Talk was a way to communicate feelings. Haley had encouraged Roy to talk about what he was going through in an attempt to help.

Funny thing about talk. She'd just unburdened herself and didn't feel the least bit better for it. She was still bummed about firing her charming volunteer. She'd enjoyed spending time with him in spite of herself. But a lie of omission was still a lie.

The truth was that Marlon Cates hadn't changed at all. Ben was right about him being trouble. He was capable of breaking her heart without breaking his stride. Firing him was for the best. Her best.

Because she was starting to look forward to seeing him every day. And that wouldn't do her any good at all.

After a restless night dreaming about kissing Marlon, Haley drove into town with Roy. She had to work the breakfast shift at The Hitching Post, but couldn't order the teen to sit at a back table with some crayons and a coloring book to keep him out of trouble. As he pointedly said, he wasn't a baby and she wasn't his mother. She couldn't tell him what to do. After that he'd left and she hoped he was staying out of trouble.

There was a cockiness to Roy that reminded her of Marlon Cates, and she didn't mean that in a good way.

Apparently she had a weakness for bad boy charmers of all ages.

After her shift ended, she left her truck parked at work and walked over to ROOTS. The basics were there—TV, fridge, furniture. She'd hoped to have more on the walls, give the place a personality, but that would come eventually. School opening was still a few weeks away and a bad economy meant fewer jobs and more kids with time on their hands who needed a hangout.

She'd made some phone calls to Tori Jones and Allaire Traub, English and art teachers respectively at Thunder Canyon High School, and asked them to spread the word that ROOTS was open. Haley planned to spend every minute that she wasn't working or taking her own part-time college classes at her new venture.

Key in hand, she prepared to open the door, but then she looked in the window and saw a group of kids inside. But how did they get in? No one was supposed to be here without adult supervision.

Haley walked inside, struggling for calm. "Hi."

A chorus of four voices answered "hi" back. Roy was sitting on the sofa with Kim Wallace, a sixteen-year-old blue-eyed blonde. On the loveseat, C. J. McFarlane was rubbing shoulders with his best friend Jerilyn Doolin. Both of them were fifteen. He was a good-looking boy with auburn hair forever in need of a trim. A slender girl with dark hair and eyes, Jerilyn was dealing with her widower dad's drinking problem. The two kids hung out together and they made a cute couple. But she didn't want them to be a couple here at ROOTS without supervision.

"So, I see you've all met Roy," she said as casually as possible. She stared at the runaway and asked, "You didn't break in again, did you?"

"Nah. Marlon let us in."

Haley followed his look to the TV stand in the corner where the man in question had his broad back to the room and was dealing with what looked like a video game.

Marlon glanced over his shoulder. "Hi. I still have the key you gave me yesterday."

She'd completely forgotten. "I see."

He stood and walked over to stand beside her in front of the teenagers. "I ran into Roy this morning and we decided to come over here. Shoot some hoops. Watch TV. Hang out."

Would she have worried about the kid more or less if she'd known he was with Marlon? She would never know.

"Then C.J. and Jerilyn stopped by and he hooked us up," Roy said.

"And I was just walking by and saw them inside," Kim volunteered. "I needed to get out of the house."

"Why is that?" Marlon asked.

She tossed a long strand of blond hair over her shoulder. "My parents. They're fighting."

Haley's heart went out to the girl. "I'm sorry to hear that."

Kim squirmed on the sofa. "They're getting a divorce."

"Didn't I hear that your parents divorced, C.J.?" Marlon folded his arms over his wide chest as he looked down at the teens.

C.J. nodded. "It was hard."

Kim looked at him. "Did you get the 'we both love you but fell out of love with each other' speech?"

"Something like that," he agreed.

"I think the divorce manual has a chapter on how to talk to the kids." Kim looked sad and angry in equal parts. "If love has a short shelf life, why should I believe they won't decide not to love me?"

"A parent's relationship with a child is different than with each other," Marlon said. "It's unconditional."

"He's right," C.J. confirmed. "For a while my mom and dad were fighting over me. My mom sued him for full custody and was going to make me go to boarding school in Switzerland."

"Cool," Roy commented.

"That stinks," Kim and Jerilyn said together.

Haley remembered agreeing with Marlon about girls and boys thinking differently, and she'd just seen proof.

"What happened?" Marlon asked the teen.

"Mom's fiancé is all about family and made her see it wasn't a good idea to come between me and my dad, and they finally came together on what was best for me. I like it here in Thunder Canyon. Dad and Tori are getting married, which is cool." He shrugged. "It all worked out."

Kim didn't look convinced. "I can't see my mom coming

around. She's driving me nuts. Has to know where I am every second. Calls my cell phone all the time. There are so many rules I can't even remember them all, let alone not break them."

"It's her way of trying to control an uncontrollable situation." Marlon sat on the sofa beside her. "If she didn't love you, there wouldn't be any rules."

"Oh, please," Kim scoffed.

"Seriously. Think about it. If you break a rule, does she come down on you?"

"Like a manufactured home in a tornado," the girl confirmed. "I can't even remember how long I'm grounded for."

"I'm willing to bet your mom knows and will follow up. And don't you think it would be a lot easier for her to just let you do whatever you want? Less work for her." He met her gaze. "That's what love is."

"I never thought about it like that," Kim admitted.

"A different perspective can be good." He stood and walked back over to the TV.

Who was this insightful man and what had he done with the real Marlon Cates? Haley wondered. It was all she could do not to let her mouth drop open. This was the first time she'd actually hung out with him. She'd seen him flirt and pick up women at the Hitching Post and judged him harshly. He wasn't the one-dimensional man she'd thought.

Haley looked at the kids. "There are sodas in the fridge if anyone is thirsty."

"Cool," C.J. said.

They all mumbled agreement and went into the back room to check out the drink situation. Haley walked over to Marlon. "Could I have a word?"

"Of course. It's your place."

"That's right." When she was this close to him it was hard to think straight, let alone come up with words. "This is my place and I fired you yesterday."

He frowned thoughtfully. "Can you actually dismiss someone who's a volunteer?"

"Yes."

"But there's no salary involved. So there's nothing to keep me from just showing up." One corner of his mouth lifted and there was a twinkle in his brown eyes that made it awfully difficult to maintain the proper level of mad. "I really don't think you can terminate the services of a volunteer."

"Watch me."

"You're going to throw me out?" He looked down at her, drawing attention to the fact that he was bigger and stronger.

"Not personally," Haley said. "But I've got friends in town who can do it."

"So you're going to call in reinforcements?"

"If I have to," she confirmed.

"Even though I've got the legal system on my side?"

"Way to spin the bad stuff," she said. "Technically they're not on your side. It's community service and law abiding citizens don't get sentenced to it. You're bending the perception."

No surprise there. He excelled in bending perceptions along with rules.

"Look, Haley, I don't want to argue with you."

"Since when?"

And didn't that sound childish? She was a grown woman, but he made her feel like an insecure teenage girl. Her stomach fluttered, her legs barely held her up, and her palms were sweaty. It happened every time she was close to him and she didn't know what to do about that. So tossing him out seemed like a good idea and she was prepared to go to the mat on it.

"You've been arguing with me since you came back to town. And doing it under false pretenses," she added.

"I was trying to tell you about the community service."

"Only because you knew I'd find out sooner or later," she accused.

"You're right."

"And because—" She blinked when his words sank in. "I am?"

He nodded. "I saw what you're doing here and it's a good thing. You're a good person. I didn't want you to think less of me." He pointed at her in warning. "And don't say that's not possible."

Her lips twitched as she suppressed a smile. "Okay."

"Now you know the truth. I'm here until I complete my service and get my license back. That should be the end of August. Basically I'm running MC/TC long distance by phone, fax and computer. Your free time is stretched to the limit. Mine is flexible. And there needs to be supervision for this place to be open."

"Adult supervision," she clarified.

"I guess speeding tickets cast some doubt, but I am of age." His expression turned wry. "Roy thinks I'm old."

"And you did convince him to hang out here," she said grudgingly. "I suppose that's better than being at loose ends on the street and getting into trouble."

"See? I've already earned my keep." He slid an arm across her shoulders and pulled her against him. "Come on, Haley. We can help each other."

"Well," she said, thinking out loud. "That would mean ROOTS hours could be expanded during the last days of summer before school starts in September."

"See?" He hugged her closer. "You need me."

He was right. But she would never admit that in a million years, let alone say it out loud. "It's community service, Marlon. I'm doing you a favor."

"So that's a yes?"

"It is."

And she wasn't sure whether it was his logical debate or the feel of his warm, strong body next to hers that had tipped the scales in his favor. She really could not think straight when she was close to him. But she'd agreed and wouldn't take it back.

That didn't mean she had to like it—or him.

So she had to assume that liking wasn't necessarily a prerequisite for attraction. Because if her hammering heart was anything to go by, she was more attracted to Marlon than ever. And she'd just said he could hang out here at ROOTS.

She'd be okay as long as he didn't kiss her.

Chapter Six

Marlon knew that anyone who wanted action on Friday night in Thunder Canyon could find it at The Hitching Post. This Friday was no exception and, while not really wanting action, it was more of a distraction. He was hanging out with three of his high school football buddies. Steady Eddie Stevens, Jimmy "Evil E" Evanson and Big Mike "Tuck" Tucker. They were in a corner at one of the bistro-style high tables and chairs, the best place to see the whole room. In the past he'd found that advantageous for scoping out women. But tonight there was only one woman he was looking for.

Haley.

He saw her weave between tables, taking orders and delivering drinks and food. She was both graceful and gorgeous. It ticked him off that she was the only one he wanted to look at.

He dragged his gaze away from her and glanced around

the table at his friends. "So let's catch up. What's going on with you guys?"

"I'm getting ready to expand my business." Eddie used to be a wide receiver in high school—tall, wiry and fast. The dark-haired, blue-eyed athlete-turned-rancher had always been surrounded by girls. "I'll be taking in guests nine months of the year. In the summer it'll be a kids' camp."

"You're starting a dude ranch?" Marlon asked.

"It's still a working ranch," Eddie protested.

"And more," redheaded Jimmy said. He'd played on special teams. "The kids coming to the camp have been through some kind of trauma. It's going to be a special program."

"Sounds impressive."

"I'll still do what I do." Eddie shrugged. "Raise horses. But in this economy diversification is the best way to stay afloat."

"Can't argue with that." Marlon took a sip of his beer. A camp for traumatized kids was a good thing; Haley would approve. In fact, the two of them were probably made for each other, but that thought made him want to put his fist through a wall. "Sounds like a chick-magnet scenario."

"No way." Eddie's voice was emphatic. "Been there, done that. Sworn off for good. I'll never understand women and it's my experience that putting in the energy trying isn't worth the kick in the teeth you get out of it."

Marlon's eyebrows rose and he looked at the other two who appeared as clueless as himself. "Want to talk about it?"

"I'd rather chew off my arm."

"Okay, then. Moving on." He looked at Mike. The guy was built like a mountain, big and beefy with sandy brown hair and gray eyes. He'd been a defensive end when they played football and rarely did anyone get by him. "What about you?"

"Still with Cates Construction," he said wryly. "I'm working on the McFarlane place. Your dad's a good boss and when Matt takes over I don't expect anything will change."

Marlon made a mental note to talk to his twin about that. He figured his brother already knew he was expected to eventually run the business, but would check it out. "Anyone special in your life?"

"Stella Dunlay."

"The cheerleader?" Marlon asked.

"Yeah. We're each other's rebound relationship." He shrugged, slightly uncomfortable talking about the personal. "We're having fun. Nothing serious."

"Way to keep it light," Marlon agreed. Two down, one to go. He raised an eyebrow at Jimmy.

He was tall, muscular, good-natured and funny. All attributes that kept him from getting picked on because of his red hair. Now he taught science and math at Thunder Canyon High and coached the football team. "This is probably as good a time as any to announce that I'm getting married. Penny Carlson."

The other two guys looked as surprised as Marlon felt. But they regrouped, slapped him on the back, clinked their beer mugs in congratulations and drank to the good news.

"When?" Marlon asked.

"Soon. She's pregnant," he added. "I was going to ask her to marry me anyway, but the unexpected news sort of speeded up the timetable. We're happy about it."

He looked it, Marlon thought. So they slapped him on the back again, clinked glasses and congratulated him on more good news.

"You, with a wife and kid. I can't believe it," Marlon said.

Jimmy shrugged. "It's easy. I love her."

If the place wasn't dark, Marlon knew his friend's face would be as red as his hair. He couldn't ever remember talking about feelings with these guys. It was always babes, boobs and butts. Those were great memories, but he didn't miss the old days. They'd all grown up. And Jimmy was going to be a husband and father… Marlon felt a stab of envy and figured Roy was right about him being old.

Just then he spotted Haley across the room, balancing a tray with a pitcher of beer and four mugs. She smiled and charmingly set it all down for four guys he didn't know. Then one of them slid an arm around her waist and she smiled, making Marlon want to put his fist through a wall again. If he didn't get over whatever this was, he'd be generating a lot of drywall repair business for Cates Construction.

"Earth to Marlon."

He looked at Mike. "Did you say something?"

"Yeah." The big guy followed his look and nodded knowingly. "So what's up with you?"

"Same old, same old."

"If that were true," Jimmy said, "the women of Thunder Canyon would be looking at the dust your car kicked up on the way out of town. Yet here you sit. Don't take this the wrong way, but why are you still here?"

"He's right." Eddie drained the last of the beer in his glass. "What's up with you?"

"Everything okay with your family?" Jimmy asked. Mr. Sensitive.

"Yeah. They're all good."

"Then I don't get it. Especially the part where you're working at Haley Anderson's teen program," Mike said.

You had to love small towns. Of course news of him at

ROOTS would spread. Haley knew the worst so there was no point in blowing off his friends.

"Okay. You got me. Here's the short version. One too many speeding tickets got my license revoked and a month of community service. I'm doing it at ROOTS and when it's over at the end of August, I get my license back."

"And you're outta here." Jimmy wasn't asking.

"Yeah. I'm gone."

The declaration had him searching the crowded place for Haley. She was leaning over the bar talking to the bartender. With her brown, silky hair swept up in a ponytail, she didn't look old enough to drink liquor, let alone serve it. Her full mouth curved into a dazzling smile that he wished was for him, and his palms itched to cup her hips and pull her against him. But that wasn't likely to happen since she had no respect for him and thought commitment wasn't his strength.

He looked at his friends. "Yeah, I'll be outta here."

"Then we need to have another round while we can." Eddie held up a hand to get Haley's attention.

Seconds later she zigzagged through the maze of tables and stood beside Marlon, but looked at his friends. "What can I get you guys?"

"Another pitcher of beer," Mike said.

"Coming right up."

Marlon recognized the sweet fragrance of her skin, floating over the smell of burgers, fries and beer that permeated the place. It was like she had a special frequency just for him that teased his hormones. She wasn't more than an inch away and he could feel the heat of her body. Normally he looked down at her but the height of the table and chairs put them close, so close he would hardly need to move to touch his mouth to hers.

"This is like déjà vu all over again," Mike said.

"What the heck are you talking about?" Jimmy just asked what they were all thinking.

"It's like high school." The big guy grinned as if that explained it clearly.

Haley frowned. "I can't speak for anyone else, but I didn't drink beer in high school."

Of course she didn't, Marlon thought. She didn't break the rules. He found that incredibly appealing, especially when he remembered kissing her and the eager way she'd responded.

"You guys are missing the point," Mike complained.

"Because you haven't made one yet," the guys said together.

"Okay. I'll spell it out," the big guy said patiently. "Marlon, seeing you and Haley together reminds me of that high school football fundraiser. Remember?"

Jimmy snapped his fingers. "Yeah. It's the annual carnival. We had it last month. The kissing booth. It's still a big draw."

"Right," Eddie agreed. "I remember now. Haley was there taking tickets and Marlon kissed her. No one was ever sure quite how it happened, but we all said the two of you should get a room."

"That's right," Marlon said, pretending he just recalled the incident instead of thinking about it just minutes ago.

That was six years ago. He'd come home for the summer after his first year of college. The carnival was a big deal and he'd gone to support his former team. He'd thought Haley had volunteered to be the kissee. He'd handed her his ticket, pulled her close and kissed her until everything around them had disappeared.

He could still hear the breathless little moany noises she made and could still see the dazed expression on her face when they came up for air. Now all he saw in her expression was confusion with a little panic around the edges.

"I don't remember that," she said.

His friends hooted at him and Mike grinned. "So the Marlon magic isn't as all powerful as we were led to believe."

"Seriously?" Marlon shifted away and studied her. "You don't recall that carnival?"

"Sure I do. It happens every year. But kissing you?" She shrugged. "Not so much."

"Ouch, buddy." Eddie's expression was dripping with pity.

"Not that it hasn't been fun walking down memory lane," she said looking around the table. "But I'll go get that pitcher now."

After she was gone, his friends hooted, hollered and continued to razz him about losing his touch with the ladies. The taunting wasn't what made him follow her. It was the fact that Miss-Play-By-The-Rules was lying through her beautiful, straight, white teeth.

At the bar, he reached out and took the circular tray away from her and set it down. When she started to protest, he grabbed her hand and tugged gently. "Come with me."

"I have stuff to do here," she protested.

"Take a break."

He took her out the back door to the parking lot filled with cars. "What the heck are you pulling?"

She yanked her hand away, then folded her arms over her chest. "I have no idea what you're talking about."

"You don't remember kissing me?"

"No." Her chin lifted just a little higher but her gaze shifted off to the left.

"I don't believe you."

"Really? Why do you care that I don't remember? You're more into dating volume than substance. Once a heart-breaker, always a heartbreaker."

He ignored the dig and pointed at her. "I think you remember that kiss but you don't want to."

She made a scoffing sound. "Your ego is getting bigger by the second."

"So is your nose. You're lying, Haley. More to yourself than to me. You don't want to admit that there's something simmering between us."

"In your dreams," she denied.

He tapped her on the nose. "It's growing with every lie."

"I'm telling the truth," she protested.

"For someone who puts so much energy into sincerity, you've got a double standard going on."

"Oh, please. I've got work to do." She turned away and disappeared inside.

Marlon stared after her for a long time, then grinned. Her intense reaction all but confirmed his suspicions. If she didn't care about him, teasing would have been the go-to response. But it hadn't. She'd denied everything, then headed for high ground. Because she liked him.

That made him want to kiss her again, kiss her so thor-oughly that if anyone saw the two of them locking lips they'd suggest getting a room. What would Miss-Play-By-The-Rules do if they did?

He wanted an answer to that question more every day.

The next day Haley still couldn't forget her conversa-tion with Marlon the night before. She stacked dirty lunch dishes in a big, plastic rectangular container and took them into the back where Jeff, the teen Linda had hired for the summer, was waiting to load them into the industrial-sized washer. It kept her hands busy, but her mind kept going back to Marlon calling her a liar. Maybe starting ROOTS would cancel out the sin.

For every kid who found a job, there were a whole lot more with too much time on their hands and money worries on their minds. At least during these few weeks before school started and the teens would have homework, sports and activities to keep them busy, she'd managed to get ROOTS up and running.

And Marlon Cates had made that possible. MC—major crush. Still? She didn't want to believe it, but there was very little evidence to the contrary. Even worse, Marlon had noticed.

Walking from the kitchen back through the restaurant, she saw a familiar face. Carleigh Benedict from Thunder Canyon Social Services was sitting alone in a booth, holding her phone and probably looking at messages. Haley liked to think her tight-knit community was immune to the problems that were rampant in big cities, but that wasn't the case. Women and children were still abused and abandoned. Carleigh was far too busy and her time advising Haley about the youth center had been very much appreciated.

Haley stopped at the end of the table. "Hi, there."

The woman looked up and smiled. "Haley. I was hoping to see you. Are you busy?"

She shook her head. "Just finished my shift. Can I get you anything?"

"Someone just took my order. I don't remember seeing her here before."

"She's new. Her name is Erin Castro."

"Very pretty," Carleigh commented.

And the new girl wasn't the only pretty one. Carleigh Benedict was a green-eyed blonde—sweet, smart and stunning. Everything Haley wasn't, but she liked the social worker anyway.

"Would you join me? I hate eating alone."

Haley was anxious to get to ROOTS, but Marlon was there to supervise the kids who'd stopped in. "Sure. I've got time for my favorite mentor. How ungrateful would I be to let you sit here by yourself?"

She slid onto the bench seat just as Erin delivered a Cobb salad, bleu cheese dressing on the side.

"Can I get you anything else?" Erin smiled automatically.

"Nothing, thanks," Carleigh answered.

"Okay, then." She looked at Haley. "My shift is over. See you tomorrow?"

"I'll be here." Haley watched the other woman walk away. What *was* her story? So far she'd been long on questions and short on personal details.

Carleigh dipped her fork into the dressing then speared some lettuce and egg. "So, I just came from ROOTS. It's really shaping up."

The social worker had been incredibly generous with her suggestions for dealing with the kids and setting down reasonable rules. She'd shared information on behaviors that were within normal teenage parameters, which ones to watch and when to get involved. Haley wished she'd had Carleigh when her brother was acting out after their mom died.

Haley smiled across the table. "It all came together really fast." Thanks to Marlon. Just thinking his name made her heart skip a beat and she tried to ignore it.

"The mural is terrific. Who did you get to do it?"

"Me."

Carleigh's eyes opened wide in surprise. When she finished chewing, she said, "You're pulling my leg. I had no idea you were so talented."

Haley shrugged off the compliment. "I've been taking art classes at the junior college."

"It shows." The other woman's gaze was intense and perceptive. "You really should think about a career in that field."

"I have thought about it."

"And?"

"It will never be more than a hobby." That didn't stop her from thinking about it, though. "Creative endeavors are time-intensive without guarantee of any reward. I've got bills to pay and family to take care of."

Carleigh nodded. "I understand. But you're really good. Not that I'm an expert. But I know what I like."

"Thanks." *Now let's change the subject,* Haley thought.

"I met some of the kids while I was there," her friend said.

"Don't tell me. Roy. Kim. Jerilyn and C.J." The four had come in every day since that first time and seemed to enjoy hanging out.

"Yeah. Along with a few others. Seth. Ilene. Eric and Danielle."

"Word is spreading. They're checking out the new place. Boredom must be setting in after all these weeks of summer."

"Then your timing in getting it open is perfect. Imagine what they'd be doing if there was no ROOTS." Carleigh set her fork down for a moment. "I met Marlon Cates, too."

Just hearing his name made Haley's chest feel funny and she shifted to ease it. "Without him, the place couldn't be open until I got off work. It gives the kids more time to hang out with supervision."

"He told me about his community service."

Haley looked up quickly, hoping that wouldn't be a problem for her fledgling project. "He's just temporary. He won't be around long enough to have a negative effect on the kids."

"I'm not second-guessing your decision."

Haley wished she could say the same. Every time she saw him her heart beat too fast and she could barely breathe. That wasn't a neutral reaction when neutral was how she so desperately wanted to feel.

"No?" she asked.

Carleigh shook her head. "When I was there he was explaining to Seth why he was ordered by the court to do community service. He broke the rules and got caught. It's good for the kids to see someone taking their punishment like a man."

Man being the operative word. Broad shoulders, wide chest, strong arms, a face to make women sigh with longing. He was a man all right.

"I'm glad you think it's okay for him to be there."

"I definitely do." The other woman smiled. "We all make mistakes. No one is perfect. That doesn't mean you can't be successful. Part of flourishing is being able to admit when you're wrong and take responsibility for your actions."

Haley blinked. "So you're saying he broke the law and is a good role model anyway?"

"I wouldn't exactly put those two thoughts together back to back without qualifying them," Carleigh explained. "But yes. If a mega-successful businessman like Marlon Cates isn't above answering to the law, what chance do teenagers have against it? He's rich, powerful and doing his time. It sends a very strong positive message. It's a good lesson for the kids."

Not just the kids, Haley thought. Marlon had tried to tell her he could give the teens a different point of view, but she hadn't really bought into it. Not until she'd seen him with Roy and the other kids. The truth was, she'd been looking for excuses to push him away in order to keep him from hurting her again. In the end, getting ROOTS open had to take priority over her feelings.

"He's been a big help," she admitted.

"Another plus is that he's not hard on the eyes." An appreciative smile curved up the corners of Carleigh's mouth.

Haley wasn't surprised when once again she felt a twinge of jealousy in her chest.

"I didn't notice," she lied.

"You're kidding, right?"

Haley's cheeks heated when she realized it was the second time in the last couple of days that she'd been caught. Marlon had seen through her when she'd claimed not to remember kissing him. In her mind, she could still picture that moment when their lips touched. It hadn't been her only kiss, but nothing else had even come close to the way Marlon had made her heart race and her body hum. And she had thought far too much about doing it again.

He'd said she wouldn't admit that there was something simmering between them, and he was right about that. She refused to let it be true. Even if it were, there was no point in admitting as much. It would just make everything harder when he was gone.

Now Carleigh accused her of not telling the truth. Was it still a lie if the person it was directed at didn't believe you?

"Okay. You're right. I have noticed. He's pretty cute."

"But?" Carleigh frowned.

"What makes you think there's a 'but'?"

"I can tell by the look on your face. What's wrong, Haley?"

"I like him."

Carleigh toyed with her paper napkin and started to shred it. "And that's bad...why?"

"Because it's not good," she hedged.

"Again I ask...why?"

"He's not staying. And even if he were, he's experienced with women."

"So?"

"I'm not. Experienced with men, I mean." She met the other woman's gaze and the words came tumbling out. "I was too busy studying in high school to date. Then I went away to college and met a guy. We were heading in *that* direction—"

"You mean sex?"

"Yeah." Again heat flared in her cheeks. "My mom always said I should wait, make sure I loved the person before taking the step."

"And did you?"

She shook her head. "I never had the chance. My mom was killed in the car accident and I came home to take care of Angie and Austin. That was the end of my college experience."

Carleigh knew her story, but the expression on her face was sympathetic. "And sex?"

Haley couldn't answer, just stared across the table, feeling the warmth of embarrassment creep up her neck.

"You've never had sex?" Carleigh asked, struggling unsuccessfully to act as if that didn't make Haley a mutant in this day and age.

"The technical term is virgin." She shrugged. "I've been raising my siblings and working. There's been no time, energy, or even a guy who interested me."

"Until now?" Carleigh's eyebrow rose questioningly.

Haley nodded miserably. "My lack of worldliness never bothered me before. But what if things between Marlon and me go *there?* What if he laughed at me?"

Carleigh was making a pile of white confetti with her napkin as she thought about what to say. "Can we agree that I'm a pretty good judge of character?"

Haley knew her friend saw all kinds of people and sized them up quickly and accurately. "Yes."

"Okay. I observed your Marlon interacting with those teenagers and did not see a man who would hurt a woman's feelings by laughing at her. He appeared to be sensitive, smart and insightful."

"Okay."

She looked at the watch on her wrist and sighed. "I've got to run. But let me leave you with this thought. Life is not a spectator sport."

True enough, thought Haley. But if one just observed there was little danger of getting beaned by a fastball. Status quo didn't rip your heart out or turn your life upside down. She knew how that felt and was determined to stay in status quo territory.

Marlon was right about her being the queen of denial, but that was okay with her, because he wasn't now and never would be *her* Marlon.

Chapter Seven

Marlon paced the length of his room above The Hitching Post for the umpteenth time. Fridays in Thunder Canyon were fun, but Monday night the place was dull as dirt. TV wasn't his thing and nine-thirty was too early to turn in. He knew the devil had a seat in hell with his name on it when thoughts of going to bed made him picture Haley lying by his side.

He walked to the window and lifted aside the lace covering for a better view of Main Street and ROOTS. Light from inside the teen center spilled onto the wooden walkway in front, which meant someone was there. It had to be her.

He'd only seen Haley for a few minutes earlier that day. She'd dropped into ROOTS a couple of times to check on things. Then she'd relieved him of duty after her shift at the bar and grill ended. Clearly she hadn't wanted to chat. The last time they had, he'd accused her of lying. He'd bet everything he owned that she remembered kissing him. And bringing it up with her earlier had been tempting, but with kids wandering in and out it wasn't appropriate.

Maybe she was alone now.

The thought was too tempting to resist. He left his room and went down the rear stairs, taking his usual back route to Main Street. There weren't a whole lot of folks around, but he didn't want to chance running across someone who felt like chatting him up. He wasn't in the mood for idle conversation. Only one brown-eyed girl was on his mind and he was pumped for a chat with her.

The dull thud of his boots sounded on the wooden sidewalk outside the teen center. He was right about her being here. Through the window Marlon could see her sitting on the sofa, with pencil in hand and a pad of paper on her lap. No one else was with her.

She was sketching something and looked especially cute and far too appealing with her forehead furrowed in concentration. One foot was tucked up underneath her and she'd caught her bottom lip between her teeth.

He'd like to bite her bottom lip. Not hard. Just a nip, something to show her that thoughts of her mouth had cost him a decent night's sleep ever since that first day he'd seen her here working on the mural. He pushed open the door and decided leading with that particular revelation would *not* be the best way to go.

She looked up. "Marlon. What are you doing here?"

"I could ask you the same thing."

"This place is my project. What's your excuse?"

His punishment, he wanted to say. But he wasn't talking about legal obligations. Thoughts of her tortured him pretty much all the time.

He moved farther into the room, just on the other side

of the coffee table. "I saw your light on. Isn't it kind of late?"

"Kids have been in and out all day. Because they're still on summer break it hasn't been quiet." She shrugged. "I'm keeping the place open until ten. Just in case someone wants to come by and talk."

As it happened, someone did want to talk, although he probably wasn't on her approved list. But it occurred to him, and not for the first time, how selfless her dedication was to this project. She was giving up a lot of precious personal time for the benefit of teens who didn't have much of a clue how hard she was working to make this happen.

"What?" she asked, eyes narrowing on him.

"Nothing." He sat down beside her. "I was just thinking."

"About?"

"Do the kids have any idea how much time, effort and sacrifice you've put in to make this place a reality for them?"

"Is that a rhetorical question?"

"Not really," he said.

"Too bad, because I really don't have an answer for you."

"Why do you do that?"

She looked up from her sketching. "What?"

"Make light of your efforts. This has been a time-consuming venture, and I'm sure it was frustrating at times. But you didn't give up and now ROOTS is a reality." He met her gaze. "You're a giver and I'm guessing it's not because you expect to get anything out of it. Most people would rather be home with their feet up."

"Wait a second." She tilted her head to look at him and the end of her ponytail brushed her slender shoulder.

"Number one, don't make me out to be something I'm not. I get something out of this."

"What?"

"The satisfaction of giving back to the community."

He nodded. "If that was number one, there must be a number two. Care to share?"

"Right now all I'm doing is sitting here. It's exactly what I'd be doing at home. No big deal."

He leaned over to get a look. "What are you sitting here doing?"

"Sketching." Quickly she flipped the cover over her work. "Just doodling really."

"Looked like more than that to me." He reached out a hand to take the pad, but she hopped up and backed away.

"It's nothing."

"I'd like to see it." He stood and moved toward her.

"You don't have to be polite."

"I'm not. Trust me. It's genuine interest."

"Like I believe that. This is you we're talking about." But she put the sketch pad behind her back.

Marlon stared at her. "If I weren't so secure and self-confident, that dig might have hurt my feelings. But I'm pretty sure you're trying to pick a fight in an effort to distract me."

He moved closer until they were practically touching. Her eyes widened and the pulse in her neck fluttered wildly. While he had her where he wanted her, he reached around her and tried to snag the notebook.

They wrestled for several moments, her small firm breasts brushing against his chest. Now that almost distracted him but he persevered. In the end, it wasn't his superior strength that finally won out. He had his arms around her and they were both breathing hard. Her lips parted and her chest was rising and falling rapidly. It was either kiss her or take advantage of her guard being down.

The latter seemed a wiser choice and he easily grabbed the sketch pad from her limp fingers.

"Hey," she said. "That was cheating."

"Define cheating." When she didn't, he continued. "I simply saw an opportunity and made my move."

But not the one he'd wanted most. And when she pressed her full lips together, he was pretty sure she felt the frustration, too. But he'd missed his chance with her after kissing her six years ago. He needed to let the whole thing go. Leaving town right now wasn't an option and when he finally did, he didn't want any regrets. While he was stuck, he couldn't make a move on her.

He turned around and started flipping through her notebook. She made several attempts to take back her work but he was taller and quicker, evading every grab. As he turned the pages and saw her sketches, something buzzed in his businessman's brain. The drawings were of jeans, shirts, jackets, scarves, and handbags. She didn't just use charcoal pencil, but colored ones as well. The purses especially caught his eye.

The designs had fringe, buckles, snaps and zippers. Inside, the lining was done in plaids, polka dots, and different patterns. Some had snowflakes. Horses. Saddles.

He looked at her. "These are really good, Haley."

"You're just saying that to make up for being a jerk."

"I'm not that nice."

"No kidding." Her look was wry.

"Seriously." He looked down at the sketches. "You're very talented."

"Now you're starting to scare me."

"Whatever your opinion is of me personally, I probably deserve," he said. "But when it comes to business success,

I've earned that, too. I didn't take MC/TC to where it is by being an idiot. Or being nice. The fact is that I know talent when I see it. And these are very good ideas."

"Thanks." She blinked up at him. "So the company is doing well?"

"As well as can be expected in this economy. Well enough that I've had buyout offers and I'm considering them."

"You'd sell it?"

"I'm weighing the pros and cons."

"But you started it all by marketing your merchandise at D.J.'s Rib Shack at the resort," she reminded him. "I thought MC stood for Marlon Cates and TC is Thunder Canyon."

"It is," he admitted.

"Your company has local roots. I think that's worth holding on to."

A whole lot of heart was shining in her eyes and he couldn't say what he wanted to. Business was all about the bottom line. Sentiment didn't make a company worth fighting for. But as he studied her drawings his mind was going a mile a minute.

"MC/TC could use fresh and innovative products to give it new life and jump start sales. Your designs could do that." He didn't realize he'd said that out loud until she responded.

"That would be exciting."

His mind was still racing when he said, "Let me take you to dinner. We'll discuss the opportunity."

"I don't know." She slid her fingertips into the pockets of her worn jeans. "Who will be here at ROOTS?"

"You have to eat. Closing the door for an hour won't make a difference, will it?"

He wanted to take her out to dinner and business was

probably the last reason on his list. This definitely went under the personal column. Sales were his thing and now he was selling himself.

"Maybe Austin would hang out here while you have a night off," he suggested.

"I hate to ask. He works hard at the resort and—"

"And you don't? Work hard, I mean." He handed back her notebook. "Isn't he the one who inspired this place? The one who saw the error of his ways because of community involvement? The one who's a college graduate because of it?"

"Yes, but—"

"If you don't ask him, I will. You're getting a night off and I'm not taking no for an answer."

She didn't look happy, but there was surrender in her eyes. "I'll work it out."

"Good. Tomorrow night. Seven o'clock."

"Okay."

Marlon nodded and walked out without another word. Never jeopardize the deal by talking too much after you got what you wanted. But grinning was allowed, which was good since he wasn't sure he could wipe the smile off his face.

Funny how things could change in a heartbeat. Just like that, he was looking forward to another night in Thunder Canyon.

Seemed like a good idea at the time. Caught up in the moment. What harm could it do?

All of the above described why Haley had agreed to dinner with Marlon. A simple *No, thank you* was what she wished she'd said last night when he'd asked. But she hadn't.

Now she was locking up ROOTS while he waited behind

her to walk to The Hitching Post just down the street. Really, she decided, what could happen?

Taking a deep breath, she turned and smiled. "All secure."

"Good." Looking uncertain, he met her gaze. "Are you okay with The Hitching Post? You already spend most of your time there."

"It's fine." She knew everyone and would be among friends. It would help her relax, although she wasn't sure that was possible no matter where they went. "I have inside knowledge of just how good the food is there."

"When I get my driver's license back, I'll take you to a place where you don't know the kitchen like the back of your hand."

"It would probably be best if you didn't make promises."

She hadn't meant to sound so curt, but his track record in keeping them wasn't good. Granted it was just the one time, but that had been enough for her. She'd wasted a lot of time and energy waiting for a call that never came. It hurt a lot and she'd felt stupid for believing. That wasn't a feeling she wanted to repeat.

"Despite what you think, I can keep my word," he said quietly.

"I just meant," she said, "that you don't owe me anything. Let's just be in the moment and let tomorrow take care of itself."

He looked down at her for several moments, then finally said, "Okay."

"Okay." Their footsteps scraped on the wooden walkway and she kept trying to keep her distance as they walked. But somehow, with the uneven boards, she kept rubbing up against him. A brush of bare arms. Bumping her shoulder into his muscular biceps. The scent of his skin. The combination ganged up on her senses and made rational thought a challenge. Without coherent ideas conversation wasn't easy. But she'd do her best to soldier through.

"So tell me more about how your company works. What happens to sketches like mine?"

"My creative team looks at concepts with potential. When they find something that really gets their juices going, we meet with marketing and pinpoint our target demographic. We evaluate the chances of success before pouring millions of dollars into a project."

She stopped in her tracks and stared up at him. "Excuse me, I could have sworn you just said millions."

"I did. First you have to come up with something people will want to have, then create that product. Labor, materials and marketing costs have to be paid before anything is even sold."

"So the saying is true. It really does take money to make money."

He nodded. "I got lucky in college with the MC/TC brand. There was a venue to display my product and someone with money was staying at Thunder Canyon Resort. He was looking for an investment and liked what he saw. The rest is history."

"That must be a lot of pressure. Putting capital into something without any guarantee that it will be successful."

"You learn to trust your instincts," he said. "Listen to the voice in your head, the feeling in your gut. When you see something you know it."

"And you saw something in my sketches?" She just couldn't believe her doodles could be turned into something profitable.

"They're original and imaginative, Haley." He stopped suddenly and when she tripped on an uneven board in the walkway, he curved his fingers around her arm to steady her. "I knew there was something the first time I saw you—"

They stared at each other for what felt like a lifetime and Haley couldn't breathe. Lights along Main Street illuminated the intensity in Marlon's dark eyes. What was he thinking? What should she do?

Keep walking, that's what. It was hard to hit a moving target.

But as her muscles tensed to take a step, his fingers closed a little tighter, keeping her right where she was. When he threaded the fingers of his other hand into her loose hair, her heart skipped. Then it started again, and beat so fast and hard she was afraid he could hear.

"Haley," he whispered. "I've wanted to do this for a long time. Since that day you were painting the mural at ROOTS."

What was he talking about? That day she looked like something the cat yakked up? So what—

And then his mouth took hers and she couldn't think at all. The world stopped and inside her it was like the Fourth of July—bottle rockets going off. The flash, bang and colors of fireworks and sparklers sparkling.

His lips moved softly, nibbling hers as his arm encircled her waist and pulled her more securely against him. She froze. *What do I do with my hands?* she thought. She wanted to feel his chest, put her arms around his neck. The sensation of her breasts crushed against him was amazing and stole the breath from her lungs. All she could think about was getting closer, as near as possible to the hard lines of his muscular body.

He took control, tipped his head to the side, making the fit of their mouths more firm, more perfect. The sparks he was creating short-circuited her nerve endings and sent sharp thrills of excitement pulsing through every part of her. She could have stayed like this forever.

Then he traced her lips with his tongue and uncertainty fueled the panic waiting in the wings. She wasn't sure what he wanted her to do. She had no experience with a man like him and he would know that if she didn't put a stop to this. She couldn't bear it if he made fun of her. Or worse, pitied her.

She put a palm on his chest and felt the tingle as part of her longed to explore the wide contours. But she couldn't risk it. He'd know her secret and she'd be humiliated. Putting pressure into the touch, she pushed him away, then backed out of the circle of his arms and started walking.

"Haley?" He caught up with her outside The Hitching Post. "Is something wrong?"

"No."

"Should I not have kissed you?" He dragged his fingers through his hair.

"Whatever."

"You're mad," he guessed.

She couldn't make herself meet his gaze. "Should I be?"

"You tell me."

Tell him what? He was the first guy who'd kissed her in years? Should she explain that the last one was in college and he'd barely progressed to kissing her good-night before she'd had to leave? Or maybe she could say that her world and her dreams shattered when she got the call that her mom was dead and any sort of personal life was put on hold indefinitely? Now too much time had passed and her social learning curve had been stunted?

Any man would have a reasonable expectation of experience from a twenty-four-year-old woman, but she was the exception to that rule. And it was too humiliating to explain, especially to Marlon Cates, that she was a social freak.

He'd been written up in *People* magazine. He'd dated actresses and models. Haley just knew she couldn't compete.

"Haley? Talk to me." He stopped at the door to the bar and grill and blocked it with his big body.

Without answering, she edged around him and inside the bar, where she knew what she was doing. Sort of. "Let's find a table."

It wasn't crowded on a weeknight and she grabbed menus from the hostess stand before choosing a booth not far from the door. A private table in the back *wasn't* on tonight's menu.

"Tuesday's special is pot roast," she said, working hard at looking over the food choices when the words wouldn't come into focus. It helped that she knew the menu by heart.

"Look," he said, "About what happened—"

"Hi." Erin Castro appeared beside them and smiled. "You two just can't stay away from this place."

Haley appreciated perkiness as much as anyone, but not at the moment. "I'd like an iced tea and tonight's special. Can you put a rush on that? I need to get back to ROOTS."

"Make it two." Marlon handed over his menu without looking at the waitress. His gaze never left Haley's face. When they were alone, he continued. "Obviously you didn't want me to kiss you."

He couldn't be more wrong. She'd wanted it more than anything. This was one time she wished she hadn't gotten what she'd wanted because now it was so messed up.

"Forget it," she said.

"I think we should talk about what happened."

"Okay." But only because he wouldn't let it drop until she did. "I'm involved with the teen program and you're busy with your business." She forced herself to look at him and shrug. "The timing isn't right."

"You're hiding, Haley. You're burying your head in the sand."

"I don't know what you're talking about."

"Lying again. But let's leave that for now." His expression turned wry. "You know, when you bury your head in the sand it leaves your backside exposed."

"I'm not doing that. It's called being realistic." Before he could back her farther into the corner, Erin showed up with their meals.

"Let me know if you need anything else," she said, before slipping discreetly away.

Haley managed to dodge further talk about what happened but that didn't make the next thirty minutes any more comfortable. It was pretty awful. She brought up everything from weather to Thunder Canyon politics and Marlon asked her for some sketches of purses for a signature line at MC/TC. She couldn't remember ever being more miserable in her life and just played with her food until mercifully the plates were removed.

When Erin moved toward them, she knew a pitch for dessert was coming. Haley was better prepared for that than she'd been for Marlon's kiss.

"No dessert for me," she said to the other girl. "Can we just have the check?"

"Sure thing," the pretty blonde answered, pulling the receipt from her pocket.

"I'd like to split it," Haley said.

"No. I'm buying," Marlon protested.

"I pay for myself." Her tone was adamant.

With a puzzled frown, Erin looked from one to the other.

"I'll just go get some experience doing separate checks while you two discuss this amongst yourselves."

When she was gone, Marlon said, "I insist on paying for your dinner. Tonight was my idea."

Not one of his better ones. Haley was sure he'd agree. This god-awful experience should take care of any possibility that he'd risk investing in her—either personally or professionally.

"Doesn't matter who suggested it. I want to pay for myself." She pulled out her wallet and put a twenty on the table. "Tell Erin to keep the change."

She slid out of the booth and left, listening for the sound of his footsteps behind her. When she didn't hear anything, she was both disappointed and relieved. The definition of conflict. The story of her life. She'd found out firsthand what harm socializing with Marlon could do.

Tonight she'd also found out she cared deeply what he thought of her. If she didn't, she'd have wise-cracked her way out of the awkwardness. Instead she froze. That was irrefutable evidence that the major crush she'd had on Marlon Cates years ago was not dead. That hadn't changed.

But *she* had. She was older, smarter, and knew better than to wait and hope for something more from him. If there was any silver lining in this fiasco, it was that her feelings were out in the open. She could protect herself. Maybe she was burying her head in the sand but that was the best way to circle the wagons and guard her heart.

As always she'd taken care of herself, had paid her own way. But she hoped that didn't mean paying a personal price for seeing Marlon outside of work. It could be very costly.

She would not let him hurt her again.

Chapter Eight

Haley stood by the bar at The Hitching Post and blew out a long breath. Of all the days to have a busier than usual lunch crowd, why did it have to be the day after she'd hardly slept? Of course, she'd hardly slept because of the loop in her head that continuously flashed images of the disastrous dinner with Marlon.

From breathtaking kiss to dinner check, it was hard to count the ways she'd made a fool of herself. *He* was probably counting his lucky stars that his community service was almost half over. Or he was looking for another way to pay his debt to society so that he never had to see her again. Well, she was on board with that because then she wouldn't have to see him, either. On top of that, she never wanted to hear his name again for as long as she lived.

Erin Castro plopped down on the bar stool beside her and heaved a tired sigh. "Is it always that busy?"

"No." Haley levered herself onto the other high chair.

"Good."

"I noticed a lot of moms with kids," Haley said. "My guess is that they're shopping for back-to-school stuff and topping off the outing with lunch. A last hurrah to the summer."

"Again I say good." Erin put an elbow on the bar and rested her cheek in her palm. "I'm getting too old for this."

Haley laughed. "You're what? Twenty-one?"

"Twenty-five." The blonde grinned. "But thanks. And you didn't have to be so charitable after the generous tip you left me last night."

It was a testament to willpower that Haley managed to hold in a wince. Apparently it was too much to hope that the other woman hadn't noticed the tension. Brush it off, she thought.

"Waitresses are the best tippers," she said.

"You were already gone, so you couldn't know, but Marlon's tip was better."

"He can afford it." Haley had meant the words to be casual, teasing, light, but the delivery had a snap to it.

"Word on the street is that he's a high-powered businessman. A millionaire. And my own experience is that he gives good gratuity. I wonder if he ever worked in the food service industry," Erin mused.

"So you made pretty good money last night." Change the subject, Haley thought. No Marlon talk. "You're doing a great job for having been here such a short time, Erin. If you can handle a crowd like we just had, you'll be fine."

"Thanks. Coming from you that's a real compliment. So how long have you worked here at The Hitching Post?"

It felt like forever. And when ungrateful thoughts like that crept in, she reminded herself that she was lucky to have the job. Lucky the manager of the bar and grill had taken a chance on a desperate eighteen-year-old without skills who badly needed a way to take care of her family. But there were times when she wished for more. And Marlon's reaction to her sketches had resurrected the dream. For all the good dreaming did.

"I've worked here going on six years now," Haley answered.

"Wow. That's a long time." Erin's blue eyes sparked with interest. "You probably know a lot about the people in Thunder Canyon. Working in a place like this."

"I'm not sure I follow." Haley stared at the other woman.

"It's just that everyone in town comes in here. Dinner. Drinks. They talk." She shrugged. "You're bound to hear things."

Haley did hear things. She got information about the folks in Thunder Canyon, but gossiping seemed wrong. Taken out of context or repeated from person to person, details got fuzzy until nothing about the original story was the truth. Was Erin a gossip? Or simply wanting to bond with her over Thunder Canyon?

"I talk to a lot of people every day," she hedged.

"I'm a newbie." Erin laughed and there was a tinge of self-consciousness. "But you already know that. And I'm trying to get to know everyone."

"It's a small town. That's not hard." Haley could understand that she was trying to fit in.

"Not if you grew up here." Erin looked eager. "I'm trying to put names and faces together. Let's take Marlon. There's another guy who comes in. Looks just like him—"

"Matthew Cates—Marlon's twin."

"Which would explain why they look alike. Don't they have another brother?"

"Two, actually," Haley answered. "Marshall and Mitchell

are both older. The twins are the youngest of the Cates boys."

"Don't they have a lot of cousins?" Erin asked, a little too casually. It looked forced.

"You might be thinking about the Traubs. D.J. and Dax. But they're brothers. No relation to the Cates family. Just longtime friends."

Erin's forehead puckered in concentration. "What about Bo Clifton? The guy who's running for Mayor?"

"You heard about that?"

"It's all over town," Erin confirmed. "Doesn't he have cousins?"

Haley tapped her lip as she thought. "Grant Clifton. He's the manager at Thunder Canyon Resort."

"It seems like I heard he has a sister?"

"Elise. She's my best friend," Haley confirmed. And how she missed her friend these days. She'd give anything to have someone to talk to about Marlon. Maybe talking would help to get him off her mind. Sounded like the theme of a country western tune. "But she lives in Billings now."

Erin nodded thoughtfully, then said, "So how long has Marlon been your boyfriend?"

"He's not."

"Really?" The other waitress tucked her blond hair behind her ear. "I thought you guys had hooked up. After last night…"

Haley squirmed. Erin's social cues and interpersonal observations were really out of whack if she thought last night's events were about a relationship. "What makes you think he's my boyfriend? Based on what you saw?"

"You mean because you were fighting?" Erin waved her hand dismissively. "A lovers' quarrel."

Way off the mark—and not very likely now. Haley

had acted like he had the plague because she had no idea how to kiss him back. He would never risk a repeat and that was too bad. Because she could definitely see how a kiss—especially from Marlon—could be life-altering. Ever since last night's close encounter of the personal kind, her hormones had been giving her a hard time. There was a knot in the pit of her stomach that felt like frustration on crack.

And she didn't know how to make it go away.

Since Marlon didn't plan to stay in Thunder Canyon, it was probably for the best that she got a failing grade in Kissing 101. A repeat of the experience would not help her stay aloof. Which she needed to do if she planned on not getting attached to him.

"We're not lovers," Haley finally said. "In fact, I'm not sure we're even friends."

"Really? He seemed pretty upset. So did you, for that matter. If there's nothing between you, there'd be no reason for that."

He was upset when she left? That information sent a small shimmy of pleasure through her. But hope was a place she couldn't afford to go.

"Trust me, there's nothing between Marlon and me."

"Too bad. He's really cute. And he's got a lot of money?" Erin looked like she was working very hard at appearing barely interested. But there was an underlying intensity to her questions that made Haley wary.

She was about to say they should get back to work and end this conversation when an older couple came into the restaurant and were seated in Erin's section.

"Gotta go." She'd noticed, too. "We should get together for a drink some evening."

"Maybe." Haley wasn't ready to commit. She was almost sure that something was up with Erin and didn't want to jump into a friendship based on hidden agendas. "I'm pretty busy with ROOTS right now."

"The teen mentor program." Over her shoulder Erin said, "Let me know if I can help."

Haley watched her smile at the customers and wondered about her over-enthusiastic interest in Marlon. Jealousy reared its ugly head again. It was one of her less attractive qualities, but acknowledging it was half the battle in suppressing the tendency. At least she hoped so.

Since Marlon had come back to Thunder Canyon, she seemed to be acknowledging and suppressing a lot where he was concerned—both her attraction to him and the crush that refused to die.

She sighed and shook her head as she slid down from her bar stool, muttering to herself. "This whole suppression thing needs work. A *lot* of work."

Marlon sat beside Roy in the folding chairs that faced the corner TV at ROOTS. They were playing a video game and he was getting his ass kicked because his head was on what happened between him and Haley last night.

When the door behind them opened, he knew right away it wasn't a group of kids. They were usually so noisy it would be impossible to sneak up on a glass of water. Even outside on the sidewalk you could hear talking, teasing, laughing. And if girls were there, the decibel level went up loud enough to shatter glass in the next county.

The person who'd just come in was too quiet and suddenly it felt as if the temperature in the room dropped to sub-zero. Plus the smell of her perfume made his blood hum, his skin burn.

Haley.

He couldn't wait to see her and dreaded it at the same time. That was just whacked for a decisive guy like himself.

Somehow he'd ticked her off when he'd kissed her last night and he didn't have a clue what he'd done wrong. It wasn't as if that was his first time kissing a girl. He'd had a lot of experience. Tons. He knew what he was doing and all the signs said Haley had been into it. She'd been breathing just as hard as he was; she'd made that turned-on, breathy little sound that drove him completely nuts.

Then all of a sudden she had pushed him away and treated him like an ax murderer. What was up with that?

Haley walked into the storage room leaving the scent of her drifting behind him. His skin felt too tight and another, stronger flash of heat rolled through him.

"Hi, Roy," she called out.

"Hey." The kid glanced sideways, game forgotten. "That was weird."

Marlon set his control on the floor. "What?"

"She didn't say hi to you."

"I noticed." There was a lot she wasn't saying to him. Volumes. And there were no signs that would be changing anytime soon. He'd sure like to be a mind reader right about now.

"What did you do?"

Since Marlon didn't think it was appropriate to discuss kissing her, he said, "Nothing."

Roy looked at him. "Must be somethin', dude. She's glacial."

"Yeah, well, if global warming can melt the polar ice pack maybe it will work on her, too." Marlon stood. "You've got supervision now. I've been relieved of duty. I'll see you later."

"You're bailing on me?" Roy complained.

Marlon looked down. "Are you going to tell me where you live?"

The teenage mask of intensity slipped into place. "No way."

"Then I'm bailing on you."

Without another word, Marlon walked outside and started down the wooden sidewalk. He was halfway to The Hitching Post when he heard a horn honk behind him. Turning, he recognized the Cates Construction truck as it pulled over and stopped beside him.

His twin, Matt, was behind the wheel. "Hey, bro."

Marlon leaned his forearms on the passenger-side window frame. "What's up?"

"I'm on my way back to a job. We're doing the foundation for Connor McFarlane's house."

"Need some help?" Marlon could sure use some physical work to get rid of the restless energy that made him want to put his fist through a wall.

His brother studied him for several moments before saying, "Hop in."

Marlon remembered Haley asking him if it was like looking in a mirror when he was with his brother. Their faces were practically identical, as was their dark hair and eyes. But they were different in a lot of ways. Matt was more muscular, a side effect of physical labor, working with his hands. He was also more serious, some said somber. According to their mother, he was just more mature. And loyal to a fault. Haley would never tell Matt that commitment wasn't his strength.

"That's a pretty fierce look on your face," his brother observed.

Marlon met his gaze for a moment. "I've got a lot on my mind."

"Want to talk about it?"

"No."

What was there to say? Haley was mad. He had no idea

why. But he was only there to do his community service, so what did it matter whether or not she liked him? Except the hell of it was that it *did* matter and he wanted it to stop mattering.

Matt knew him well enough to leave him to his thoughts and they were quiet until they got to the construction site. And it was a beaut, Marlon thought when the truck pulled into the clearing. Connor McFarlane had picked a nice piece of land outside of town. A few trees had been cleared, but the majority were saved. The way the earth was dug out for the foundation showed him the general layout of the house, giving the front a spectacular view of the mountains, the best possible view as a matter of fact. Matt would have spent a lot of time getting the orientation just right for maximum panorama potential. His brother was incredibly good at his job.

He opened the driver's-side door and jumped out of the truck, then reached in for his tool belt and buckled it on. Marlon followed him over the uneven ground to a stack of lumber.

"This is going to be a great house," he said.

"Big." Matt studied the ground and nodded with satisfaction. "It will be good for the Cates Construction portfolio."

"Where's the rest of your crew?"

His brother grabbed a piece of wood. "They're done for the day. Can't afford to pay overtime, but there's still a couple more hours of daylight and I don't want to waste it." He looked up and suddenly grinned. "And I found some free labor."

"It'll cost you," Marlon warned. "You won't know when or how much, but it will."

"I'm scared." Matt positioned the board where he wanted

it and fitted another in. "We're pouring the foundation soon and it needs to be framed first."

"Yeah. I figured," Marlon said wryly. "I lift a hammer from time to time—when I have the time. It hasn't been that long since I worked for Cates Construction."

"You're a pansy," Matt joked. "Soft and sweet with your cushy job behind your desk in L.A."

"Never judge a man until you walk a mile in his shoes." Marlon smiled.

Unlike dealing with the mercurial Haley Anderson, this back and forth with his brother was familiar. The house foundation wasn't there but the same couldn't be said of the one he had with Matt. It felt good. And the truth was they hadn't worked like this for a while. Or talked.

"So what's new?"

Matt glanced up. "I guess you haven't heard."

"What?"

"Dillon Traub is going to take over for Marshall as the on-site sports doctor at Thunder Canyon Resort."

Dillon was Dax and D.J. Traub's cousin. Through them, Marlon had met him and liked him a lot. He was fun, casual and confident without being obnoxious. Then a thought hit him.

"Why is he filling in? Where's Marshall going?"

Matt slid him a pitying look that said he really needed to stay in the loop. "Marshall and Mia, that's his wife in case you haven't heard—"

"I know he's married. And I've actually met Mia. She's great. What I didn't know is that they're going somewhere."

"In September he's taking her on an extended working vacation," Matt explained.

"Working how?"

"Mia has finished nursing school and they'll be doing

some sightseeing as well as visiting counseling centers that she hopes to model her own after."

"I didn't know that," Marlon said.

His twin nodded. "She's using her inheritance to start a grief counseling center for women."

Marlon thought about Haley, the overwhelming anguish she must have experienced after her mom died. "Sounds like a really worthwhile undertaking. The Anderson family could have used something like that."

Matt swiped his forearm over his sweaty forehead as he nodded. "Yeah. I don't know how Haley did what she did. Raising Angie and Austin at the same time she was dealing with her mother's loss…and she did a great job of it."

"Yeah." Haley was a hell of a woman, Marlon thought. As was his sister-in-law. "Good for Mia. I hope the two of them have a great trip. And I can't think of anyone better than Dillon to fill in for Marshall."

Too bad he wouldn't be around when the other man took over for his brother. Moving around a lot was the downside of doing what Marlon did. And that meant missing out on a lot of stuff. It never used to bother him, but now? Discontent was the best description he could come up with.

Marlon watched his brother fit more wood together and nail it in place. "You know, it's a good thing Dillon is rich and the heir to Traub Oil Industries."

"I'm sure Dillon wouldn't argue with you on that point." Matt looked up, a wry expression on his face. "But why do you think so?"

"Because he's not locked into a nine-to-five job and can pick and choose where and when to practice medicine."

Matt rested his forearm on his thigh. "Now that I think about it, he always knew he wanted to be a doctor when he grew up."

"Don't sound so envious." Marlon handed his brother another two-by-four. "You always liked building stuff. From Tinkertoys to Erector sets, you'd make things. I envied that."

"You think I've always been sure of myself?" Matt asked.

"Duh," Marlon answered.

"Not so much. Have you forgotten that I'm a law school dropout?"

"Only because it was never really your dream," Marlon defended. "Mom and Dad wanted you to be a lawyer."

"That's not an excuse," Matt retorted.

"I'm not saying it was. Just that kids try to please their parents."

Marlon thought of Roy and wondered if he'd run from parental pressure to do or be something he didn't want. Then he thought about Haley, who hadn't had the guidance of parents nearly as long as she should have. And now she was trying to help other kids who needed a steadying hand. Again he realized that she was a very special woman.

"In the long run, life is all about finding something you love to do," Marlon said. "And you like working with your hands. It's what you're good at. Construction is a no-brainer for you."

"Like you're good at business."

"Yeah. But it fries my ass that you're good at business, too." Marlon grinned when his twin made a scoffing sound. "Really. It's not fair that you can do both equally as well. And you really love it."

Matt looked up. "How do you feel about what you're doing?"

"You mean my company?"

"No, the community service. The need for speed brought you down, bro. How's it going at ROOTS?"

"It's living up to its name," he said ruefully. "I'm planted in one spot. At least until the end of August."

"You might be stuck in one spot, but at least the scenery is good. Haley is hot. You could be stuck working for a crabby ninety-year-old with a gray bun in her hair and a stick up her butt."

No argument there, Marlon thought. Haley was pretty as a picture and twice as sweet. Until last night. "She's not ninety and I've never seen her hair in a bun."

"So what's wrong?"

"Nothing."

Matt's expression was scornful. "This is me, Mar. I know you better than anyone."

"You don't know everything."

"Then tell me."

Marlon met his brother's gaze. "I was engaged in college and she took me for a bundle of money."

"I hate it when you're right." Matt stared at him. "I didn't know that."

"She played the purity card. Said she didn't believe in sleeping together before marriage. So I proposed and wanted to set a date."

"Don't tell me. She was in no hurry to do that."

"Right in one," Marlon said ruefully. "She claimed she had a lot of debt from her father's medical problems and didn't want to burden me with it."

"So you wrote her a check," Matt guessed.

"With too many zeroes. After which she disappeared." He hated being made a fool of. "It's not something I look back on with pride."

"I can understand that. But don't let that put you off women altogether."

"Who says I'm doing that?" Marlon asked, suddenly defensive.

"Something's going on. What's up?"

He knew there was no point in putting his twin off. Matt knew him too well and wouldn't let up until he had the information he wanted. "Haley. All grown up, I mean."

Matt stood and rested his hands on his hips. "You're hung up on her. And running scared because of the girl who ripped you off."

Marlon waved his hand dismissively. "What have you been smoking?"

"There it is again," his brother said, pointing. "Defensive. Another sign that something's different with you this time."

"You're crazy."

"No, you are. You need to embrace it, bro. She could be 'the one.'"

"The one?"

"To finally tame my restless twin," Matt explained.

"No way." Marlon shook his head. "Just call me the happy wanderer."

"The more they protest, the harder they fall," Matt teased.

Marlon didn't like the turn of this conversation and it was time to put it out of its misery. "Even if I was interested in Haley, and that's a big if, I'm not the settling down sort."

"Where have I heard that before?" Matt snapped his fingers. "Oh, yeah. Big brother Marshall said it right before he met Mia. Maybe even after they met. He swore up and down he wasn't the kind of man who did relationships. He was just like you, carefree and commitment-phobic."

"And your point is?"

"He's married and getting ready to go on his honeymoon. I've never seen him happier."

"Again I ask, what's your point?" Marlon knew he'd be

sorry for asking, but the words were out before he could stop them.

An unfortunate byproduct of verbal sparring with his brother was getting backed into a corner. Fighting his way out didn't always make his comebacks very smart.

"Just saying. Haley could be the one." Matt smiled. "Never say never."

There was no way to win this argument so Marlon didn't try. No matter how much he'd liked kissing Haley, how much he liked the lady herself, clearly the feeling wasn't mutual. Although he would swear the attraction was. But could he trust it? Was pushing him away some kind of game with her?

There was no point in sorting out the questions. The bigger problem was finding a way to shut down his festering feelings, because he had two more weeks of community service left. That was more than enough time for a lot to happen.

And he didn't want anything to happen. Not with Haley. He would rather walk barefoot over broken glass than do anything else to hurt her.

Chapter Nine

"Guys don't make cookies."

Haley looked up as Roy stirred chocolate chips into the second batch of thick dough. They were in her small, cozy kitchen working on the old oak table. The six chairs were against the wall where inspirational sayings were hung beside her mother's copper pots and decorative plates. With walls painted a soft yellow, the white cotton curtains at the window pulled everything together as they overlooked the front yard.

Thank goodness she'd been able to hang on to this place after her mother died. Not only for Austin and Angie's sake, but for her own, as well. She still felt her mother's presence and wondered what her response would have been if Austin griped about baking like Roy just did.

"Is there a rule somewhere that says guys can't make cookies?" she asked.

He looked up from his job. "It's chick work."

"Has anyone ever mentioned to you that whining is marginally tolerable in a two-year-old, but incredibly unattractive not to mention annoying in a teenager?"

"Just saying." Roy grinned. "If any of my friends saw me with a wooden spoon and a bowl of dough, I'd never live it down."

"Do your friends live close by? Is there a chance they could see what you're doing?"

"Did you think I wouldn't notice that?"

"I wasn't subtle?" she asked innocently.

"Not even a little bit." He grinned again. "Nice try."

"Okay then. Back to cookies. You might be surprised how many men know their way around a kitchen. Some of the top chefs in the world are men."

She studied him, his blue eyes unreadable, light brown hair shaggy around his lean face. Definitely a hottie as the teen girls had mentioned more than once. Yesterday he'd said longingly how good home-baked cookies tasted and she realized how long it had been since she'd baked them. This was a rare day off, giving her time to do just that. Angie and Austin had left for work at the resort a while ago and she'd nudged Roy into helping her. A dollop of guilt had been judiciously applied in the nudging process. Apparently he needed another dose.

The muscles in his biceps bunched as he wielded the wooden spoon, grunting from the effort. "I hate baking."

"Me, too." She met his surprised gaze. "What? Just because I'm a girl I have to like it?"

"I didn't say anything."

"It's written all over your face." She lifted one shoulder in a shrug. "There's my shocking secret. I hate cooking."

He stood the spoon up straight in the thick mixture. "Then why are you doing it?"

"You said the kids like homemade better than store-bought cookies."

"So? They can survive without 'em. Everyone has to live with disappointment."

She happened to be looking at him when he made the comment. Was he quoting someone who'd said it to him? Was he running from some form of disappointment? Sooner or later this had to be sorted out because the situation couldn't go on much longer. The call to his mother had been a while ago and all the poor woman knew was that he'd been alive then.

If she and Marlon couldn't get Roy to open up pretty soon, they'd have to involve the authorities. It wasn't her first choice because she wanted the kids to feel they could trust her with anything. But talking through problems was the first step in facing them. Roy was simply hiding.

"Yeah," she finally said. "Everyone does have to live with disappointment. But not when it comes to chocolate chip cookies. They've been known to make stronger men than you sing like a canary."

"Not me." He glanced at a grouping of pictures on the wall behind her.

There was one about parenthood and a saying that children learned what they lived. Another of a cow because her mother had liked cows. And a cross-stitch of a breadbasket. Her favorite was the embroidery that her mom had made. Just words on a linen square. "There are but two lasting bequests we can give our children—roots and wings."

Haley glanced at it, then said, "My mother made that. She said it means that kids should always know where they come from, where home is. Where they're loved. But a parent should also infuse their children with the courage to strike out and find their own destiny. Never be afraid to follow a dream knowing you can go home again. It's where the name of the mentoring program came from."

"ROOTS," he said.

She nodded. "It's my dream. To help kids, like the people here in Thunder Canyon helped me when my mom died."

"I get it," he said.

"Good." Hoping he would say more about where he came from, she waited, but he just looked thoughtful. It wasn't quite time to push yet. Sighing, she indicated a pan full of cooled cookies beside the stove. "Why don't you put those in that plastic container."

"Okay." He lifted a spatula from a crockery jar on the counter and went to work. "So, speaking of ROOTS—"

Something in his voice made her look up. A hint of vulnerability that maybe he'd tell her more about himself. "Yes?"

"What's up with you and Marlon?"

Hearing the name of the man she kept trying to put out of her mind was unexpected and she missed the cookie sheet when she scraped dough off her spoon. It plopped on the distressed wood floor. No way this floor could be as distressed as her, she thought. Talking about the man who'd kissed her wasn't her idea of a good time. Odd, now that she thought about it. There was a time she'd dreamed about kissing Marlon and it finally happened, in front of ROOTS, the dream that she'd made happen. She was one for one on the dream front. One was going well, the other? Not so much.

"There's nothing up with me and Marlon." Turning her back, she grabbed a paper towel, then stooped to clean up the mess. It was a good way to hide the reaction she couldn't conceal. Kids didn't miss much.

But Roy was persistent. "Then why didn't you say hello to him yesterday?"

"What? Where?" She threw the gooey paper in the trash, then picked up the two teaspoons and resumed dropping dough on the cookie sheet.

"You came in to ROOTS after work and said hi to me but not to Marlon. You always say hello to everyone. What's up with that?"

"Really? I didn't realize." She brushed a knuckle on her cheek and remembered what Marlon had said about lying. Was her nose growing? "I'm sure it wasn't a big deal."

"Was, too. He bailed right after that. It was tense. And don't tell me it's just my imagination. Or I don't know what tension is, because I do. He was tense and so were you."

"It's nothing you need to worry about. The fact is, his community service will be over soon. He'll be leaving town."

Her attempt to sound upbeat was a dismal failure. Even she heard the sadness in her voice. Something about saying those words out loud made her chest squeeze so tight it was a challenge to draw in a breath of air. So much for the unspoken lie that his kiss didn't change anything.

"I think you really like him," Roy stated firmly.

Keep it light, she thought. Uncomplicated. And as truthful as possible. "Of course I like him. I like everyone. You shouldn't read anything into it."

"I wish you'd stop treating me like a kid."

"Why would you think I am?" she asked.

"I've got eyes. I've been around. I know stuff. I'm almost eighteen. A man."

Haley rested her spoons on the lip of the big bowl as she looked at him. "Reaching a milestone age doesn't automatically mean you're a man, or a woman either, for that matter. It's what you do day in and day out that makes you an adult."

He put the lid on the big plastic container. "You mean like what you did? Stepping up for Angie and Austin after your mom died?"

"That's right."

"What about your dad?" he asked. "Was he dead, too?"

To her he was. His leaving had broken Nell Anderson's heart. Haley remembered being a little girl and asking her mom about him. The soul-deep sadness in her eyes when Nell had answered that he just didn't love them enough to stay. He'd already been gone a long time, but her mother was still sad and lonely. The child Haley had been wished she and her brother and sister were enough for their mom, but the sadness never went away.

And Haley never resented the man who'd fathered her more than when he wasn't there for his kids after losing their mother. It had been six years, but anger still made her voice shake and her hands tremble when she talked about him. The feelings were real and raw and maybe Roy should know he wasn't the only person on the face of the planet with problems. He needed to see, so she turned off her own emotional sensors and let her feelings show.

"My father was never a man," she said angrily. "Real men don't walk out on a wife and three children who need him."

The hostile tone got Roy's attention. "Do you remember him?"

"No." It was on the tip of her tongue to say she was glad, but that was childish. Running away. "It makes me sad and angry. I try to tell myself that he's the one who missed out, but the truth is Angie, Austin and I all lost out on something because we didn't know our father. He disappeared and avoided his responsibilities."

Thoughtfully, Roy leaned back against the Formica countertop. "So you do think I'm a kid."

"It doesn't matter what I think. Only you can decide whether or not you're running away from something."

"Marlon isn't running," he said out of the blue.

It was official. Marlon Cates was a favorite of everyone. Women wanted to be with him and guys wanted to be his friend. She was the only one who fell into some gray area of pretending he didn't do a thing for her.

"I'm not sure what you mean," she said.

"Community service. He's here and doing what he has to do. He's not running out on his punishment. He's sticking around. That makes him a man."

Wow, was he a man, she thought as memories of their kiss popped into her head. Roy blinked at her and, for just a second, she was afraid she'd said the words out loud. Then his expression turned pensive, making him look like the confused teenager she was trying to help.

"He's taking the consequences for his actions. Like a man. I can't argue with that."

Roy suddenly grinned. "And I still say you like him."

She couldn't argue with that either, much as she wished she could. She'd like to believe that Roy was just a kid who didn't really understand grown-up relationships. It was a fact that Marlon was doing the responsible thing and making a difference. The teens looked up to him. That was all good.

It was her liking him that was bad.

Unlike how her father had walked out, Marlon's leaving wasn't going to be a surprise. She had fair warning. There was time to prepare. And yet she didn't know how to stop the runaway, out-of-control freight train her feelings had become. Every indication was that they couldn't be stopped. She'd tried, but even this teenager had seen through her.

Since she couldn't seem to get a handle on what was simmering between them, maybe Marlon could stop it. Who could blame him after the way she'd acted. Even Roy had noticed. From now on she expected Marlon to be just as cool toward her, maybe put the brakes on her feelings.

She had to keep trying. There was a time limit on how long Marlon was sticking around, but heartbreak had no shelf life. It could last forever.

She could be THE ONE.

Ever since yesterday, when his twin had said that about Haley, the words had been capitalized in Marlon's mind and wouldn't leave him alone. He'd come for breakfast at The Hitching Post and so far was just having coffee, wishing it wasn't too early for something stronger. He was still brooding about Matt comparing him to their older brother Marshall, who'd sworn that he wasn't the marrying kind.

For the record, Marlon's situation was completely different. He didn't live in Thunder Canyon. He had a life in Los Angeles and Haley hadn't bothered to hide her opinion of the place. Plus she'd made no secret of the fact that she didn't respect him much. Even Roy had noticed the cold shoulder.

How could she be "the one"? In order to tame the restless Cates twin, she needed to show some interest. If she was interested, she had a funny way of showing it.

"You're in my seat."

The deep voice and hostile tone made Marlon look up. Ben Walters was looming over him, a walking, talking crabby sign that this day could actually get worse. The two of them had never gotten along and Marlon wasn't in the mood to play nice now.

"I don't see your name on it," Marlon said.

"If you were around more, you'd know they call this Ben's booth." The other man pointed to the erotic picture of Lily Divine over the bar. "Old guy like me knows the best seat in the house when he sees it."

Marlon studied the portrait of the scantily clad woman. It had nothing to do with why he'd sat here, but now that the benefits had been brought to his attention, he grinned. "Old has nothing to do with it."

The man's mouth twitched, as if he were fighting a smile. "Still, this is my usual place."

"Maybe we could share it." The fact that this geezer was a close friend of Haley's wasn't his primary motivation, but it wasn't exactly a deal breaker either.

Ben looked thoughtful for several moments, then nodded. "On one condition."

"Name it."

"You sit on the other side of the booth."

"Done." Marlon slid his coffee mug across the table, then got up and sat with his back to Lily Divine.

Ben had just settled on the seat when Hitching Post manager Linda Powell brought over two menus and a steaming mug of black coffee. The pretty brunette put it down in front of the older man and smiled.

"This is a first." She glanced at the two of them and one of her dark eyebrows lifted questioningly. "Has there been a shift in the universe and no one told me?"

"Some things Marlon and me see eye to eye on." Ben slid a look at the portrait and a corner of his mouth lifted.

"Are you ready to order or do you need a minute?" She was talking to Marlon. "It seems like you should know that menu by heart. You're going to give Ben some competition as our best customer."

"The food is good." Marlon shrugged and without any

waitress prompting said, "I'll have the special. Eggs over medium. Hash browns. Sausage. And a side of pancakes with maple syrup."

"Make it two."

"I thought you were watching your cholesterol." Linda stared at the other man over the half glasses sitting on the end of her nose.

"Here's the thing." Ben handed her the menu. "I quit smoking. Gave up beer for a glass of red wine now and then. And never touch a salt shaker. Every once in a while a man's gotta get wild."

"With sausage and eggs?" Marlon's mouth curved up. "Are you sure the excitement won't be too much for you?"

"Smart aleck." Ben pointed a finger at him, but a twinkle lurked in his light blue eyes. "You should learn to respect your elders, son."

Marlon met his gaze—man to man. "I have a great deal of respect for you."

"I'll have these orders up in a jiffy." The brunette flashed another flirty smile at Ben before taking both menus and moving away.

Marlon watched the older man stare appreciatively at the sway of her hips as she walked and wondered if the widower was involved with the waitress. If so, he was happy for them.

He couldn't resist saying, "She's sweet on you."

"Yeah."

"There's no accounting for taste," Marlon teased.

"Can't argue with that."

A shrewdness slid into those wise eyes and Marlon had a feeling they were no longer talking about Ben and Linda. But if he meant Haley was sweet on Marlon, he was wrong. Her taste didn't run to businessmen from Los Angeles.

That thought made him wonder… How did her taste in men run?

Maybe she was dating someone and thought Ben knew about it. Because in a small town, people always knew that kind of stuff.

He took a sip of cold coffee and said as casually as possible. "You and Haley are pretty close."

"That we are." Ben nodded once. "She's like the daughter I never had."

"Then you'd probably know if she's seeing someone."

"Sees lots of people. Goes with the territory when you work in a place like this."

"That's not what I meant. Is she—"

"I know what you meant. Wasn't born yesterday, which we've already established."

Marlon sighed. "You're not making this easy."

"Good." The older man nodded with satisfaction.

"Is there a guy?" Marlon held up his hand before a witty comeback came in his direction. "I mean is there someone she goes out with on a regular basis?"

The idea of her with another guy tied his gut in knots and made his chest feel like an elephant plopped his backside down right smack in the center of it. Haley dating someone else felt wrong on every level.

Ben thought about the question for several moments then simply said, "Nope."

Linda picked that moment to come back carrying a tray loaded with food. She set plates of steaming potatoes, eggs and pancakes in front of them. Marlon had been starving when he sat down, but had lost his appetite in the last couple of minutes.

"Nope, what?" Linda asked.

"Marlon wanted to know if Haley has a boyfriend."

As the two stared at him, Marlon was now fidgeting

like a teenager meeting his girlfriend's parents for the first time. He could change the subject, but now that he'd popped open this can of worms, his squirmy curiosity refused to slither back inside.

Linda slid the empty plastic tray under her arm and looked at Ben. "I can't recall Haley going out with anyone. At least not around here. Can you?"

"Like I said... Nope."

"Not in Thunder Canyon. If she did we'd know."

That was pretty much what Marlon figured. But her behavior when he'd kissed her made him suspicious. Something was up. "What does that mean? Not here in Thunder Canyon?"

"She went away to college."

Marlon tried to remember if he'd known that and couldn't. Now it seemed vitally important.

"It was just for a couple of months," Linda continued, her forehead creased as she thought back. "Then her mom was killed and she had to come back for Angie and Austin. Poor thing."

He knew that. What he wanted was current events in her life. He was impatient for information and tamped down the urge to hurry them up.

"Now that you mention it, wasn't there a guy at college that she talked about?" Ben pushed a pat of butter over the top of his pancakes and poured on syrup from the small glass container on the side of the plate.

A guy? In college?

"Were they...close?" Marlon asked, hearing the edge in his voice.

"Must have been if she mentioned him to you," Linda commented.

"But you never met the guy?" Marlon looked from one to the other, trying to figure out what all this meant.

Ben took a bite of egg and chewed thoughtfully. "I'd remember if he'd showed up. Never did. And believe me, that girl could've used another pair of shoulders to hold up all the crap going on."

Marlon's imagination went full throttle and filled in the blanks. She'd gone away to school and hooked up with someone. It was hot and heavy then tragedy brought her home. For good. But the guy wasn't there to support her during the worst time of her life. He'd disillusioned her. Broke her heart.

Marlon stabbed his fork into the stack of pancakes. "The bastard wasn't there when she needed him most. That would make it pretty hard for her to trust anyone."

"That'd be my guess." Ben nodded. "She tries to hide it, but there's a sadness in her eyes. Too much. She's been hurt pretty bad."

And she didn't want to take a chance again.

It made sense.

Then Marlon had to go and kiss her. Just like he'd done all those years ago. He'd kissed her at the football fundraiser. Just like that, quiet and timid Haley Anderson had really gotten his attention. He'd been surprised at the passion simmering beneath her shy surface and wanted to get to know her better. Asking her for a date had been the plan and she'd seemed eager for him to call.

But apparently Ben Walters had heard about it. Gotta love the way things spread in a small town. It had ticked him off when Ben warned him away, told him not to mess with Haley. He'd wanted to tell the old meddler to mind his own business, then changed his mind and told Ben he wouldn't make trouble. That'd be a first, the old man had said.

Marlon met the older man's gaze and knew he was

remembering it, too. "All those years ago… Staying away from Haley was the best thing to do. You were right about me."

Ben shook his head. "Nope."

"Excuse me?" Marlon had thought he'd agree and rub it in.

"Frank and Edie Cates are good parents. All you boys grew up to be fine men."

"I didn't think you liked me. I'm flattered."

"Don't be." Ben shifted his bulk on the bench seat. "Not trying to be your friend. Just honest. Word around town is you're taking responsibility for what you did wrong and actually helping those kids at ROOTS. Not to mention Haley. Just saying…I was wrong about you. You're a good man."

Try telling that to Haley, Marlon thought darkly. She'd been smart to push him away. He had a reputation with women. The kind he dated were into fun, games and publicity. But Haley was different. Not so shy and timid anymore, but solid and sweet and sexy. She was an all or nothing kind of girl who had him thinking more about *all* while the nothing part looked less and less inviting.

Something about Haley pulled at him with a steady strength that was becoming increasingly difficult to ignore. But she'd had more bad stuff happen to her than most people did in a lifetime.

The last thing he would do was be one more thing on her bad list. While he was stuck in Thunder Canyon he had to find the willpower to leave her be before he had to leave for good.

Chapter Ten

It was getting late, almost time to close ROOTS up for the night. But the three teenage girls, two flanking Haley on the sofa and one leaning over the back of it, were really into critically assessing her drawings in general, and handbag designs in particular.

In the corner of the room opposite the TV and video games, Roy and Austin were huddled around the donated computer on its donated desk. The girls had teased them about hiding in their "man cave."

Haley picked up a red pencil, made a few strokes and added a bow on the evening bag. "This would look really nice in black satin. Maybe some sequins on the bow."

"Ooh," the girls all said together.

"I've never seen anything in the store as cute as that," said Becky Harmon, a hazel-eyed brunette new to ROOTS.

Kim and Jerilyn had brought her with them tonight.

Haley had heard rumors about her older brother, a senior running back on the Thunder Canyon High School football team. Word on the street was that he'd been caught using performance-enhancing drugs to increase his chances of getting notice from college scouts and possibly a scholarship. Money was tight since their dad was out of work. That would mean even more trauma and tension at home.

It made Haley feel good that she'd provided somewhere the girl could go and forget about real-life problems for a while. She could laugh, be silly and talk about girly stuff.

On her sketch pad, Haley drew a small, slim bag with a shoulder strap and snap closure. Then she sketched a rear view of the same purse. "What do you think about a decorative zipper?"

"Awesome." Kim was leaning over the back of the sofa.

Jerilyn tapped her lip thoughtfully. "Maybe a sort of big, chunky one with fringe on the tab."

"Great idea." The scratchy sound of Haley's pencil was the only sound in the room as the teen audience watched her bring the idea to life on paper. "There. What do you think?"

"I want to buy one," Kim said, enthusiastically. "It's just the right size. Not too big. Not a murse."

"A what?" Haley glanced over her shoulder at the pretty blonde.

"You know. Murse. Mom purse."

No, she didn't know and the thought made her a little sad. That flash of pain at missing her mom only happened rarely now, but this was one of those times. Some of it was hearing the kids talk about their parents and remembering why this program was so important to her. She glanced over at Austin, who was pointing something out to Roy on the computer monitor. Her mom would be proud of this place and her three kids, who had turned a horrible loss into something positive.

The thought didn't take away her fear of going through more pain and darkness again. She had her family and would protect them with everything she had. But the remembered sadness made her more determined than ever not to let anyone else close.

The front door opened and Marlon Cates walked in, all loose-limbed dash and swagger. Her heart skidded and popped, a completely involuntary reaction. It seemed loud and felt like an earthquake aftershock, but when she glanced around no one else seemed to notice.

"Hi." He lifted a hand in greeting and everyone responded. "I saw the lights still on. Obviously this is the happening place on a weeknight in Thunder Canyon."

"That's for sure. Come see what Haley is drawing." Becky waved him over. "Look at how awesome these purses are. She even designed different linings, with a coordinating trim on the outside. Just small touches of it."

"I like the paisley," Kim commented.

"My favorite is the sun, crescent moon and stars," Jerilyn said.

"You're such a brainer geek." Becky looked at her friends and added, "I mean that in the best possible way."

The girls' chatter faded as Marlon moved closer to see what she was doing.

"Can I see?" he asked.

"Sure." Heart pounding in spite of her resolve not to react, she handed him the sketch pad.

While he flipped through it, she worked on getting her reaction in check. The spicy, clean scent of his aftershave wasn't making it easy.

Finally he looked at her. "These are good."

"Thanks."

"Good?" Becky sounded miffed. "That's the best adjective you can come up with?"

"They're awesome," Kim said again. "We'd buy them in a second."

"Haley knows how much I like her—designs," he added, his eyes dark with a thrilling intensity.

His slight hesitation before that last word had her pulse racing again.

"I do." Haley managed to keep her voice steady and normal. "He told me they have promise."

"I also said I'd like to send them to my assistant in L.A. Get her opinion on whether or not they're marketable."

"Of course they are." Jerilyn slid to the edge of the sofa in her earnestness. "They're different. Young. Fun and funky."

"Elegant, too," Becky added.

Kim came around and sat on the sofa arm, presenting a united female front. "Haley's designs are really good. If your assistant doesn't get it, then you need a new assistant."

"Down, girl." He handed the pad to Haley, then backed up a step. "I said I'm on board. So far Haley hasn't given me the go-ahead."

Only because he'd kissed her and she freaked out. He'd invited her to dinner to discuss the possibility of doing business, but they didn't talk much after that kiss. It wasn't his fault she'd come unglued, then got sidetracked by insecurity and humiliation. Come to think of it, the idea of putting her designs out publicly brought up those same kinds of feelings.

"It's not an easy decision." She started putting her art supplies away in the pencil box.

"Why?" Kim demanded.

"Seems like a no-brainer." Jerilyn's dark eyes narrowed.

"You're scared." Becky nodded knowingly.

Haley looked at each girl in turn and finally nodded. "Yeah, I am. What if they're really awful?"

"That would mean we have no fashion sense," Kim said. "And that's just not possible."

"You don't understand," Haley protested.

"Sure we do." Jerilyn met her gaze. "It's like when I tried out for chorus at school. I didn't know if I was good enough. And I wanted so badly to make it because a lot of my friends belonged. I wanted it enough to risk someone telling me I was terrible. And this is high school where public is really public, if you know what I mean."

"They nailed you," Marlon said to Haley.

She saw laughter in his eyes and knew there would be no support from him. "But this is like putting my baby out there and giving the public a chance to say it's ugly."

"You need a name for the line," Marlon said, clearly unsympathetic to her insecurity. "A brand."

"Use your initials," Becky suggested. She picked up the last pencil—a green one—and wrote H-A on the sketch pad. "HA!"

"I like it." Marlon nodded approvingly. "All you have to do is give me the go-ahead."

A horn honked outside and through the window they could see a car at the curb.

"It's my mom," Kim said standing. "She's here to pick us up."

"Good." Haley was relieved that they had transportation after dark, and that she'd gotten a reprieve from the pressure.

Kim walked to the door with Jerilyn and Becky trailing behind. "See you, Roy. Austin. Bye, Marlon."

"Take a chance, Haley." Becky poked her head back in. "What have you got to lose?"

Then they were gone and Marlon watched from the window as they got safely into the car and drove away. Haley thought about what the girls had said and wondered who was mentoring whom. They were wise beyond their years.

Roy walked over and dropped into the chair. "Can we be done talking about chick stuff?"

"That works for me," Haley answered.

Austin joined them and shook hands with Marlon. "I hate to agree with Roy, but women's purses are boring. And the fact that you don't think so scares me." Her brother slid Marlon a skeptical look.

"It is boring," Marlon agreed. "But potentially lucrative. And I don't havc to talk about it. That's what I have an assistant for."

"Lucrative? As in lots of money?" Austin was interested now.

"Some designers can get upwards of a thousand dollars for a handbag."

Austin's jaw dropped. "You're kidding me."

"No way," Roy said.

"Money is something I never joke about." Marlon looked dead serious.

"Me, either," Austin agreed. "Especially when you don't have any."

Haley knew what he was getting at and felt the need to explain. "Austin is talking about going to graduate school. To get a master's degree in engineering."

"Really?" Marlon looked impressed.

"Yeah." Austin rubbed a hand across his neck. "Green energy is the way of the future. We need to be oil-independent and I'd like to be a part of finding a way to do that in an environmentally responsible way."

"Good for you."

"Boring," Roy said.

Marlon reached over and ruffled the teen's hair. "Don't listen to him. If that's your dream, go for it."

"I'd like to, but—" Austin hesitated.

"The Anderson family budget spreadsheet doesn't have a column for graduate school tuition." Haley tried to make a joke, but it was hard when she knew how much her brother wanted this. It hurt that she couldn't give it to him.

Marlon folded his arms over his chest. "I could help. A loan maybe."

"Thanks," Haley said. "But we'll figure it out."

"A thousand dollars a pop?" Austin picked up the sketch pad and stared at her drawings in amazement. "I don't care what Haley says. Take this with my blessing. If someone says they're ugly, I'll beat them up for her."

Marlon laughed. "It's her decision. And nothing may come of it. There are no guarantees." He looked at her. "What do you say?"

She blew out a long breath and met his gaze, then echoed Becky. "What have I got to lose?"

"I'll send them to my assistant tomorrow." He nodded. "Good for you. There's no harm in trying."

Unlike giving in to her attraction for him. That could be incredibly harmful. She knew how it felt to lose someone she loved, how the sadness never completely went away. Marlon simply walked into the room and her body reacted as if she hadn't just warned herself not to care. Adrenaline-fueled hormones flooded her system and it was exciting. He was acting as if nothing was wrong between them and that felt good, too.

How was she going to be okay when he left town? How

would she be all right when she couldn't look forward to him walking into the room anymore?

"I'm surprised that Roy left with Austin." Marlon looked at the front door the duo had just walked out of, then back at her.

Haley hit the Off switch on the computer and monitor. "I guess he needed a male bonding moment after all the chick talk without his wingman. C.J.'s dad had just picked him up before you came in and the girls and I started talking fashion."

"Has Roy given you any clue about where he's from or why he ran away?"

"Nothing." She turned away from the now dark monitor. "I tried to torture it out of him by forcing him to help me bake chocolate chip cookies."

"You made cookies?" He looked around the room.

"Sorry. The kids ate them all before you got here."

"And making them is an ordeal?"

"Yes for those of us who don't love baking. But this method of extracting information has sometimes been wildly successful."

"Austin doesn't count," Marlon said wryly.

"Darn." She turned serious. "It didn't count much with Roy, either. And he had the nerve to say I wasn't subtle, followed quickly by a declaration that no facts would be forthcoming."

"Too bad."

"Although he did say something about having to live with disappointment and I'm pretty sure he didn't mean the kids here who wouldn't have homemade cookies if we didn't bake."

Frowning, Marlon slid his fingertips into the pockets of his jeans. "He wasn't more specific?"

She shook her head. "For a teenage boy, disappointment could be anything from not getting a coveted video game to being shut down by the head cheerleader."

"I remember."

"Which one?"

"Both," he said ruefully. "You might not believe this, but I was fooled by a pretty face once."

"No. Really?" That shocked her. It didn't seem like bad ever happened to him. But the dark and angry expression on his face told her differently.

"I thought it was love at first sight, but she was after money." He shrugged. "I fell for it."

"Wow, Marlon, I don't know what to say." She wasn't happy he'd been hurt, but it made him more human somehow. Less godlike and untouchable.

"It was a long time ago."

"I guess she didn't get the Marlon magic?" she said, trying to tease a grin out of him.

It worked and his expression turned wry. "Not even a little bit. A guy never forgets something like that."

"Even an old guy like you?" Apparently she liked teasing him. The words just fell out of her mouth.

His gaze jumped to hers as he grinned. "Yeah. Even an old guy like me can remember that high school is like the wild wild west of hormones."

She hadn't been in high school for years, but every time he was near, her hormones zigged and zagged, dropped, rolled and ducked like a shootout at the OK Corral. "I've never heard it put quite like that."

"Doesn't make it any less true."

She sighed. "The thing is, Marlon, if he doesn't tell us something soon, I'm going to have to get Social Services involved. He's under eighteen."

"I know. And school will be starting soon. Covering for him too much longer isn't in his best interest."

"I just can't help feeling that it would be better if he volunteered the information instead of forcing it out of him."

"Teenage boys can be stubborn," he said.

"Is that the voice of experience?"

He looked at her. "I refuse to answer on the grounds that it may incriminate me."

"I'll take that as a yes." She smiled. It felt good. Being mad at him took a lot of negative energy. That flash of insight made her remember something else. "Roy made another comment."

"About himself?"

She shook her head. "He noticed the tension between us."

"Yeah, well…" He dragged his fingers through his hair. "You weren't very subtle about being peeved at me."

The kiss had embarrassed her and anger was the go-to emotion. She'd taken it out on him and that wasn't fair. "I'm sorry for the way I treated you."

He looked surprised, leaning more toward shocked or stunned. "I don't quite know what to say."

She shrugged. "There's no excuse really. I've just had a lot on my mind and you were a handy target."

"No problem." There was warmth and sincerity in his expression when he added, "I was serious about helping Austin with graduate school expenses."

She smiled at the extraordinarily sweet and generous offer. And she was incredibly grateful that he went there instead of the real source of what was uppermost in her mind.

Him. MC. Major crush. Marlon Cates. Hottie and home-town hero.

When he left town after completing his community service, it might be easier on her if she were mad at him. But she didn't want the short amount of time he had left to be highlighted by anger and animosity. Teasing him was so much more fun.

"It's really kind of you to offer financial help, but Austin is looking into scholarships, grants and student loans first."

"If none of the above works out, you'll let me know?"

"Promise."

"Okay."

They smiled at each other and her pulse quickened as the blood seemed to rush to her head, pounding in her ears. It was time to go before she embarrassed herself again.

"It's getting late," she said. "I need to make sure everything is shut down and locked up."

"I'll give you a hand."

"Thanks."

They walked around turning off lights, TV and the video game. As Haley moved toward the back room, she heard the front door dead bolt slide home and knew Marlon had secured it. She grabbed her purse and keys from the closet, then hit the On switch for the angel night light in the powder room, making the dark not quite so absolute.

Marlon appeared in the doorway. "All set?"

"Yeah."

"I'll walk you to your truck."

"Okay."

There was a chilly breeze blowing when he followed her out and watched her secure the door. Her truck was parked under an outside light just a few steps from where they stood. Haley walked around to the driver's-side door and unlocked it. Marlon, standing behind her, reached around and opened it. She tossed her purse onto the passenger seat, then turned to say good-night.

"I appreciate you helping me out with my sketches."

"I'll come by in the morning and pick them up so I can overnight them to my assistant."

"Thanks for trying, even if nothing comes of it."

"Don't mention it. Whether you believe it or not, you're incredibly talented."

His deep, husky voice sent shivers over her skin. The truck was to her back and Marlon stood in front of her, blocking the wind. He was tall and broad, the sleeves of his T-shirt strained against the muscles bunching in his biceps. She instantly flashed on how good it had felt to be wrapped in his arms and a soft, yearning sound involuntarily slipped from her throat.

"Haley?" Intensity slid into his eyes making them darker, more dangerous.

"I—I should go—"

He reached out, cupping her cheek in his palm, and she leaned into the warmth, her eyelids drifting closed.

"Haley, I really want to kiss you…"

She opened her eyes and met his searching gaze. On some level she realized that he understood the last kiss had sparked the recent tension. This time, though, he was asking—and she couldn't have said no if her life depended on it.

"Okay," she whispered.

He slid the fingers of both hands into the hair around her face, brushed it off her cheeks. Then he lowered his head and softly touched his lips to hers. The achingly sweet contact made her eyes drift closed again as she sighed contentedly into his mouth. When his tongue touched hers, sparks of electricity arced through her and she opened wider. He dipped inside, stroking and caressing, making her breathe harder, faster, until she could hardly breathe at all.

His hand dropped to her waist and squeezed gently. Almost of their own accord, her arms tangled around his neck and she lifted up on her toes, trying to get closer. He pulled her snugly against him and held her there as he nibbled kisses over the corner of her mouth, jaw and neck. She could hear his own raspy breathing and joy surged through her.

They were as close as a man and woman could be. *Almost,* she thought as longing sliced through her, knotting uncomfortably in her chest. She snuggled and squirmed against him, instinctively trying to get nearer, and felt the hard ridge of his desire. He wanted her, she thought. And she wanted him right back. Her body throbbed with a powerful need, a feeling like she'd never felt before and had never known was there.

Marlon had awakened it and she wanted to know everything there was to know about being a woman. She slid her fingers into the hair at his nape and brushed her thumb over his neck. His deep groan of yearning made her heart sing. She wanted to touch him again, explore the wide expanse of his chest, the bare skin beneath his shirt. And she wanted him to do the same to her.

Just then the headlights of a car pulling into the far side of the lot flashed over them and they jumped apart. Both of them were breathing hard and Marlon hunched protectively over her, hiding her.

The knee-jerk reaction was sweet, but unnecessary, although five minutes longer and there might have been a whole lot more to hide.

"You better go." Marlon dragged his fingers through his hair.

"Can I drop you off at The Hitching Post?" Her voice

was a breathless, wanton whisper that didn't sound at all like her.

There was a slight hesitation before he shook his head. "The walk will do me good."

"Are you sure, because it's on my way—"

He settled his hands at her waist and lifted her into the truck. "Go, before it's too late."

He shut the door, not letting her question what that meant. But she knew. If he asked her to his room, she would go without a second's thought. She wanted him to make love to her, make her a woman. She might be a naive virgin, but the ache deep inside her didn't need explanation.

More important, the longing to be with him was impossible to ignore.

Chapter Eleven

Haley had never been more grateful for small-town traffic patterns than she was on the drive home. It was late, and she passed only a handful of cars and trucks. That was fortunate since part of her attention was focused on the aftereffects of kissing Marlon. This time was so much better because she didn't freeze up and freak out.

Her spirits were flying and her body hummed. Every part of her felt keyed up in the most wonderful way. Her nerve endings were highly sensitive. But the best part? She couldn't ever remember being this happy.

Marlon had wanted her.

She was sure of it.

For some reason, he hadn't wanted to take things to third plate, or home base, or whatever the slang was for going all the way. She was sure that's what he'd meant when he told her to go before it was too late. But she was way past late and had a lot of catching up to do.

And she wanted to catch up with Marlon.

She'd had a thing for him as long as she could remember and that teenage kiss had made her want more even then. But the timing had been all wrong. Now wasn't much better; he was leaving town soon. All the more reason to catch up while she could.

This time when he left, she didn't want any regrets. No one got through life without them, but some you could control and making love with Marlon fell into that column.

She was a grown up now and knew the score. No expectations for tomorrow, just live in the now. Of course her mother had advised her to wait for the right man—someone she cared about who cared about her. The L-word was never spoken, just implied during "the talk" all those years ago.

There wasn't a doubt in Haley's mind that she and Marlon cared about each other. It felt very right for him to be the first.

And only.

"Not going there," she muttered to herself.

No expectations; no promises. There was just now.

And that's when Haley made up her mind.

She was going back to town and knock on Marlon's door upstairs at The Hitching Post. If she was wrong about him wanting her, so be it. She was getting pretty good at surviving humiliation. Regrets, not so much. There was a very good chance that this state of wanting and not having him would make her implode.

Since she was almost home, she decided to stop in and let Austin and Angie know what she was doing. Well, not precisely *what*, just that she had to go back to Thunder Canyon and they shouldn't worry.

Haley pulled into the driveway and parked the truck beside her brother's small, aging compact, then grabbed her purse. When she walked up to the front door, she heard male voices. Loud voices. Arguing. She went inside and the chaotic scene matched the feelings bouncing through her, but for a very different reason.

Austin was in Roy's face. "I know what I saw."

"You don't have a clue, dude."

"Don't call me dude."

"Stop, Austin," Angie cried. "It's not what you think."

"You put the moves on my sister." Austin poked Roy in the chest.

Angie grabbed her brother's arm. "He didn't. How many times do I have to tell you?"

Haley dropped her purse just inside the door. "What's going on?"

Without looking away from Roy, Austin said, "He made a pass at Angie."

"No way," Roy protested. "Haley, I wouldn't do that."

Angie met her gaze. "He's like a little brother. We're friends."

"Then why was he on top of you when I walked in the room?" Austin demanded.

"We were wrestling for the cookies," Roy said defensively, blue eyes blazing.

Haley saw the empty plastic cookie container on the rug in the front room, by the couch. The cookies were broken and chocolate chips ground into the carpet. Roy's T-shirt was ripped and Austin's sports shirt was only partially tucked into his jeans. She was no forensics expert, but it didn't take top-notch detective skills to see the two had scuffled. Quickly scanning their faces, she saw no evidence that punches were thrown. So far it was only pushing and shoving.

A muscle in Austin's jaw bunched. "You're taking advantage of Haley's kindness. In return you're hitting on my other sister. You're not getting away with it. I'm not going to stand by and let some jerk I know nothing about hurt my family."

"I'm not doing that—" Roy moved closer and Austin shoved him back.

When that escalated to grappling, Haley snapped out of her shock. She moved forward and with Angie's help shoved between them.

"Stop it right now." She shouted to be heard over the grunting and heavy breathing from exertion.

"He started it," the teen said.

"I stopped it before you could start anything," Austin argued.

"Do something, Haley," Angie begged. "Austin's gone all macho and over-protective."

"Someone has to." Austin's dark eyes snapped with anger. Breathing hard he looked at Haley and said, "What do you know about this kid?"

"I know he needs help," she defended.

"And what if he's playing you? He won't say where he's from or why he won't go home. He could be taking advantage of your soft heart. A user. Someone has to look out for *you*."

"I can take care of myself," Haley said.

"Me, too," Angie chimed in. "I don't need Rambo coming to the rescue."

Austin shook his head. "That's not the way it looked to me."

"I have no reason not to believe or trust Roy," Haley said. "Let's all take a deep breath and calm down."

"So you're taking his side over your own brother?" Austin looked even angrier.

"I'm not taking anyone's side. There's no side to take. It was a misunderstanding."

"When are you going to wake up?" Austin challenged. "Make him tell you where he's from or toss his backside out."

"What if I do that and Roy gets hurt?" Haley demanded. "Where would you be now if people had treated you that way when you were a teenager with problems?"

"Are you ever going to let me forget that?" he demanded. "Just so we're clear, you're not my mother. I grew up, got my head on straight. It's what a guy does." Austin glared at Roy, then turned his fierce expression back to her. "You and Angie are way too trusting."

"I don't need anyone telling me what to do." Angie looked first at her, then Austin. "Especially my brother. Just because you have a bachelor's degree doesn't mean you have a brain. I don't need you fighting my battles. I'll give my trust to whoever I darn well please."

Haley would give anything to have Marlon here, and his understanding of the male point of view along with him. Everything that came out of her mouth was wrong and seemed to make this situation even more tense.

With an effort, she pulled the tatters of her patience together. "Saying derogatory things to your brother isn't helping, Angie."

"And neither is he," she argued, pointing at her sibling.

Haley looked at her sister. "Doesn't he get points for the sentiment? He's just trying to be a good big brother."

Angie shook her head. "He's interfering in my life. Don't even talk to me about points."

"How about the point on top of your head?" Austin snarled.

"Very funny. Is that the best you've got?"

"I've saved the good stuff," Austin retorted. "Get ready. Here it comes—"

"Look, dude, don't pick on Angie," Roy interrupted.

The two made a threatening move toward each other until Haley put a palm on each of their chests to keep them separated. There was so much testosterone in the room it was a wonder she could stand her ground at all. And again she wished Marlon was there to back her up.

When had she started to rely on him so much?

Right now she couldn't think about the downside of that. First she had to get a cease-fire from these two.

"Everyone stand down," she ordered. "Take five and we'll talk about this without punching and yelling."

"I'm not a kid. Don't even tell me to use my words." Angie glared at her. "Let me say this one more time. We're just friends. Austin is being an ass. I'm a grown-up and don't need you hovering. You need to back off." She stalked out of the room and moments later her bedroom door slammed.

Haley felt as if she'd been punched in the stomach. "Okay, she needs to cool off. Roy— Austin—"

"She's right. Talking is a bunch of crap." Austin stared angrily over her head at Roy. "I manned up. I did what I thought was right. I make my own decisions. You need to let go, Haley." He left and the house shook when his bedroom door crashed closed.

Double punch to the gut. She was reeling, almost as if the words had been physical blows. Why was she suddenly the bad guy? She'd taken care of them when she was just a kid herself. What had she done that was so wrong?

If they wanted space, they could have it. But Roy needed help and she wouldn't let him down.

"That went well." She blew out a long breath. "Kind of makes you glad that I'm not part of America's diplomatic corps."

"Whatever." The teen flopped on the sofa, his body still vibrating with pent-up anger.

Now what? Roy had been sleeping on an air mattress in Austin's room, but that didn't seem like a good idea.

"I think for tonight it would be best if you spent the night on the couch." When he looked at her and shrugged, she said, "I'll get some bedding for you."

Without waiting for an answer, she left him and went down the hall to the linen closet for sheets, blanket and pillow. On her way she passed closed doors and couldn't help feeling left out in the cold. And just the tiniest bit sorry for herself.

All she'd wanted was to smooth over the incident and be one big happy family. Instead her family, the only people she had in this world, was mad at her. She'd never felt more alone in her life.

She remembered the warm feel of Marlon's arms around her and desperately wanted to go to him. But she couldn't leave. If World War III broke out again, someone had to be Switzerland. That made her feel even more alone.

The morning after kissing Haley Marlon was wound so tight he felt ready to explode. It had probably been the most boneheaded move he'd ever made. His body was revved and sent his mind to a place where he longed to spend the night with her in his arms, his mouth on hers.

Just like that his body tensed all over again. He remembered her contented sigh, the needy little sounds she'd made. The short walk from ROOTS to The Hitching Post hadn't come close to taking the edge off his need. It would be right there when he saw her again later this morning.

He still didn't know how he'd come up with the willpower to turn down her offer of a ride, but somehow he'd resisted the almost irresistible temptation. Maybe because he knew he'd invite her up to his room. Possibly he hadn't wanted to hear her say no. Or yes. Or tell him yet again that he didn't do commitment. The problem was, now that she'd put the idea of commitment in his head, it wouldn't leave him alone. And she was the only one he could think about.

But that was crazy. Maybe not as nuts as falling for a woman's con to get money out of him, but nuts all the same. Haley's life was here in Thunder Canyon and his wasn't. He was going back to L.A. When had the initial impatience to get his license back turned into regret at having to leave Haley?

He paced his room, trying to pin down the moment, all the while knowing it wouldn't change anything. Stopping beside the king-size bed, he couldn't help picturing Haley there with him, which couldn't—wouldn't—happen. Somehow he knew that if it did, walking away from her would be like ripping his heart out.

Poetic thoughts like that were pretty lame for a guy who'd never been accused of having a sensitive side. And all this pacing and regret was just putting off the inevitable—seeing her. She'd be working the breakfast shift downstairs. There were other places in town to eat, but not as good. And sooner or later he would have to see her because he still had community service hours to perform.

"Might as well get it over with," he said to the empty room. At least he'd gotten her sketches off to L.A. first thing that morning. "I can tell her that my assistant will be looking at them this time tomorrow."

He was bracing himself for the punch-to-the-gut sensation Haley always gave him when there was a knock on his door. The sound was startling because he never had visitors.

He opened the door, and got the punch-to-the-gut feeling when he saw who was there. "Haley."

"Hi, Marlon. Sorry to bother you."

"You're not." At least not in a way he could share. "I'm glad you stopped by. I wanted you to know that I overnighted your sketches to my assistant first thing this morning. I—" He noticed something on her face that clued him in. She hadn't come about her drawings. "Is something wrong?"

She twisted her fingers together. "Is Roy here by any chance?"

"No. I haven't seen him since he left ROOTS last night with Austin."

The hopeful expression on her expressive face turned to disappointment, then worry. "Okay. Thanks."

"Wait." He reached out and grabbed her arm when she started to turn away. "Why are you looking for him?"

"He was gone this morning."

"I see." Marlon leaned a shoulder against the doorjamb and slid his fingertips into the pockets of his jeans. "Maybe he went home."

"I think he would have said something, don't you?"

"He's a runaway. By definition that makes him unpredictable."

"I think that's part of the age. The thing is, I thought we connected. And for him to leave without a note or anything feels wrong to me. That's why I thought he might be here with you."

There was something she wasn't telling him. He'd bet money on it. And when had he gotten to know her that well? "Did something happen before he took off?"

Her gaze jumped to his and she was chewing on her bottom lip. Finally she said, "There was an awful scene last night."

He straightened away from the door frame. It didn't sound like this was something she'd want to discuss in the hallway. "Come in. Tell me what happened."

She passed him and walked into the room. They were alone, but this wasn't the way he'd pictured having her all to himself.

"When I got home last night," she started, "Roy and Austin were arguing."

The two had seemed like best buds when they'd left the teen center. "What happened?"

"I guess Austin walked in on Roy and Angie goofing around and assumed the worst."

"That Roy was hitting on his sister?" he guessed.

She nodded. "They insisted they're just friends and Austin was overreacting. I tried to get everyone to shake hands and apologize, but the next thing I knew they were all telling me to get off their case and butt out."

"Roy, too?"

She shook her head. "He was back to his default response."

"Whatever?" he guessed.

"That's the one," she said grimly. "This morning my brother and sister were barely speaking to me or each other. And Roy was just gone."

"Have you checked with C.J.? Or Jerilyn? Or some of the other kids from the center?"

"Not yet." Worry clouded her eyes. "I was hoping I wouldn't have to because I'd find him hanging out here with you. But I'll start making phone calls. Thanks, Marlon. Sorry to bother you."

"Stop saying that. You're not bothering me. I want to help." He dragged his fingers through his hair. "What if no one has heard from him?"

"I'll keep looking."

"Why?"

"Because he ran away from home and now he's run away from me. I feel responsible."

"Haley, you did nothing but try to help that kid. It's not your fault."

"Maybe not, but he could be out there alone. Just because he's a guy doesn't mean he's not at the mercy of predators—" Her voice caught and she pressed her full lips together.

"Do you have a plan?" he asked, wanting to fix this for her. He wanted to be her knight in shining armor and chase the apprehension from her face. He knew it was stupid, but that didn't make the feeling go away.

"Yeah. If he's nowhere to be found in Thunder Canyon, I'm going to Billings."

That surprised him. "Why?"

"When he was hanging out at the center with the other teens, I overheard him say he has a friend there."

"Did he happen to mention the name of this friend?"

"No, but—"

"Haley, that's like spitting into the wind."

"I don't care." She threw up her arms in frustration. "Sitting around isn't an option."

Determination was a good quality, but Marlon wished she had a little less. He hated the idea of her going all alone. As she'd so graphically stated, there were predators out there. Unlike Roy, she wasn't a guy.

"Is there any way to talk you out of this?"

"Unless you've been lying to me and Roy is hiding under the bed... No. You can't change my mind."

"That's what I thought you'd say." He grabbed his wallet and room key from the desk. "In that case, I'm going with you."

"That's not necessary. You should open the center—"

"The kids will survive if it doesn't open for a day. I'll help you make phone calls. It will be faster. If no one's heard from him, we'll cruise Thunder Canyon and look for him." He held up his hand to stop her when she opened her mouth. "Two pairs of eyes are better than one and you're driving."

"Really, I can handle this."

Without acknowledging her protest, he continued, "If our search doesn't produce any results, we'll go to Billings together. I'm not letting you look for him by yourself."

"I won't be," she protested. "My best friend, Elise Clifton, lives there. She knows the town and can give me a hand."

He shook his head, determined to out-stubborn her. "That doesn't solve the problem of you driving there alone. What if you have a flat tire? A problem with your truck? It's not getting any younger."

"I'm used to handling stuff."

"So you've said."

He couldn't refute that she'd had to handle stuff. Life had smacked her down, but she didn't stay there. She thumbed her nose at fate, picked herself up and thrived in spite of everything. She was a beautiful, talented woman who was also determined, obstinate, persistent and caring. The problem of her going alone wasn't hers. It was his.

He wasn't used to worrying about anyone, but that didn't seem to stop the protective feeling rolling through him. He didn't like worrying about her and was going along whether she liked it or not.

Staying here in Thunder Canyon while she went to look for an impulsive teenager all by herself wasn't an option.

"Here's the deal, Haley. We can stand here and argue, wasting precious time. Or you can give in gracefully and let me help you cut the work in half. Because I'm not taking no for an answer." He rested his hands on his hips and stared her down. "So what's it going to be?"

She took his measure for several moments, then said, "Okay. You can help."

"Good choice. Let's go find the bonehead."

She grinned for the first time since he'd opened the door and made him feel like he'd given her the moon and stars.

Later he would worry about why that reaction was a bad thing.

Chapter Twelve

Haley could admit to herself that she was happy Marlon had accompanied her to Billings, but never out loud for him to hear. For one thing, nothing good would come of it. And she had to focus on finding Roy. The man she'd believed Marlon to be just a few short weeks ago would never have inconvenienced himself for anyone. She'd learned he wasn't that man.

But *this* man could break her heart if she wasn't careful.

They climbed back into her truck after talking to a representative for the Billings police and Marlon said, "Now what?"

"I'm thinking."

Not entirely about finding the teen, but that would stay her secret. "The cops weren't much help."

"They'll do what they can. Keeping an eye out for anyone meeting Roy's description is something. And the sketch you did of our boy was a pretty good likeness. Distributing the copies they made to patrol officers may produce results."

"It doesn't feel like enough," she grumbled, glancing at him in the passenger seat.

His expression was wry. "Unfortunately they can't mobilize a task force for every runaway kid. It happens too often and is usually nothing more than a grounded teenager hiding out to punish a parent who dared not be their friend."

"And who really gets punished?" She knew how awful it felt to worry about someone you love. But he was right, although that didn't make her feel better.

"I know you're concerned, but there's no reason to believe he won't be fine. Roy will probably have kids someday. The fruit doesn't fall far from the tree. DNA and all that. He'll almost certainly have one a lot like him. What goes around comes around and he'll live to regret this. Live is the operative word." He reached over and squeezed her shoulder reassuringly.

She wasn't reassured, but his touch made her concentrate on catching her breath instead of the lost boy. Was it only hours ago that she'd made up her mind to go to Marlon's room and finish what he'd started with that kiss in the ROOTS parking lot? It felt like a lifetime ago. Even worse, another missed opportunity.

She sighed. "We can phone shelters. They might be able to give us leads about where homeless teens tend to hang out."

He nodded. "We need a local phone book."

"I know just where to find one."

She started the truck and pulled out into traffic. A short time later, they stopped in front of a book store. It was located on a quaint street with retail shops sporting western facades and wooden walkways, not unlike the ones in Thunder Canyon.

Marlon looked at the storefront. "Books and More?"

"Elise works here. I called her. She's expecting us."

"And she'll have a phone book," he guessed.

Haley nodded. "And she knows the town. She might have some ideas of her own about where to look for a teenager who doesn't want to be found."

They got out of the truck and walked to the door. The bell above it rang when the door was opened. Haley had been here before, managing to take a couple of days off to visit her friend. But it never seemed long enough. And suddenly excitement shot through her along with acute impatience.

She glanced anxiously around at book shelves lining the store's perimeter and displays of the current bestsellers straight ahead. Beyond that were rows of genres—mystery, thrillers—and her personal favorite—romance.

Before she could decide which way to go, a blue-eyed blonde in navy slacks and a white blouse moved from behind one of the racks. Instantly a pleased smile lit up her pretty face.

"Haley!"

There was hugging, talking at the same time, and laughing.

"It's so good to see you, Haley. How long has it been?"

"Too long." She looked up at the man beside her. "You remember Marlon Cates."

Elise nodded. "You're not easy to forget."

"Should I be scared or flattered?" His expression was half-teasing, half-wary.

"Both." She grinned. "I was a year behind you in school. You always seemed to travel with an entourage. And having a twin brother for a wingman didn't hurt. Everyone wanted to be your friend."

"I'm not quite sure how to respond to that."

Elise laughed. "You don't have to say anything."

She and Elise were the same height, same age, although the other woman looked younger and always had. The small brown birthmark on the bridge of her nose, right side, hadn't gone away. She watched her friend's easy exchange with Marlon and waited for a flash of jealousy, like she'd felt when he'd talked to Erin Castro. But it never came. Maybe because he was treating Elise like a little sister.

Haley felt guilty about Roy taking off in the first place, but the silver lining of that particular cloud was the chance to see her friend.

"Elise, you look so good. Your hair's different. Longer." The golden blond strands brushed her shoulders and barely curved under.

"That's my cue," Marlon said.

Haley glanced up. "For what?"

"To leave. So you can engage in girl talk."

"Have you had lunch yet?" Elise asked.

It was after one o'clock and Haley had forgotten about eating, but her stomach chose that moment to growl. She put a hand on her abdomen and laughed ruefully. "That would be no."

"There's a cute little café two doors down. They make a great club sandwich."

"Any place is fine." Haley glanced at Marlon again. "You have to eat."

"I saw a fast food place up the street. I'll just grab a burger there." He looked at Elise. "If I can borrow your phone book, I'll make some calls and see if I can get some leads on our boy." He snapped his fingers. "And if you have a copy machine, I'll duplicate a sketch Haley made and circulate it."

"That's a good idea," Haley said. "But I should help you."

He shook his head. "Give yourself a break. Take an hour. I insist."

She knew once he'd made up his mind, trying to change it would be as impossible as moving the mountains that surrounded Thunder Canyon. So she gave in gracefully. "Okay, then."

Elise nodded toward the back of the store. "Let me just tell my boss I'm going to lunch."

Fifteen minutes later she and Elise were sitting at a round table covered with a red checkered cloth. Club sandwiches and fries nestled in white plastic baskets and diet sodas were sitting in front of them and they dug in eagerly.

"So how are you?" Haley wiped her mouth with the paper napkin.

"Good. I love working at the bookstore. When it's not busy I can bury myself in a book."

Escape, Haley thought. And her friend had good reasons for wanting to. "What's new?"

Elise chewed thoughtfully, then her blue eyes lit up. "I'm going to be an aunt. Grant and his wife, Stephanie, are expecting a baby."

"That's great," Haley said. "I hadn't heard."

"I'm sure you will." Her friend grinned. "Nothing stays a secret in Thunder Canyon."

"That's so true. This is yummy," Haley said, picking up her second triangle of sandwich.

"So is Marlon." Elise's blue eyes danced with the teasing. "What's up with that?"

"With what?"

"Don't play dumb, Haley. This is me and I will not be distracted. You and Marlon? A relationship?"

"There's no relationship—"

Haley's automatic denial died on her lips. She was so used to pushing aside her feelings, putting on a perky face, pretending everything was perfect. But this was Elise, the one person she could always open her heart to. The friend she'd always been able to talk to and unburden herself. Maybe because they both shared deep personal losses. Elise's father had been murdered on his ranch years earlier. When life in Thunder Canyon became too painful, her mom had moved them to Billings. And when Haley's mom died in the car accident, she'd finally understood her friend's soul-deep sadness and their bond deepened. For whatever reason, this was a rare and precious opportunity to talk to her friend, face-to-face. No phone. And no e-mail, which was even less satisfying.

"Okay." Haley picked up a fry and took a bite. "I wouldn't call it a relationship. Not what you're implying. We're friends, I guess."

"So the spark I saw between you was just static electricity?" Elise hardly looked older than eighteen, but she missed nothing.

"Okay. He kissed me."

"Really?"

"Yeah. Twice."

"Does that tally include the one at the football fundraiser six years ago?"

Haley had told her all about that, including a blow-by-blow of the heartbreak and disappointment that followed when he didn't call. "Okay," she confessed. "Three times."

"And?"

"And nothing." She explained about him losing his

driver's license and the community service that kept them practically joined at the hip. Temporarily. "He's going back to L.A. Soon."

"And your heart is going to break again." It wasn't a question.

"Not this time. He hasn't promised anything and I know he's leaving. Older and wiser." She shrugged and took a sip from her diet soda.

"Just because you know the score it doesn't mean you can keep your emotions in check. It's not like ordering your dog to sit, stay, play dead."

How she wished her feelings were dead, but just the opposite was true. Emotions were alive, well, thriving out of control.

"I know."

"Have you slept with him?" Elise asked.

If anyone else had asked, Haley would have been shocked and embarrassed. Elise knew that she'd never had sex. "No."

"Do you want to?"

"Yes," she said simply. No point in lying. Her friend always saw through her.

"So you really do care." There was gentle understanding in Elise's soft voice.

"How did you know?"

"If you didn't, you wouldn't even consider going to bed with him." Sympathy and understanding were soft in her friend's blue eyes. "Maybe Marlon is the reason you've waited this long."

She was right. Warm feelings for this wonderful friend welled up and tears filled her eyes. She felt a little less alone because there was someone in this world who knew her so well.

"I miss you so much." She reached over and squeezed Elise's hand. "I wish we could talk like this more often."

"Well, I'll be back in Thunder Canyon for the holidays. We'll get together then."

"Christmas seems so far away."

"The time will fly," Elise promised.

"I could be more patient if it wasn't going to be a temporary visit. When Grant and Stephanie's baby is born, you're going to want to be close to your niece or nephew. A good reason to make it a permanent move. Don't blame me for keeping my fingers crossed."

"They're your fingers, but—" Deep sadness dimmed the sparkle in Elise's eyes. "I really can't live there. Too many bad memories."

Haley nodded, knowing all about the awful things that had happened. But she couldn't help hoping that the next visit would change her friend's mind about making it a move back for good. She was going to need the comfort of talks like this when Marlon went back to his regularly scheduled life and took her heart with him.

"It won't kill you to have some dinner, Haley."

Marlon lounged in the open doorway to her room. The search had taken all afternoon. They'd made phone calls, tacked up copies of his sketch all over town and driven around looking for Roy without success. It was getting late and he could see how tired she was. Her exhaustion would make the trip back to Thunder Canyon an ordeal. Without a license, he couldn't take over the driving for her.

Finally he'd made an executive decision and reserved two rooms for the night at a hotel. He'd known it was the right decision when she didn't fight him on it.

After a trip to the local Walmart for necessities, he'd come next door to convince Haley that a hunger strike wouldn't help find the teenager and would only hurt her in the long run.

"It feels wrong," she finally answered.

"Are you afraid you'll have fun?" he challenged.

"Of course not—" She stopped, a puzzled look on her face as she tried to figure out what, if anything, she'd admitted.

"Then you don't want to spend time with me."

"I do, it's just—" Again she stopped, frowning.

Marlon definitely wanted to spend time with her. He just wished there wasn't a dark cloud hovering over this trip, that she could be carefree and forget about responsibility for a while. He wanted to give her that before it was time to go.

He moved farther into the room—a duplicate of his. There was a king-size bed covered with a blue-green patterned comforter. The walls were cream-colored and dark wood nightstands bracketed the bed. A bathroom was to the right by the door. It was your basic, generic hotel room.

He should know. He'd stayed in what felt like a million of them, traveling around by himself. But just having Haley next door made it different, special and he wanted to do something for her. Buying her a nice dinner seemed right.

"What is it, Haley?" he asked again. "There's nothing more you can do tonight. We've left cell phone numbers with everyone possible. If anyone has information about Roy, they'll call. Let's stand down. Just for a little while."

Her brown eyes darkened with the conflict raging inside her. Finally her gaze lifted to his. "Is this one of those times when you're not taking no for an answer?"

"You noticed that about me?"

"Didn't have to notice. You're not shy about announcing it." She shook her head and muttered, "Darn sales personality."

"I know." He grinned as he took her elbow and guided her from the room. "Gotta love it."

"It's very irritating."

"Part of my charm." At the end of the hall, he pushed the down elevator button.

"You call it charm. I say pigheaded, obstinate and inflexible."

"Takes one to know one. And my mother calls it perseverance." When the doors whispered open, they stepped into the car. "She always said it would be a good quality in an adult. A kid? Not so much."

"Your mom is a smart lady."

"I take after her." That finally merited a smile. She'd made him work, but it was worth the reward.

There was a nice restaurant right next door and this time he didn't make the mistake of kissing her on the way. Although the memory of her response to his mouth on hers last night hinted at a more positive outcome.

They walked inside the place, which had candlelight and white tablecloths. The hostess greeted, then seated them in a quiet corner of the uncrowded dining room. It was impossible not to notice the romantic surroundings.

Haley looked beautiful in unforgiving sunshine, but by candlelight she took his breath away. Her brown hair was loose and teased her shoulders and cheeks, making him want to bury his fingers in the silky softness. This place had probably been a mistake. Somewhere called Bubba's Burgers and Beans would have been noisy and loud, not at all suited to passionate thoughts. Although he wasn't sure even that atmosphere would have completely erased his growing need to touch her.

A waitress in black pants and pristine white blouse appeared beside them. "My name is Claire and I'll be your server tonight. Can I get you a cocktail or glass of wine?"

Marlon looked at Haley and the frown told him that's where she drew the line. Fun was one thing, but keeping a clear head because of why they were here took priority.

"Iced tea for me," he said.

"Make it two," said Haley.

"Coming right up." She handed them menus and left to get their drinks.

"No beer?" One corner of Haley's full mouth lifted.

"Gotta keep a clear focus. Just in case."

The approval shining in her eyes made him feel as if he'd just gone to the head of the class. It was a potent reaction and that was dangerous. Possibly leading to promises he wasn't sure he could keep. He didn't want to risk doing anything to lead her on. There wouldn't be a repeat of not keeping his word.

He opened his menu and had to force himself to read the choices. The time for him to go back to L.A. was approaching far too quickly and it felt as if he couldn't look at her long enough. Hard enough.

"So what are you having?" he asked, not really seeing the words. He chanced a glance and she was nervously chewing on her lip. "What?"

"The prices…" She glanced up.

"I can afford it."

"You don't have to."

He wondered if she'd ever been to a restaurant more upscale than The Hitching Post. He doubted it. No one seemed to know if she dated. The jerk in college probably hadn't taken her anywhere fancy. This might be his only chance to do something for the woman who took care of everyone else.

"If you don't order whatever you want, regardless of the cost, I'm getting you the most expensive dinner they have."

Her eyes widened. "There are things listed without the cost. It says market price."

"Live dangerously."

"Really?"

He was. Just by being here. "Yeah."

When Claire came back with drinks and said, "Are you ready to order? Or do you need a few minutes."

"I'm ready," Haley said. "Petite filet mignon, medium rare, with a baked potato and house salad."

"Good choice," said Marlon. "I'll have the same."

"Coming right up."

Fifteen minutes later they were digging into their meals. The pleasured expression on Haley's face was a mixed blessing. It was good to see her enjoying an experience that he took for granted. Bad because blood flow went south of his belt as thoughts of other ways to pleasure her refused to leave him alone. He was a jerk and the seventh level of hell wouldn't be low enough for him.

When she declared herself too full to eat another bite, half her steak still sat on her plate. He finished it for her.

"I had a feeling that would happen," he said.

"Is that why you ordered the smaller cut? Because the women you take to dinner leave half of theirs?"

And just like that the sad, guarded expression was back in her eyes. Before he could ask her about it, Claire returned and they declined dessert, so she took his credit card.

"What's wrong, Haley?" he finally said.

"I was just wondering if Roy had dinner tonight."

The "women he took to dinner" remark told him it was

more than that, but he didn't want to go there. Instead, he asked, "Why do you do that?"

"What?"

"Shut down the fun. Punishing yourself doesn't do anything except make you feel sad. It doesn't change the fact that bad stuff happens and none of it is within your control."

She slapped her cloth napkin on the table and glared. "You don't think I already know that?"

"I know you know," he said. "More than anyone you should understand how important it is to live in the moment. You can't walk around waiting for the other shoe to fall."

"That's easy for you to say. When you went to college, left home for the first time, no one called a few weeks later to tell you your mother was dead. You didn't have to rush home in a state of shock to a brother and sister even more traumatized than you.

"One day you're the oldest child and the next you're parenting the only family you have left in the world." She drew in a shuddering breath. "Do you have any idea what it's like to be dumped into a responsibility that you didn't ask for and in no way deserve?"

"You did an unbelievable job," he said sincerely.

"If that's true, I couldn't have done it without Ben Walters. He was like the father I never had."

"Even more than you know."

"What does that mean?" she demanded. "Why don't you like him?"

"I think you've got that reversed."

He hadn't meant to say anything to her, but couldn't be sorry he had. It was important before he left to let her know that when he'd said he was going to call her, he'd fully intended to do just that. He needed her to know that he wasn't a heartless player, that she was wrong when she'd mocked his commitment capability. He wanted to clear the air.

"Six years ago I kissed you at the football carnival and told you I'd call. Somehow Ben Walters found out." He shrugged. "No secrets in a small towns."

"I don't understand."

"Ben warned me to stay away from you. That you weren't my type and he wasn't too old to make me sorry if I hurt you."

"Ben threatened you?"

"It was a guy thing. And he was right to do it." Marlon watched her jaw drop. "For what it's worth, recently he told me he was wrong about me."

"I never knew that." Surprise chased the sadness from her eyes. "All this time I've been thinking the worst about you."

"So what you said about commitment not being one of my strengths…" he teased.

"I'm sorry."

He wasn't looking for an apology, just clarification. And he definitely didn't want to make her feel bad. "Please don't look like that. I just thought you should know why I didn't call back then. I didn't mean to hurt you."

And if there was a God in heaven he wouldn't hurt her now. Or ever.

"I believe that," she said. "But it happened. And that wasn't the worst. It's hard for me to live in the moment, let my guard down and have fun. Taking a chance, moving forward…that hasn't worked out so well for me—"

Her voice broke and her lips trembled. She put her hand over her mouth, looking completely destroyed by the collapse of her composure. Without another word, she stood up and hurried out of the restaurant.

Marlon quickly signed the credit card receipt Claire had unobtrusively slipped on the table, then followed Haley. He couldn't stand to see her look like that.

But it was worse to stand back and do nothing. She wasn't alone; he was there. The least he could do was hold her while she cried.

Chapter Thirteen

Haley wasn't sure how she managed to find her way to her room, what with tears blurring her eyes. But she did, and stopped outside her door, fumbling in her jeans pocket for the card key.

It had been six years since her mother died. She'd managed to get everything under control. *She* was under control, always. So, what had made her melt down like that after so long?

Why tonight?

Why with Marlon?

Just thinking his name brought a fresh wave of emotion and she couldn't see to get her key in the slot. It didn't help that her hand was shaking.

"Damn it," she said brokenly.

"Haley?"

She'd felt him behind her even before he'd spoken. All

she wanted was to be alone and have her little scene in the privacy of her room.

"Please go away." Was that too much to ask?

"I can't leave you like this."

Apparently it was. "I'm fine."

"All evidence to the contrary. What's wrong?"

Too much to put into words. How could she tell him that she'd lost it because the future couldn't include him when they both wanted different things?

Just like that a fresh wave of tears trickled down her cheeks and she pressed a hand over her mouth to stifle a sob.

"Nothing's wrong."

"I don't believe you." His hands on her shoulders turned her. "Come here."

He wrapped his arms around her and pressed her close. She rested her cheek on his chest, comforted by the steady beat of his heart, the warmth of his body.

"Don't cry, Haley. We'll find Roy."

"I know."

It was easier to let him think that was the problem than explain she wasn't as selfless as he thought. This emotion was all about her. "I didn't mean to spoil the evening. You didn't need to follow me back."

But she couldn't manage to be sorry that he had.

"I can't stand to see you so upset. I had to make sure you were okay or do something to fix it."

"Stand down." She sniffled. "I'll dry."

He backed her up a step and looked down. "Promise?"

"Yes."

They stared at each other for several moments and she knew the exact moment he went from comfort mode to something else entirely. His brown eyes darkened and a muscle in his jaw tensed.

"You need to go in your room." His voice was deep, dangerous.

In a brief, blinding flash of clarity she knew that this was one of those turning points in life. A place where choices happened along with regrets. She could choose to live and look back with pride or duck and run and be sorry about it for the rest of her days. Was it only last night that she'd planned to go to his room and take the step? Fate had given her a second chance and she couldn't throw it away.

"No," she said. "Take me to your room."

Surprise jumped into his eyes, but the darkness was back a moment later. "That's a bad idea."

"Then you don't want me?" The brazen words were out and she couldn't believe she'd actually said it.

"I wouldn't say it like that."

"Then how would you say it?"

He shook his head. "Don't look at me like that."

"How?" she asked.

"Like I yanked the funding on your project. I'm trying to be a gentleman and it's not easy."

"Why isn't it easy?"

"Oh, God—" He swallowed hard. "Because you're beautiful. The feel of you— Your skin is— So soft. You've completely destroyed the sliver of self control I've managed to retain until this second."

Her heart pounded and her spirit soared. She'd made him feel like this? "Really?"

"Hell, yes. I want you more than I've ever wanted any woman in my life."

"I want you, too." She heard his sigh of surrender and knew she'd won.

Like a gunslinger pulling a six-shooter from a holster, suddenly his card key was in his hand and a second later the door to his room was open. Flipping the switch, he led her inside as the entry lit up. The door had barely closed before she was in his arms with his mouth on hers.

Haley slid her arms around his neck and pressed against him. The muscles in her legs were going lax and she hung on for all she was worth. Marlon's kiss was filled with hunger and any insecurity she once had disappeared as instinct and need took over.

His tongue traced the seam of her lips and she gladly opened to him. When he swept inside and boldly claimed her, the tempo of her breathing increased. The moan of need in her chest refused to be contained and the sound of it fueled the tension in his body as his hands seemed to explore everywhere. He caressed her back, curved his fingers at her hips to pull her against his hardness. Sliding his palms up above her waist, he stopped and brushed his thumbs over her breasts, making her nipples erect and sensitive.

She wanted him to touch her bare skin, ached to feel her breasts in his palms. As if he could read her mind, he tugged at the hem of her T-shirt, pulling it up and over her head. With a flick of his fingers, her bra loosened and he slid the straps down her arms before dropping it on the floor.

And then he was holding her in his hands and the feeling was too wonderful. Blood pounded through her veins and between her thighs, a steady throbbing started.

"Oh, Haley," he breathed. "You're so beautiful."

She closed her eyes and drew in a shuddering breath. "That feels so good."

Such an inadequate word.

Especially when he lowered his head to her right breast and took it in his mouth. The sensation was like a jolt of sensuous electricity when he flicked his tongue over the tip. She thought the pleasure was too much to bear until he turned his attention to the left side. Unable to restrain the tension building inside her, she nearly whimpered with need.

Marlon straightened and looked at her, his eyes burning with passion. His chest was rising and falling fast and furiously. He took her hand and led her to the side of the bed.

"Are you sure about this?" he asked.

"Absolutely."

That was all he needed to hear before sweeping aside the quilt, blanket and sheet in one move. She toed off her sneakers as he unfastened the button on her jeans and slid them down with her panties. Embarrassment and shyness threatened until he dragged his shirt off. The sight of his naked chest, the contour of muscle, stole the breath from her lungs. Then he kissed her and they were skin to skin from the waist up. Shyness disappeared as the exquisite intimacy set fire to her blood.

He pulled back reluctantly and reached into his jeans' pocket for his wallet. Reaching inside with two fingers, he pulled out a square packet and set it on the nightstand. Protection. Thank goodness he'd remembered because she hardly knew her own name.

Then his heated gaze settled on her face as he unfastened his jeans and pushed them down and away. She barely had time to admire the strength of his body, the muscular arms and legs, before he easily lifted her into his arms and settled her in the center of the big bed.

Before she had a chance to get cold, he was beside her, sliding an arm beneath her and pulling her close. He cupped her cheek in his palm and kissed her. With his teeth, tongue and touch, he stoked the fire inside her. He dragged his hand over her breast and down her belly. With one finger he parted the folds of her femininity, then entered her, preparing her. His thumb brushed over the bundle of nerves coiled at the juncture of her thighs and it was like the best electrical shock she'd ever had. The jolt nearly brought her up off the bed.

But that was just the beginning. He began to stroke her—over and over—building the pressure. She writhed, unable to hold still. Her hips lifted, seeking, as the throbbing in her center grew unbearable. And then there was an explosion of pleasure like a nuclear blast. Wave after wave shuddered through her and Marlon tenderly held her until it was over.

"Oh, my God—"

He smiled. "Yeah."

Words could never describe such a feeling. Finally, she understood what all the fuss was about. Her next thought was that she didn't know it all because she was still a virgin. Before she could figure out how to phrase a question, he was reaching for the condom he'd put on the nightstand.

After covering himself, he gathered her into his arms and whispered against her hair, "You're even more passionate and responsive than I imagined."

She was stunned that he'd thought about her like this.

"You imagined me?"

"After that first kiss." He grinned. "It made me wonder. You were so quiet and shy in high school. But just that once, I felt something."

"Wow."

If only she'd known he noticed her. The revelation made her daring and she lifted a hand to his neck, then slid her fingers into the hair at his nape. Pulling him down, she settled her lips on his and felt his breathing quicken, his heart pound. He rolled over her, bracing his weight on his forearms as he nudged her thighs apart with his knee.

"Put your legs around me." There was an intensity in his husky voice, an urgency in his movements.

She did as he asked, anxious now to take the final step, know this last secret. She felt him push into her and braced herself. When he thrust gently, there was a sharp pain when the resistance was gone. But she felt him tense.

He froze for a moment, confused. "Haley?"

"Don't stop," she whispered, holding him fast. "Please."

The discomfort faded and then she wrapped her legs more securely around him, drawing him in deeper. He groaned and his hips started to move. In moments, his body went completely still, then tensed as he cried out with pleasure. She held him tight as release surged through him. Now that she knew the awesomeness of the sensation, she smiled. Her heart soared at the wonder of giving him that. When he lifted his head, she dropped her arms. He rolled out of bed, then grabbed his pants from the floor before disappearing into the bathroom.

Her body was a little sore in the best possible way and she had a flash of insight. Sex didn't make her a woman. It just made her glory in being one.

Unfortunately, the glow only lasted until Marlon came back and handed her the hotel robe that had been hanging in his closet. "We need to talk."

Not the words she'd wanted to hear. It couldn't be a good sign. "Okay."

While she slid her arms into the sleeves and tied the robe around her waist, he turned his back. But when he spoke, she didn't have to see his face to know he was upset.

"You're a virgin?"

"Not anymore." She turned on the nightstand light.

He whirled around. "Did it occur to you at any point that it was information I should have?"

"No." She leaned against the headboard. "It's kind of a catch twenty-two. I didn't know what you needed to know because I'd never done it before."

"You're twenty-four years old. How is that possible?"

"Life intervened. I got busy. And my mom always told me not to rush into sex because there's only one first time and it should be special."

He winced. "If I'd known, I would have made it special."

"It was," she protested. "I'm glad it was you. I really wanted you to be the one."

"The one?" He couldn't have looked more surprised if she'd slapped him.

"You said yourself there was something simmering between us."

"Yeah." Regret shadowed every angle of his face. "And I was stupid for saying that. I was doing my damnedest to resist temptation—"

"I'm glad you didn't." That was an attempt to tease him out of this severe mood, but the muscle jerking in his cheek told her she'd failed.

"It's no use, Haley. Maybe if I were a different man…"

"Shouldn't that be my call?"

"How can you make the right one? You have nothing to compare."

She stood up and walked over to him, close enough to feel the anger rolling off him and let him feel hers. "Sex is just a physical act. The fact that it's my first time doesn't mean I don't know my own mind. I know who I like and don't like. I've been around."

"So have I. Enough to know I'm not good enough for you. I'm not the right guy. I can't be what you need."

The words pierced her heart and drew blood. It was vital

that she be alone when the pain of it hit. Without a word, she grabbed up her clothes. She'd waited to be with a man, wanting it to feel right. And it had. So wonderful, so right. And she hated that Marlon thought it was wrong.

But *he* was wrong. A woman who'd saved herself for the right man shouldn't feel as if she'd made a mistake.

Haley wasn't sure how she managed to find her way to the door connecting their rooms. Even more surprising was how she held back the tears. But they didn't fall until she'd made it safely to her side and was alone.

They fell *because* she was alone and always would be.

The next morning Haley bought a cup of coffee and a scone from the Starbucks next door to the hotel. She was steering clear of Marlon. Her eyes were swollen and achy from crying, but that wasn't the reason for her evasive actions.

What was she going to say to him about last night?

In her fantasy of first-time sex, cuddling afterward had been a component. Followed closely by falling asleep wrapped in a pair of strong arms. Her anxiety about the scenario had been more in the nature of what to do about morning breath.

Physically, she was a little sore and couldn't help being glad of the proof that she was no longer pure as the driven snow. If she'd told him, what would he have done to make it different? Most likely he'd have sent her away.

With no clear answer to the questions, she walked back to the hotel and through the Western-themed lobby. To her left was the registration desk, a replica of a saloon bar with brass foot rail. The ceiling was made of natural pine open beams and there was a river rock fireplace in the corner. A leather couch and two wing chairs formed a conversation area around it. On the coffee table stood a metal sculpture of horse and rider. Somehow the artist had managed to convey the illusion of motion, of racing across the plains.

If anyone could appreciate creativity in any medium, it was her. Sketching had always been her serenity and she figured after last night she'd be churning out a lot of stuff when she got home.

She wished she was there now and was tempted to hop in her truck and go. But she just couldn't skip out on Marlon, no matter how big a jerk he'd been. That didn't mean she wouldn't take the coward's way out and avoid him just a little while longer.

She scurried through the hotel lobby and went outside to the courtyard. Sitting on a wrought-iron bench, she scanned her surroundings. It was a landscaped rectangular area surrounded on three sides by the four-story buildings. A fenced-in pool was at the far end with grass, trees, flowers and shrubs in the middle. It was a peaceful place, or might have been if she wasn't in the middle of a personal crisis.

She should have stayed in Thunder Canyon. The trip had been a waste of time. Roy was still missing and she'd slept with her major crush. On the failure scale, she was two for two.

"Here you are."

She jumped at the sound of Marlon's voice behind her. Lost in thought and wallowing in a healthy portion of self-pity, she hadn't heard him approach.

"Here I am." She didn't turn to look at him.

"Do you mind if I join you?"

Yes. But it would be best to get this over with. She shrugged. "Suit yourself."

He sat down beside her with his own Starbucks cup in hand. "I've been looking all over for you."

"And you found me."

She dug into her bag and broke off a piece of scone—not

out of hunger because her appetite had deserted at the sound of his voice, but just for something to occupy her hands. The longer she could keep from looking at him the better.

If only she couldn't smell the spicy fragrance of his aftershave, the clean manly scent of his skin after a morning shower. Her insides quivered with excitement in spite of the rational voice warning that it was a waste of energy.

He took a sip of coffee. "Are you all right?"

"Of course." She chewed the pastry without tasting anything. "Don't I look all right?"

"That's not what I meant and you know it."

"What *did* you mean?"

She could have taken pity on him and answered the question she knew he was asking, but her charitable streak was nowhere to be found. If it was up to her, ignoring the whole thing would be the way to go.

He let out a long breath. "We need to talk about last night."

"No, *we* really don't."

"Okay then. I need to. You can just listen."

"No, I really can't." She started to stand, but his hand shot out and tugged her back down. She hated that his slightest touch put a hitch in her breathing.

"Don't be stubborn."

"Can't help it. I was made that way." She set the bag and coffee on the bench between them.

"Why didn't you tell me you'd never been with a man?"

The words felt like an accusation and she went on the defensive. "It's not something I should have to apologize for."

"God, no—" There was adamant agreement in his tone. "I'm the one who should apologize."

"Darn right." She chanced a look at him and the sincere regret in his expression deflated the serious case of mad she was carrying around. "Why?"

"I should have known," he said miserably.

That shocked her. "How could you?"

"There were signs. Your reaction to that kiss on the way to dinner, for one."

"It just surprised me. I haven't kissed that many guys." The defensive words just popped out. She prayed he wouldn't pity her. That was something she couldn't bear.

"How many?"

"A few." She glanced at him and it didn't look like he was feeling sorry for her. "Including you? Two."

"The guy when you were in college?"

"How did you know that?"

"I asked around because—" He raked his fingers through his hair. "Your reaction when I kissed you was— I was afraid I'd screwed up. Ben and Linda didn't remember you going out with anyone in Thunder Canyon, but thought there might have been someone when you went away to school."

"You made inquiries into my personal life?"

"I was trying to understand," he defended. "I figured someone hurt you and that's why you pushed me away. Now I know the truth."

Could they just be done with this conversation? "It's no big deal."

"You're wrong. It's an incredibly big deal. When a woman gives herself to a man for the first time, it's a gift."

"Really?" Her gaze snapped up to his and she couldn't detect anything but honesty there.

"A gift and a responsibility."

"Why?"

He was quiet for several moments. "A woman's first time can affect her attitude about sex forever. A guy feels pressure to make it good. I wish I'd known—"

That was so sweet. It was the subtext of what her mom had said from the male point of view. And she knew without a doubt that her mom would have liked Marlon.

"I handled it badly," he continued. "I'm really sorry about that. Somehow I'll make it up to you."

A glow spread from her midsection outward until every part of her was tingling. Obviously he didn't consider her an alien from the planet Zatu and that boded well for a second time. She was all in favor of that.

She touched his arm and the warm skin melted any lingering insecurities. "For the record, my attitude about sex is alive and well."

He studied her for several moments, then wrapped her fingers in his big hand. Apparently he decided she was telling the truth because his mouth softened into a smile. "Good."

As much as Haley wanted to hold on to this moment, they needed to figure out their next move. "What are we going to do about Roy?"

He let go of her hand and picked up his coffee, taking a sip as he thought. "I think we've done everything we can here."

"But he's still out there somewhere."

"Billings has a population of over a hundred thousand," Marlon pointed out. "It's like looking for a needle in a haystack. There are kids in Thunder Canyon who want to hang out at ROOTS. They need to be your priority."

She sighed. "You're right. It's just—"

"The ones who run away need the most help?" he guessed.

"Yeah."

"He knows how to find you." He squeezed her fingers reassuringly, then released her and stood up. "Let's go home."

"Okay."

They walked back into the lobby and she started for the elevator when he put a hand on her arm.

"I'm going to check out at the front desk since we're down here," he said.

"I'll go with you."

They talked to Paul, the clerk on duty, who charged the credit card Marlon had given them yesterday. He'd insisted on paying for her room, too, and said she could reimburse him later. Something told her he wouldn't take her money, though.

Marlon folded the printout of the charges and slipped it into the back pocket of his jeans. "Thanks."

"No problem," the young man said. He smiled and looked at each of them in turn. "Come back and see us again, Mr. Cates. Mrs. Cates."

Haley was trying to process the fact that Paul thought they were a couple even though they'd had separate rooms. He'd probably only looked at the total, not the itemized charges. It was an honest mistake. The real surprise was Marlon's reaction.

"We're not married." His tone was adamant and he couldn't get the words out fast enough.

He could have let the misunderstanding slide. Who cared if a man they would never see again thought they were married?

Obviously Marlon cared. He'd been incredibly uncomfortable with the idea. Setting the guy straight and in that sharp tone was the equivalent of backing up several steps and putting his hands up to distance himself from any part of her being his Mrs.

It was a sad and sobering reality check. Just moments ago she'd been a starry-eyed lover looking forward to a second time. But the truth was, he regretted the first time. If she'd told him she'd never done it before, he'd have sent her to her room with a pat on the head. He didn't want the responsibility.

He didn't want to be tied down to a place *or* a person.

Especially a person.

And her reality check went one awful step further. This whole time she'd been worried about her crush on Marlon. Worried about making the same mistake. She wouldn't have slept with him if she didn't care. A lot. So she hadn't made the *same* mistake. This was so much more than a major crush.

She'd fallen in love with him.

Chapter Fourteen

It was a quiet afternoon at ROOTS. Marlon and Haley were the only ones there. They'd been back in Thunder Canyon for twenty-four hours and still no word from Roy. He hoped the kid was on her mind and not what happened between them.

Sex.

Awesome.

He still couldn't believe that she'd picked him to be her first. And if circumstances were different, if he wasn't leaving, he would show her everything he could about seduction and tenderness. But nothing had changed and something made her go distant. One minute she'd shyly told him her attitude about sex was alive and well. The next they'd checked out of the hotel and on the drive back, she got quiet and broody.

Marlon had tried more than once to draw her out. Every time he'd asked if something was bothering her she went all female on him and said everything was fine. He was beginning to hate that word.

So here they sat. Not talking. He was working on his laptop at the tiny computer desk and she was sitting behind him on the couch, with her legs tucked up beneath her and a sketch pad in her lap. The only sound in the room was her charcoal pencil scratching on the paper.

Marlon liked quiet when he worked, but the air was vibrating with tension and making him nuts. He was just about to take her on regarding the silent treatment when his phone rang.

He reached for the case on his belt and retrieved his cell. After looking at the caller ID, he smiled and answered. "Dana. How's the world's best personal assistant?"

"Crabby. When are you getting out of the slammer?" she asked.

"Technically I was never in the slammer."

"You know what I mean."

"My community service will be satisfied in about a week." So soon? When did that happen? It had gone too fast, he thought, swiveling his chair around to look at Haley. She didn't look back.

"Good. I need a vacation," Dana said.

"Because?"

"I'm running MC/TC by myself."

"I've been pulling my weight," he protested.

"Oh, please. Long distance just makes more work for me."

"I'll make it up to you when I get home."

"Don't try to get on my good side with false promises. I'm mad at you."

He leaned back in the chair and slid another quick look at Haley who was still pretending not to listen. "So the whole purpose of this call was to yell at me and make me feel guilty?"

"Of course."

"Come on, D. I know you better than that. How's business?"

"The numbers have improved slightly. Not dance-of-joy good yet, but there's reason for cautious optimism. The downward spiral has leveled off and some of the profit graphs are actually starting to go up."

"That's great news. Might be a good time to counter the buyout offer."

"So you've decided to sell?" Dana asked, disapproval leaking into her tone.

Marlon had discussed the pros and cons with her at length and knew, like Haley, she favored hanging in there. "I'm still considering all the options."

"Before you go to the dark side, consider this." He heard papers rustling. "The sketches you sent me from— What's her name?"

"Haley," he said and saw her glance up.

"Right. Haley's drawings are incredibly promising."

"I thought so."

"Boss, we could do a whole line. Love the name, by the way. A great way to brand it. HA! It's sassy and sexy."

Just like the woman herself. He glanced at Haley who was looking at him now, probably at the sound of her name and the excitement in his voice.

"That's good," he said.

"If we push it, I think we can get the product into our trial market in time for Christmas. It will be a lot of work and more up-front cost to do it. But the payoff could be really big."

"I'm glad you approve."

"You found her," Dana said. "I assume the designer is a her."

"Yes, indeed."

"She's there, isn't she?"

He met Haley's curious-but-trying-not-to-be look. "Yup."

"You can't talk?"

"I thought I was," he said.

"You know what I mean."

"Yeah. And that would be an affirmative."

"This covert conversation doesn't work for me," Dana said, going into crabby mode again. "When are you coming home?"

"I'll be back when my community service is done."

"About a week," she repeated. "Good. I'll get moving on these new designs. See you soon, boss."

"Excellent. I can't wait to see what happens." He hung up.

"Problem?" Haley didn't look distant as much as troubled.

"Actually, no." He stood and walked over to the sofa. "That was my assistant."

"I gathered. The 'world's best personal assistant' remark was a big clue."

"Dana Taylor," he confirmed. "We met in college. A business class." For some reason he felt compelled to explain. "When MC/TC started to take off, she was the first person I hired. It was a good decision."

"So everything's okay?"

"Very. She called to let me know how much she likes your designs." He waited, but there was no response. Maybe she didn't understand the potential. "She wants to try and get them in the stores by the end of the year."

Her eyes widened, but there was no excitement. "You sound anxious to get back to work."

"Dana thinks your designs will really take off. But if we're going to make it happen, there will be a lot of overtime required." He'd expected laughing, squealing, possibly dancing and hugging. What he didn't expect was no reaction at all.

She put her pad and pencil down on the table and stood. "Then I wouldn't dream of keeping you. After all the overtime here at ROOTS you've more than satisfied the court's expectations. And mine. I'll sign off on your community service right now so you can go."

Leave?

Early?

When he'd started here at ROOTS, those words would have made him pump his arm in triumph. Now? Not so much. He still had a week. He *wanted* that week.

"Are you trying to get rid of me?" The words were raw and angry.

The thought of leaving her was like a punch to the gut and knocked the air out of him, a lot like being tackled by a two-hundred-fifty-pound linebacker who wanted to rip his head off. Every instinct he had pushed back.

He liked Haley, everything about her.

She was beautiful. Smart. Prickly. Stubborn. Creative, sweet and funny. Pure of heart.

He liked walking into ROOTS and seeing her eyes light up at the sight of him. He liked knowing she had no idea her reaction was so obvious. Making her laugh made him happy. He especially enjoyed nudging the sad look from her eyes and wanted to make that expression disappear for good. But somehow he'd etched it even deeper and that was unacceptable.

And just like that it all became clear to him. He wanted to be in her life and to keep her in his. "Haley, I—"

"You're off the hook, Marlon. Go back to L.A." She turned and disappeared into the back room followed by the sound of the rear door opening and closing.

Marlon didn't want her to leave any more than he wanted to. It was as clear to him as the mountains around Thunder Canyon on a windy day. Maybe he should accept the offer on the table to buy his business. He could stay here. Go to work for Cates Construction. It would be great to see more of his family.

More important—he would be with Haley.

Somehow she'd gotten under his skin. All he'd ever wanted was to be a successful businessman and he'd done it. He had no idea when success had stopped being enough.

That was a lie. The seed was planted six years ago when he kissed Haley, then never followed through. Being forced to stay and work with her, his feelings had taken root and blossomed.

He had to go after her this time.

Just as he turned toward the back room where she'd disappeared, the bell over the front door clanged. Marlon did a double take when Roy Robbins strolled casually inside as if he hadn't a care in the world.

"Hey, dude—"

"Don't you dare 'hey dude' me, you pinhead."

"Haley says it's not nice to call people names."

"Well, Haley's not here right now. I am." Marlon pointed at the kid, anger rolling through him. "What the hell happened? Haley's been worried sick about you. She insisted on going all the way to Billings because you have a friend there. Obviously we didn't find you."

Marlon realized *he'd* found something on that trip, though.

Himself.

"Where the hell have you been?"

"Lighten up, man."

"Not a chance. I'm leaning on you hard. And you know why? You used Haley—"

"It wasn't like that," Roy protested.

"Bull. You took advantage of her good heart. Stayed at her house. Let her feed and take care of you. You used this mentoring program, one that means everything to her, as your own social network. For completely selfish reasons. Then there's a little dust-up and you can't take the heat like a man. Gone without a word like a spoiled brat." Marlon took half a step closer. "You made Haley worry. I don't like it when she worries."

"Peace, man." Roy made a *V* with his index and middle fingers. "I thought it would be best for me to split."

"Best for who?"

"For Haley."

"Again I say bull. You took the chicken way out because facing her was too tough."

"She talked to me about how to man up."

"And apparently wasted her breath," Marlon accused.

Something that looked a lot like surrender flickered in the boy's eyes. And somewhere in the hazy, rational part of Marlon's mind he knew he was taking out his own frustrations on the kid. He dragged in a cleansing breath of air.

"Look, dude—" Roy caught himself and stopped. "Marlon, I didn't mean to worry her. I thought she'd be relieved if I was gone."

"You thought wrong." Some of Marlon's anger slipped away when it became clear to him that the kid regretted his actions.

"I know that now. I'll apologize to Haley before I go."

"What?"

Marlon wasn't sure whether to be surprised or pissed off. What would Haley do in this situation? Probably bake cookies and grill Roy like raw hamburger with a touch so gentle he wouldn't realize the secrets he was giving away. Connecting to people was effortless for her. As simple as a long-ago kiss that had changed his life.

"You thirsty?" Marlon finally asked.

Roy looked wary as he nodded. "But maybe I should go find Haley—"

"That's a good idea. But it might also be a good idea to run what you're planning to say by me. I'll get a couple of sodas." Marlon pointed at him. "Stay put."

"Cool." Roy sat on the couch.

When he came back with the drinks, the kid hadn't moved. He handed Roy a cold can, then sat in the worn chair beside him and popped the tab on his own soda.

"So we know why you took off from Thunder Canyon. Where did you go?"

"Helena." Roy lifted the tab on his drink and took a long swallow of the cold liquid.

Helena? What the heck?

"Why there?" Marlon asked calmly.

"It's where my cousin lives."

"So when you ran away from home, why didn't you go to your cousin's in the first place instead of Thunder Canyon?"

"He'd have ratted me out to my folks and I didn't plan to go home ever again. Then," he added.

"Do you want to talk about it?"

"Not really." A small smile curved the corners of his mouth. "But Haley says talking is a good way to sort things out."

"You should listen to her," Marlon advised.

Roy nodded. "There was this girl—Whitney."

"A woman. Why doesn't that surprise me?" He took a drink of his soda to stop any more editorial comments from slipping out. *Not helpful,* Haley would have said. "Go on."

"She's a cheerleader. A real fox. Extremely hot." Roy met his gaze to see if his meaning sank in.

"I'm old, but the teenage boy/cheerleader fantasy is an unforgettable classic for guys of all ages," Marlon explained wryly.

Roy grinned, but it faded a moment later. "She dumped me. It was on her Facebook page. The whole school was tweeting about it."

"It happens."

"But, dude, I never saw it coming. We were voted the couple most likely to last until graduation." Roy's eyes were full of teenage tragedy. "And she didn't even give me a reason. She said I didn't do anything, but the relationship just ran its course and we were over."

"That's rough." Marlon sincerely meant that.

"Everyone knew. I just couldn't stick around. The pity was a total drag."

"I can see where you'd feel that way." And this was the part Marlon really wanted to talk about. "But Haley will be upset if you take off again."

"It's not taking off." Roy looked up. "I'm going home. My mom is on her way. I just came back to thank Haley for everything she did for me. I don't know how I'll ever repay her for—"

"Thanks will be enough. She doesn't want anything but for you to be okay." Marlon reached over and squeezed the kid's shoulder approvingly. "You gonna be okay? When you get home? Maybe you could talk to Whitney."

Roy nodded thoughtfully. "I'd sure like to know why

she dumped me. To understand what was going through her mind."

Good luck with that, Marlon thought. Fortunately the words didn't come out of his mouth. "Talking is good. Just don't forget that the female mind is a dark and complicated place."

"Dude, you're talking about Haley, aren't you?"

"That's a pretty big leap." It was true, Marlon thought, but still a big leap.

"You didn't deny it, so I must be right." Roy pointed at him. "You like her."

"Of course I do. Everyone in town likes her."

"That's what Haley said when I asked her about you."

"What?" Marlon asked.

"You want to hook up with Haley. A blind man could see that."

No way was he telling this kid that they'd already hooked up and all it accomplished was to make everything even more complicated. "It's not that simple."

"Why do adults always say that about their relationships? Do you think for us kids it's a day at the beach?"

"You have a point," Marlon admitted.

"I know Haley likes you."

"Really? Did she say so?"

What was this? Junior high? Should he pass her a note in study hall?

"Not exactly." Roy shrugged. "But when I called her on it, she said the same thing you just did. That she likes everyone. It was an answer, but not really. You know what I mean? Like you just now. And it was the way she said it, also just like you."

Haley liked him? Of course she did. She'd gone to bed with him. She'd chosen him to be her first. That filled him with pride followed closely by humility. But did it mean that they had a chance for something real and lasting? Was she the *one?*

"Look, dude, you can't run away. Reaching a milestone age doesn't make you a man. It's staying put and dealing with stuff that does it."

Marlon suppressed a smile. The kid wasn't so much a pinhead any more. He'd recently acquired some wisdom and was paying it forward. Following Haley's example. When they'd played one-on-one basketball, Marlon had taken him down a peg or two. Maybe it was time to hand back his ego.

Marlon heard the back door open and close just as he said, "What do you suggest I do?"

"You like Haley, right?"

"Yeah."

Roy nodded with smug satisfaction about guessing correctly. "You gotta tell her how much you care."

There was a small sound behind them and Marlon turned.

Haley stood in the doorway. "You care about me?"

Chapter Fifteen

Haley wanted to take back the question. If Marlon added that he cared about her "as a friend", the humiliation would be so much worse than not knowing how to kiss.

And then it sank in that he was talking to Roy, and relief flooded her. "You're okay," she said to the teen.

"I was with my cousin." He was standing between the old sofa and coffee table. "I didn't mean to make you worry. Or cause trouble with your family. Marlon said you looked for me in Billings."

"You said something about a friend there." And if she hadn't eavesdropped, none of what happened in Billings would have happened.

It hurt a lot that Marlon's heated protest at being mistaken as part of a couple confirmed that he was a contented bachelor. But she would never be sorry he'd made love to her. It was a memory she would hold close to her forever.

"Say something, Haley," Roy begged.

She smiled. "Next time leave a note."

"I thought it would be best to just go, that it would be better for you."

"I appreciate your concern, really. But there was no need to disappear." She moved farther into the room, keeping the sofa between her and the two guys. "There is something we need to talk about, though. You know I care about you, but sooner or later you have to go home."

"Done."

She blinked at him. "Really?"

"I called my mom. She's on her way and was pretty cool on the phone. Said we have to talk about stuff, but it can wait till we get home."

Haley was happy for him. "No threats of grounding for the rest of your life?"

"Not yet. But I'm sure there will be consequences," the teen said ruefully.

"I hope so. It means they care."

"Then the state of Montana cares big time about Marlon," Roy joked, glancing at the man in question. "What with his community service consequences."

Haley didn't even want to peek at him. It was hard enough hanging on to her composure when she pretended he wasn't there. But looking at him with all his masculinity, magnetism and charisma, not to mention charm, broke her heart just a little more every time.

"The state of Montana doesn't give a rat's behind about me. It's all about rules to keep civilization civilized." Marlon's voice was laced with humor but underneath it had an edge.

Haley could feel his gaze and her skin grew warm as her heart beat too fast. "I'm glad you're working things out with your family."

"It was a girl," Roy said.

"What?" She was confused at the sudden change of topic.

"The reason I ran away. She dumped me and wouldn't say why. I didn't want to face anyone. My parents blew me off. Said everyone goes through it and we all have to learn to live with disappointment. They didn't understand." Roy folded his arms over his chest. "But running away was immature. I'm going to talk to Whitney about it when I get home."

"Very grown-up decision."

"Marlon mentioned that it might be a good idea."

It was. Darn him. She wanted him to be a jerk so she could elevate her anger to a certain level and keep out the pain. He was taking that away from her, too.

"When's your mom coming?"

"Not long," Roy answered. "I wanted to tell you first. Then I need to say good-bye to C.J. and the others before I go."

Haley nodded her approval. "Good plan."

He hesitated for a moment. "Would it be okay if I gave you a hug? I mean, Austin's not going to break down the door and beat me up or anything, is he?"

"He's at work. The coast is clear." She opened her arms and he walked around the sofa into them.

"Thanks, Haley. For everything. Seriously."

"You're welcome." Her throat was thick with emotion and her feelings were mixed. She was incredibly glad the program she'd started had helped him, but would miss him terribly. "You're part of the family, kiddo. Don't be a stranger."

"No way." He shook hands with Marlon, then walked out the door.

Through the big window she saw him look back and grin. He waved once and was gone. Now she was alone with Marlon and the question she'd asked just a few minutes before. Maybe he hadn't heard or didn't remember.

He looked at her. "I do care about you, Haley."

Heard and *remembered,* she thought.

"That's nice of you to say."

"Nice has nothing to do with anything. It just is."

He didn't sound happy about that, but join the club. She wasn't happy about her feelings either. "Anyway, thanks for all your help."

There was an angry expression in his dark eyes when he rounded the sofa and stood in front of her. "What are you doing?"

"Saying good-bye." It was a miracle that she kept her voice from cracking. She couldn't show any weakness that would betray the raging emotions churning inside.

"I'm not going anywhere."

"Your community service is complete."

"Signing off on it early doesn't mean you're getting rid of me."

"News flash, Marlon, you don't live here any more."

"About that—" He rubbed a hand across the back of his neck. "I'm seriously considering taking the buyout offer for my company."

And completely sever any ties he had to this town? Every part of her protested and she wondered if it was about losing even that small connection to him.

"But your business was born in Thunder Canyon," she argued. "You'd be putting your dream in someone else's hands. Like giving your baby away."

"Some things are more important than business."

"Like what?

"You." Intensity burned in his eyes.

"I don't understand." Her heart was hammering and

blood roared in her ears. She couldn't possibly have heard him right.

"I'm thinking about going to work in the family construction business. Permanently settling in Thunder Canyon."

For her? She wasn't the sort of woman that a man gave everything up for. That just wasn't possible. She wasn't a woman who could be played with, either.

"Look, Marlon, I'm not sure where this is coming from. It's out of character for you."

"I think I know my own character pretty well, so I'm confused about your reaction." His eyes narrowed on her.

"Then let me explain. When you checked out of the hotel in Billings the clerk called us Mr. and Mrs. Cates. Just the misunderstanding made you start to sweat. The words were barely out of his mouth and you were jumping down his throat, correcting him. That shows pretty clearly how much commitment is still not one of your strengths." Her chin lifted. "So, I'm not sure what's going on with you, but don't expect me to fall into your arms. I don't want to be someone you settle for."

A multitude of emotions rolled through his eyes like thunderheads until anger locked into place. "I suppose I should have expected that from the status quo queen."

She winced at the ice in his tone. "Excuse me?"

"You have an exciting opportunity, Haley. The chance to design a line of products for my company, a major national brand. It's a chance to achieve your dream. But were you excited?" He shook his head. "I didn't see it."

"Because there's a lot to consider. How can I leave my family? They count on me. And ROOTS? Who would keep it going? It's an important program." She sucked in a deep breath. "Thunder Canyon is my home."

"You didn't even discuss options. A move away might not be necessary and Thunder Canyon is just geography. Home is where you make it. And if you think staying here is about community loyalty, you're not just lying to me this time. You're lying to yourself."

"Who do you think you are?" she said angrily.

"The guy who's keeping it real. You're a coward, Haley Anderson." He pointed at her to underline his words. "You call it noble and everyone here thinks you have wings and a halo. But the truth is you're afraid to leave."

Marlon turned and his broad back was the last thing she saw before he slammed the door. His accusations ricocheted around the empty room, stirring up a host of painful memories.

She'd been brave once. She'd left Thunder Canyon and life as she'd known it came crashing down around her.

It was going to happen again even though she wasn't the one leaving. This time Marlon was and he'd be taking her heart with him.

This time she would never be whole again.

Nell Anderson—Beloved Mother.

Haley's eyes filled with tears and her throat was thick with emotion as she stared at the headstone in Thunder Canyon cemetery. Feelings welled up that were about losing Marlon and not the loss she'd suffered so many years ago.

Beloved Mother.

The words were deceptively simple.

"I do love you, Mom. And I miss you now more than ever," she whispered. "I could sure use someone to talk to."

The sun was shining in a cloudless blue sky. A perfect Montana day. She set the bright bouquet of yellow daisies, purple mums and baby's breath on the grass. "I'm in love with Marlon Cates. Can you believe it? Sensible, practical me and Thunder Canyon's legendary bad boy?"

A sudden gust of wind swirled around her as if Mother Nature was responding to a disclosure that turned the universe on its ear. It had definitely taken Haley by surprise. On the road behind her she heard a car door close. She felt more than heard footsteps on the grassy ground and the hair at her nape prickled with awareness. Somehow she knew it was the bad boy in question.

"Haley?"

Her heart was beating too fast when she met Marlon's gaze. It had been a couple of days since she'd seen him. Worn jeans fit his muscular legs as if they were tailor-made for him. A black T-shirt hugged his wide chest and aviator sunglasses hid his eyes. He looked every inch worthy of his reputation, but now she knew it was nothing more than a façade. His heart was good.

"What are you doing here?" she asked.

"I wanted to see you."

"How did you find me?"

"Ben." He took off the glasses and hung them from the neck of his shirt and moved to stand beside her, their arms nearly brushing. "He told me you come here almost every Sunday to put flowers on your mother's grave."

"I do." She looked down. "I guess the court reinstated your driver's license."

"I'm legal again. Got my wheels back," he confirmed.

"And this joyride to the cemetery is to celebrate?"

"Not exactly. I needed to talk to you."

He was leaving; she could hear it in his voice. The realization was like a physical blow. It knocked the wind out of her and hurt clear through to her soul. She desperately wanted to curl into fetal position and fold in on herself to keep the pain from spreading, but dignity trumped weakness.

"You didn't have to come all this way outside of town to say good-bye."

"I didn't." He looked sheepish. And too cute for words. "I mean, I did. I'm here. But not to say good-bye."

Haley was confused. He had a license to leave. Why was he making this harder? "What did you want to talk about?"

"I wanted to tell you that I love you, Haley. I'm *in* love with you."

The direct statement knocked the wind out of her and felt like a punch to the gut, but there was no pain. Shock and awe, yes, just before disbelief crept in. "Is this some kind of joke?"

"Look, I know you're ticked off about how I handled that situation at the hotel in Billings." He looked down. "It was a knee-jerk reaction. Jerk being the operative word. I was still processing the fact that you'd never been with a man before and chose me to be the one. Mostly I was dealing with not deserving you."

"So you're here out of a sense of responsibility?" She folded her arms over her chest. "No, thanks. I can take care of myself."

"Of course you can. That's not—" He raked his fingers through his hair. "I'm really messing this up. In my own defense, let me say that I've only recently acquired any experience talking about feelings."

"I don't get it."

"Roy and I discussed his reaction to getting dumped by a girl. My comments were sensitive and reasonable."

"You're the expert on the male point of view," she said wryly.

"And in the past I'd have just taken him out for a beer and called it a day."

"He's not old enough to drink."

"You know what I mean. I didn't blow off his feelings. Because now I know what love feels like. Thanks to you."

Haley studied his expression. She'd gotten to know him really well and knew when he was teasing or when something bothered him. She could tell when he was angry, annoyed or getting his stubborn on. She was absolutely certain that he was telling her the truth.

"You really do love me."

"Finally," he said grinning. "I didn't have to work that hard to convince a venture capitalist to invest in my company." He curved his fingers around her upper arms, then pulled her close. "And you're in love with me, too."

Liquid heat poured through her and pooled in her belly when he touched his lips to hers. She sighed and sank into him, every nerve ending in her body doing the happy dance. Until reality set in.

Haley pulled away. "It doesn't matter how I feel because you're leaving."

"Says who?" When she opened her mouth to answer, he touched a finger to her lips. "You're wrong, Haley. Staying in Thunder Canyon wouldn't be settling. Not if you were with me—" He hesitated, then intensity darkened his eyes. "If you were my wife, anywhere we were together would be home. It's where the heart is and you have mine. I've traveled a lot but I've never met anyone who made me want to stay. Not until you. The most beautiful woman, inside and out, was right in my own backyard."

"Really?"

He nodded. "You gave me back my roots."

She glanced beside her, to her mother's final resting

place. As the word sank in she remembered the sampler. "There are but two lasting bequests we can give our children—roots and wings," she whispered.

"Amen."

She looked up. "You're right about me, Marlon. I'm a lying coward and I don't see how you could love me."

"What?"

"I fibbed about not remembering that kiss at the football fundraiser. And I felt what was going on between us that very first day when you walked into ROOTS. It was easier to pretend not to care."

"Why?"

"Because I'm afraid of change, afraid to go." The breeze blew a strand of hair into her eyes and she pushed it away. "The last time I left—the *only* time—I lost the most important person in my life. Everything turned upside down."

"I know, sweetheart." He reached a hand out, but she backed away. "Okay, I'm going to say something that you already know because you told me that night at dinner in Billings. But it's the truth and I'll keep repeating the words until the message finally sinks in."

"What?" she asked when he hesitated.

"Bad stuff happens. No one can control it. Not you, or me, or anyone. Losing your mom was the worst. But it had nothing to do with the fact that you weren't here. You didn't cause the accident just because you went away."

His gaze was magnetic, willing what he said to sink in. And finally she allowed it through. All these years she'd been winging it, telling herself that's what the wings part of roots and wings meant. Now she realized her mom's lasting legacy was to not be afraid to take flight. To follow her dream wherever it took her.

Now she could let herself see that her dream was Marlon.

The weight Haley had been carrying lifted from her shoulders. Or maybe her burden felt lighter because there was another, stronger, pair of shoulders to share it.

"You're right. So right." Haley walked into his arms and rested her cheek on his chest. "I love you, Marlon. If what you said was an actual proposal, I would love to marry you."

"I'm going to hold you to that," he said fervently. "I'll spend the rest of my life proving to you that commitment *is* one of my strengths."

"I was wrong about that. You do commitment pretty darn well." A warm feeling slid down her spine that felt a lot like the comforting touch of her mother's hand. In her heart, Haley knew it was her mother's approval of this man, their marriage. She looked up at him and smiled. "My mother gave me roots and you fixed my broken wings. I'll follow you anywhere."

Epilogue

Haley had been afraid no one would come to the grand opening of ROOTS and had never been happier to be wrong. A week after she'd accepted Marlon's proposal, she'd managed to get everything here. Her mother's sampler was hanging on the wall with a commemorative plaque dedicating the Nell Anderson ROOTS Teen Center to her memory.

She and Marlon looked around the crowded storefront-turned-teen center where a good portion of the Thunder Canyon community was helping themselves to cookies, brownies, coffee and punch. He hugged her, pride in his eyes. "It's certainly an impressive turnout."

A lot of faces she knew. One she'd just met. Dillon Traub. He was the good-looking doctor filling in for Marlon's brother Marshall, who was taking a delayed honeymoon trip with his wife, Mia.

She leaned into Marlon and said, "I love you."

"Of course you do." The familiar twinkle gleamed in his eyes when he looked at her.

Marlon's twin, Matt, moved beside them. "Rumor has it that you're turning down the buyout offer on the company, bro."

"Not a rumor. Fact." He smiled proudly at her. "I'm recruiting some new designing talent to breathe life into it. We're tightening the belt to ride out the tough economic times. Then we'll be poised to kick some serious retail butt. Did I mention that I plan to marry the talent and make sure I've got her locked in for life?"

Matt nodded. "You two look happy."

"There's a good reason for that." Haley felt all aglow, even if no one could tell and her feet hadn't touched the ground for a week. "Marlon's taking me to Hawaii. He wants my first time seeing the ocean to be in paradise."

Marlon shot a warning look at his brother. "Don't you dare say it."

"You mean I told you so?" Matt grinned.

"What did you tell him?" Haley demanded.

"That you might be *The One.*"

"Well, he's the one for me," she said. "But not because of Hawaii. If he took me to a laundromat, I'd still be the happiest, luckiest girl on the planet."

"Don't you have a speech to give?" Marlon asked, before his twin could rib him unmercifully.

"Yes, I do. But it's so loud in here, I'm not sure how to get everyone to listen."

Marlon guided her to the far end of the room and then put his fingers to his lips. The next sound out of him was an earsplitting whistle. Conversation stopped and everyone looked at them.

"Attention, everyone," he said. "Haley has something to say."

She smiled her appreciation, then nervously cleared her throat. "Thanks for coming. This is an awesome turnout. A lot of you know this program has been a dream of mine ever since my mom died. Without the help of the people here in Thunder Canyon my brother, sister and I wouldn't have made it through that awful time. This center is my way of saying thank you."

She looked out at the smiling faces. Ben Walters was there with Linda Powell beside him. Marlon's folks, Frank and Edie Cates, nodded approvingly. They'd given a big thumbs up to her engagement to their son. Austin and Angie were clapping. The two of them had been in touch with Roy, who, it turned out, didn't live far away. He'd started his senior year and was doing great.

She looked up at Marlon, who smiled his encouragement. Turning back at the crowd, she said, "I have some good news and bad. Some of you already know, but for those who don't, Marlon Cates and I are going to be married."

The announcement was greeted by applause, whistles and cheers. She held up her left hand and wiggled the ring finger with the breathtaking diamond. Just the night before Marlon had gone down on one knee and formally popped the question, then sealed the deal with the impressive jewelry.

"The thing is," she continued, "I'm moving to Los Angeles and that means I have to step down as the director of ROOTS." When the crowd made noises of disappointment, she held up her hands. "I appreciate that. You'll never know how much. But the center will continue to operate with a dedicated staff of volunteers. My brother, Austin, promised to put in some time before he goes to graduate school, courtesy of the Marlon Cates scholarship fund." Her future husband wouldn't take no for an answer on that front. "My sister, Angie, will also put in some hours. So will Linda Powell and Ben Walters—" When she looked at the older man, he pointed to Marlon and gave her a nod of endorsement. She took a deep breath. "And last but definitely not least, Carleigh Benedict of Thunder Canyon Social Services is going to take over as director. She was my adviser, mentor and friend, and the kids will be lucky to have her. Please give her your legendary Thunder Canyon support."

The pretty blonde waved and smiled when the crowd clapped enthusiastically.

"That's the spirit," Haley said. "In conclusion, I'd like to say that donations to the program are always gratefully accepted. It's sad to say good-bye, but Marlon and I will visit all the time. ROOTS is in very good hands."

And so am I, she thought as her Montana millionaire pulled her into his arms.

* * * * *

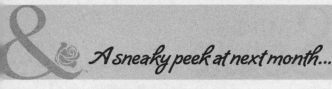

A sneaky peek at next month...

Cherish™

ROMANCE TO MELT THE HEART EVERY TIME

My wish list for next month's titles...

In stores from 16th September 2011:

❑ Nikki and the Lone Wolf — Marion Lennox

& Mardie and the City Surgeon — Marion Lennox

❑ The Lonesome Rancher — Patricia Thayer

& Finding Happily-Ever-After — Marie Ferrarella

❑ The Mummy Proposal — Cathy Gillen Thacker

In stores from 7th October 2011:

❑ From Doctor...to Daddy — Karen Rose Smith

& When the Cowboy Said "I Do" — Crystal Green

❑ Her Italian Soldier — Rebecca Winters

Available at WHSmith, Tesco, Asda, Eason, Amazon and Apple

Just can't wait?

Visit us Online

You can buy our books online a month before they hit the shops! **www.millsandboon.co.uk**

0911/23

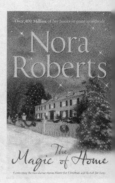

New Voices
MILLS & BOON
Starts 13th September!

Top Writing Tips from Mills & Boon Editors

We're looking for talented new authors and if you've got a romance bubbling away in your head we want to hear from you! But before you put pen to paper, here are some top tips...

Understand what our readers want: Do your research! Read as many of the current titles as you can and get to know the different series with our guidelines on www.millsandboon.co.uk

Love your characters: Readers follow their emotional journey to falling in love. Focus on this, not elaborate, weird and wonderful plots.

Make the reader want to walk in your heroine's shoes: She should be believable, someone your reader can identify with. Explore her life, her triumphs, hopes, dreams. She doesn't need to be perfect—just perfect for your hero...she can have flaws just like the rest of us!

The reader should fall in love with your hero! Mr Darcy from *Pride and Prejudice*, Russell Crowe in *Gladiator* or Daniel Craig as James Bond are all gorgeous in different ways. Have your favourite hero in mind when you're writing and get inspired!

Emotional conflict: Just as real-life relationships have ups and downs, so do the heroes and heroines in novels. Conflict between the two main characters generates emotional and sensual tension.

Have your say or enter New Voices at:
www.romanceisnotdead.com

Visit us Online

NEWVOICESTIPS/A

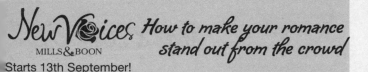

New Voices
MILLS & BOON

How to make your romance stand out from the crowd

Starts 13th September!

Avoiding the dreaded cliché

Open your story book with a bang—hook your reader in on the first page and show them instantly that this story is unique.

A successful writer can use a conventional theme and twist it to deliver something with real wow factor!

Once you've established the direction of your story, bring in fresh takes and new twists to these traditional storylines.

Here are four things to remember:

- Stretch your imagination
- Stay true to the genre
- It's all about the characters—start with them, not the plot!
- M&B is about creating fantasy out of reality. Surprise us with your characters, stories and ideas!

So whether it's a marriage of convenience story, a secret baby theme, a traumatic past or a blackmail story, make sure you add your own unique sparkle which will make your readers come back for more!

Good luck with your writing!

We look forward to meeting your fabulous heroines and drop-dead gorgeous heroes!

Have Your Say

You've just finished your book.
So what did you think?

We'd love to hear your thoughts on our
'Have your say' online panel
www.millsandboon.co.uk/haveyoursay

- Easy to use
- Short questionnaire
- Chance to win Mills & Boon® goodies